DARK DISCOVERY

Luke hesitated for a fraction of a second, then moved through the doorway.

Inside the small stone chamber, he saw what was left of the Jedi candidate. The body lay crisped and blackened on the floor, rising wisps of steam curling from the remaining fabric of a Jedi robe.

On the floor, the newly constructed lightsaber lay where it had been dropped, as if the student had tried to fight something—and lost.

Luke caught his balance by leaning against the cool stone wall. His vision blurred, but he could not tear his gaze from his student sprawled in front of him.

By now the eleven other trainees had gathered. Luke turned, trembling, and grasped the worn stone bricks at the edge of the door until even the rounded corners bruised his fingers. He applied a Jedi calming technique three times before he felt confident enough to trust his voice. The words tasted like wet ash in his mouth.

"The dark side is always with us," he said.

STAR WARS®

The Jedi Academy Trilogy

Volume II

DARK APPRENTICE

Kevin J. Anderson

BANTAM BOOKS

NEW YORK · TORONTO · LONDON · SYDNEY · AUCKLAND

DARK APPRENTICE
A Bantam Spectra Book / July 1994

ISBN 0-553-29799-6

Published simultaneously in the United States and Canada

PRINTED IN THE UNITED STATES OF AMERICA

OPM   0 9 8 7 6 5 4 3 2 1

Dedication

To LUCY AUTREY WILSON, of Lucasfilm Licensing . . . who gets thrilled just to see her name in the acknowledgments of a book; no telling what she'll do when she sees a dedication! Lucy has always been enthusiastic, willing to listen to ideas and offer her own, and a pleasure to work with on all my STAR WARS projects.

Acknowledgments

I'd like to shower thanks upon: Lillie Mitchell for transcribing piles of my microcassettes with lightning speed; my wife Rebecca Moesta Anderson for just about everything, from brainstorming to copyediting to personal support to helping dialogue make sense; the exhaustive Star Wars expertise of Bill Smith at West End Games (not to mention all the wonderful source material available from West End); Tom Veitch for helping me create the entire history of Exar Kun (so much, in fact, that we are writing his story and the Great Sith War in twelve issues of *Dark Lords of the Sith* to be published by Dark Horse Comics); Ralph McQuarrie, whose imagination and original painting inspired the temple of Exar Kun; my editor Betsy Mitchell, who helped develop this story, and her successor Tom Dupree, who came aboard the starship when we were already leaping into hyperspace; Heather McConnell, who helps keep all systems under control; Karen Anderson for custom-designing the word "praxeum"; Sue Rostoni at Lucasfilm for helping things run smoothly; Rose Guilbert for the sentient mollusks; Dave Wolverton and Timothy Zahn for their invaluable assistance and cooperation; David Brin for the *Startide*; my agent Richard Curtis; Rita Anderson; Chuck Beason; and of course, George Lucas, for creating such a marvelous universe in the first place.

STAR WARS®

The Jedi Academy Trilogy

Volume II

DARK APPRENTICE

1

The huge orange sphere of the gas planet Yavin heaved itself over the horizon of its fourth moon. Soft, misty light shone across the ever-stirring jungles and the ancient stone temples.

Luke Skywalker used a Jedi refreshing technique to remove weariness from his body. He had slept soundly—but the future of the New Republic and the fate of the galaxy weighed heavily upon him.

Luke stood atop the squared pyramid of the Great Temple that had been abandoned millennia before by the lost Massassi race. During the Alliance's early struggles against the Empire, they had built a secret base in the ruins, from which they had launched their desperate attack against the first Death Star. Now, eleven years after the Rebels' departure, Luke had returned to the fourth moon of Yavin.

Now he was a Jedi. A Jedi Master. He would be the first of a new generation, like those who had protected the Republic for a thousand generations. The old Jedi

Knights had been respected and powerful, until Darth Vader and the Emperor had hunted and slaughtered virtually all of them.

Luke had received support from Mon Mothma, the New Republic's Chief of State, to seek others who had a potential to use the Force—trainees who might become part of a new order of Jedi. Luke had managed to bring a dozen students to his "academy" on Yavin 4, but he felt uncertain about the best way to train them.

His own instruction by Obi-Wan and Yoda had been abbreviated, and Luke had since discovered facets of Jedi lore that made him realize just how much he still did not know. Even a great Jedi like Obi-Wan Kenobi had failed with his student and had let Anakin Skywalker become a monster named Darth Vader. Now Luke was expected to instruct others and make no mistakes.

Do or do not, Yoda had said, *there is no try.*

Luke stood on the smooth, cool stones of the rooftop and looked out across the awakening jungle, smelling the myriad sharp and sweet scents as the air warmed in the morning light. The spicy tang of blueleaf shrub and the perfume of lush orchids drifted up to him.

Luke closed his eyes and let his hands hang at his side, his fingers spread. He let his mind open and relax; he drew strength from the Force, touching ripples made by the life-forms crowding the jungles below. With heightened senses he could hear the rustle of millions of leaves, twigs scraping, small animals scurrying through the underbrush.

Letting out a yelp of pain and terror, a rodent thrashed and died as a predator crushed it in its jaws. Flying creatures sang mating songs to each other through the dense treetops. Large grazing mammals fed on leaves, tearing tender shoots from high branches or grubbing for fungi in the forest debris.

A wide warm river, sapphire-blue overlaid with muddy swirls of brown, flowed past the Great Temple, barely visible under the thick trees. The river bifurcated to send a tributary past the old Rebel power-generating station, which Luke and Artoo-Detoo had repaired during their preparation for the Jedi academy. Where the river sloshed around a submerged, half-rotted tree, Luke could sense a large aquatic predator lurking in the shadows, waiting for smaller fishlike creatures to swim by.

The plants grew. The animals flourished. The moon awakened to a new day. Yavin 4 was *alive*—and Luke Skywalker felt energized.

Listening intently, he heard two people approaching from far off in the dense foliage. They moved quietly, without speaking, but he could sense the change in the jungle as two of his Jedi candidates made a path through the undergrowth.

Luke's introspective moment had ended. He smiled and decided to go down and meet them.

As he turned to go back into the echoing stone halls of the temple, Luke looked up at the sky to see the streaking trails of a shuttlecraft descending through the humid atmosphere. He realized with a start that they were due for another delivery of supplies.

Luke had been so focused on training new Jedi that he had lost touch with galactic politics. Upon seeing the shuttle, he felt a deep longing to know about Leia and Han and their children. He hoped the pilot would bring news.

He shrugged down the hood of his brown Jedi cloak. The garment was too warm for the jungle humidity, but

Luke had stopped noticing minor physical discomfort. He had walked across fire on Eol Sha and gone to the spice mines of Kessel, and he could not be bothered by a little perspiration.

When the Rebels had first set up their hidden base in the Massassi temple, they had scoured the thick plant life from the chambers. Across the river stood another prominent temple, and according to orbital surveys, more structures lay buried under the implacable vegetation. But the Alliance had been far too wrapped up in its war against the Empire to bother with detailed archaeological inspections. The vanished race of temple builders remained as much a mystery now as when the Rebels had first set foot on Yavin 4.

The temple's flagstoned corridors were uneven but remarkably unscathed after centuries of exposure to the elements. Luke took a turbolift from the pinnacle down to the third level, where other students slept or meditated in the early morning. As he stepped out of the turbolift, Artoo-Detoo puttered out to greet him. The droid's wheels hummed along the bumpy flagstones, and his hemispherical head rotated back and forth, chittering at Luke.

"Yes, Artoo, I saw the shuttle coming down. Would you go down to the clearing to meet it for me? Gantoris and Streen are returning from their sojourn in the jungle. I want to greet them and learn what they've found."

Artoo acknowledged with a bleep and trundled over to a stone ramp. Luke continued through the cool confines of the temple, smelling the mustiness of the enclosed air, the powdery tang of crumbling stones. Along the halls, some of the old Alliance banners still hung outside empty quarters.

Luke's Jedi academy was by no means luxurious; in fact, it was barely even comfortable. But he and his students had concerns that absorbed their energy far more than simple conveniences. Luke had not repaired all of the damage caused by time, but he had refurbished the glowpanels, water systems, and food-prep facilities the Alliance had installed.

When he reached the ground level of the temple, the partially raised hangar-bay doors stood like the dark slit of a mouth. Luke sensed echoes of the past inside the hangar bay, a faint residue of starfighter fuel and coolant, clinging dust and grease in the corners. He stepped outside to the jungle, blinking in the washed-and-faded sunlight as evaporating mists rose from the damp undergrowth.

Luke's timing was perfect. As he walked through the lush foliage, he heard his two Jedi trainees approach.

As an exercise in resourcefulness and as an opportunity for uninterrupted concentration, Luke sent his students in pairs into the wilderness. Alone, with no other abilities but their own, they worked on powers of concentration, sensing and studying other life-forms, touching the Force.

Luke raised his hand in greeting as the two stepped through feather ferns and thick blueleaf shrubs. Tall, dark Gantoris parted heavy branches and came forward to meet Luke. His high forehead had been shaven clean of eyebrows; his skin looked chapped and weathered. Though Gantoris had calmly lived among geysers and lava flows on Eol Sha, he seemed startled to see the Jedi Master; but he covered his reaction instantly.

On his hellish world, Gantoris had used an innate talent with the Force to keep a small group of forgotten colonists alive. Gantoris had had nightmares of a terrible "dark man" who would tempt him with power and then destroy him. At first he had thought Luke was that man—Luke, who appeared in his dark Jedi robe, striding through a geyser field to ask Gantoris to come to his academy. Gantoris had tested Luke by making him walk across lava and climb through geysers.

Behind Gantoris came Streen, the second candidate Luke had found in his Jedi search. Streen had lived as a gas prospector in an abandoned floating city on the planet Bespin. Streen had been able to predict eruptions of valuable gases from deep within the cloud layers. Luke had tempted him with the ability to shut off the clamoring voices Streen heard in his head whenever he went to populated areas.

As the trainees bowed, Luke clasped their hands. "Welcome back. Tell me what you've learned."

"We found another Massassi temple!" Streen said breathlessly, looking back and forth. His wispy pale hair was tangled, matted with flecks of vegetation.

"Yes," Gantoris said. The man's ruddy face and his braided dark hair were smudged with sweat and dirt. "The new temple isn't as large as this one, but it seems more potent somehow. It's made of obsidian, sitting out in the middle of a shallow glassy lake, with a tall statue of a great lord."

"A site of great power!" Streen said.

"I felt the power too," Gantoris added. He straightened, tossing his thick braid behind him. "We should learn all we can about the Massassi race. They seem to have been very powerful, but they vanished entirely. What happened to them? Is there something we need to fear?"

Luke nodded gravely. He, too, had sensed the power in the temples. The first time he had come to Yavin 4, Luke had been little more than a boy thrust headfirst into the Rebellion against the Empire. He had barely realized the extent of the Force; in fact, he had learned of its existence only days before.

But he returned to the jungle moon a Jedi Master, and he could sense many things that had been hidden to him before. He knew the dark power that Gantoris had detected, and although he told his students they must share what they learned, Luke felt that certain knowledge could be deadly.

Darth Vader had discovered the wrong kind of knowledge. Luke could not dismiss the possibility that one of his students would be seduced by the dark side.

Luke clapped his hands on their shoulders. "Come inside. Take a drink. A supply shuttle is landing, so let's go greet our guest."

When they reached the cleared landing pad, Artoo-Detoo waited next to the grid-control kiosk, chittering coordinates to a descending X-23 StarWorker space barge.

Craning his neck, Luke watched the craft descend with a grinding whine of engines and a blast of jets. The StarWorker barge looked like a trapezoidal cargo container with Incom sublight engines strapped on. The intrasystem craft had seen better days: its gray metallic hull showed discolorations from blaster fire and countless pitted scabs from meteor encounters. But the engine sounded loud and strong as the landing gear kicked in.

The space barge flashed its running lights around its belly, then settled down gently. Luke tried to squint through the tiny front port as a group of flying creatures in the treetops burst into flight, screeching and scolding the metal thing that had lumbered into their forest.

Heavy plasteel support struts extended, locking to the ground with a hiss of hydraulic pressure. The bitter-oil smell of exhaust hung in the humid air, mixing with the peppery and sweet scents of jungle flowers and leaves.

The mechanical smell reminded Luke of the bustling metropolis of Imperial City, the governmental center of the New Republic. Though he had been at peace for months now on Yavin 4, Luke felt a tingle of sweat down his back. He could not let his guard slip for one second—he had a mission to do for the New Republic. This was not a vacation.

The hull of the space barge continued to mutter to itself as it settled. With a coughing hiss the rear cargo doors slid apart slowly as if two giants pushed them back one step at a time. Bluish-white light shone down on crates and boxes wrapped in storage nets or bolted to the walls—food, communications equipment, clothing, and amenities.

Moving softly across the packed clearing, Gantoris and Streen came up beside him. Streen's eyes went wide with a sense of wonder, but Gantoris wore a puzzled, sour expression. His skin remained dark, as if in a constant angry blush. "Do we need these things, Master Skywalker?"

Luke glanced at the contents. Judging from the material—the unnecessary material—included in the shipment, Leia herself must have compiled the cargo list. Exotic food synthesizers, comfortable clothes, heaters, humidity-neutralizers, even a few hollow Ithorian wind chimes.

"We'll make do," he said.

A narrow ramp extended with a groan of pistons and rollers from the raised pilot compartment. The silhouette of a man appeared on the ramp, booted feet, wrinkled and padded flightsuit, rounded helmet. He descended, yanking his white helmet off as his gloved hands covered the blue scooped-arc symbol of the New Republic. The pilot shook his head, tossing short dark hair from side to side.

"Wedge!" Luke grinned and shouted. "Doesn't the New Republic have anything better for its generals to do? A delivery driver in space!"

Wedge Antilles stuffed his helmet under the padded orange sleeve of his flightsuit and extended a hand to Luke. Luke embraced Wedge in the greeting of two friends who had not seen each other in far too long.

"You've got to admit I'm qualified for the job," Wedge said. "Besides, I got tired of doing demolition work in the armpit of Imperial City, and before that I got tired of cleaning up wrecked spacecraft in orbit around Coruscant. I figured a delivery driver was better than a garbageman."

Wedge flicked a glance over Luke's shoulder, and another smile dimpled his cheeks. Gantoris came forward from the cargo bay and gave Wedge a quick, almost brutal handshake as he locked eyes with the pilot. "General Antilles, have you any word from my people? I trust they have all been safely shuttled to their new home on Dantooine?"

"Yes, Gantoris, they're all settled in and doing fine. We drop-lifted an entire settlement of self-erecting living modules. We sent them programming units and agricultural droids so they could establish a viable colony right away. Dantooine is a very mild planet—plenty of animals to hunt and native vegetation to eat. Trust me, they'll be much more comfortable than they were on Eol Sha."

Gantoris nodded solemnly. "That I do not doubt." His glittering eyes looked past Wedge to the treetops. Orange light from the rising gas giant made his eyes flicker like the lava pools he had made Luke walk across on Eol Sha.

"Gantoris, Streen—please start unloading the supplies," Luke said. "I don't think you'll have trouble lifting the crates with a little nudge from the Force. Consider it a test. Artoo, please call Kirana Ti and Dorsk 81 from their quarters to help."

Streen and Gantoris moved to the corrugated ramp from the loading bay. Artoo-Detoo hummed across the landing grid and disappeared into the shadowy hangar of the Great Temple in search of the other Jedi candidates.

Luke clapped his friend on the shoulder. "I'm starving for news, Wedge. I hope you brought some gossip with you."

Wedge raised his eyebrows. His narrow chin and soft features made him look more youthful than Luke. They had been through a lot together: Wedge had flown beside Luke on his triumphant run down the Death Star corridor, had assisted in the defense of Echo Base on the ice planet Hoth, and had fought against the second Death Star over Endor.

"Gossip?" Wedge asked, laughing. "That doesn't sound like something that would interest a Jedi Master."

"You got me there, Wedge. How are Leia and Han? How is Mon Mothma? How are things on Coruscant? When is Han going to bring Kyp Durron to my training center? That boy had enormous potential, and I want to start working with him."

Wedge shook his head at the volley of questions. "Kyp will be here, Luke, don't worry. He spent most of his life in the spice mines of Kessel, and he's only been out a month. Han's trying to show the kid how to live a little first."

Luke remembered the dark-haired teen Han had rescued from the black spice mines. When Luke had used a Jedi testing technique to see if Kyp had potential to use the Force, the boy's response had knocked Luke across the room. In his entire Jedi search, Luke had never encountered such power.

"And what about Leia?"

Wedge considered, and Luke appreciated that he didn't just answer with a simple "Of course everything's fine." "She seems to be spending more and more time with her duties as Minister of State. Mon Mothma has been handing off a lot of important responsibilities to Leia while she herself stays in her private chambers and rules from a distance. It's got a lot of people disturbed."

That behavior seemed highly unusual for the strong, compassionate ruler Luke remembered. "And how is Leia handling it?" He longed to know a thousand things at once, wishing he could be in the thick of it all again . . . while another part of him preferred the peace of Yavin 4.

Wedge sat on the edge of the sloping ramp. He propped one leg next to a support strut, then balanced his helmet on his knee. "Leia's doing a wonderful job, but she's trying to do too much, if you ask me. Even with baby Anakin still in hiding, she does have the twins to watch over now. Threepio helps, but Jacen and Jaina are still only two and a half years old. It's more than a full-time job, and Leia is getting exhausted."

"She could come here for a rest," Luke suggested. "Have her bring the twins, since I need to get them started on basic Jedi skills."

"I'm sure Leia would love to come here," Wedge said. They turned and watched as Streen and Gantoris emerged from the barge carrying tall crates. The two Jedi candidates walked smoothly, carrying loads that seemed impossible, and Wedge's eyes widened at the impressive feats of strength. "I had to have labor droids put those boxes onboard. I couldn't budge one myself."

"Then my students must be showing some progress." Luke nodded. "What about you, Wedge? You going to be a delivery driver the rest of your career?"

Wedge smiled; then with a flick of his wrist he tossed the helmet up the ramp and into the open cockpit. It clacked and thumped across the floor. "No. In fact I came here because I have a new assignment, and I won't get a chance to see you again for some time. The New Republic Council feels that Dr. Qwi Xux may be in danger from espionage. Admiral Daala is still out there somewhere with her fleet of Imperial Star Destroyers, and any time now I expect her to start blasting planets at random with hit-and-run strikes. She may try to get Qwi back."

Luke nodded gravely. Qwi Xux had been the top scientist in the Imperial research facility from which Han Solo had escaped—with Qwi's help. "If Admiral Daala doesn't want Dr. Xux back, I'm sure someone else will."

"Yeah," Wedge said, "that's why I've been assigned as her personal bodyguard and escort. In the meantime the Council still hasn't decided what to do with the Sun Crusher weapon that Han captured." Wedge sighed. "That's just scratching the surface of everything going on back on Coruscant."

Luke stared at Gantoris and Streen as they continued to unload the cargo bay, marching across the clearing to deposit their crates in the empty, cool hangar. Artoo-Detoo rattled out of the temple, leading two other students.

"Sounds like you need the new Jedi Knights more than ever," Luke said.

Wedge agreed emphatically. "More than you can know."

2

Fidgeting from the long voyage in the expanded B-wing fighter, Leia Organa Solo rode in silence beside Admiral Ackbar. The two of them sat in the cramped, metallic-smelling cockpit as the ship plunged through hyperspace.

Being Minister of State kept Leia on the move, shuttling from diplomatic event to ambassadorial reception to political emergency. Dutifully, she hopped across the galaxy, putting out fires and helping Mon Mothma hold together a fragile alliance in the vacuum left by the fall of the Empire.

Leia had already reviewed the background holos of the planet Vortex dozens of times, but she could not keep her mind on the upcoming Concert of the Winds. Diplomatic duties took her away far too often, and she used quiet moments to think about her husband Han, her twin children Jacen and Jaina. It had been too long since she had held her youngest baby, Anakin, who remained isolated and protected on the secret planet Anoth.

It seemed that whenever Leia tried to spend a week, a day, even an *hour* alone with her family, something interrupted. She seethed inside each time, unable to show her feelings because she had to wear a calm political mask.

In her younger days Leia had devoted her life to the Rebellion; she had worked behind the scenes as a princess of Alderaan, as Senator Bail Organa's daughter; she had fought against Darth Vader and the Emperor, and more recently against Grand Admiral Thrawn. Now, though, she felt torn between her duties as Minister of State and her duties as Han Solo's wife and as mother to three children. She had allowed the New Republic to come first. This time. Again.

Beside her in the cockpit Admiral Ackbar moved his amphibious hands fluidly as he manipulated several control levers. "Dropping out of hyperspace now," he said in his gravelly voice.

The salmon-colored alien seemed perfectly comfortable in his white uniform. Ackbar swiveled his gigantic glassy eyes from side to side, as if to take in every detail of his craft. Through the hours of their journey, Leia had not seen him fidget once.

He and the other inhabitants of the watery world Calamari had suffered much under the Empire's iron grip. They had learned how to be quiet, yet listen to every detail, how to make their own decisions, and how to act upon them. Working as a loyal member of the Rebellion, Ackbar himself had been instrumental in developing the B-wing class of starfighters that had taken such a huge toll on the Imperial TIE fighters.

As Leia watched him pilot the stretched-out, cumbersome-looking fighter, Ackbar seemed an integral part of the gangly craft that appeared to be all wings and turbolaser turrets mounted around a dual cockpit. Ackbar's crew of fishlike Calamarians, led by his chief starship mechanic, Terpfen, had expanded the former one-man craft into Ackbar's personal diplomatic shuttle, adding a single passenger seat.

Through the curved dome of the cockpit windows, Leia watched as multicolored knots of hyperspace evaporated into a star-strewn panorama. The sublight engines kicked in, and the B-wing streaked toward the planet Vortex.

Leia's dress uniform felt damp and clingy, and she tried to adjust the folds of slick fabric to make herself more comfortable. As Ackbar concentrated on the approach to Vortex, Leia pulled out her pocket holopad, laying the flat silvery plate on her lap.

"Beautiful," she said, peering out the viewport to the planet beneath them. The blue and metallic-gray ball hung alone in space, moonless. Its atmosphere showed complex embroideries of cloudbanks and storm systems, racing spirals of clouds that swirled in horrendous gales.

Leia remembered her astronomical briefings about Vortex. The sharp tilt of the planet's axis produced severe seasonal changes. At the onset of winter, a vast polar cap formed rapidly from gases that froze out of the atmosphere. The sudden drop in pressure caused immense air currents, like a great flood going down a drain; clouds and vapor streamed southward in a battering ram to fill the empty zone where the atmosphere had solidified.

The Vors, hollow-boned humanoids with a rack of lacy wings on their backs, went to ground during storm season, taking shelter in half-buried hummock dwellings. To celebrate the winds, though, the Vors had established a cultural festival renowned throughout the galaxy. . . .

Deciding to review the details one more time before they landed and the diplomatic reception began, Leia touched the icons etched into the synthetic marble frame of her datapad. It would not do for the New Republic's Minister of State to make a political faux pas.

A translucent image shimmered and grew out of the silvery screen in a miniaturized projection of the Cathedral of Winds. Defying the hurricane gales that thrashed through their atmosphere, the Vors had built a tall ethereal structure that had resisted the fierce storm winds for centuries. Delicate and incredibly intricate, the Cathedral of Winds rose like a castle made of eggshell-thin crystal. Thousands of passageways wound through hollow chambers and turrets and spires. Sunlight glittered on the structure, reflecting the rippling fields of windblown grasses that sprawled across the surrounding plains.

At the beginning of storm season, gusts of wind blew through thousands of different-sized openings in the honey combed walls, whipping up a reverberating, mournful music through pipes of various diameters.

The wind music was never the same twice, and the Vors allowed their cathedral to play only once each year. During the concert thousands of Vors flew into or climbed through the spires and windpipes, opening and closing air passages to mold the music into a sculpture, a work of art created by the weather systems of the storm planet and the Vor people.

On the holopad Leia skimmed to the next files. The music of the winds had not been heard for decades, not since Senator Palpatine had announced his New Order and declared himself Emperor. Objecting to the excesses of the Empire, the Vors had sealed the holes in their cathedral and refused to let the music play for anyone.

But this season the Vors had invited representatives from the New Republic to come and listen.

Ackbar opened a comm channel and pushed his fishlike face closer to the voice pickup. Leia watched the bristly feelers around his mouth jiggle as he spoke. "Vortex Cathedral landing pad, this is Admiral Ackbar. We are in orbit and approaching your position."

A Vor voice like two dry twigs rattling together crackled back over the speaker. "New Republic shuttle, we are transmitting landing coordinates that take into account wind shear and storm systems along your descent. Our atmospheric turbulence is quite unpredictable and dangerous. Please follow precisely."

"Understood." Ackbar settled back into his seat, rubbing broad shoulder blades against the ridged back of the chair. He pulled several black restraint strands across his chest. "You'd better strap in, Leia," Ackbar said. "It's going to be a bumpy ride."

Leia switched off her holopad and tucked it beside her seat. She secured herself, feeling confined by the webbing, and took a deep breath of the stale recycled air. The faintest fishy undertone suggested Calamarian anxiety.

Staring ahead, Ackbar took his B-wing into the swirling atmosphere of Vortex, straight toward the storm systems.

• • •

Ackbar knew that humans could not read expressions on broad Calamarian faces. He hoped Leia did not realize how uneasy he felt flying through such hellish weather patterns.

Leia did not know that Ackbar had volunteered to take the mission because he trusted no other person to pilot someone as important as the Minister of State, and he trusted no other vehicle more than his personal B-wing fighter.

He turned both of his brown eyes forward to watch the approaching cloud layers. The ship cut through the outer layers of atmosphere, zooming into buffeting turbulence. The sharp wings of the starfighter sliced the air, curling wind in a rippling wake. The wing edges glowed cherry-red from the screaming descent.

Ackbar gripped the controls with his flipper-hands, concentrating on fast reactions, split-second decisions, making sure everything worked just right. In this landing there would be no room for error. He cocked his right eye down to scan the landing coordinates the Vor technician had transmitted.

The craft began to rattle and jitter. His stomach lurched as a sudden updraft knocked them several hundred meters higher and then let them fall in a deep plunge until he managed to wrestle control back. Blurry fists of high-rising clouds pummeled the transparisteel viewports, leaving trails of condensed moisture that fanned out and evaporated.

Ackbar tracked from side to side across the panels with his left eye, verifying the readouts. No red lights. His right eye cocked back to catch a glimpse of Leia sitting rigid and silent, held in place by black restraint cords. Her dark eyes seemed almost as wide as a Mon Calamarian's, but her lips were pressed together in a thin white line. She seemed afraid, but afraid to show it, trusting in his ability. Leia said no word to distract him.

The B-wing headed down in a spiral, skirting an immense cyclonic disturbance. The wind hooked the rattling wings of the fighter, knocking the craft from side to side. Ackbar deployed the secondary aileron struts in an attempt to regain stability and retracted the laser-cannon turrets to minimize wind resistance.

"New Republic shuttle, we show you off course," the brittle-twig voice of the Vor controller came over the speaker, muffled by the roaring wind. "Please advise."

Ackbar turned his left eye to double-check the coordinate display, and saw that the starfighter had indeed veered off course. Calm and focused, he tried to force the craft back onto the appropriate vector. He couldn't believe he had gone so far astray, unless he had misread the coordinates in the first place.

As he yanked the B-wing toward a wall of spiraling clouds, a blast of gale-force winds hammered them into a roll and slammed Ackbar against his pilot seat. The fighter spun end over end, battered by the wild storm.

Leia let out a small scream before clamping her mouth shut. Ackbar hauled with all his strength upon the levers, firing stabilizer jets in a counterclockwise maneuver to counteract the spin.

The B-wing responded, finally slowing its crazed descent. Ackbar looked up to see himself surrounded by a whirlwind of mist. He had no idea which direction was up or down. He accordioned out the craft's set of perpendicular wings and locked them into a more stable cruising position. His craft responded sluggishly, but the cockpit panels told him that the wings were in place.

"New Republic shuttle, please respond." The Vor did not sound at all concerned.

Ackbar finally got the B-wing upright and flying again, but found he had missed his coordinates once more. He angled back into them as easily as he could. His mouth felt desiccated as he checked the altitude panels and saw with alarm how far the ship had dropped.

The metal hull plates smoked and glowed orange from tearing through the atmosphere. Lightning slashed on all sides. Blue balls of discharge electricity flared from the tips of the wings. His readouts scrambled with racing curls of static, then came back on again. The cockpit power systems dimmed, then brightened as reserve power kicked in.

Ackbar risked another glance at Leia and saw her fighting wide-eyed fear and helplessness. He knew she was a woman of action and would do anything to help him out—but there was nothing she could do. If he had to, Ackbar could eject her to safety—but he did not dare risk losing his B-wing yet. He could still pull off a desperate but intact landing.

Suddenly, the clouds peeled away like a wet rag ripped from his eyes. The wind-whipped plains of Vortex spread out below, furred with golden-brown and purple grasses. The grasslands rippled as the wind combed invisible fingers through the blades. Concentric circles of bunkerlike Vor shelters surrounded the center of their civilization.

He heard Leia gasp in a deep wonder that sliced through even her terror. The enormous Cathedral of

Winds glinted with light and roiling shadows as clouds marched overhead. The high lacy structure seemed far too delicate to withstand the storms. Winged creatures swarmed up and down the sides of the fluted chambers, opening passages for the wind to blow through and create the famous music. Faintly distant, he could hear the lilting, eerie notes.

"New Republic shuttle, you are on the wrong course. This is an emergency. You must abort your landing."

With a shock Ackbar saw that the displayed coordinates had changed again. The B-wing did not respond as he fought the controls. The Cathedral of Winds grew larger every second.

Cocking an eye to look through the upper rim of the domed viewport, Ackbar saw that one of the perpendicular wings had jammed at a severe angle, yielding maximum wind resistance. The angled wing slapped against the turbulence and jerked the starfighter to the left.

His cockpit panels insisted that both wings had deployed properly, yet his own vision told him otherwise.

Ackbar jabbed the controls again, trying to straighten the wing, to regain control. The bottom half of his body felt cold and tingly as he channeled reserves of energy into his mind and his hands on the control levers.

"Something is very wrong here," he said.

Leia stared out the viewport. "We're heading straight for the cathedral!"

One of the aileron struts buckled and snapped from the plasteel hull, dragging power cables as it tore free. Sparks flew, and more hull plates ripped up.

Ackbar strangled an outcry. Suddenly the control lights flickered and dimmed. He heard the grinding hum as his main cockpit panels went dead. He hit the second auxiliary backup he had personally designed into the B-wing.

"I don't understand it," Ackbar said, his voice guttural in the confines of the cockpit. "This ship was just reconditioned. My own Calamarian mechanics were the only ones who touched it."

"New Republic shuttle," the voice on the radio insisted.

On the crystalline Cathedral of Winds, multicolored Vors scrambled down the sides, fleeing as they saw the craft hurtling toward them. Some of the creatures took flight, while others stared. Thousands of them were packed into the immense glassy structure.

Ackbar hauled the controls to the right, to the left—anything to make the craft swerve—but nothing responded. All the power had died.

He couldn't raise or lower the ship's wings. He was a large deadweight falling straight toward the cathedral. Desperately he hit the full battery reserves, knowing they could do nothing for the mechanical subsystems, but at least he could lock in a full-power crash shield around the B-wing.

And before that, he could break Leia free to safety.

"I'm sorry, Leia," Ackbar said. "Tell them that I am sorry." He punched a button on the control panel that cracked open the right side of the cockpit, splitting the hull and blasting free the tacked-on passenger seat.

As it shot Leia into the clawlike winds, Ackbar heard the wind screech at him through the open cockpit. The crash shield hummed as he hurtled toward the great crystalline structure. The fighter's engine smoldered and smoked.

Ackbar stared straight ahead until the end, never blinking his huge Calamarian eyes.

Leia found herself flying through the air. The blast of the ejection seat had knocked the breath out of her.

She couldn't even shout as the wind caught and spun her chair. The seat's safety repulsorlifts held her like a gentle hand and slowly lowered her toward the whiplike strands of pale-hued grasses below.

She looked up to see Ackbar's B-wing shuttle in the last instant before it crashed. The starfighter smoked and whined as it plunged like a metal filing toward a powerful magnet.

In a frozen moment she heard the loud, mournful fluting of winds whistling through thousands of crystalline chambers. The breeze picked up with a gust, making the music sound like a sudden gasp of terror. The winged Vors scrambled and attempted to flee, but most could not move quickly enough.

Ackbar's B-wing plowed into the lower levels of the Cathedral of Winds like a meteor. The booming impact detonated the crystalline towers into a hail of razor-edged spears that flew in all directions. The sound of tinkling glass, the roar of sharp broken pieces, the shriek of the wind, the screams of the slashed Vors—all combined into the most agonizing sound Leia had ever heard.

The entire glasslike structure seemed to take forever to collapse. Tower after tower fell inward.

The winds kept blowing, drawing somber notes from the hollow columns, changing pitch. The music became a thinner and thinner wail, until only a handful of intact wind tubes were left lying on their sides in the glassy rubble.

As Leia wept with great sobs that seemed to tear her apart, the automatic escape chair gently drifted to the ground and settled in the whispering grasses.

3

The polar regions of Coruscant

reminded Han Solo of the ice planet Hoth—with one crucial difference. Han was here *by choice* with his young friend Kyp Durron for a vacation while Leia went off with Admiral Ackbar on yet another diplomatic mission.

Han stood atop the crumpled blue-white ice cliffs, feeling warm in his insulated charcoal-gray parka and red heater gloves. The ever-present auroras in the purplish skies sent rainbow curtains flickering and refracting off the ice. He drew in a deep breath of crackling cold air that seemed to curl his nostril hairs.

He turned to Kyp beside him. "About ready to go, kid?"

For the fifth time the dark-haired eighteen-year-old bent over to adjust the fastenings on his turbo-skis. "Uh, almost," Kyp said.

Han leaned forward to peer down the steep turbo-ski run of rippled ice, feeling a lump form in his throat but unwilling to show it.

Blue and white glaciers shone in dim light from the months-long twilight. Below, ice-boring machines had chewed deep tunnels into the thick ice caps; other excavators had chopped broad terraces on the cliffs as they mined centuries-old snowpack, melting it with fusion furnaces to be delivered via titanic water pipelines to the dense metropolitan areas in the temperate zones.

"You really think I can do this?" Kyp said, straightening and gripping his deflector poles.

Han laughed. "Kid, if you can pilot us single-handed through a black hole cluster, I think you can handle a turbo-ski slope on the most civilized planet in the galaxy."

Kyp looked at Han with a smile in his dark eyes. The boy reminded Han of a young Luke Skywalker. Ever since Han had rescued Kyp from his slavery in the spice mines of Kessel, the young man had clung to him. After years of wrongful Imperial imprisonment, Kyp had missed the best years of his life. Han vowed to make up for that.

"Come on, kid," he said, leaning forward and igniting the motors of his turbo-skis. With thickly gloved hands Han held on to the deflector poles and flicked them on. He felt the cushioning repulsorfield emanating from each point, making the poles bob in the air to keep his balance.

"You're on," Kyp said, and fired up his own skis. "But not the kiddie slope." He turned from the wide ice pathway and pointed instead to a side run that branched off over several treacherous ledges, across the scabby ice of a rotten glacier, and finally over a frozen waterfall to a receiving-and-rescue area. Winking red laser beacons clearly marked the dangerous path.

"No way, Kyp! It's much too—" But Kyp launched himself forward and blasted down the slope.

"Hey!" Han said. He felt sick in the pit of his stomach, sure he would have to pick up Kyp's broken body somewhere along the path. But now he had no choice but to blast after the boy. "Kid, this is really a stupid thing to do."

Crystals of powdery snow sprayed behind Kyp's turbo-skis as he bent forward, touching the ground at occasional intervals with his deflector poles. He kept his balance like an expert, intuitively knowing what to do. After only a second of the thundering descent, Han realized that Kyp might be more likely to survive this ride than he was.

As Han rocketed down the slope, the snow and ice hissed beneath him like a jet of compressed air. Han hit a frozen outcropping that sent him flying, and he somersaulted through the air, flailing with his deflector poles. Stabilizer jets on his belt righted him just in time as he slammed into the snow again. He continued down the slope with the speed of a stampeding bantha.

He squinted behind ice goggles, concentrating intensely on keeping himself upright. The landscape seemed too sharp—every razor-edged drift of snow, the glittering sheared-off face of ice—as if every single detail might be his last.

Kyp let out a loud *whoop* of delight as he slewed left onto the dangerous offshoot turbo-ski path. The whoop echoed three times around the sharp-edged cliffs.

Han began cursing the young man's recklessness, then experienced a sudden inner warmth as he realized he had expected little else from Kyp. Making the best of it,

Han let out an answering whoop of his own and turned to follow.

Red laser beacons flared, warning and guiding the foolish turbo-skiers along the path. The rippled surface whispered beneath the soft cushioning fields of his turbo-skis.

Ahead, the icy roadway seemed foreshortened and continued at a different elevation. Han realized the danger an instant before he reached the precipice. "Cliff!"

Kyp bent low, as if he had simply become another component of his turbo-skis. He tucked his deflector poles close to his sides, then fired up the rear jets of his skis. He rocketed over the edge of the cliff, arcing down in a long smooth curve to the resumption of the trail.

Barely in time, Han activated his own jets and launched himself over empty space. His stomach dropped even faster than gravity could tug him down. Wind ruffled the edges of his parka hood.

In front of him Kyp landed smoothly without so much as a wobble and shot downslope.

Han had time to take only one gulping breath as the plateau of ice rushed up to meet his turbo-skis with a loud *crack*. He gripped his deflector poles, desperate to maintain his balance.

A powdery ribbon of drifted snow curled across their path. Kyp jammed down with his deflector poles, hopping up into the air and cleanly missing the drift—but Han plowed straight through.

Snow flew into his goggles, blinding him. He wobbled and jabbed from side to side with his poles. He managed to swipe a gloved hand across his goggles just in time to swerve left and avoid smashing into a monolithic ice outcropping.

Before he had recovered his balance, Han launched over a yawning chasm in the rotten glacier that fell out beneath him. For a timeless instant he stared down at a drop of about a million kilometers, and then he landed on the far side. Behind him, he heard a *whump* as a block of age-old snow lost its precarious grip on the wall and plunged into the crevasse.

Ahead, Kyp encountered a blocky, rubble-strewn glacier field. More widely spaced now, the laser beacons seemed to give up and let foolhardy turbo-skiers choose their own path. Kyp wobbled as he struck hummocks of ice and snow. He raised the repulsorfield to skim higher over the surface.

As the crusty glacier grew rougher, clogged with grainy blown snow, Han muttered complaints and curses through gritted teeth. He kept his balance somehow, but Kyp had lost ground. Han found himself breathing the boy's wake, pushing closer and faster—and suddenly the race meant something to him again. Afterward, while sitting around in a cantina and swapping stories, he would somehow convince himself that the whole thing had been a great deal of fun.

Feeling a bit of the recklessness he had just cursed Kyp for, Han pulsed the jets, lunging forward in an adrenaline-filled burst of speed that brought him side by side with Kyp.

A snowfield sprawled in front of them, sparkling white and unsullied by other turbo-ski tracks—even though it had not snowed for more than a month in this arid frigid climate—demonstrating exactly how few people had been foolish enough to attempt the dangerous path.

Ahead, the roped-off receiving-and-rescue area lay like a sanctuary: communications gear, warming huts, powered-down medical droids that could be reactivated at a moment's notice, and an old hot-beverage shop that had long since gone out of business. Home free—they had made it!

Kyp glanced sideways at him, his dark eyes crinkled at the corners. He crouched down and blasted his skis at full power. Han hunched over to decrease his air resistance. Pristine snow flew around him, hissing in his ears.

The line of laser beacons switched off like metallic eyes blinking shut. Han had no time to wonder about it before the smooth blanket of snow ahead bulged, then sloughed inward.

A crunching, grinding sound accompanied the straining of massive engines. Gouts of steam erupted from the collapsed snowfield as the glowing red nose of a mechanical thermal borer thrust into the open air. The screw-shaped tip continued to turn as it chewed its way out of the solid ice.

"Look out!" Han yelled, but Kyp had already veered off to the left side, leaning hard on one deflector pole and jabbing at the air with his other. Han punched his stabilizing jets and streaked to the right as the mammoth ice-processing machine chewed the opening of its tunnel wider, clutching the walls with clawed tractor treads.

Han skimmed past the gaping pit, feeling a blast of hot steam across his cheeks. His goggles fogged again, but he found his way to the steep ice waterfall, the final obstacle before the finish line. The edge of the precipice flowed with long tendrils of icicles like dangling cables that had built up over centuries during the brief spring thaws.

Kyp launched himself over the edge of the frozen river, igniting both ski jets. Han did the same, tucking his poles against his ribs, watching the packed snow fly up to strike the bottoms of his skis with a loud slap that echoed along the ice fields in unison with the sound of Kyp's landing.

They both charged forward, then slewed to a stop in front of the cluster of prefab huts. Kyp peeled down the hood of his parka and started laughing. Han held on to his deflector poles, feeling his body tremble with relief and an overdose of excitement. Then he, too, began chuckling.

"That was really stupid, kid," Han managed at last.

"Oh?" Kyp shrugged. "Who was stupid enough to follow me? After the spice mines of Kessel, I wouldn't consider a little turbo-ski slope too dangerous. Hey, maybe we could ask Threepio to tell us the odds of successfully negotiating that slope when we get back."

Han shook his head and gave a lopsided grin. "I'm not interested in odds. We did it. That's what counts."

Kyp stared across the frozen distance. His eyes seemed to follow the arrow-straight lines of nonreflective water conduits ringed with pressure joints and pumping stations.

"I'm glad we've had so much fun, Han," he said, staring into something only he seemed to see. "I've done a lifetime's worth of healing since you rescued me."

Han felt uncomfortable at the thick emotion he heard in Kyp's voice. He tried to lighten the mood. "Well, kid, you had as much to do with our escape as I did."

Kyp didn't seem to hear. "I've been thinking about what Luke Skywalker said when he found my ability to use the Force. I only know a little bit about it, but it seems to be calling me. I could do a huge service to the New Republic. The Empire ruined my life and destroyed my family—I wouldn't mind getting a chance to strike back."

Han swallowed, knowing what the boy was trying to say. "So you think you're ready to go study with Luke and the other Jedi trainees?"

Kyp nodded. "I'd rather stay here and have fun for the rest of my life, but—"

Han said in a soft voice, "You deserve it, you know."

But Kyp shook his head. "I think it's time I start taking myself seriously. If I do have this gift of using the Force, I can't let it go to waste."

Han gripped the young man's shoulder and squeezed hard, feeling Kyp's rangy frame through his bulky gloves. "I'll see that you get a good flight to Yavin 4."

The whirring hum of repulsorlifts broke the quiet moment. Han looked up as a messenger droid approached, streaking like a chromium projectile over the ice fields. The droid arrowed straight for them.

Han muttered, "If that's a representative from the turbo-ski resort, I'm going to file a complaint about that ice-mining machine. We could have been killed."

But as the messenger droid hovered over them, lowering itself to Han's eye level, it snapped open a scanning panel and spoke in a genderless monotone. "General Solo, please confirm identification. Voice match will be sufficient."

Han groaned. "Aww, I'm on vacation. I don't want to bother with any diplomatic mess right now."

"Voice match confirmed. Thank you," the droid said. "Prepare to receive encoded message."

The droid hovered as it projected a holographic image onto the clean snow. Han recognized the auburn-haired figure of Mon Mothma. He straightened in surprise—the Chief of State rarely communicated with him directly.

"Han," Mon Mothma said in a quiet, troubled voice. He noticed immediately that she had called him by his first name instead of his more formal rank. A fist of sudden dread clenched his stomach.

"I'm sending you this message because there has been an accident. Admiral Ackbar's shuttle crashed on the planet Vortex. Leia was with him, but she's safe and unharmed. The admiral ejected her to safety before his ship flew out of control, directly into a large cultural center. Admiral Ackbar managed to power up his crash shields, but the entire structure was destroyed. So far at least 358 Vors are confirmed dead in the wreckage.

"This is a tragic day for us, Han. Come home to Imperial City. I think Leia might need you as soon as she returns." Mon Mothma's image wavered, then dissolved into staticky snowflakes that faded in the air.

The messenger droid said, "Thank you. Here is your receipt." It spat out a tiny blue chit that landed in a puff of snow at Han's feet.

Han stared as the droid turned and streaked back toward the base camp. He squashed the blue chit into the snow with the base of his turbo-ski. He felt sick. The excitement he had just experienced, all the joy with Kyp, had evaporated, leaving only a leaden dread inside him.

"Come on, Kyp. Let's go."

• • •

See-Threepio thought that if his fine-motor control had allowed it, his entire golden body would be chattering with cold. His internal thermal units were no match for the frozen polar regions of Coruscant.

He was a protocol droid, fluent in over six million forms of communication. He was able to perform an incredible number of diverse tasks—all of which seemed more appealing at the moment than baby-sitting a pair of wild two-and-a-half-year-olds who saw him as their plaything.

Threepio had taken the twins to the snow-play area at the bottom of the ice slopes, where they could ride tame tauntauns. Little Jacen and his sister Jaina seemed to enjoy the spitting, cumbersome creatures—and the Umgullian rancher who had brought the furry animals to Coruscant seemed delighted to have the business.

Afterward Threepio had stoically endured as the twins insisted on making a "snow droid" of him, packing layers of snow around his shiny body. He still felt ice crystals caked inside his joints. As he enhanced the output from his optical sensors, Threepio thought that his golden alloy had taken on a decidedly bluish tinge from the low temperature.

On a sledding slope the twins spun around, giggling and shrieking as they bounced against padded restraints in a child's snow skimmer. Threepio waited for them at the bottom, then began the long trudge back up the hill so the children could do it all over again. He felt like a low-capacity labor droid with too little computing power to understand the drudgery of its own existence. "Oh, how I wish Master Solo would get back soon," he said.

At the top of the ramp he secured Jacen and Jaina snugly into their seats. In tandem they looked up at him with rosy-cheeked faces. Humans claimed to find the winter chill exhilarating; Threepio wished he had outfitted himself with more efficient low-temperature lubricants.

"Now, you children be careful on the ride down," he said. "I shall meet you at the bottom and bring you back up." He paused. "Again."

He launched the children in the spinning snow skimmer. Jacen and Jaina laughed and squealed as feathers of snow sprayed down the slope. Threepio began to move with a rapid gait down the long ramp.

When he reached the bottom, the twins were already attempting to unstrap themselves. Jaina had managed to disconnect one buckle, though the attendant at the equipment-rental station had assured Threepio that the restraints were utterly childproof.

"Children, leave that alone!" he said. He refastened Jaina's restraint and switched on the hoverfield beneath the snow skimmer. He grasped the handles and began to climb back up the slope to the launching platform.

When he reached the top, both twins shouted, "Again!" in unison, as if their minds were linked. Threepio decided it was time to lecture the children about overindulgence in enjoyment, but before he could formulate a speech with the appropriate levels of sternness and vocabulary, a crowded shuttle skimmer arrived. Han Solo emerged, pulling back the hood of his gray parka and balancing his turbo-skis on his left shoulder. Kyp Durron followed him out of the transport.

Threepio raised a golden arm. "Over here," he said. "Master Solo, over here!"

"Daddy!" Jaina said. Jacen echoed her a fraction of a second later.

"Thank heavens," Threepio said, and started to unfasten the restraints.

"Get ready to go," Han said as he marched forward, his expression unaccountably troubled. Threepio reached forward, about to begin his litany of complaints, but Han dropped the bulky turbo-skis into the droid's arms.

"Master Solo, is something wrong?" Threepio tried to balance the heavy skis.

"Sorry to cut your vacation short, kids, but we have to get back home," Han said, ignoring the droid.

Threepio straightened. "I'm very glad to hear that, sir. I don't mean to complain, but I was *not* designed for temperature extremes."

He felt an impact against the back of his head as a large lump of snow splattered him. "Oh!" he said, raising his arms in alarm, barely managing to keep hold of the skis. "Master Solo, I must protest!" he said.

Jacen and Jaina giggled as they each picked up another snowball to throw at the droid.

Han turned to the twins. "Stop playing with Threepio, you two. We have to get back home."

Down in the repair bays of the revamped Imperial Palace on Coruscant, Lando Calrissian couldn't imagine how Chewbacca managed to cram his enormous furry body inside the *Falcon*'s narrow maintenance crawlway. Standing in the corridor, Lando saw the Wookiee as a tangle of brown fur wedged between the emergency power generator, the acceleration compensator, and the anticoncussion field generator.

Chewbacca let out a yowl as he dropped a hydrospanner. The tool bounced and fell with a series of ricocheting clangs until it landed in a completely inaccessible spot. The Wookiee snarled and then let out a yelp as he banged his shaggy head on a coolant pipe.

"No, no, Chewbacca!" Lando said, brushing back his sleek cape and sticking his arm into the maintenance crawlway. He tried to point toward the circuitry. "That goes here, and *this* goes there!" Chewbacca grumbled back, disagreeing.

"Look, Chewie, I know this ship like the back of my hand, too. I owned her for quite a few years, you know."

Chewbacca made a string of ululating sounds that echoed inside the enclosed chamber.

"All right, have it your way. I can work the access hatches on the outside hull. I'll retrieve your hydrospanner. Who knows what other junk we'll find there?"

Lando turned and made his way to the entry ramp, stomping down into the cacophony of shouted requests and engine noises in the starship mechanic bay. The air smelled oily and stifling, tainted with gaseous coolants and exhaust fumes from small diplomatic shuttles to large freighters. Human and alien engineers worked on their ships. Stubby Ugnaughts clambered inside access hatches and chattered at each other, requesting tools and diagrams for fixing troublesome engines.

Admiral Ackbar's carefully picked crew of Calamarian starship mechanics oversaw special modifications to small vessels in the New Republic fleet. Terpfen, Ackbar's chief mechanic, wandered from ship to ship, status board in hand, verifying requested repairs and scrutinizing the work with his glassy fish eyes.

Lando pried open the access hatch on the *Falcon*'s outer hull. The hydrospanner clattered out and fell into his outstretched hands, along with burned-out cyberfuses, a discarded hyperdrive shunt, and the wrapper from a package of dehydrated food.

"Got it, Chewbacca," he shouted. The Wookiee's answer was muffled inside the cramped access hatch.

Lando looked at the scorch marks along the *Falcon*'s battered hull. The ship seemed to be one massive collection of patches and repairs. He ran a callused hand along the hull, caressing the metal.

"Hey! What are you doing to my ship?"

Lando jerked his hand away from the *Falcon* and looked around guiltily to see Han Solo approaching. Chewbacca bellowed a greeting from the maintenance crawlway.

Han's face reflected a thunderstorm of bad moods as he strode across the debris-strewn floor of the mechanic bay. "I need my ship right now. Is she ready to fly?" Han said.

Lando put his hands at his side. "I was just making some repairs and modifications, old buddy. What's the problem?"

"Who told you you could make any modifications?" Han looked unaccountably angry. "Chewie, we've got to fly right away. Why did you let this clown mess around with my engines?"

"Wait a minute, Han! This used to be my ship, you know," Lando said, not knowing what had provoked such anger in his friend. "Besides, who rescued this ship from Kessel? Who saved your tail from the Imperial fleet?"

See-Threepio hastened stiffly into the mechanic bay. "Ah, greetings, General Calrissian," he said.

Lando ignored the droid. "I lost the *Lady Luck* rescuing your ship. I'd think that deserves a little gratitude, don't you? In fact, since I sacrificed my own ship to save your hide, I thought maybe you'd be grateful enough to give me back the *Falcon*."

"Oh, my!" Threepio said. "That *is* an idea that might warrant some consideration, Master Solo."

"Shut up, Threepio," Han said without glancing in the droid's direction.

"Looks like you've got an attitude problem, Han," Lando said with a grin he knew would annoy his friend. But Han had stepped over the bounds of common courtesy with his snappish accusations, and Lando had no intention of letting him get away with it.

Han looked ready to explode. Lando couldn't figure out what was bothering him. "My problem is you've been sabotaging my ship. I don't ever want you touching her again, do you understand? Get your own ship. Seems to me that with the million-credit reward you got at the blob races on Umgul, you could buy just about any ship you want and stop messing around with mine."

"An excellent idea, sir," Threepio added helpfully. "With that amount of money, General Calrissian, you could indeed buy a fine ship."

"Be quiet, Threepio," Lando said, putting his hands on his hips. "I don't want to buy another ship, old buddy." He stressed the last two words with thick sarcasm. "If I can't have the *Lady Luck*, I want the *Falcon*. Your wife is the Minister of State, Han. You can have the government provide you with any sort of transport you want—why not get yourself a new fighter right from the Calamarian shipyards?"

"I'm certain that could be arranged, sir," Threepio agreed.

"Shut up, Threepio," Han said again, keeping his eyes on Lando. "I don't want any old ship. The *Falcon* is mine."

Lando glowered at Han. "You won her from me in a sabacc game, and to tell you the truth—old buddy—I've always suspected you cheated in that game."

Han became livid, backing away. "You're accusing *me* of cheating? I've been called a scoundrel before, but never a cheat! In fact, it seems to me," he said in a low, threatening voice, "that you won the *Falcon* yourself in a sabacc game before I came along. Didn't you also win the Cloud City Tibanna gas mines from the former Baron Administrator in a sabacc game? What could you possibly have used as collateral for a bet like that? You're a dirty no-good swindler, Lando. Admit it."

"And you're a pirate!" Lando said, stalking forward, his fists bunched at his side. He had made his reputation as an expert gambler.

Chewbacca growled from within the *Falcon*, making loud clangs and thumps as he extricated himself from the cramped passage. He stumbled down the entry ramp and stood gripping the piston supports.

As Han and Lando closed to within striking distance, Threepio wriggled in between them. "Excuse me, sirs, but might I make a suggestion? If indeed you both won the ship in a sabacc game, and if you are contesting the results, could you perhaps simply play another game of sabacc to settle this issue once and for all?" Threepio turned his glowing optical sensors first at Lando, then at Han.

"I just came down here to get my ship," Han said, "but now you've made it into a point of honor."

Lando glared at Han without flinching. "I can beat you any day of the week, Han Solo."

"Not this day," Han said, lowering his voice even further. "But not just sabacc. We'll make it *random* sabacc."

Lando raised his eyebrows, but met Han's gaze stare for stare. "Who's going to keep track of the plays?"

Han jerked his chin to the side. "We'll use Threepio as our modulator. Goldenrod doesn't have enough brains to cheat."

"But, sir, I really don't have the programming to—" Threepio said.

Han and Lando snapped in unison, "Shut up, Threepio!"

"All right, Han," Lando said, "let's do it before you lose your nerve."

"You're going to lose more than nerve before this game is over," Han said.

As Lando set up the cards and the sabacc table, Han Solo ushered the last of the off-duty bureaucrats toward the door of the small lounge. "Out. Come on! We need to use this place for a while."

They grumbled and objected in a variety of languages, but Han assisted them through the entryway with gentle shoves. "File a complaint with the New Republic." Then he closed and sealed the door, turning to Lando. "You ready yet?"

This was far different from the stuffy, smoke-filled parlors where he used to play sabacc, such as the underground game where he had once won a planet for Leia in an attempt to buy her affections.

At the sabacc table Lando spread out a handful of rectangular cards with crystalline screens sandwiched between metal layers. "Ready when you are, buddy." But he looked uneasy. "Han, we don't really have to do this—"

Han sniffed the air, frowning at the cloying smells of deodorizing mists and ambassadorial perfumes. "Yes, I do. Leia's been in an accident on one of her diplomatic missions, and I want to escort her back home, not some hospital ship."

"Leia's hurt?" Lando said, standing up in surprise. "So that's what has been bothering you. Forget it, take the ship. I was just kidding anyway. We'll do this some other time."

"No! We do it now, or you'll never be off my case. Threepio, get in here. What's taking so long?" Han said.

The golden droid scooted in from the back-room computer station, looking flustered, as usual. "I'm here, Master Solo. I was just reviewing the sabacc-rules programming."

Han punched his selections into the console of the bartender droid, smiling as he selected a fruity, prissy drink for Lando—complete with a blue tropical flower as a garnish—and a spiced ale for himself. He sat down, slid the drink across the surface to Lando, and sipped his ale.

Lando took a swallow of the mixture, winced, and forced a smile. "Thanks, Han. Should I deal?" He held the sabacc cards in his hand, leaning over the table's projecting field.

"Not yet." Han held up a hand. "Threepio, double-check to make sure those card surfaces are completely randomized."

"But, sir, surely—"

"Just do it. We want to make sure nobody gets an unfair advantage—don't we, old buddy?"

Lando managed to retain his forced smile as he handed the deck to Threepio, who ran the cards through a scrambler at the side of the table. "They are completely mixed, sir."

Threepio meticulously dealt five of the flat metallic cards each to Lando and to Han. "As you know, this is *random sabacc,* a combination of variant forms of the game," Threepio said, as if reciting the programming he had just uploaded. "There are five different sets of rules, shifted by chance, and changed at random time intervals as determined by the computer's random generator—that's me!"

"We know the rules!" Han growled, but he wasn't so certain. "And we also know the stakes."

Lando's deep, flinty eyes met his across the table. "Winner takes the *Falcon.* Loser takes Coruscant public transit from now on."

"Very well, sirs," Threepio said, "activate your cards. The first player to reach a score of one hundred points will be declared the winner. Our first round will be played according to . . . " He paused briefly as his randomizing function made a selection from the scrambled list of rules. "—Cloud City Casino alternate rules."

Han stared at the images appearing on his cards as his mind raced to remember how Cloud City Casino rules differed from the Bespin Standard form of the game. He stared at a mixed-up assortment of the four suits in sabacc—sabres, coins, flasks, and staves, with various positive and negative scores on each.

"Each player may select one and only one of his cards for a spin-change, and then we tally to see who comes closest to a score of positive or negative twenty-three, or zero."

Han scanned his cards, concentrating, but found no set that would add up to an appropriate tally. Lando wore a broad smile—but Lando *always* carried such an expression when he gambled. Han took a sip of his bitter spiced ale, swallowed hard, and chose a card. "Ready?" He raised his eyes to look at Lando.

Lando pushed the small scrambler button on the bottom left corner of a card. Han did the same, watching the image of the eight of coins flicker and re-form into a twelve of flasks. Together with a nine of flasks in his hand, he added to twenty-one. Not great. But when he saw Lando scowl at his own new card, he hoped it would be good enough.

"Twenty-one," Han said, slapping his cards on the table.

"Eighteen," Lando answered with a scowl. "You get the difference."

"Change of rules! Time has elapsed!" Threepio said. "Three points in favor of Master Solo. Next round is by . . . Empress Teta Preferred system."

Han looked at his new hand of cards, delighted to see a firm straight—but, if he remembered right, under Empress Teta rules the players swapped one card at random, and when Lando reached over to pluck a card from the right side, Han hoped to replace it with a Commander of Sabers—but the hand failed. Lando won the round and came out with a small lead, but before they could tally the scores, Threepio chimed in with another "Change of rules!" This time, scored under the Bespin Standard system, Lando's lead doubled.

Han cursed to himself as he stared at a chaotic mess in the next hand, not knowing what to bid, what to throw away. Before he made his decision, though, the random clock in Threepio's electronic brain forced him to call another rules change. "Corellian Gambit this time, sirs."

Han whooped in delight, for under the new rules the suits fit together with a completely different pattern. "Gotcha!" he cried, laying down his hand.

Lando grumbled, showing a wild card that, while valuable only moments before, now cost him fourteen points under the new scoring system.

Han crept ahead over the next several hands, then lost ground when rules changed back to Cloud City Casino style, which deemed all wild cards forfeit. Han reached forward to snatch one of Lando's cards, just as Lando selected one of his cards to change at random. They both froze. "Threepio, tell us again which rules we're playing under."

"New time interval anyway," the golden droid said. "Change to Bespin Standard. No, wait—new time interval again! Back to Empress Teta Preferred."

Han and Lando looked at their new cards again, minds whirling in confusion. Han took another sip of his spiced ale, and Lando drained his fruity concoction with a grimace. At the bottom the bright-colored flower had begun to sprout writhing roots that crawled on the bottom of his glass.

"Threepio, tell us the scores one more time," Lando said.

"Calculating for the last rules change, sirs, the total is ninety-three points for Master Solo and eighty-seven for General Calrissian."

Han and Lando glared at each other. "Last hand, buddy," Han said.

"Enjoy your remaining few seconds of ownership, Han," Lando said.

"Corellian Gambit rules, last-hand special case," Threepio announced.

Han felt his head pounding, trying to remember what happened in the last hand of the Corellian Gambit. Then he saw Lando locking in the denomination of only one of his cards, making ready to place his hand into the flux field in the center of the sabacc table.

Han studied his high-ranking face cards, Balance and Moderation, either of which would nudge him over the total score of a hundred. He pushed the retainer button on Balance, for eleven points, then thrust the rest of his hand into the flux field.

Han and Lando leaned over, staring in suspense as the images on the cards swirled and changed, flickering from one value to another in a blur until they stabilized, one by one.

Lando stared at low-demonination numeric cards, nothing at all spectacular, while Han got the best deal he had seen throughout the entire game. All face cards, Demise, Endurance, The Star, and The Queen of Air and Darkness, along with the Balance card he had kept. His score handily passed the goal, leaving Lando in the dust.

He cheered at the same instant Threepio declared another "Change of rules!" Han glared at the golden droid, waiting.

"This hand will be scored under the Ecclessis Figg Variation," Threepio said.

Han and Lando looked at each other, mouthing the words. "What is the Figg Variation?"

"In the final round the scores of all odd-numbered face cards are subtracted instead of added to the final score. This means, Master Solo, that while you gain ten points for Endurance and The Queen of Air and Darkness, you forfeit a total of forty-one for Balance, The Star, and Demise."

Threepio paused. "I'm afraid you lose, sir. General Calrissian gains sixteen points for a total score of one hundred three, while you are left with a final score of sixty-two."

Han blinked in shock at his half-empty glass of spiced ale as Lando pounded the tabletop in triumph. "Good game, Han. Now go on off to fetch Leia. Want me to come with you?"

Han kept staring at the table, at his ale, at anything but Lando. He felt hollow inside. Not only had he learned of Leia's tragedy today, but he had also lost the ship he had owned for more than a decade.

"Take her, she's yours," Han mumbled. He finally looked up to meet Lando's eyes.

"Come on, Han. You're distraught. You never should have made the bet in the first place. Just—"

"No, the *Falcon* is yours, Lando. I'm not a cheat, and I made the deal going into the game." Han stood, turning his back on Lando, leaving the rest of his ale untouched. "Threepio, authorize a change of registration for the *Falcon*. And you'd better get in touch with central transportation control. Arrange a diplomatic transport for Leia. I won't be picking her up after all."

Lando shifted uncomfortably. "Uh, I'll take good care of her, Han. Not a scratch."

Without another word Han went to the door of the lounge, unsealed it, and walked out into the echoing halls.

4

With **black-gloved hands**
clasped behind her back, Admiral Daala stood at attention on the bridge of the Imperial Star Destroyer *Gorgon*.

In front of the bridge viewport, brilliant gases illuminated by a knot of blue-giant stars turned the Cauldron Nebula into a spectacular light show. Beside her in parking formation hung the *Basilisk* and the *Manticore*. The ionized gases played havoc with ships' sensors, making the nebula a perfect hiding place for her three fully armed battleships.

Daala heard a tentative bootstep behind her and turned to face Commander Kratas. "Yes, Commander?" As she moved, her olive-gray uniform clung like a second skin, while her mane of coppery hair trailed behind her like the tail of a comet.

Kratas snapped off a perfect salute and remained standing one step below her observation platform. "Admiral," he said, "as of oh-nine-hundred hours we have completed our assessment of the losses suffered during our battle at Kessel."

Daala formed her lips into a tight, emotionless line. Kratas was a short man, recruited into the Imperial Navy from an occupation force on one of the conscripted planets. He had dark hair trimmed to regulation length, wide watery eyes set under beetling brows, and a jutting chin that hung below almost nonexistent lips. The best part of Kratas, though, Daala thought, was that he always followed orders. He had been trained well in the Imperial Military Academy on Carida.

"Give me the breakdown, Commander," Daala said.

Kratas did not blink as he rattled off the numbers from memory. "Together, we lost a total of three TIE squadrons, and of course all hands and resources on board the *Hydra*."

Daala felt a cold stab of anger at the mention of her wrecked battleship. Kratas must have seen something in her expression, because he flinched, though he did not move aside.

The *Hydra*, Daala's fourth Star Destroyer, had been torn apart in one of the Maw cluster's black holes. It had been Daala's first significant loss in combat, one fourth of her destructive capability wiped out by Han Solo and the traitorous scientist Qwi Xux, who had stolen the Sun Crusher superweapon and fled the Empire's closely guarded Maw Installation.

"However," Kratas continued. His voice quavered the smallest bit, then he straightened. "Forty TIE fighters from the *Hydra* did manage to reach safety inside the other Star Destroyers, which makes up somewhat for the other losses."

Daala's Star Destroyers had emerged from the Maw cluster, expecting to engulf and obliterate Han Solo—but her ships had run headlong into Kessel's ragtag fleet like frenzied battledogs. Though her Star Destroyers had defeated nearly two thirds of Kessel's ships, the *Basilisk* had suffered severe damage and had to be linked with the *Gorgon*'s navicomputers for escape to a secret location in the Cauldron Nebula.

"What is the status of repairs to the *Basilisk*?" she said.

Kratas clicked his heels smartly as if pleased to give good news. "Three of the four damaged turbolaser cannons have been refurbished and are now operational. We expect to finish repairs on the fourth battery within the next two days. Armored spacetroopers have completed work on the breached external hull. Decks 7 through 9 are airtight again, and we are currently replenishing the atmosphere. The damaged flight-control circuitry has been rerouted, and the navicomp and targeting consoles are now fully operational."

He drew in a deep breath. "In short, Admiral, I believe our entire fleet is ready for battle again."

Daala leaned closer to the observation window, curling her long fingers around the simulated wood of the railing. She tried unsuccessfully to stop a smile from creeping across her lips. The metallic smell of the air comforted her. She had lived on the *Gorgon* for over a decade now. The air had been reprocessed and replenished until pungent organic odors had been scoured away, leaving only sterile smells, the tang of metal and lubricating oils, the reassuring scent of pressed Imperial Navy uniforms and polished stormtrooper armor.

"If I might ask a question, Admiral," Kratas said, glancing around to see the other personnel at their stations, every head turned studiously away from the conversation, pretending not to listen. Daala raised her eyebrows, waiting for him to continue.

"With the information we gained from interrogating Han Solo, and with transmissions we've received, we know that the Emperor is no longer alive, that Darth Vader and Grand Moff Tarkin are also dead, and that the Empire has fragmented into civil war." Kratas hesitated.

Daala spoke for him. "You are wondering, Commander, who our Commander in Chief is?"

Kratas nodded vigorously. "Grand Admiral Thrawn has been killed, as has Warlord Zsinj. We know of several commanders still fighting over the remnants of the Empire, but they seem more interested in destroying each other than in battling the Rebellion. If I may make a suggestion? The Imperial Military Academy on Carida still appears to be stable and loyal, with a great many weapons at their disposal. Perhaps it would be best to—"

"I don't think so," Daala said sharply, turning from him to smother her scowl. She had been trained and trounced in the harsh military academy on Carida. Because she was female, Daala had been passed over for promotion after promotion; she had been given the worst assignments. She had been brutalized. And that had only increased her drive to succeed.

Finally she had created a false identity for herself through Carida's vast computer networks and used that identity in combat simulation rooms. She had won repeatedly, creating breakthrough tactics that had been adopted by many of the Imperial Army's ground assault forces. After Moff Tarkin had discovered Daala's true identity and realized her talent, he had secretly whisked her away, using his new authority as Grand Moff of the Outer Rim territories. He had promoted her to the rank of admiral—as far as she knew, the only female admiral in the entire Imperial Fleet.

Yet because of the Emperor's own prejudices against women and nonhuman races, Tarkin had kept the truth about his new admiral a secret. Daala and Tarkin had become lovers, and to keep her from coming to the Emperor's attention, he had given her command of four Star Destroyers assigned to guard the supersecret think tank inside the black hole cluster.

But now that she had come out with her battleships, ready to devastate any planet loyal to the Rebellion, Daala could not conceive of handing over that authority to her former persecutors on Carida.

She took a deep breath again and faced Commander Kratas. He stood without moving, still waiting for her response. Around the bridge other crew members looked up from their stations; but when Daala glanced at them, they quickly found other things to do.

"Since the factions seem to have forgotten that our true enemy is the Rebellion, I think we will set an example for them. We must focus their attention on the appropriate enemy—the Rebels who killed Grand Moff Tarkin, who destroyed the Death Star, who murdered the Emperor. Since Grand Admiral Thrawn was the only person in the Imperial fleet with a rank higher than my own, I must assume that my rank is now at least as high as any of the pretenders."

Kratas's eyes widened, but Daala shook her head. Her long hair swirled like flickering flames. "No, Commander, I have no intention of putting in my bid for what is left of the Empire. That's not a job I would relish. We'll leave that to the petty dictators. I just want to cause damage. Lots of it."

Her lips curled in a snarl, and her voice grew husky. "I think our best chance is to rely on hit-and-run tactics, guerrilla warfare. We have three Star Destroyers. That's enough to wipe out the civilizations on any number of worlds. We must hit fast and run fast. We will continue to pound the Rebels for as long as we can."

She glanced around the bridge to see that all personnel stood staring at her, some with wide eyes and gaping mouths, others grinning. Her crew had been bottled up for so long in the Maw, ready to fight but denied any chance at action because they were forced to guard the group of prima donna weapons scientists.

Daala glanced out at the Cauldron Nebula, saw the bright lights of other star systems piercing the haze of ionized gas. Many targets waited out there.

She turned to the navigator's station. "Lieutenant, I want you to plot a course for the last-known shipping lanes closest to our position."

"Yes, Admiral," the lieutenant said, practically leaping toward his station.

"Inform all personnel on the three ships," Daala said. A bold grin lit her face; she felt as if her blood had become molten copper. Her green eyes seemed to sparkle with laser bolts ready to be fired on unsuspecting prey.

The fight was about to begin.

"Let's go hunting," Daala said, and a spontaneous cheer erupted from the bridge crew.

Deep in space, the pack of Imperial Star Destroyers waited, sensors alert and scanning for the ripples of approaching ships. They hung at a hyperspace node on the far end of the Corellian Trade Spine, where all ships bound for Anoat or Bespin or other planets along the line would drop out of hyperspace to recalibrate their course and set off on a new vector.

Daala paced the *Gorgon*'s bridge, keeping her gaze moving, watching her personnel as they waited. Waited. Her scrutiny kept them on edge, nervous, intent on performing flawlessly. She was proud of her crew. She felt confident that they could wrench a proud victory from the Rebel scum.

One of the lieutenants straightened at his sensor console. "Admiral! Fluctuations indicate a ship arriving in hyperspace. Tracking . . . it's coming through."

Daala snapped commands. "Full alert. Instruct *Basilisk* and *Manticore* to power up their turbolaser batteries."

Commander Kratas whirled from his station to delegate tasks. The intense alarm signal whooped through the decks of the Star Destroyer. Stormtroopers rushed to their posts, armor and boots clattering.

"Gunners," Daala shouted through the intercom, "target to disable only! We must take the ship."

"Here it comes!" said the lieutenant.

Daala spun to stare at the black emptiness of space, at the stars hanging motionless in complex patterns. A ripple appeared, like a scratch on black-painted glass, and a midsized ship broke through into normal space and hung at a preprogrammed halt for navigational recalibration.

Daala smiled, trying to imagine the expression on the captain's face as he suddenly found himself blockaded by three Imperial-class Star Destroyers.

"A Corellian Corvette, Admiral," Kratas said, as if Daala could not identify it herself. She glanced at the distinctive hammerhead shape of the bridge section and the bank of twelve enormous hyperdrive and sublight rocket motors glowing blue-white with exhaust. "They're the most common galactic transports. Might just be merchants."

"What does that matter?" Daala said. "Prepare to fire. Let's test the *Basilisk*'s repaired turbolaser batteries."

"Admiral, the captain of the Corvette is signaling us," the comm officer called.

"Ignore it. *Basilisk*, open fire. Two surgical shots. Take out the rear hyperdrive units."

Daala watched, feeling the electric thrill of command. Two blinding green arrows lanced out. The first bolt spattered and diffused against the Corvette's increased shields, but the second blast punched through the weakened area and crippled the rocket engines. The Corvette rocked in space, then slowly spun like a dead rodent on a wire. Red-yellow glow diffused from a ruptured power core.

The three Star Destroyers loomed over the crippled ship.

"The Corvette's captain is signaling surrender," the comm officer said.

Daala felt a brief twinge of disappointment but brought it under control. She could not allow herself to make stupid mistakes. She had already been overeager in pursuing Han Solo and the stolen Sun Crusher—and that zealousness had caused her to lose the *Hydra*.

Commander Kratas stepped behind her, lowering his voice. "What if this ship is not part of the Rebel Alliance? Many smugglers also use Corellian Corvettes."

"A point well-taken," Daala said. Long ago Tarkin had impressed upon her that a good commander always listened to the opinions and suggestions of her trusted officers. "If the captain has connections with a smuggling network rather than the Rebellion, then perhaps we can put him to work for us. We could hire some spies, saboteurs."

Kratas nodded at the suggestion.

"Engage a tractor beam," Daala said. "Open the lower-bay doors, and we'll draw the Corvette into our hangar."

Daala toggled the narrow-beam comm system by her station, and an image of an Imperial Army general rose from the holo dais. His form flickered blue at the fringes from transmission distortion. Daala bent over the image, like a giant contemplating a toy. "General Odosk, prepare your boarding party. Have you briefed your troops?"

"Yes, Admiral," came the filtered voice. "We know what to do."

Daala whisked his image into thin sparkles of static. It would be fitting to let survivors from the *Hydra* be the boarding party of their first captured ship.

The crippled Corvette, still leaking thermal emissions from its breached power core, rose on invisible strings of the *Gorgon*'s tractor beam. The lower bay of the Star Destroyer slid open like the jaws of an enormous carnivore.

The comm officer spoke again. "Admiral, the captain of the Corvette continues to ask for instructions. She sounds rather distraught."

Daala snapped around. "*She*? The Corvette has a female captain?"

"It's a female voice, Admiral."

Daala tapped her fingers together, pondering the new information. Women seemed to have a much easier time at gaining command in the Rebel Alliance—but the extra burden of brutal struggle had made Daala stronger.

"Keep her in suspense."

"Capture complete, Admiral," Commander Kratas said. "The Corvette offered no resistance. Boarding parties are ready."

"Close the hangar-bay doors," Daala said. "Send a slicer team to drain the prisoner's computer core for information. We need maps, history tapes. We have too much to learn."

"Didn't you just order General Odosk and his special crew to board the ship?" Kratas said.

Daala frowned sharply at him. "They have other orders. You follow yours."

"Yes, Admiral," Kratas said in a small voice.

"Bring the captain of the Corvette to the interrogation chambers. We may need to encourage a bit of truthfulness." Kratas nodded and walked briskly off the bridge.

The door of the grim interrogation room sighed open with a discouraging hiss. When Daala entered, she was disappointed to see the captured captain: a short, mouse-faced Sullustan with thick rubbery jowls hanging around a weak chin. His great glassy eyes, pitch-dark and glittering, reminded her of the black holes in the Maw cluster.

The Sullustan captain jabbered in a panic, his lips wet with foaming drool. Beside him marched an old-model chrome protocol droid that served as his translator. The droid moved arms and legs with humming, ratcheting motivators as if its computer brain was so scrambled it could no longer control all of its systems at once.

The droid spoke in a brusque female voice. "Admiral! I'm so glad we've finally been brought to someone in charge. Can we straighten out this difficulty? We have done nothing wrong."

Beside the droid, the Sullustan captain pushed on the tight skin-cap covering his sloping head. He jabbered away with a monotonous *blub-blub-blub*.

The droid translated, "Captain T'nun Bdu demands an explanation—" The Sullustan babbled in alarm and clutched the platinum arm of the droid. "Correction, the captain respectfully requests that you be so kind as to explain your actions. Please tell us if there is anything he can do to avoid a diplomatic incident, as he has no wish to initiate any conflict."

The Sullustan captain nodded vigorously. A froth of saliva collected on his lips and ran in runnels between his flappy jowls.

"Wipe your chin," Daala said. She looked at the horrendous interrogation chair strapped in the shadows of the room. The walls were covered with unfinished iron plates, held in place by large blocky bolts. Stains marked various places that had not been cleaned after earlier interrogations. The chair itself had angled pipes and tubing, restraints, chains, spikes, most of which served no purpose other than to increase a victim's terror.

"What we would like from the captain right now," Daala said, turning back as if ignoring the chair, "is some information. Perhaps you can provide it to us without our needing to resort to any . . . unpleasantness."

The captain flinched in terror. The platinum female droid shifted from foot to foot and then seemed to reach a decision. The droid looked with apparent adoration at the Sullustan captain and then straightened herself and spoke in a clear, unfluttered voice. "Admiral, I can provide that information. There is no need for you to torture my captain."

The Sullustan *blub-blub-blubb*ed again, but the droid seemed not to hear. "We are on a mission to provide supplies and new living units for a small colony on the planet Dantooine. The colony is not affiliated with the Rebellion as of this moment. The colonists are harmless refugees."

"How many are in this colony?" Daala asked.

"Approximately fifty, taken from the old mining outpost Eol Sha. They are not presently armed."

"I see," Daala said. "Well, Captain, we must liberate your assets. I believe that the cargo hold of a Corellian Corvette routinely carries provisions for up to a year without restocking. I am commandeering those provisions for the service of the Empire. This colony on Dantooine will have to get their supplies some other way."

The Sullustan chittered in dismay, and Daala skewered him with a glare. "Perhaps, Captain, you would like to step outside the airlock and file a complaint?"

The Sullustan shut up instantly.

The door of the interrogation chamber sighed open again, revealing two stormtrooper guards and Commander Kratas. "Take the captain and his droid back to his ship," Daala said, then cocked her head down to stare at the Sullustan. "Our crew is already emptying your cargo holds, but General Odosk has set his men to repairing and bypassing the damaged engine. Enough that you could limp to another system."

The Sullustan bowed, speaking nonstop in his rodent-like language. The female droid stood at attention and spoke in an astonished voice. "Why thank you, Admiral. That is most respectful of you. We appreciate your hospitality."

The stormtroopers took them away, clomping down the sterile halls of the Star Destroyer. The doors sealed shut again, leaving Daala alone with Commander Kratas. He turned to her with wide dark eyes below his beetling brows. "Admiral, have we lowered ourselves to the level of space pirates? Attacking transport ships and stealing supplies?"

Daala removed a datapad from her hip and punched a button to call up her latest readout. She turned it toward him so he could look at the information. "I appreciate your respect for the honor of the Imperial Navy, Commander. However, before I came to see the captives, I received a report regarding the contents of the Corvette's cargo hold. There are indeed supplies for a new colony, but we also found heavy weaponry, communications gear, and prefabricated equipment for starfighter hangars."

She gestured toward the door. "Back to the bridge. I want to see what happens next."

"What do you mean?" Kratas said.

Daala switched off the datapad and looked at him. "You'll see. Be patient for now."

As they left, the door of the interrogation chamber slid shut, sealing behind it the darkness and the smell of fear trapped in the room.

The close-up image of General Odosk flickered, but she could see the self-satisfied grin on his wide, swarthy face. "Mission accomplished, Admiral."

"Excellent, General. I trust you are at a good vantage point?"

Odosk nodded. "I wouldn't miss it. Thank you."

Daala turned back to the viewing window on the bridge. The wounded Corellian Corvette dropped out of the *Gorgon*'s hangar bay and drifted free in space. "Back away," she told the navigator. "Order the *Basilisk* and the *Manticore* to do the same."

"Yes, Admiral."

The three Star Destroyers spread out and moved away from the much smaller ship. The Corvette's damaged rocket engine no longer glowed.

Kratas shook his head. "I still can't believe you're letting him go."

Daala intentionally spoke loud enough for the rest of bridge crew to hear. She rarely felt the need to explain her orders to underlings, but at certain times explaining her reasoning might make them respect her even more.

"Ships vanish all the time, Commander," Daala said. "If we simply destroyed this ship, it could be written off as some accident in transportation. A meteor storm, a breached reactor plate, bad navigation through hyperspace. But if we let this captain send a message first, then the Rebel Alliance will know what we have done. We can accomplish the same task, but increase the terror and chaos. Do you agree?"

Kratas nodded, but he still looked doubtful.

The comm officer spoke up. "The transponder we implanted in his comm system has activated. He's sending a tight-beam transmission to specific coordinates."

Daala smiled. "Good, I didn't think he'd wait until he got clear."

The comm officer pressed an ear jack to the side of his head. "He's reporting the situation, Admiral. Three Star Destroyers . . . fired upon without warning . . . taken prisoner and interrogated."

"I think that's enough," Daala said. She opened the comm channel. "General Odosk, proceed." She shielded her eyes.

The thermal detonators planted against the reactor walls of the twelve rocket pods detonated simultaneously, blasting the inferno open and sending a tidal wave of deadly radiation through the Corellian ship. An instant later the raging heat evaporated the entire hull, turning it into metallic steam. The rocket pods blew up in brilliant sunbursts; then the rest of the ship expanded outward in a blinding glare.

Daala nodded. "I think the survivors of the *Hydra* have had their revenge."

In stunned admiration Kratas smiled. "I believe so, Admiral."

She turned to face the rest of her bridge crew. "We now have accurate maps and information on the political situation of the Rebel Alliance. We have struck our first blow—the first of many."

Daala drew a deep breath, feeling vibrant and alive with euphoria. Grand Moff Tarkin would have been proud of her.

"Our next stop will be the planet Dantooine," she said. "We have a colony to visit."

5

Luke Skywalker, Jedi Master, gathered his twelve students in the grand audience chamber of the Massassi temple.

Diffuse orange light trickled through the narrow sky-lights. Lush vines climbed the stone walls, spreading out in verdant webs in the corners. Most of the flat stones were a nonreflective smoky gray; other lozenges of dark green and vermilion and ocher stone ornamented the enormous chamber.

Luke remembered standing here as a young man after their brief victory celebration following the destruction of the Death Star. He smiled as he recalled how Princess Leia had presented medals to him and Han Solo and Chewbacca. Now the grand audience chamber stood empty except for Luke and his small group of Jedi candidates.

Luke watched the students file toward him along the broad promenade. Wearing dark-brown Jedi robes, the candidates walked in eerie silence across the slick floor that had long ago been polished smooth by the mysterious Massassi.

Streen and Gantoris moved first, side by side; Gantoris looked full of self-importance. Of all those Luke had gathered at his Jedi training center, Gantoris had so far shown the most progress, the most inner strength—yet the man from Eol Sha did not seem to realize that he stood at a crossroads. Gantoris would soon need to decide exactly how he would proceed in his growth with the Force.

Behind the two of them came Kirana Ti, one of the young and powerful witches of Dathomir, who had left the other Force-wielding, rancor-riding women on her homeworld to learn better control. Kirana Ti and the other witches had been instrumental in helping him recover an ancient wrecked space station, the *Chu'unthor*, in which resided many records of old Jedi training—records that Luke had studied to develop exercises for his Jedi trainees.

Beside Kirana Ti came Dorsk 81, a bald green-and yellow-skinned humanoid from a world where all family units were genetically identical, cloned and raised to carry on the status quo. But Dorsk 81, the eighty-first reincarnation of the same genetic attributes, had somehow been dramatically changed. Though he seemed identical in every way, his mind worked differently, his thoughts moved along different paths, and he could feel the Force working through him. With the hope of becoming a Jedi Knight, Dorsk 81 had left his homeworld of identical people for something new.

Then came Kam Solusar, an older man, son of a Jedi that Vader had slaughtered long ago. Solusar had fled the Empire after the great Jedi purge and had spent decades in isolation beyond the inhabited star systems. Upon returning, Solusar had been captured and tortured by evil Jedi, twisted to the dark side of the Force, but Luke had bested him in the game of Lightsider. Solusar had received advanced training in certain areas, but because of his self-imposed exile, he still knew little about many aspects of the Force.

As the rest of the candidates gathered at the raised platform, Luke shrugged back his hood and tried to mask his pride at seeing the group. If he successfully completed their training, these candidates would form the core of a new order of Jedi Knights, champions of the Force, to help protect the New Republic against dark times.

He heard them stirring, not speaking to each other, each one no doubt wrapped up in thoughts of touching the Force, finding new pathways to inner strength and windows to the universe that only Jedi teachings could open for them. Their collective talent amazed him, but he hoped for even more trainees. Soon Han Solo would send his young friend, Kyp Durron; and Luke had strongly hinted for his former opponent Mara Jade to join them, since they had struck an uneasy truce during the battle against Joruus C'baoth.

At the podium Luke tried to stand tall. He found the core of peace inside him that allowed him to speak with a firm voice. "I have brought you here to study and to learn, but I myself am still learning. Every living thing must continue to learn until it dies. Those who cease to learn, die that much sooner.

"Perhaps it was misleading when I called this an 'academy' for Jedi. Though I will teach you everything

I know, I don't want you merely to listen to me lecture.

"Your training will be a landscape of self-discovery. Learn new things and share what you have learned with others. I will call this place a *praxeum*. This word, made up of ancient roots, was first used by the Jedi scholar Karena, distilling the concepts of learning combined with action. Our *praxeum*, then, is a place for the learning of action. A Jedi is aware, but he does not waste time in mindless contemplation. When action is required, a Jedi acts."

Luke repositioned a small translucent cube on the raised dais behind him. He ran his fingers over the cool surface of the ancient knowledge repository Leia had stolen from the resurrected Emperor. The Jedi Holocron.

"We will invoke a past Jedi Master from the Holocron," Luke said. "We have used this device to learn the ways of the old Jedi Knights. Let us see what stories it has for us this morning."

He activated the precious artifact. In the distant past it had been traditional for each Jedi Master to compile his life's knowledge and store it within a great repository such as this, which was then passed to one of his students. Luke had only begun to fathom its depths.

An image formed both inside and outside the cube, a half-tangible projection that was more than just a stored bit of data; it was an interactive representation of the Jedi Master—a stubby alien, part insectile, part crustacean. It seemed to be bent with age or too much gravity. Its head extended into a long funnel, like a beak from which dangled whiskery protuberances. Close-set, glassy eyes stared like glittering pinpoints of knowledge.

The creature leaned on a long wooden staff, its legs spindly and knobby as it swiveled its funnellike face to contemplate the new audience. Tattered rags covered its body, sticking out in odd directions like clothing or external skin. Its voice came out in a reedy melody, like high-pitched music played under fast running water.

"I am Master Vodo-Siosk Baas."

"Master Vodo," Luke said, "I am Master Skywalker, and these are my apprentices. You have seen many things and recorded many thoughts. We'd be honored if you would tell us something we should know."

The image of Master Vodo-Siosk Baas hung his beaklike head on a jointed elbow of neck, as if in contemplation. Luke knew that the Holocron was simply uploading and sifting through reams of data, choosing an appropriate story through a personality algorithm stored with the Jedi Master's image.

"I must tell you of the Great Sith War that occurred—" Here the image paused as the Holocron assessed the current situation. "Four thousand years before your time.

"This war was caused by a student of mine, Exar Kun, who found forbidden teachings of the ancient Sith. He imitated the ways of the long-fallen Sith and used them to form his own philosophy of the Jedi Code, a distortion of all we know to be true and right. With this knowledge Exar Kun established a vast and powerful brotherhood and claimed the title of the first Dark Lord of the Sith."

Luke stiffened. "Others have claimed that title," he said, "even to this time." *Including Darth Vader.*

Master Vodo-Siosk Baas seemed to lean more heavily on his walking stick. "I had hoped Exar Kun and his kind were defeated once and for all. Exar Kun joined forces with another powerful Jedi and great warlord, Ulic Qel-Droma. Exar Kun worked his invisible threads into the fabric of the Old Republic, bringing downfall through treachery and his distorted abilities with the Force."

Master Vodo looked at the gathered students. Gantoris seemed incredibly eager to hear more, leaning forward and staring with wide, dark eyes. The image of the long-dead Jedi Master turned to face Luke. "You must warn your students to beware of the temptations of conquest. That is all I can tell you for now."

The image flickered and wavered. With a feeling of deep uneasiness Luke silenced the Holocron. The images returned to swirling pearlescence inside its cubical walls.

"I think that's enough for this morning," Luke said. "We all know that other Jedi have followed the wrong path, bringing not only themselves but millions of innocent lives to doom and suffering. But I trust you. A Jedi must trust himself, and a Jedi Master must trust his apprentices.

"Explore yourselves and your surroundings, in teams or alone, whichever makes you comfortable. Go to the jungle. Go to other parts of this temple. Or simply go back to your chambers. The choice is yours."

Luke sat down on the edge of the raised stage and watched the students file out of the grand hall. The translucent cube of the Holocron stood mute beside him, a vessel filled with valuable but dangerous knowledge.

Obi-Wan Kenobi had been Luke's teacher. Luke had listened to every word the old man had said, trusting it; yet Luke had later learned how often Obi-Wan had obscured the facts, had distorted information—or as Obi-

Wan explained it, simply offered the truth "from a certain point of view."

Luke watched the robed forms and wondered if his students could handle the knowledge they might discover. What if, like ancient Exar Kun in Master Vodo's story, they were tempted to uncover the forbidden teachings of the Sith, that so subtly yet crucially differed from the Jedi Code?

Luke feared what might happen should one of his students travel down the wrong path. But he also knew that he had to trust them—or they could never become Jedi Knights.

Deep into the night Gantoris hunched over the cluttered worktable, secretly constructing his own lightsaber.

A blanket of shadows surrounded him, obliterating distractions that might keep him from his task. His dark eyes had adjusted to the tight-beam glowlamp that spilled a harsh pool of light over his debris-strewn work surface, leaving the rest of the room in murk. As Gantoris moved to pick up another precision tool, his shadow flapped like a bird of prey across the ancient stone walls.

The Great Temple sat silent, like an ancient trap to stifle sound. The other students in Master Skywalker's Jedi academy—his *praxeum,* as he called it—had retired to their private chambers to fall into an exhausted sleep or to meditate on Jedi relaxing techniques.

Gantoris's neck ached, and his shoulder muscles burned from holding his cramped position for hours. He breathed in and out, smelling the thickness of old smoke and the scratchy moss that had worked for millennia to pry through cracks in the precisely placed temple blocks.

The moss had withered not long after Gantoris had taken up residence in the chambers. . . .

Outside, the jungle of Yavin 4 simmered with restless life, rustling, chittering, singing, and shrieking, as stronger creatures fed, as weaker creatures died.

Gantoris continued to work. He no longer needed sleep. He could draw the energy he required using different methods, secrets he had been taught that the other students did not suspect. His unbraided black hair stuck out in wiry shocks, and an acrid, gunpowdery smell clung to his cloak, his skin.

He focused on the components scattered across the table: silver electronics, dull metal, glinting glass. He slid his fingertips across the cold bits of wire, picked up a sharp-edged microcontrol box with trembling hands. Widening his eyes in annoyance, Gantoris stared at his hands until the trembling stopped, then set to work again.

He understood how the pieces would all fit together. Once he *knew*, once he had drawn together sufficient Jedi knowledge, everything seemed obvious to him. Obvious.

The elegant energy blade served as the personal weapon of the Jedi, a symbol of authority, skill, and honor. Cruder weapons could cause more random destruction, but no other artifact evoked as much legend and mystery as the lightsaber. Gantoris would settle for nothing else.

Every Jedi built his own lightsaber. It was a rite of passage in the training of a new student. Master Skywalker had not yet begun to teach him, though Gantoris had waited and waited. He knew he was the best of the students—and he chose not to wait any longer.

Master Skywalker did not know everything a true Jedi Master must teach new apprentices. Skywalker had gaps in his knowledge, blank spaces he either did not understand or did not wish to teach. But Master Skywalker was not the only source of Jedi knowledge. . . .

Once he had forsaken sleep, Gantoris had taken to roaming the halls of the Great Temple, sliding barefoot and in silence along the cold floors that seemed to drink heat, no matter how warm the jungle had become during the day.

Sometimes he wandered out into the rain forest at night, surrounded by mists and singing insects. The dew splashed his feet, his robe, making indecipherable patterns across his body like coded messages. Gantoris walked unarmed, silently daring any predator to challenge him, knowing that his Jedi skills would be proof against mere claws and fangs; but nothing molested him, and only once did he hear a large beast charging away from him through the underbrush.

But the dark and mysterious voice that came to him in his nightmares had given him instructions on how to build a lightsaber. Gantoris had been driven with a new purpose. A true Jedi was resourceful. A true Jedi could make do. A true Jedi found what he needed.

Using his ability to manipulate simple objects, he had broken past the seals into the locked Rebel control rooms in the temple's lower levels. Banks of machinery, computers, landing-grid panels, and automated defense systems sat covered with grime from a decade of abandonment. Master Skywalker had repaired little of the equipment. Jedi apprentices had no need for most of it.

Quietly and alone, Gantoris had removed access panels, stripped out microcomponents, focusing lenses, laser diodes, and a cylindrical casing twenty-seven centimeters long. . . .

It had taken him three nights, tearing apart the silent equipment, stirring up dust and spores, sending rodents and arachnids scurrying to safety. But Gantoris had found what he needed.

Now he assembled the pieces.

Under the garish light Gantoris picked up the cylindrical casing. He used a spot laser-welder to cut notches for the control switches.

Each Jedi built his own lightsaber to a range of specifications and personal preferences. Some included safety switches that shut off the glowing blade if the handle was released, while other weapons could be locked on.

Gantoris had a few ideas of his own.

He installed a small but efficient power cell. It snapped into place, connecting precisely. Gantoris sighed, concentrated a moment to still his trembling hands again, then picked up another set of delicate wires.

He flinched, whirling to look behind him in the shadows. He thought he had heard someone breathing, the rustle of dark garments. Gantoris stared with his red-rimmed eyes, trying to discern a dim human form in the corner.

"Speak, if you're there!" Gantoris cried. His voice sounded harsh, as if he had swallowed burning coals.

When the shadows did not answer him, he sighed with cool relief. His mouth tasted dry, and soreness worked its way through his throat. But he willed away the feeling. He could drink water in the morning. A Jedi endured.

Building the lightsaber was his personal test. He had to do it alone.

Next, he took out the most precious piece of the weapon. Three corusca jewels, cast out from the high-pressure hell of the gas giant Yavin's core. When he and his addlebrained companion Streen had discovered the new Massassi temple far out in the jungle, Gantoris had found these gems on the steep obsidian walls. Embedded among the hypnotic pictographs etched into the black volcanic glass, the jewels had glinted in the hazy orange daylight.

Though they had remained untouched for thousands of years, these three gems had flaked off as Gantoris stared at them. They fell to his feet in the crushed lava rock surrounding the lost temple. Gantoris had picked up the gems, cupping the warm crystals in his hands as Streen wandered among the obelisks, chattering to himself.

Now Gantoris removed the jewels—one watery pink, another deep red, and the third starkly transparent with an inner electric blue fire along the edges of the facets. He was *meant* to have these jewels; they were destined for his own lightsaber. He knew that now. He understood all of his former nightmares, his former fears.

Most lightsabers had only a single jewel that focused the pure energy from the power cell into a tight beam. By adding more than one gem, Gantoris's blade would have unexpected capabilities to surprise Master Skywalker.

Finally, his fingers raw and aching, Gantoris sat up. Pain embroidered firelines across his neck, shoulders, and back, but he washed it away with a simple Jedi exercise. Outside the Great Temple he could hear the changing symphony of jungle sounds as nocturnal creatures found their dens, and daylight animals began to stir.

Gantoris held the cylindrical handle of his lightsaber and inspected it under the glowlamp's unforgiving light. Craftsmanship was everything in a weapon like this. A barely noticeable variance could cause a disastrous blunder. But Gantoris had done everything right. He had taken no shortcuts, allowed no sloppiness. His weapon was perfect.

He pushed the activator button. With a *snap-hiss,* the awesome blade thrummed and pulsed like a living creature. The chain of three jewels gave the energy blade a pale purplish hue, white at the core, amethyst at the fringes, with rainbow colors rippling up and down the beam.

Accustomed to the dimness, Gantoris squeezed his eyes to block out the glare, then gradually opened them again, staring in amazement at what he had made.

He moved the blade, and the air crackled around him. The hum sounded like thunder, but none of the other students would hear it through the mammoth thickness of the stone walls. In his grip the blade felt like a winged serpent, sending the sharp scent of ozone curling to his nose.

He slashed back and forth. The lightsaber became a part of him, an extension of his arm connected through the Force to strike down any enemy. He sensed no heat from the vibrating blade, only a cold annihilating fire.

He deactivated the blade, awash in euphoria, and carefully hid the completed lightsaber under his sleeping pallet.

"Now Master Skywalker will see I am a true Jedi," he said to the shadows along the walls. But no one answered him.

6

The private investigatory pro-
ceedings of the New Republic's ruling Council stood
closed against Admiral Ackbar. He waited in the ante-
room outside, staring at the tall steelstone door as if it
were a wall blocking the end of his life. He stared
unblinking at the designs and scrollwork modeled by
the Emperor Palpatine after ancient Sith hieroglyphics,
and they disturbed him.

Ackbar sat on the cold synthetic-stone bench, feeling
only his misery, despair, and failure. He nursed his
bandaged left arm and felt pain slice up and down
his biceps where tiny needles held the slashed salmon-
colored skin together. Ackbar had refused standard
treatment by medical droid or healing in a bacta tank
programmed for Calamarian physiology. He preferred to
let the painful recuperation remind him of the destruction he had caused on Vortex.

He cocked his enormous head, listening to the rise
and fall of heated voices through the closed door. He

could make out only a mingled murmur of mixed voices, some strident, some insistent. He looked down and self-consciously brushed at his clean white admiral's uniform.

His remaining injuries seemed insignificant compared to the pain inside him. In his mind he kept seeing the crystalline Cathedral of Winds shatter around him in an avalanche of shards, hurling a storm of glassy daggers in all directions. He saw the bodies of winged Vors tumbling around him, slaughtered by the razor-edged crystal sabers. Ackbar had ejected Leia to safety, but he wished he had been brave enough to switch *off* the crash field, because he did not want to live with such disgrace. Ackbar had been piloting the deadly ship, no one else. *He* had crashed into the precious Cathedral of Winds. No one else.

He looked up at the sound of shuffling footsteps and saw another Calamarian approaching tentatively down the rose-hued corridors. The other ducked his head, but swiveled his great fish eyes up to look at his admiral.

"Terpfen," Ackbar said. His voice sounded listless, like words dropped onto the polished floor, but he tried to dredge up enthusiasm. "You've come after all."

"I could never desert you, Admiral. The Calamarian crewmen remain your firm supporters, even after. . . . "

Ackbar nodded, knowing the unshakable loyalty of his chief starship mechanic. As with many of his people, Terpfen had been taken away from his watery homeworld, kidnapped by Imperial enslavers, and forced to work on designing and refining their Star Destroyers with the renowned Calamarian starship-building expertise. But Terpfen had attempted sabotage and had been tortured. Severely. The scars still showed on his battered head.

During the Imperial occupation of the planet Calamari, Ackbar himself had been pressed into service as a reluctant aid to Moff Tarkin. He had served Tarkin for several years until he finally escaped during a Rebel attack.

"Have you completed your investigation?" Ackbar asked. "Have you gone over the records that survived the crash?"

Terpfen turned his head away. He clasped his broad flipper-hands together. His skin flushed with splotches of bright maroon, showing his embarrassment and shame. "I have already filed my report with the New Republic Council." He looked meaningfully at the closed door of the chamber. "I suspect they are discussing it even now."

Ackbar felt as if he had just attempted to swim under an ice floe. "And what did you find?" he said in a firm voice, trying to resurrect the power of command.

"I found no indication of mechanical failure, Admiral. I've gone over the crash tapes again and again, and I have simulated the flight path through the recorded wind patterns on Vortex. I continue to come up with the same answer. Nothing was wrong with your ship." He looked up at the admiral then turned away again. Ackbar could tell that this report was as difficult for Terpfen to say as it was for Ackbar to hear.

"I checked your ship myself before you took off for Vortex. I found no indications of mechanical instabilities. I suppose I could have missed something. . . . "

Ackbar shook his head. "Not you, Terpfen. I know your work too well."

Terpfen continued in a quieter voice. "I can reach only one conclusion from the data, Admiral—" But Terpfen's voice cut off, as if he refused to speak the inevitable.

Ackbar did it for him. "Pilot error," he said. "I caused the crash. It's my fault. I've known it all along."

Terpfen stood; his head hung so low that he showed only the bulging, sacklike dome of his cranium. "I wish there was some way I could prove otherwise, Admiral."

Ackbar extended a flipper-hand and placed it on Terpfen's gray crewman's uniform. "I know you've done your best. Now please do me one more favor. Outfit another B-wing for my personal use and provision it for a long journey. I'll be flying alone."

"Someone might object to having you fly again, Admiral," Terpfen said, "but don't worry. I can find some way around the problem. Where will you be going?"

"Home," Ackbar answered, "after I tend to some unfinished business."

Terpfen saluted smartly. "Your ship will be waiting for you, sir."

Ackbar felt a hard knot in his chest as he returned the salute. He stepped forward to the closed steelstone door and pounded on the ornate surface, demanding to be let in.

The heavy door groaned open on automatic hinges. Ackbar stood at the threshold as the members of the ruling Council turned to look at him.

The flowstone seats were sculpted and polished to a high luster, including the empty chair that still bore his own name. The air was too dry for his nostrils and stank with the underlying dusty smell of a museum. He could detect the pungent nervous odor of human sweat mixed with the peppery steam from their chosen hot drinks and refreshments.

Obese Senator Hrekin Thorm waved a pudgy hand at Ackbar. "Why don't we make *him* lead the reparations team? That seems appropriate to me."

"I wouldn't think the Vors want him anywhere near their planet," Senator Bel-Iblis said.

"The Vors haven't asked us to help them rebuild at all," Leia Organa Solo said, "but that doesn't mean we should ignore it."

"We're lucky the Vors are not as emotional as other races. This is already a terrible tragedy, but it does not seem likely it will turn into a galactic incident," Mon Mothma said.

Gripping the edge of the table, she stood and finally acknowledged Ackbar's presence. Her skin looked pale, her face gaunt, her eyes and cheeks sunken. She had skipped many important meetings lately. Ackbar wondered if the Vortex tragedy had worsened her health.

"Admiral," Mon Mothma said, "these proceedings are closed. We will summon you after we have taken a vote." Her voice seemed stern and cracking, devoid of the compassion that had launched her career in galactic politics.

Minister of State Leia Organa Solo looked at him with her dark eyes. A flood of sympathy crossed her face, but Ackbar turned away with a stab of anger and embarrassment. He knew Leia would argue his case most strongly, and he expected support from General Rieekan and General Dodonna; but he did not know how Senators Garm Bel-Iblis, Hrekin Thorm, or even Mon Mothma herself would vote.

That doesn't matter, Ackbar thought. He would remove their need to decide, remove the possibility of further humiliation. "Perhaps I can make these deliberations easier on all of us," Ackbar said.

"What do you mean, Admiral?" Mon Mothma said, frowning at him. Her face was seamed with deep lines.

Leia half rose as she suddenly understood. "Don't—"

Ackbar made a decisive gesture with his left fin-hand, and Leia reluctantly sat down again.

He touched the left breast on his pristine-white uniform, fumbling with the catch as he removed his admiral's-rank insignia. "I have caused enormous pain and suffering to the people of Vortex. I have brought immense embarrassment to the New Republic, and I have called down terrible shame upon myself. I hereby resign as commander of the New Republic Fleet, effective immediately. I regret the circumstances of my departure, but I am proud of the years I have served the Alliance. I only wish I could have done more."

He placed his insignia on the creamy alabaster shelf in front of the empty Council seat that had once been his own.

In shocked silence the other Council members stared at him like a mute tribunal. Before they could voice their mandatory—and probably insincere—objections, Ackbar turned and strode out of the room, walking as tall as he dared, yet feeling crushed and insignificant.

He went back toward his quarters to pack his most prized possessions before heading to the hangar bay, where he would take the ship Terpfen had promised him. He had one place to visit first, and then he would return to his homeworld of Calamari.

If General Obi-Wan Kenobi could vanish into obscurity on a desert planet like Tatooine, Ackbar could do the same and live out the rest of his life among the lush seatree forests under the seas.

With the pretense of taking out a B-wing fighter to test its response under extreme stress, Terpfen soared away from Coruscant. The other distraught Calamarian crewmen wished him luck before he departed, assuming he intended to continue his desperate work to clear Admiral Ackbar's name.

But just before the jump into hyperspace, Terpfen entered a new series of coordinates into the navicomputer.

The B-wing lurched with a blast of hyperdrive engines. Starlines appeared around him, and the ship snapped into the frenzied, incomprehensible swirl of hyperspace. He reflexively slid the nictating membrane over his glassy eyes.

Terpfen felt shudders pass through his body as he strained to resist the calling. But he knew by now, after all these years, that he could do nothing to fight it. Screaming nightmares never let him forget his ordeal in the hellish conditioning on the Imperial military training planet of Carida.

The scars on his battered head were not just from torture, but from Imperial vivisection, where the doctors had sawed open his skull and scooped out portions of his brain—segments that controlled a Calamarian's loyalty, his volition, and his resistance to special commands. The cruel xenosurgeons had replaced the missing areas of Terpfen's brain with specially grown organic circuits that mimicked the size, shape, and composition of the removed tissue.

The organic circuits were perfectly camouflaged and could resist the most penetrating medical scan, but they made him a helpless cyborg, a perfect spy and saboteur who could not think for himself when the Imperials wanted him to think their thoughts. The circuits left him sufficient mental capacity to play his part, to make his own excuses each time the Imperials summoned him. . . .

After guiding his ship for several standard time units, Terpfen looked at the chronometer. At the precise instant indicated he pulled the levers that switched off the hyperdrive motors and kicked in the sublight engines.

His ship hung near the lacy veil of the Cron Drift, the gaseous remnants of a multiple supernova where four stars had simultaneously erupted some four millennia ago. The wisps of gas crackled with pinks, greens, and searing white. The residual x rays and gamma radiation from the old supernova caused static over his comm system, but it would also mask this meeting from prying eyes.

A dark Caridan ship already hung there waiting for him. With a flat stealth coating on its hull, the Caridan ship looked like a matte-black insect that swallowed starlight, leaving only a jagged silhouette against the starfield. Protrusions of assault blasters and sensor antennas stuck out like spines.

A burst of static came across Terpfen's comm system; then the tight-beam holotransmission of Ambassador Furgan's head focused itself inside the B-wing cockpit.

"Well, my little fish," Furgan said. His huge eyebrows looked like black feathers curling up on his forehead.

"What is your report? Explain why our two victims were not killed in the crash you engineered."

Terpfen tried to stop the words from coming, but the organic circuits kicked in, providing all the answer the Imperial ambassador needed. "I sabotaged Ackbar's personal ship, and that should have meant death for both passengers—but even I underestimated Ackbar's skill as a pilot."

Furgan scowled. "So the mission failed."

"On the contrary," Terpfen said, "I believe it is even more successful. The New Republic is far more affected by this chain of events than it would be if a simple crash had killed the Minister of State and the admiral. Their fleet commander has now resigned in disgrace, and the ruling Council is left without an obvious replacement."

Furgan considered for a moment, then nodded as a slow smile spread across his fat, dark lips. He changed the subject. "Have you made any progress in uncovering the location of the third Jedi baby?"

During his torturous conditioning, Terpfen had spent four weeks with his head entirely encased in a solid plasteel helmet that kept him blinded, sent jabs of pain at random and malicious intervals. He could not speak or drink or eat, fed entirely through intravenous nutritional supplements. Now, as he sat trapped inside the cockpit of the B-wing fighter, he felt swallowed up in that black pit again.

Terpfen answered in a steady, uninflected voice. "I have told you before, Ambassador. Anakin Solo is being held on a secret planet, the location of which is known only to a very few, including Admiral Ackbar and the Jedi Master Luke Skywalker. I think it highly unlikely that Ackbar will divulge it in casual conversation."

Furgan looked as if he had just bit into something sour and wanted to spit it out. "Then what good are you?"

Terpfen would have taken no offense even if his organic circuitry had allowed him to. "I have set into motion another plan that may provide the information you seek."

Terpfen had performed the task with parts of his mind he did not own. Flipper-hands moving not of his own volition had completed what the rest of him wanted to scream against.

"Your plan had better work," Furgan said. "And one last question—I've noticed that Mon Mothma has avoided public appearances for several weeks. She has not attended many important meetings, sending proxies instead. Tell me, how is dear Mon Mothma's health?" He began to chuckle.

"Failing," Terpfen said, cursing himself. The laughter in Furgan's face suddenly vanished, and his holographic eyes stared into Terpfen's great watery disks.

"Go back to Coruscant, my little fish, before they notice you've disappeared. We wouldn't want to lose you, when there is so much work left to do."

Furgan's transmission winked out. A moment later the beetlelike ship turned and, with a blue-white flare of its hyperdrive engines, burst into a fold of space and vanished.

Terpfen hung alone in the darkness, looking out at the glowing slash of the Cron Drift, surrounded by the echoing walls of his own betrayal.

7

Bearing only a dim glowlamp, Luke Skywalker led a procession of his Jedi students deep into the lower levels of the Massassi temple. Dressed in hooded robes, none of them voiced objections to Luke's nighttime journey; by now they had grown accustomed to his eccentric training methods.

Luke noted the cold, smooth stone against his bare feet, then dismissed the sensation. *A Jedi must be aware of his environment, but must not let it affect him in ways he does not desire.* Luke repeated the phrase to himself, focusing on the state of perfect control he had learned only gradually through the teachings of Obi-Wan Kenobi, Yoda, and his own exercises of self-discovery.

He initially noted the silence of the temple, then scolded himself as he broadened his perceptions. The Great Temple was not silent: The stone blocks ticked and trembled as they cooled in the deepening night. Air currents danced in faint breaths, slow-motion rivers through the enclosed passageways. Tiny, sharp-footed arachnids clicked across the floors and walls. Dust settled.

Luke led his group down the flagstoned steps until he stood facing a blank stone wall. He waited.

Dark-haired Gantoris was the first to notice a tenuous wisp of pale mist through a flaw in the rock. "I see steam."

"I smell sulfur," Kam Solusar said.

"Good," Luke said. He worked the secret panel that slid aside the stone door to a maze of sunken and half-collapsed passages. The tunnel sloped down, and the students followed as he ducked into the deeper shadows. His glowlamp spilled a flickering pool of light in a faint, washed-out circle. His own shadow looked like a hooded monster, a distortion of Darth Vader's black form against the cramped walls.

The underground passage hooked to the left, and now Luke could smell bright and sharp brimstone fumes; the lumpy rock wept condensed moisture. In a moment he could hear the simmering of water, the whisper of steam, the stone sighing with escaping heat.

Luke emerged into the grotto and paused to draw a deep breath of the acrid air. The stone felt slick beneath the soles of his feet, warm and wet.

The other trainees joined him, looking down at a roughly circular mineral spring. Pearllike chains of bubbles laced the clear water as volcanic gases seeped through the rocks. Steam rose from the pool's surface, twisting in stray air currents. The water reflected the glowlamp with a jewel-blue color from algae clinging to the sides. Ledges of stone and crusted mineral deposits made footholds and shallow seats on the walls of the hot spring.

"This is our destination," Luke said, then switched off the glowlamp.

The underground darkness swallowed them, but only for a moment. Luke heard two trainees draw in deep breaths—Streen and Dorsk 81—but the others managed to restrain their surprise.

Luke stared into the blackness, willing it to peel back. Gradually light did filter back, a distant gleam of reflected starlight from an opening in the ceiling high above.

"This is an exercise to help you concentrate and attune yourself to the Force," Luke said. "The water is a perfect temperature: you will float, you will drift, you will reach out and touch the rest of the universe."

He shed his Jedi robe in the near darkness and slipped without a splash into the spring. He heard the rustle of cloth as the others disrobed and moved toward the edge.

The water's sudden heat stung his skin, and the foam of rising bubbles tingled against him. Ripples traversed the pool as the Jedi candidates slid in one at a time. He sensed them floating, relaxing, allowing themselves to gasp with pleasure and warmth.

Luke drew slow, deep breaths as he lay back, drifting, purging his mind and body. The bite of sulfur in the air scrubbed his throat raw and clean; the heat and bubbles opened his pores.

"There is no emotion; there is peace," he said, echoing words from the Jedi Code that Yoda had taught him. "There is no ignorance; there is knowledge. There is no passion; there is serenity. There is no death; there is the Force."

He heard mingling voices as the twelve others repeated his words. But this was too formal for him, too stiff and stilted—he wanted them to *understand* him, not memorize mantras. "Right now you are floating in warmth, in near darkness. Imagine yourselves totally immersed, surrounded, free. Let your minds wander of their own accord, travel along the ripples in the Force."

He swirled his hands, gently stroking back and forth to generate waves in the pool. The other students stirred. He could sense them around him, concentrating, trying too hard.

"Look up," he said. "First you must find the place where you *are* before you can journey elsewhere."

Overhead, high up in the rocky ceiling, a slash of stars spilled through a crack. The pinpoints winked and shimmered with currents in Yavin 4's atmosphere.

"Feel the Force," he said in a whisper, then repeated the words with greater strength. "*Feel* the Force. You are part of it. You can travel with the Force, down into the core of this moon, and out into the stars. Every living thing strengthens the Force, and everything draws strength from it. Concentrate with me and observe the limitless vistas your skills will show you."

Drifting in the warm water, feeling the fizz of bubbles against his skin, Luke looked up at the confined patch of stars through the broken ceiling, then looked back down to the darkened pool. "Can you see it?" he said.

The bottom of the pool flickered, opening a gateway to the universe. He saw the glory of stars, arms of the galaxy, stars exploding in titanic death throes, nebulae coalescing in a blazing wash of birth.

He heard unbridled gasps as the Jedi candidates saw the same vision. They each seemed to be a self-contained form hovering over the universe, where they could get the ultimate perspective, a true view from a height.

Luke felt the wonder pulsing through him as he identified Coruscant and the Emperor's Core worlds. He saw the embattled systems where tattered Imperial remnants fought each other in civil warfare; he saw the empty systems that had once been controlled by the Ssi Ruuk Imperium, until they had been defeated by the combined Empire and Rebel forces at Bakura. Luke recognized and named planets he had known, Tatooine, Bespin, Hoth, Endor, Dathomir, and many others—including the secret world of Anoth, where he and Admiral Ackbar had hidden Han and Leia's third baby.

But then the names and coordinates of the planets soured in his mind, and Luke scolded himself for thinking like a tactician, like a starship pilot. Names meant nothing, positions meant nothing. Every world and every star was a part of the whole of the galaxy, as were Luke and his trainees at the Jedi *praxeum*. As were the plants and creatures in the jungle above—

His attuned senses picked up a change deep within the subterranean chambers, sleeping volcanic outlets that provided geothermal heat to the mineral spring. Somewhere deep in the crust of Yavin 4, a bubble had burst, spewing hot gases upward, simmering through cracks in the rock, rising, seeking an escape route. Coming toward them.

A dark rift appeared in the image of the galaxy below them. With a sudden wave of alarm, four of the Jedi trainees sloshed in the warm water, attempting to reach the edge. Others clenched themselves in panic.

Luke fought down his own fear and made his voice rich and forceful, as he had once tried to sound when negotiating with Jabba the Hutt. His words came out rapidly, filling the remaining seconds.

"A Jedi feels no heat or cold. A Jedi can extinguish pain. Strengthen yourselves with the Force!" Luke thought of the time he had walked across lava in one of the tests Gantoris had imposed upon him. He willed extra protection into his body, forming an imaginary sheath around his exposed skin, thin as a thought and *strong* as a thought.

He scanned the concerned faces in a flash, saw Kirana Ti close her green eyes and grit her teeth; middle-aged Kam Solusar stared at nothing, yet maintained a confident air; Streen, the Bespin cloud hermit, seemed not to understand, but he instinctively increased his protection.

As the large, shifting bubbles boiled to the surface, Dorsk 81, the yellow-skinned clone from the bureaucratic planet, scrambled toward the edge. Luke saw that he would never make it in time; unless Dorsk 81 set up his personal defenses in the next few seconds, he would be boiled as the hot gas escaped into the air.

Before Luke could move, Gantoris reached Dorsk 81, gripping the alien's naked shoulder with his callused hand. "Ride it with me!" Gantoris said, raising his voice above the hissing noise. Volcanic gas bubbles surged to the surface of the hot spring. Luke saw a wall of protection surround Gantoris and Dorsk 81, incredibly strong—and then the primal, potent gases belched around them, churning the water into a foaming fury.

Luke felt the stab of intense heat, but he willed it away. He could feel the strength grow as the candidates also understood and reinforced each other. The scalding onslaught lasted only a few seconds, and the boiling surface of the pool began to return to stillness.

The window to the universe had vanished.

"Enough for tonight," Luke said, sighing in satisfaction. He heaved himself dripping over the lip of the mineral spring and stood. He could smell sulfurous steam rising from his body as he found the rough folds of his Jedi robe piled on the floor. "Think about what you have learned."

With that the trainees began laughing and congratulating each other. They climbed out, one by one. Gantoris assisted Dorsk 81, who thanked him before donning his robe. "Next time I will be stronger," Dorsk 81 said in the dimness.

"I know you will be."

Luke met the dark-haired man as he pulled the robe over his head. "That was a good thing you did, Gantoris."

"It was only heat," Gantoris said, and his voice became grim. "There are far worse things than heat." He paused, then spoke as if divulging a secret. "Master Skywalker—you are *not* the dark man who haunted my nightmares on Eol Sha. I know that now."

The confession took Luke aback. He could not see Gantoris's expression in the dim light. On Eol Sha, Gantoris had suffered horrifying premonitions, but he had not spoken of his nightmares since arriving on Yavin 4. Luke tried to ask why he had mentioned it now, but the other man turned, gliding past the gathered trainees as they made their way back up the gloomy tunnels.

• • •

In the humid morning the trainees gathered in the ship-landing area to continue their exercises. Mists rose to the crown of the Great Temple. Sounds of the stirring jungle buzzed around the students as they practiced preposterous lessons to improve their supernatural balance, to encourage simple feats of levitation.

Luke paced among them as they attempted the things Yoda had taught him in the steamy swamps of Dagobah. He smiled as Kirana Ti and the young minstrel/historian Tionne joined forces. Laughing and concentrating, the two women lifted Artoo-Detoo in the air as the little droid puttered about, clearing the ever-encroaching weeds from the landing grid. Artoo vented electronic beeps and whistles as he floated; his treads spun in the air.

Behind them Gantoris emerged from the shadowy mouth of the temple, striding into the hazy light. Luke turned to watch him approach.

"Glad you could join us, Gantoris!" he said with a combined touch of good humor and scolding as he looked significantly up at how high the orange gas giant had risen to fill much of the sky.

Gantoris's face looked rough and red, as if scorched; tough, smooth skin covered his forehead where his eyebrows should have been. He had braided his thick black hair into a long strand that hung past his shoulders.

"I have been preparing for a new test," Gantoris said, and reached into the folds of his robe. He removed a black cylinder.

Luke blinked his eyes in astonishment at seeing a newly constructed lightsaber.

Artoo crashed to the ground with a terrified squeal as both Kirana Ti and Tionne lost their concentration. The others ceased their lessons and stared in astonishment.

"Fight me, Master Skywalker," Gantoris said. He removed his robe to display the padded captain's uniform he had worn as the leader of his people on Eol Sha.

"Where did you get a lightsaber?" Luke asked cautiously, his mind whirling. None of his students should have been able to master the technology or the discipline yet.

Gantoris fingered the controls on the handle, and with a loud spitting sound the glowing blade extended, a white incandescent core of energy fringed with deep violet. He moved his wrist, flicking the blade back and forth, testing it. A bone-vibrating hum scalded the air. "Isn't it the test of a Jedi to build his own lightsaber?"

Luke proceeded carefully. "The lightsaber may seem the simplest of weapons, but it is difficult to master. An unpracticed wielder is as likely to injure himself as his opponent. You aren't ready for this, Gantoris."

But Gantoris stood like a weathered Massassi colossus, holding the blazing edge of his lightsaber vertically in front of his face. "If you don't ignite your lightsaber and fight me, I will cut you down right here." He paused with a smirk. "That would be a rather embarrassing fate for a Jedi Master, wouldn't it?"

Reluctantly, Luke shrugged out of his robe. He pulled his own lightsaber from the waist of his comfortable gray flightsuit and, feeling the Force thrum through him, ignited the yellow-green blade.

The other trainees watched in amazed silence. Luke wondered how he could have miscalculated so greatly, how Gantoris had gained access to information that only an advanced student should have obtained.

He stepped forward, raising his blade. Gantoris stared unblinking. Luke saw his red-rimmed eyes burn with a depthless intensity, and he felt a twinge of fear.

They crossed blades with a crackle of dissipating power, testing each other. He felt the resistance of the energy blades, the flow of the Force. He and Gantoris struck again, harder this time, and sparks flew.

Abandoning all pretense of testing, Gantoris launched himself at Luke, hacking and slashing with the white-violet saber. Luke blocked each blow, but fought only defensively to keep from provoking his student.

Gantoris made no sound as he struck again and again. The lightsabers intersected with a flash of multicolored lightning. The fury in Gantoris astonished Luke, and he backed toward the jungle's edge, unnerved by the violence.

Gantoris pressed his advantage. Luke blocked away all thoughts of the other trainees watching.

"Am I a Jedi now?" Gantoris asked in a husky voice.

Luke parried, then blocked another blow, locking both blades in a snapping, sizzling spray of discharged energy. He spoke through clenched teeth. "Training requires diligence and commitment. And control. A Jedi needs to know more than how to build a lightsaber. He must also learn how and when to use it!"

Luke drove forward, suddenly taking the offensive. He struck and struck, careful not to injure Gantoris but confident in showing his mastery. "The lightsaber is the weapon of a Jedi Knight, but a true Jedi rarely uses it to settle a dispute. It is better to outthink and outmaneuver your opponent. But when forced, a Jedi strikes quickly and decisively!" He slashed down, hard.

Clumsily defending himself, Gantoris backed into a tangle of jungle. Dew sprayed from underbrush as they trampled stands of climbing ferns. Startled flying creatures flapped away with squawks. Gantoris swung and slashed wildly at Luke's lightsaber, using brute force but no finesse. He bumped against a wide-boled Massassi tree, and flakes of purplish bark fell to the ground in an uneven patter.

Luke stood over him, intending to call an end to the duel, but Gantoris's eyes blazed brighter. As if springing a trap, he fingered a button on his lightsaber handle— and the violet-edged blade suddenly *extended* like a spear, flashing outward to nearly double its length.

Reacting with lightning reflexes, Luke jerked aside, and the point of Gantoris's energy blade slashed through the sleeve of his gray flightsuit, leaving a smoldering gash.

He stared at Gantoris in disbelief for a precious fraction of a second. Not only had Gantoris built his own lightsaber, but he had constructed a blade with multiple jewels, allowing him to adjust the amplitude of his blade. Such a weapon was at least twice as difficult to make as a traditional lightsaber, and Gantoris had done it by himself!

Without pausing Gantoris pressed his advantage, lunging with his longer blade, knowing that Luke could not come close enough to touch him.

The thin, wavering voice of Streen called out, "Gantoris!" unheeded by Luke or Gantoris. The other students pressed toward the edge of the jungle, but this battle was between Luke and Gantoris alone.

He was dismayed to see the recklessness in Gantoris—it reminded him of his own last battle with Darth
Vader as the Emperor gloated, encouraging Luke to feel
the anger flow through him. Luke had almost fallen then,
almost allowed himself to give in to his anger and begin
the journey to the dark side. But he had been strong
enough in the end.

Gantoris seemed dangerously close to the edge.

Luke coiled his muscles, gathered his strength, and
leaped upward. With a boost of his levitating ability, he
soared high enough to reach a thick lower branch of the
Massassi tree. He landed gently, keeping his balance as
he looked down at the outraged Gantoris.

"How did you learn all this?" Luke called over the
hum of lightsabers, trying to break through Gantoris's
intensity.

The fiery-tempered man turned his face up, glaring
with red-rimmed eyes. "You are not the only teacher of
the Jedi way!"

With a low-throated outcry, Gantoris held his lightsaber with both hands and slashed sideways, sizzling
through the massive trunk of the tree. Sparks and smoke
and the wet cinnamon smell of scalded sap spilled into
the air. The ancient tree shifted sideways, then crashed
through clinging upper branches as it toppled.

Luke leaped free and landed easily in a rotting tangle
of moss and fallen branches. He needed to end this soon.
Gantoris seemed possessed by an anger he could not
control, and simple Jedi calming techniques could not
reach him.

Gantoris shortened his blade to a more usable length,
matching Luke's as he came in for the attack. Luke
let his student press him back, through climbing ferns

and brilliant nebula orchids. He reached out through the Force, sensing the jungle around them, looking for a useful diversion.

And found it.

He faked a stumble against a broken fungus-covered rock and lurched sideways toward a thicket. Gantoris charged after him, slashing vines out of the way in puffs of gray steam. Gantoris would never hear the burbling grunting noises coming from the thicket.

Luke jumped aside as Gantoris hammered down with his lightsaber. The violet-white blade sliced through thorns and interlocked twigs—and a startled, outraged beast charged out of the underbrush with an operatic range of bellows.

The snorting runyip flailed from side to side as it stampeded past them. It was a massive, clumsy creature covered with oily fur and clods of dirt stuck to its flexible nose where it had been rooting among the decaying vegetation.

The outburst distracted Gantoris for only a second. But Luke used the moment to reach out with the Force. Grasping with invisible hands, he yanked the lightsaber handle out of Gantoris's grip and used his skill to push the button that deactivated the blade.

Luke snatched Gantoris's weapon from the air, gripping it with his left hand, and switched off his own lightsaber. Suddenly, without the roaring hiss of dual blades, the jungle seemed disturbingly silent.

Gantoris stared at him, unmoving. Both of them panted with trembling exhaustion. They stood close to each other, within arm's reach. Pearls of sweat appeared on their foreheads.

Reaching his decision, Luke broke the frozen moment. He flipped the handle of Gantoris's lightsaber forward and extended it toward the other man. Gantoris tentatively took his weapon back, glanced at it, then met Luke's gaze again.

"Good exercise, Gantoris," Luke said, "but you must learn to control your anger. It could be your undoing."

8

Through the simmering haze of a security field deep within the steelcrete mazes of Coruscant, Kyp Durron looked at the thorn shape of the Sun Crusher.

He squinted to get a better view, leaning forward until three heavily armed New Republic guards strode to bar his way. Within the hangar he could see another crew of guards standing around the Sun Crusher itself. Just inside the electrostatic security field, a huge blast door hung ready to clang down at a moment's notice.

With his small wiry frame, free grin, and tousled dark hair, Kyp didn't think he could possibly pose any threat, but the three guards pointed their blaster rifles at his chest. "This is a restricted area," the sergeant said. "Leave immediately, or we will shoot."

"Hey, relax," Kyp said, raising his hands. "If I wanted to steal the thing, I would never have flown it here in the first place."

The sergeant looked at him skeptically. It was obvious he didn't have a clue what Kyp was talking about.

"I'm Kyp Durron. I *flew* the Sun Crusher with Han Solo from Maw Installation. I just wanted to have another look."

The sergeant's stony expression did not change. "I don't know General Solo personally," he said, "but I have orders to restrict all access. No exceptions."

Kyp shifted to one side to see between the guards. He disregarded their presence, looking again at the angular superweapon that had been developed by the captive scientist Qwi Xux at Maw Installation.

Dr. Xux had innocently designed a weapon that could trigger a star to explode, wiping out all life in an entire solar system. Qwi had done it as an exercise to test the limits of her scientific abilities; but Han had broken through her brainwashing and made her realize what she had created. Qwi had then helped them steal the superweapon and escape from Admiral Daala and Maw Installation.

Kyp was glad the Sun Crusher was now in the hands of the New Republic, but it concerned him that the Senate couldn't decide what to do with it. The existence of such a powerful weapon seemed to change the attitudes of even good people in the government.

Kyp watched as engineers and mechanics attempted to understand how the Sun Crusher worked. They used laser-welders against the ultradense quantum-plated armor, but nothing could scratch the indestructible craft.

Two mechanics clambered out of the upper hatch, carrying a metal cylinder a meter and a half long and half a meter wide. Three engineers at the bottom of the hangar bay craned their necks to look up at the cylinder and dropped their hydrospanners in horror. Another engineer put down her precision calibrator and backed away very slowly.

"It's one of the supernova torpedoes!" an engineer said.

The two mechanics carrying it suddenly froze. Someone sounded a squawking alarm. The guards inside the security field ran about looking for targets to shoot. The trapped engineers and mechanics screamed for the deadly security field to be dropped so they could evacuate. The three guards outside whirled and leveled their blaster rifles at Kyp, as if he had become a threat after all.

He laughed. "It's only a message cylinder," he said. "Have them open it up—they'll see. It's where the log recorders are kept so vital data can be ejected if the Sun Crusher ever gets destroyed."

But as alarms hammered through the air, and people inside the restricted hangar ran around in panic, the guards showed no interest in Kyp's explanations. "You'd better leave now, young man. Immediately!" the sergeant said.

Shaking his head, part in amusement and part in annoyance, Kyp circled back up the long corridors, wondering how long it would take the supposed experts to figure it out.

Wedge Antilles watched with admiration as the beautiful and ethereal alien scientist, Qwi Xux, stepped forward and prepared to address the New Republic Assembly.

Qwi did not like to talk in front of an audience, and she had been nervous for days after setting up this speech. A solitary person, she had begun to confide in Wedge now that he spent most of his time as her official bodyguard and liaison. Wedge had encouraged her in every way, trying to calm her, insisting that she would do a wonderful job. He supported her belief that she could no longer ignore the Sun Crusher.

Qwi had looked at him gratefully. Her wide indigo eyes were in striking contrast to her pale, pale blue skin and the gemlike cap of pearlescent feathers that draped from her head down to her shoulders.

Now Qwi stared at Mon Mothma and the other ministers. She straightened her back, letting her thin arms hang at her sides. She spoke with a flutey voice that sounded like birdsong.

"Mon Mothma and esteemed representatives of the New Republic government," Qwi said, "when I first came to you seeking sanctuary and bringing the Sun Crusher, you invited me to speak to you whenever I felt the need. Now I must tell you of my grave concerns. I will try to be brief, because you must come to a decision."

Beside Wedge, the enormous form of Chewbacca rumbled a low growl of displeasure; but Wedge was impressed at how quiet and restrained the Wookiee had managed to hold himself. Chewbacca was not known for his ability to sit still.

Threepio spoke in a soft voice. "Calm down, Chewbacca. You'll have a chance to speak soon enough. Are you quite certain you don't want me to edit your words into more appropriate language? I *am* a protocol droid, you know, and I am familiar with the requirements."

Chewie blatted a quiet but definite negative. Wedge shushed them both so he could hear Qwi as she spoke. Her musical voice didn't falter, and Wedge felt a warm pride spreading in his chest.

"The Sun Crusher is the most formidable weapon ever devised," Qwi said. "I know this better than anyone, because I designed it. It is an order of magnitude more dangerous than even the Death Star. It is no longer in the clutches of Imperial powers—but I'm concerned about what the New Republic intends. I have refused to divulge its workings for a reason, but you have kept it locked in your research bays for weeks, tinkering with it, studying it, trying to unlock its secrets. It will do you no good."

She paused to take a long breath, and Wedge worried that she might lose her nerve. But Qwi straightened her slender form and spoke again. "I urge you to destroy the Sun Crusher. A weapon of such power should not be trusted in the hands of any government."

Mon Mothma looked weak and weary as she gazed down at Qwi. Below and to her left, old General Jan Dodonna spoke up. "Dr. Xux, according to reports from our engineers, this weapon cannot be destroyed. The quantum armor makes it impossible for us even to dismantle it."

"Then you must find some other way to dispose of the Sun Crusher," Qwi said.

Sounding flustered, Senator Garm Bel-Iblis, Mon Mothma's old nemesis, rose to his feet. "We cannot allow a weapon of such power to slip *out* of our grasp," he said. "With the Sun Crusher, we have a tactical advantage available to none of our Imperial enemies."

"Enough," Mon Mothma said in a quavering voice. Her cheeks were flushed, which served to highlight the pallor of her skin. "We have debated this many times," she said, "and my opinion stands unchanged. A weapon of such hideous destructive power is a brutal and inhuman device. The Emperor might have been monster enough to consider using it, but under no circumstances will the New Republic be party to such barbarism. We have no need for such a weapon, and its presence only serves to divide us. I shall veto any attempts to study the Sun Crusher further, and I will fight to my last breath any of you who suggest using it against any foe, Imperial or otherwise."

She looked at her military commanders, and Wedge felt intimidated by the anger and sheer conviction in her voice. The vacant seat of Admiral Ackbar, who was normally a voice of sanity and moderation, remained empty and hollow like a deep wound. Wedge silently urged Qwi to speak up again, to tell her idea.

As if on cue, she said in her melodious voice, "Excuse me, but might I make a suggestion? Since the Sun Crusher cannot be destroyed by any normal means, we should use the automatic pilot to send it into the heart of a sun, or at least to the core of a gas-giant planet, where it will be impossible to recover."

General Crix Madine spoke up. "A gas-giant planet would be sufficient. The pressures at the core are far beyond what even our most sophisticated vessels can withstand. The Sun Crusher would be out of reach for all time."

Bel-Iblis looked around, his dark eyes flashing. As if sensing defeat and realizing that a gas planet was marginally more acceptable than the blinding fury of a star, he said, "All right, dump it into a gas giant then, for whatever good it will do."

Mon Mothma raised her hand as if to issue an official directive, but Bel-Iblis interrupted. "On a related topic, I hope you have not forgotten that the Maw Installation itself remains a threat. The Imperial admiral may have taken her Star Destroyers, but the scientists are still there inside the black hole cluster. According to General Solo's report, they have a fully functional Death Star prototype." He sent a challenging look toward Mon Mothma.

Chewbacca lurched to his feet and bellowed. His roar echoed through the chamber, stopping all conversation. Threepio waved his golden metallic arms. "Not yet, Chewbacca, not yet! It's not our turn."

But Mon Mothma looked at the agitated Wookiee and acknowledged him. "You have something to say to us, Chewbacca? Please."

Chewbacca spoke a long rumbling sentence in his Wookiee language. As he spoke, Threepio stood beside him and translated quickly in his prissy synthetic voice.

"Chewbacca wishes to remind this auspicious gathering that not only is Maw Installation the home of numerous highly intelligent Imperial scientists, but it is also a prison for some number of Wookiee captives who have been held for nearly a decade. Chewbacca respectfully wishes to suggest—"

Threepio raised a metal hand in front of the Wookiee's mouth. "Slow down, Chewbacca! I'm doing the best I can." He faced forward again. "Excuse me. Chewbacca respectfully wishes to request that the New Republic Council consider an expedition to Maw Installation, both as a rescue party and as an occupation force for the installation."

Chewbacca roared but Threepio did not seem disturbed. "I know that's not what you said, Chewbacca, but it's what you *meant*—so be quiet and let me finish.

"Ahem, with such an occupation force the New Republic can ensure the security and whereabouts of whatever unpleasant weapons have been developed at Maw Installation. Chewbacca thanks you for your time and consideration, and he wishes you to have a pleasant day."

Chewbacca cuffed him, and Threepio sat down in a stiff-legged tumble of golden arms and legs. "Oh, do be quiet," the droid said. "Every change I made was an improvement."

Mon Mothma looked to the gathered Council members. All of them seemed pleased with the suggestion to send a force to Maw Installation. Qwi Xux backed toward Wedge, nervous and relieved; he squeezed her shoulder in congratulation. She smiled at him, and he smiled back.

"I believe we're all agreed on this matter," Mon Mothma said, and forced a weak smile, "for once. We shall set up a rescue and occupation force to go to Maw Installation. We must move decisively, as soon as possible, but not so quickly that we make mistakes."

As Mon Mothma looked around, she seemed to want nothing more than to leave the chamber and return to her quarters where she could rest. Wedge frowned in concern.

"If there is no other business," Mon Mothma said, "this meeting is adjourned."

9

The Imperial Star Destroyer *Gorgon* entered planetary orbit like a wide-bladed knife ready to strike. Flanking the flagship on either side rode the fully operational cruisers *Basilisk* and *Manticore*.

Commander Kratas relayed a message from the navigation console. "We have achieved orbit around Dantooine."

Daala clasped her gloved hands behind her back and turned to survey the bridge crew. "Sensor sweep," she said, and waited as the lieutenant calibrated his instruments to scan the visible face of the planet.

"A very primitive world, Admiral. No detectible industry. A few nomadic settlements . . ." He paused. "Wait. At the terminator I detect a cluster of people."

Daala studied the swirling olive, blue, and brown face of the planet, observing the edge of daylight creeping across the surface.

"I've found what appear to be the ruins of a larger base that seems mostly abandoned now. The inhabited area is not very well developed—mostly small prefabricated dwellings." The lieutenant scratched his short brown hair and bent closer to his glowing screen.

"I see excavations where new superstructures are being set up," he said, looking up at Daala. "This configuration is consistent with a large transmitting dish. Perhaps even a shield generator."

Daala's brow furrowed as she pondered how her former mentor Grand Moff Tarkin would have handled this situation.

Commander Kratas seemed to sense her hesitation and offered, "It doesn't appear that they could muster much resistance," he said.

Daala pursed her lips. "Even if they did resist, we would still defeat them. That's not the point." She ran a slender finger along her chin, then brushed her coppery hair back behind her shoulders. "To start with, we will target the abandoned base from orbit and level it with our turbolasers. It will be a spectacular display."

Daala's Star Destroyers controlled enough power to turn entire planets to slag, but she didn't want to do that here. "Dantooine is too remote for an effective demonstration," she said, "but we can make use of it nonetheless. Commander Kratas, I want you to lead a strike force. Take two AT-ATs from the *Gorgon* and a pair from each of the other two ships. Six Armored Transports should be enough."

"Me, Admiral? But surely General Odosk or one of the other Imperial Army commanders—"

"Do you have a problem with my orders, Commander?"

"No, Admiral. Not at all."

"I want you to show your versatility. Didn't they put you through those exercises on Carida?"

"Yes, Admiral," Kratas said, "I simply thought it would be more efficient just to blast them from orbit."

Daala fixed him with her emerald stare. "Consider it an exercise, Commander. We've been cooped up guarding Maw Installation for too long, and we won't have another opportunity to catch the New Republic so unprepared."

Now that he was a hopeful colonist, Warton got up in time to watch Dantooine's peaceful pastel sunrise. He stretched and stepped outside his prefab self-erecting home unit, enjoying every moment of dawn. He felt safe and at peace for the first time in his life.

His bones ached, but it was a pleasant soreness from gratifying work. He would never recover completely from his hard life on the tortured world of Eol Sha, but just spending a day without earthquakes or lava flows or scalding geysers made his life happy.

The other colony units, made of brightly colored polymers set with transparisteel windows, looked across the whispering savannas of Dantooine. All the people rescued from Eol Sha agreed that this place seemed like paradise with tall, waving lavender grasses and broad-boled, jagged-branched blba trees.

The southeastern horizon grew bright where Dantooine's amber sun would rise. Overhead in the purplish skies he saw three brilliant stars moving against the other points of light.

A cluster of six meteors streaked through the sky toward the horizon, their bright trails like slashes of claws. Then the supersonic screeching noise of their descent shattered the early-morning stillness. He saw the meteors impact; the savanna glowed with spreading flames not far from the colony.

Other colonists from Eol Sha scrambled out of their huts, roused by the noise from the sky. Not far to the east, the empty ruins of the old Rebel base rose like adobe bulwarks out of the grasses. A small team of New Republic construction engineers bustled about their encampment.

"What is it?" his wife Glena said as she stepped out of the dwelling to stand beside Warton. He shook his head, unable to answer.

Then deadly lightning began to rain down from above.

The singing of mace flies fell into silence. Blinding bolts of green laser fire shot down, striking the abandoned base and ripping up huge clouds of fragmented buildings and shards of synthetic rock.

Turbolaser beams from orbit flashed again, cutting across their earlier path. In seconds they had obliterated the entire abandoned base, leaving only a smoldering rubble-strewn scar.

The colonists ran out of their dwellings. Some screamed; others just stared in stupefied terror. Luke Skywalker had promised he would find a place of safety for the people of Eol Sha—but it seemed the Jedi had been mistaken.

As the ruins of the base continued to crackle and steam, and fires spread across the dry savannas, Warton heard a pulsating, low-pitched sound: the humming of massive engines, the clanking of metal, thunderous footfalls.

He squinted into the brightening morning, still dazzled from the green laser bolts, until he could discern the monstrous silhouettes of gigantic walking machines. Four-legged and camellike, the Imperial walkers—All Terrain Armored Transports—strode from their smoldering landing sites and marched in hulking formation across the savanna.

The cockpit "heads" of the attacking AT-ATs bent lower to aim banks of laser cannons. Precision bolts of green and red fire shot down. The ancient swollen blba trees erupted into flames that spread out in concentric circles across the dry grasses. Greasy smoke curled up, carrying the stench of burning wet vegetation and roasted small animals.

Warton shouted, "Run everyone! Get away from the dwellings. They will target them first."

The refugees from Eol Sha waded across the tall grasses as Imperial walkers plodded forward. The AT-ATs covered more distance with each step than a human could run in half a minute. The walkers took aim at the fleeing colonists, striking each individual with enough firepower to destroy a small fighter ship.

Glena yanked her hand away from Warton and shouted at him, "Wait!" She turned around to run back toward their small dwelling.

"No!" he yelled, unable to imagine anything that would cause her to turn and run into the attack.

Before she could say another word, a blinding lance of turbolaser fire exploded full in her chest, and Warton watched in utter horror as Glena vanished in a blazing, sizzling cloud of red steam.

The six walkers continued to march ahead, firing at blba trees, at colony huts, and at anything that moved. The great machines spread out to encircle the entire settlement.

Over at their encampment the New Republic engineers had managed to set up a single-ion cannon. Warton, still standing stricken and motionless, watched their tiny forms as they scrambled to rig the dish-shaped generator. He knew the people manning the ion cannon were simply construction engineers with no battle training.

"Why?" Warton wanted to know. But so many questions filled his head that he could not be more specific than that: *Why?*

The New Republic engineers powered up the ion cannon and focused a single blast toward the lower section of the closest Imperial walker. The bolt struck and fused the knee joint of the AT-AT's front foreleg, melting the servomotor mechanisms. The walker halted and tried to limp backward in a stiff-legged retreat.

The other five AT-ATs swiveled their heads in unison, targeting the single ion cannon with a river of laser blasts in a great gout of green fire—obliterating communications gear and ion cannon in a single splash of light.

The walkers advanced again, firing indiscriminately. The prefabricated colony huts exploded one by one. Hungry flames raged through the dry grasses on the savanna.

Warton's people screamed as they ran, and stumbled, and died. The roar of destruction rang in his ears, and still he could not move. He stood with his hands at his sides. His entire body trembled.

Even the blasted world of Eol Sha had never been as hellish as Dantooine.

Commander Kratas sat in the AT-AT's unfamiliar cockpit, directing the movement of his six great machines. They fired at anyone who tried to escape, igniting islands of grass and flushing out burning colonists who had attempted to hide there. Kratas intended to leave them no place to hide.

He verified that every one of the huts had been blown to pieces, and all moving colonists had been cut down as they fled. The Rebel engineers and their ion cannon had been taken out with a single strike, and the minor damage inflicted on one walker could be repaired easily in the workshops back on the *Gorgon*.

"I wish he'd move," the gunner said.

Kratas looked down to see a single man standing among the wreckage, motionless and staring.

"It's not much of a challenge to hit a stationary target," the gunner said, lifting the visor of his black helmet. "If he'd run, I could get better practice."

Kratas surveyed the devastation and the black smoke curling up from a thousand different fires. Their job here was done. "Take him out anyway," Kratas said. "We don't have time to play games."

The gunner squeezed his firing buttons, and the lone surviving man vanished in a flare of green fire.

Commander Kratas signaled the flagship, and he nodded to Daala's tiny shimmering form on the transmitter platform. "The mission is a complete success, Admiral. No casualties on our part, very minor damage to one AT-AT."

"You're sure nothing is left alive down there?" Daala said.

"Nothing, Admiral. No structure is left standing. The place is a wasteland."

"Good," Daala said with a slight nod. "You may return to the ships. I believe we've made our point. We've had our practice."

She continued with a smile, "Next time we'll choose a more important world to strike."

10

The sleep of a Jedi was rarely troubled by dreams. Pure rest brought about through concentration and meditation techniques left little room for disturbing thoughts or shadow plays. But this time nightmares did break through to Luke Skywalker.

A voice called him across a misty blank dreamscape. "Luke, Luke my son. You must hear me!"

A shadowy form rose out of the mists even as the surroundings began to sharpen. Luke saw himself in his pale-gray flightsuit, stained with sweat, grime, and pain—as he had looked when he took his father's body from the second Death Star.

The features on the spectral silhouette shimmered with a pale aura. Luke saw the firm face of Anakin Skywalker, restored from the ravages Darth Vader's evil had worked on his body.

"Father!" Luke called. His own voice had an odd, echoing quality, as if it bounced off the mists.

"Luke," the image of Anakin said.

Luke felt tingling amazement surge through him. It was another sending, just like his last contact from Obi-Wan Kenobi. But Obi-Wan had bid him farewell, claiming that he could never contact Luke again. "Father, why are you here?"

Anakin stood taller. His robes rippled in a rising wind that drove back the mists. Suddenly the world surrounding them was no longer featureless. Luke recognized that he and the image of his father stood atop the Great Temple on Yavin 4. The orange gas giant hung overhead, and the timeless jungles below looked unchanged. But the stones of the temple were white and new with bright scars from fresh quarrying. A sketchy framework of scaffolding laced one wall of the ziggurat. Far below, Luke heard mumbling and chanting, incantations from suffering slaves.

He saw people of the vanished Massassi race laboring together, straining to haul enormous stone blocks along roads they had chopped through the jungle. The grayish-green Massassi were humanoid, smooth-skinned, with large lanternlike eyes. Anakin Skywalker stood on the highest point of the temple, as if directing the work gangs below.

"Do not be deceived, Luke. Do not trust everything you think to be the truth." Anakin's words carried an odd, distant lilt, like the faint accent of an ancient race. "Obi-Wan lied to you, more than once."

Luke felt uneasiness well up within him. No matter how much he loved Obi-Wan Kenobi, he knew the old man had not always been completely forthcoming with him. "Yes, I know he hid the truth from me. He told me Darth Vader had killed you, when you had really become Vader."

Anakin turned from the illusory Massassi laborers below. He met Luke's gaze with eyes as bottomless as the universe itself. "Was that the only lie Obi-Wan told you?"

"No. He hid other things from me." Luke looked off into the jungled distance, toward the moon's foreshortened horizon to see another clearing, another tall temple being erected.

"And Obi-Wan rationalized it as being for your own *protection*. Did you ask for such protection, Luke?"

"No." Luke tried to fight back his uneasiness.

"Obi-Wan wanted you to be his student, but he wouldn't allow you the freedom to make your own decisions. Did he trust you so little? Did you always agree with his 'certain point of view'?"

"No," Luke said, feeling the words swallowed up in doubt.

Anakin's voice became tinged with anger. "Obi-Wan fought against the complex Sith teachings I had uncovered. He did not understand them himself, but he forbade me to study them—though he always insisted that I must learn for myself and choose my own path. I rebelled against him for his narrow-mindedness, and I insisted on unlocking secrets for which I was not ready. In the end it consumed me—I fell to the dark side, and I became the Dark Lord of the Sith."

Anakin looked at Luke with an anguished, apologetic expression. "But if Obi-Wan had let me learn the teachings at my own pace, I would have grown stronger. I would have remained uncorrupted. He never understood that."

Anakin's image shook his head. "If you are going to teach other Jedi, Luke, you must understand the consequences of what they may learn. You, too, must study the ancient heritage of the Sith. It is a part of your Jedi training."

Luke swallowed. "I'm afraid to believe you, Father. I have already felt the power of the dark side."

Below, Massassi labor crews hummed and sang in stuporous unison, far beyond exhaustion, as they hauled an enormous block up a mud-covered ramp made of stripped logs.

Atop the dream temple, the wavering image of Anakin Skywalker spoke more forcefully. "Yes, but the ways of the Sith can lead you to a stronger grasp of your own power. You can wipe out the last vestiges of the pitiful Empire that continues to harass your New Republic. You can become more than a mere servant to a frail and corrupt government. You can administer the galaxy yourself as a benevolent ruler.

"You deserve it more than any other person, Luke. You can control everything, if you use the Force as your tool, instead of allowing yourself to become its servant."

Luke stiffened, unable to believe what his father was saying. Then he noticed that with the rising passion in his voice, the image of Anakin Skywalker became less distinct, wavering, until it transformed into only a black outline, an engulfing hooded form that sucked energy from the air.

Slowly, Luke realized the truth. "You are not my father!" he shouted as the illusion began to crumble. "My father was a good man in the end, healed by the light side."

Streaks of brilliant light flashed across the dreamscape sky of ancient Yavin 4. Below, Massassi slaves fled into the jungles in terror as the monumental temples crumbled under a barrage of laser blasts from orbit. Old Republic battleships had arrived, immolating the moon's surface.

"Who are you?" Luke shouted at the figure through the roar of sudden blazing devastation around him. "Who?"

Instead, the hollow shadow laughed and laughed, ignoring the destruction that erupted from the construction sites—or amused by it. The Massassi temples exploded. The thick rain forests burst into flame.

The dark man's silhouette grew larger and larger, swallowing up the sky. Luke backed away from it, but his dream feet reached the edge of the imposing temple, and he stumbled backward, falling away, falling. . . .

Surrounded by the thick stone walls of his quarters, Gantoris did not even attempt to sleep. He sat on his bunk dreading the arrival of the dark man from his nightmares.

He fingered the lightsaber he had constructed, feeling its smooth cylinder, the rough spots where he had welded the pieces together, the buttons that would activate the energy blade. He wondered how he could use it against the ancient spectre who had taught him things that terrified him, things that Master Skywalker would never show his Jedi trainees.

"Do you mean to strike me down with that weapon?" the hollow voice said.

Gantoris whirled to see the oily, infinitely black silhouette ooze out of the massive stones in the wall. His impulse was to ignite the lightsaber and slash the violet-white blade across the dark form. But he restrained himself, knowing it would do no good.

The shadow man laughed, then spoke with his antiquated accent. "Good! I am glad to see you have learned to respect me. Four thousand years ago the entire military fleet of the Old Republic and the combined forces of hundreds of Jedi Masters could not destroy me. You would certainly be unable to do so alone."

The dark man had shown him how to borrow energy from other living things, to shore up his own reserves. His mind was alert, but his nerves were frayed and his body exhausted. "What do you want with me?" Gantoris said. "You don't just want to teach me."

The shadow man agreed. "I want your *anger*, Gantoris. I want you to open the doorways of power. I am barred from the physical plane—but with enough other Sith followers, I could be at peace. I could even live again."

"I won't let you have my anger." Gantoris swallowed, searching for a core of strength within himself. "A Jedi does not give in to anger. There is no passion; there is serenity."

"Don't quote platitudes to me!" the dark man said in a cold, vibrating voice.

"There is no ignorance; there is knowledge," Gantoris continued, repeating the Jedi Code. "There is no passion; there is serenity."

The dark man laughed again. "Serenity? Let me show you what is happening at this moment. Do you recall the people you saved from Eol Sha? How happy you were to learn they had been taken to a place of safety, a paradise world? Observe."

Inside the black cut-out form of the hooded man, an image appeared, displaying the grasslands of the planet

Dantooine. The scene looked familiar to Gantoris after seeing the progress tapes delivered by Wedge Antilles.

But now he saw Imperial lasers striking down, leveling colony buildings, giant armored walkers striding across the savanna, blasting anything that moved, igniting the temporary living units. People ran screaming. His people.

Gantoris recognized most of their faces, but before he could name them, they dissolved one by one in brilliant flashes as they tried to flee. The trees blazed in conical bonfires; black clumpy smoke rose in jagged swirls.

"You lie! This is a trick!"

"I have no need of lies when the truth is so devastating. You can do nothing to stop it. Do you enjoy watching your people die? Does that not spark your anger? In your anger lies strength."

Gantoris saw the old man Warton, whom he had known his entire life, standing in the middle of the holocaust. Warton stared around him, hands dangling at his sides, frozen in shock, until a thick green bolt cut him down.

"No!" Gantoris shouted.

"Let loose your anger. Make me stronger."

"No!" he repeated, turning his head away from the images of burned ruins and blackened bodies.

"They are all dead. All of them," the dark man taunted. "No survivors."

Gantoris ignited his lightsaber and lunged at the dark man.

With an insistent bleeping Artoo-Detoo woke Luke from his nightmares. He snapped awake, using a Jedi technique to dispel the weariness and shock of the sudden waking.

"What is it, Artoo?"

The droid whistled, telling him something about a message waiting in the command center. Luke shrugged into his soft robe and hurried across the cold floor in the early light of planetrise. Taking the turbolift down to the second level of the temple, he entered the once-bustling command center.

"Artoo, bring up the lights." He picked his path through the equipment, dust-covered chairs, shut-down computer consoles, document tables cluttered with debris. He powered on the communications station that Wedge had insisted on installing during his last supply run.

The image of Han Solo waited impatiently for him, fidgeting in the holofield. When he saw Luke appear in the transmission locus, Han grinned up at him. "Hey, Luke! Sorry I forgot to account for time differential. Not even dawn there, is it?"

Luke brushed his brown hair into place with his fingers. "Even Jedi need to sleep sometime, Han."

Han laughed. "Well, you'll be getting less sleep when your new student arrives. I just wanted to tell you that Kyp Durron has had enough of his vacation. I think after all that time in the spice mines, he got used to being miserable. The closest thing to the spice mines I could think of was your Jedi academy—that way he can work all day long, but at least he'll be improving himself in the process."

Luke smiled at his old friend. "I'd be honored to have him join us, Han. I've been waiting for him. He has the strongest potential of all the trainees I've seen so far."

"Just wanted to let you know he's coming," Han said. "I'm trying to arrange for the next available transport to Yavin 4."

Luke frowned. "Why don't you just bring him in the *Falcon*?"

Han hung his head, looking extremely troubled. "Because I don't own the *Falcon* anymore."

"What?"

Han seemed filled with embarrassment, eager to end the communication. "Look, I've got to go. I'll tell Leia hello for you and give the kids a hug."

"All right, Han, but—"

Han gave a sheepish grin and quickly terminated the transmission.

Luke continued to stare at the blank space where Han's image had been. First his nightmare of a dark man masquerading as Anakin Skywalker, and now the grim news that Han had lost the *Millennium Falcon*—

Luke heard a disturbance coming down the hall: clumsy footsteps slapping on the stone floor, panicked shouts. He looked up, ready to scold one of his students for such blatant lack of control, when the cloned alien Dorsk 81 rushed into the control center. "Master Skywalker! You must come immediately!"

Luke sensed waves of horror and misery spilling from his candidate. "What is it?" he asked. "Use the calming technique I showed you."

But Dorsk 81 grabbed his arm. "This way!" The yellow-olive alien urged him out of the cluttered control room. Luke sensed widening ripples of alarm traveling like an earthquake through the solid stone of the temple.

They ran along the flagstoned corridors, up the turbolift, and into the section of living quarters where the trainees made their homes.

A sour, smoky stench filled the air, and Luke felt an icy lump in his stomach as he pushed cautiously forward. Hard-bitten Kam Solusar and addled Streen both stood outside the open doorway to Gantoris's quarters, looking pasty and ill.

Luke hesitated for a fraction of a second, then moved through the doorway.

Inside the small stone chamber, he saw what was left of Gantoris. The body lay crisped and blackened on the floor, burned from the inside out. Singed stains on the flagstones showed where he had thrashed about in the conflagration. Gantoris's skin flaked in black, peeling ashes over his powdery bones. Rising wisps of steam curled from the remaining fabric of his Jedi robe.

On the floor the newly constructed lightsaber lay where Gantoris had dropped it, as if he had tried to fight something—and lost.

Luke leaned against the cool stone wall to catch his balance. His vision blurred, but he could not tear his gaze from his dead student sprawled in front of him.

By now the other eleven trainees had gathered. Luke grasped the worn stone bricks at the edge of the door until even the rounded corners bruised his fingers. He applied a Jedi calming technique three times before he felt confident enough to trust his voice. The words tasted like wet ash in his mouth, as Yoda had told him so long ago.

"Beware the dark side," he said.

11

After eight seemingly random
hyperspace jumps to shake any possible pursuit, Ackbar
took his B-wing fighter along the correct vector to the
hidden planet Anoth. Terpfen had "borrowed" the fighter
for him, claiming to have purged the records of its existence; Ackbar didn't want to know how his mechanic had
gotten through the security systems so easily.

For years isolated Anoth had been a haven for the
Jedi children, protected by its perfect obscurity and
anonymity. The twins had gone home to Coruscant
only a month or two before, but the youngest child—
one-year-old baby Anakin—remained under the protection of Leia's devoted servant Winter, far from prying
Imperial eyes or dark-side influences that could corrupt
the baby's fragile Force-sensitive mind.

As space snapped into sharp focus, Ackbar saw the
clustered multiple planet of Anoth. The world was
composed of three large fragments orbiting a common
center of mass. The two largest pieces hovered nearly

in contact, sharing a poisonous stormy atmosphere. The third and more distant fragment orbited in a precarious, almost-safe position where Ackbar, Luke, and Winter had set up a hidden stronghold.

Skittering electrostatic discharges danced from the two touching pieces of Anoth, and the ionized fury bathed the habitable chunk in electrical storms that served to mask the planet from prying eyes. The entire system was unstable, and in a blink of cosmic time it would destroy itself, but for the last century or so it had been possible for humanoid life to establish a foothold there.

Ackbar brought his B-wing in on close approach through the deep-purple skies of Anoth. Sparks discharged from the wing of his fighter, but he felt no threat. This was not like flying through the storms of Vortex.

Inside the cramped B-wing, Ackbar wore only a flightsuit over his big frame, not his admiral's uniform. Later he would leave the "borrowed" fighter in the Calamarian shipyards, where a New Republic pilot could shuttle it back to Coruscant. Ackbar would not be flying a starfighter again, so he had no need of it.

He sent a brief signal to inform Winter of his arrival, but he did not respond to her surprise or her questions. Switching off the fighter's comm unit, he rehearsed how he would tell her all that had happened. Then he concentrated on guiding the B-wing in for a landing.

Below him the surface of Anoth was a craggy forest of rocky spires, sharp ledges, and clawlike peaks that were riddled with caves left behind when volatile inclusions in the rocks had evaporated over the centuries, leaving only glasslike rock.

Inside the labyrinth of smooth tunnels Winter had made a temporary home with the Jedi babies. Now she had only one child left to care for; and in another year, when Anakin reached the age of two, Winter could return to Coruscant and to active service with the New Republic government.

The small white sun never brought much daylight to Anoth, bathing the world in Gothic purple twilight lit by stark flashes of interplanetary lightning discharges. Ackbar and Luke Skywalker had found this planet, choosing it from among the possibilities as the safest place to hide the Jedi children. And now Ackbar had come one last time before returning to his homeworld of Calamari.

He felt sympathy for baby Anakin, who had not known a more welcoming place during his first year. Ackbar had always felt a close attachment to the third child, but he had come to say goodbye before fading from public view forever.

He flew the B-wing in among the spired forests and rock outcroppings. It reminded him of the tall fluted towers of the Cathedral of Winds on Vortex. That thought gave him a stab of pain, and he tried not to think of it further.

He cruised the ship in among the rocks, flying confidently as he arrowed toward the opening to the network of caves. With landing jets and a careful manipulation of repulsorlifts, Ackbar managed to land the starfighter smoothly on the wide grotto floor.

As he powered down the engines and prepared to disembark, a metal crash door swung open. A tall rigid-looking woman stood at the doorway. Her robes and her white hair clearly identified her as Leia's ageless servant Winter. Even for a human, she looked strikingly distinctive to Ackbar.

He climbed stiffly out of his ship and turned his salmon-colored head away to keep from meeting her eyes. He saw with a backward glance that the one-year-old baby toddled at Winter's feet, making happy noises, curious to see the new visitor. Ackbar felt a shudder go through him as he realized he would probably never see the dark-haired boy again.

Winter spoke in her flat, no-nonsense voice. He had never heard her upset before. "Admiral Ackbar, please tell me what has happened."

He turned to face her, showing his flightsuit, his lack of military insignia. "I am no longer an admiral," he said, "and it is a long story."

Ackbar sat eating a meal of reconstituted rations that Winter had somehow managed to make palatable. As he told her every detail of the tragedy on Vortex and how he had resigned from his service, Winter did not appear judgmental. She simply listened, blinking rarely, nodding even less often.

Baby Anakin crouched on Ackbar's lap, cooing and reaching up in curiosity to pat Ackbar's clammy skin and touch his huge glassy eyes. Anakin giggled as the round eyes swiveled in various directions to avoid being poked by pudgy fingers.

"Will you stay here for an evening's rest—?" Winter said. Her sentence cut off sharply, as if she had been about to call him admiral.

"No," Ackbar said, holding the baby against him with flipper-hands. "I can't. No one must suspect that I have come here, and if I delay too long, they will realize I have not gone directly to Calamari."

Winter hesitated and then spoke in a voice that seemed less able to conceal emotion than it normally did. "Ackbar, you know I have the greatest respect for your abilities. It would honor me if you would stay here with me instead of going into hiding on your homeworld."

Ackbar looked at the human woman and felt a surge of emotion well up inside him. Winter's mere suggestion had been powerful enough to strip away layers of guilt and shame with which he had buried himself.

When he did not answer immediately, she pressed further. "I'm all alone here, and I could use your help. It gets lonely for the baby . . . and for me."

Ackbar finally managed to speak, avoiding Winter's gaze but giving his answer before he could change his mind. "Your offer honors me, Winter, but I am not worthy. At least not at the moment. I must go to Calamari and search for peace there. If I—" The words caught in his throat again, and he realized he was trembling. "If I find my peace, perhaps I shall return to you—and the baby."

"I—*we*'ll be here waiting, if you change your mind," she said, then escorted him back to the hangar grotto.

Ackbar felt her watching him as he climbed back into the B-wing. He lifted the ship on its repulsorlift jets and turned to see her standing at the doorway. He flicked his running lights to signal her.

Winter raised a hand in sad goodbye. Then, with her other hand, she made Anakin's pudgy arm wave to him too.

Ackbar's starfighter soared into space, leaving them behind.

Back on Coruscant, Terpfen lay sick and shivering in his private quarters, trying with all his might to resist. But in the end the organic circuitry inside what was left of his brain took over.

Moving with forced steps, he descended to the dispatching and receiving network in the lower levels of the old Imperial Palace. No one watched him in the echoing, crowded room as diplomatic droids and packages came in and left, streaking off to various embassies and spaceports on Coruscant, bearing important dispatches.

Terpfen coded his secret message, summarizing information he had received from the hidden tracking device he had planted on Ackbar's ship. He sealed the message inside a coffin-sized hyperspace courier tube and shielded the entire apparatus. He glanced around suspiciously before he keyed in Admiral Ackbar's personal diplomatic security code, which would allow it to bypass all checks and tariff points. No one would have thought to revoke Ackbar's access yet.

The routing doors opened up at the far end of the center, and the silvery message canister rose on its launching fields. In a reflex action Terpfen reached out, trying to grasp the slick sides of the canister, scraping with the sharp points of his hands—but the container rocketed out, picking up speed as it soared into the Coruscant sky.

Terpfen had programmed five alternate routes to discourage tracking. The message canister would arrive unhindered and without delay at the Imperial Military Academy on Carida. The coded message would be displayed for the eyes of Ambassador Furgan only— divulging the location of the secret planet where the last Jedi baby was hidden.

12

"**Y**ou'll do just fine, kid," Han said, trying to maintain his roguish grin.

Standing at the door of Han and Leia's quarters, Kyp Durron nodded. Han noticed a faint trembling around the young man's lips. "I'll do my best, Han. You know that."

Suddenly unable to say another word, Han embraced Kyp, silently cursing the stinging tears that rose to his eyes. "You'll be the greatest Jedi ever. You'll give even Luke a run for his money."

"I doubt that," Kyp said. He broke away and averted his face but not before Han caught the shimmer of tears in his eyes too.

"Wait," Han said, "I've got something for you before you go." He ducked back inside and returned to the door with a soft package. Kyp took it with a tentative smile and unwrapped the top layers of paper.

Han watched the young man's expression. Kyp reached into the package and withdrew a flowing black cape that glittered with subliminal reflective threads, as if it had been woven out of a clear starry night.

"Lando gave it to me—feeling guilty about winning the *Falcon*, I guess—but I can't wear stuff like this. I want you to have it. You deserve something nice, after all those years you spent in the dirty spice mines."

Kyp laughed. "You mean so I can dress up for all those formal occasions at the Jedi academy?" His expression became serious. "Thanks, Han . . . for everything. But I've got to be going. General Antilles is escorting the Sun Crusher to Yavin, and I'll be going with him. He'll drop me off at Luke's academy."

"Good luck," Han said.

Kyp said, "I'm sorry you lost the *Falcon*."

"Don't worry about it," Han said. "She's a hunk of junk anyway."

"You got that right," Kyp said with a smile, but both of them knew he didn't mean it.

"Want me to walk with you down to the hangar?" Han asked, realizing as he said it that he wasn't sure he wanted to.

"Naw," Kyp said, turning away from the door. "I hate long goodbyes. See you around."

"Sure, kid," Han said. He watched Kyp's back for a long time as the young man walked with a feigned bouncy step down the corridors to the turbolift.

Han thought about going back into his room, then decided he'd rather go for a drink instead. Leia was in yet another late-night Council meeting with Mon Mothma, and the kids were already in bed, so Han left Threepio with instructions to remain powered up so he could baby-sit.

Han eventually returned to the lounge where he and Lando had played sabacc for possession of the *Falcon*.

The window looked out across the sweeping geometrical skyline of the rebuilt Imperial City. Towering metal and transparisteel pillars stretched to rarefied heights. Warning beacons and transmitting towers blinked in multicolored patterns as flying craft swooped on the updrafts between the tall buildings.

At another table a hammerheaded Ithorian ambassador sat by himself next to a small musical synthesizer. He hummed along with the atonal noises and plucked small leaves off a fresh ferny-looking snack. A pug-faced Ugnaught chittered and played electronic dice with a well-groomed Ranat. The bartender droid drifted from one table to another, attempting to be of service.

Han soon lost himself in thought, wondering where he had come to, thinking about how much his life had changed since his years as a spice smuggler for Jabba the Hutt and then as a general in the Rebel Alliance.

He continued to do important things with his life, but it just didn't seem as *real* anymore. He had enjoyed spending time with young Kyp Durron. The young man reminded him so much of himself, and now Kyp had gone off to become a Jedi just like Luke.

"You're gonna miss the kid, aren't you?" a deep voice said. Han looked up to see Lando Calrissian standing over him with a big smile.

"What are you doing here?" Han said grumpily.

"I'm buying you a drink, old buddy," Lando said. He shoved forward one of the prissy fruity concoctions, complete with bright tropical flower, that Han had bought Lando on the night of their sabacc game.

Han scowled and accepted it. "Thanks a lot." He took a sip, grimaced, then took a gulp. Lando pulled up a chair.

"I didn't invite you to sit down," Han said.

"Look, Han," Lando said, adding a stern edge to his voice, "when you won the *Falcon* from me in a sabacc game, did I spend years pouting and not talking to you?"

Han shrugged and looked up. "I don't know. I pretty much stayed away all those years." He paused, then added quickly, "And the next time we saw each other, you betrayed us to Darth Vader."

"Hey, that wasn't my fault, and I've more than made up for it since," Lando said. "Listen, I've got a deal for you. Next time you get a chance, why don't the both of us take the *Falcon* and go back to what's left of Kessel? Maybe we can find my old ship there. If we do, I'd gladly take the *Lady Luck* back, and you can have the *Falcon*." He held out his broad hand. "Deal?"

Han grudgingly admitted that it was the best he could hope for. "All right, pal," he said, and shook Lando's hand.

"Solo," a woman's sharp voice said. "They told me I'd find you here."

"Can't a guy get some peace?" he said, and turned to see a trim, attractive woman standing at the lounge entrance. She had shoulder-length reddish brown hair the color of some exotic spice. Her features were finely chiseled: a narrow chin and a mouth that looked as if it had spent too many years frowning and was just now learning the shape of a smile. The shards of ice that were Mara Jade's eyes had warmed somewhat since the last time Han had seen her.

Lando stood up, sweeping his cape behind him and extending his hand. "Well hel-*lo*! Please join us, Miss Jade. May I get you anything? We've met before but I'm not sure you remember me. I'm—"

"Shut up, Calrissian. I need to talk to Solo."

Lando laughed and went to get her a drink anyway.

Dark patches stood out on the shoulders and sleeves of Mara's flight jacket, as if it had once borne the insignia of military service. Mara Jade had been the Emperor's Hand, a special servant to Palpatine himself, and she had seen her life crumble after his death; she had blamed Luke for that and held a vendetta against him until recently.

Now, after the retirement of the great smuggler Talon Karrde, Mara seemed to become more open and ready to participate in broader events. She had managed a tenuous coalition of smugglers to help fight against Grand Admiral Thrawn, and she still maintained a loose alliance, even though some of the worst offenders—such as Moruth Doole on Kessel—refused to have anything to do with the New Republic and the smuggler's alliance.

"What brings you back to Coruscant, Mara?" Han said. Lando returned bearing another one of his fruity drinks for her and a new one for himself. She looked at it, pointedly ignored it, and continued talking to Han.

"I'm bringing a message. You can pass it on to the appropriate people. Your Imperial friend Admiral Daala has been sending out feelers, trying to hire smugglers as spies and saboteurs. A few have taken the offer, but I don't expect many of them to trust Daala after what she did to the forces of Kessel. Even though Moruth Doole wasn't part of our alliance, he was still a smuggler, and smugglers tend to stick together—especially against Imperials."

"Yes," Han said, "we got the message that she had attacked one of the supply ships and destroyed it before it could get to Dantooine."

Mara looked at him, and her gaze became hard again. "Haven't you heard what happened to your colony on Dantooine? Daala's already been there, you know."

"What?" Han said, and Lando echoed his surprise.

"A small group of New Republic engineers is setting up a communications base there," Han said, "but we haven't contacted them in the last week or two."

"Well, there's no need to," Mara said. "Dantooine has been leveled. Every person in your colony *and* all of your New Republic engineers are dead, as of two days ago. Daala attacked with her three Star Destroyers and vanished again to wherever her hiding place is."

"And so you came here just to give us this information?" Han said, trying to recover from his shock.

Mara took a long, slow drink of the cloying concoction that Lando seemed to be enjoying so much. She shrugged. "I have an agreement with the New Republic, and I keep my agreements."

As Han felt anger and shock starting to boil inside him at what Daala had done, Lando changed the subject.

"So where are you off to now, Miss Jade?" he said. Leaning forward on the table, he seemed to be trying to melt her with his big brown eyes. Han rolled his.

"You're welcome to stay here for a while," Lando said. "I'd be happy to show you some of the sights of the city. There's some beautiful views on top of the Grand Towers." Mara looked at him as if considering how much effort it was worth for her to answer his question.

"I'll be leaving immediately," she said. "I'm going to spend some time at Skywalker's Jedi training center. It makes good business sense to learn how to use my Jedi abilities, if only for self-protection."

Han sat up in surprise. "You're going to learn from Luke? I thought you still hated Luke! You've tried to kill him often enough."

Mara's eyes stared back as if ready to blaze through him; then she softened and even smiled. "We've . . . reconciled our differences. You might say we negotiated a truce." She looked down at her drink but did not touch it. "For now, at least," she added, and then smiled even more. She stood up to leave. "Thanks for your time, Solo." She ignored Lando completely and walked out of the lounge.

Lando watched Mara leave, admiring the slick satiny gray fabric of her slacks and tight padded flightshirt. "She sure has gotten beautiful."

"Yeah, I hear that happens to most assassins once they retire," Han answered.

Lando didn't seem to hear him. "How could I have missed her in Jabba the Hutt's throne room? She was there, and I was there, but I didn't notice her at all."

"I was there too," Han said, "and I didn't see her. Of course, I was frozen in a block of carbonite at the time."

"I think she likes me," Lando said. "Maybe I'll volunteer to take the next delivery of supplies to Yavin 4, just so I can see her."

Han shook his head. "Lando, she wanted you to disappear. She didn't even acknowledge your presence."

Lando shrugged. "Sometimes it just takes my charm

a little longer to work." He flashed one of his best lady-killer smiles. "But when it does. . . . "

"Oh, brother," Han said. He finished his drink and left Lando sitting there, daydreaming as his own drink sat unnoticed beside him.

13

The next night Leia had just sat down to cherish a relaxing meal with her husband and her children when the summons from Mon Mothma arrived.

As usual, she had been wrapped up in governmental proceedings all day. After the disaster on Vortex, she had been allowed no respite, and the pressure had increased as Mon Mothma withdrew further from her responsibilities, begging off the unimportant receptions and meetings and sending Leia as her proxy.

Living on the peaceful world of Alderaan as the daughter of the powerful Senator Bail Organa, Leia had grown up surrounded by politics. She was used to the constant demands, the communiqués arriving at all hours, the sudden emergencies, the whispered negotiations, and the forced smiles. She had cho-sen to follow in Senator Organa's footsteps, knowing full well the demands that would be made of her.

But she treasured the scant quiet times she managed to steal with Han and the twins. It seemed ages since she had been able to visit baby Anakin, though Han himself had accompanied Winter twice in the last two months.

Tonight Leia had come home late, flustered and harried, but Han was there waiting with Jacen and Jaina. They had held dinner for her, which Threepio had prepared as a test of his new and dubious gourmet programming at the food synthesizers.

They sat down in the dining area, where illumination strips bathed the room in soft pink and peach colors. Han played the relaxing music of one of her favorite Alderaani composers, and they sat down to eat off fine Imperial china taken from the late Emperor's private stock.

It was not intended to be a romantic dinner with two-and-a-half-year-old twins banging their silverware and demanding constant attention—but Leia didn't mind. Han had done his best to commemorate dinner as a family.

Leia smiled as Threepio delivered their meal, a very passable-looking grazer roulade accompanied by skewers of spiced tubers and sweet marble-berry fritters. "I believe you will be quite impressed, Mistress Leia," the droid said, gently bowing and setting smaller plates in front of Jacen and Jaina.

"Yuck," Jacen said.

Jaina looked at her brother for confirmation, then said, "I don't like this."

Threepio straightened in indignation. "Children, you have not even tasted the food. I insist that you sample your dinners."

Leia and Han looked at each other and smiled. Jacen and Jaina both had bright eyes and well-defined features below thick dark-brown hair—just like their parents. The twins were extremely precocious, speaking in short but complete sentences and amazing their parents with the concepts they had already managed to grasp and communicate.

Jacen and Jaina seemed to share a kind of psychic link, speaking in half sentences to each other or somehow communicating in complete silence. This didn't surprise Leia—as Luke had told her, the Force was strong in their family.

Han claimed that the two kids knew how to use their powers more than they admitted. He had found cabinet doors mysteriously unlocked after he had fastened them securely, and sometimes shiny baubles left on high shelves were suddenly found underfoot as if they had been played with. The food synthesizers, far out of reach, had once been reprogrammed to add a double portion of sweetening to all recipes, even the soup.

Perplexed with the mysterious occurrences, Threepio had dug through diverse and obscure data records, insisting that the best explanation could be found in an ancient superstition of *poltergeists*—but Leia suspected it had more to do with small Jedi children.

She took a bite of her thinly sliced, herb-crusted grazer. It smelled wonderfully nutty as the aroma curled up to her nose. It was tender and perfectly seasoned to counteract the pungent unpleasant aftertaste often found in imported grazer filet. She considered complimenting Threepio, but decided that it would probably make the protocol droid altogether too pleased with himself.

"Look what Jaina's doing!" Jacen said.

Leia stared in astonishment as the little girl balanced her delicate skewer of spiced tubers impossibly on its tip and used the Force to twirl it around like a top.

"Mistress Jaina, please stop playing with your food," Threepio said.

Leia and Han met each other's gaze in amazement. She was glad that Luke had formed his Jedi academy, so these children would learn to understand the powerful and beautiful gift they had been given.

The door chime sounded like a tubular bell through their living quarters. The noise startled Jaina, and her delicately balanced skewer toppled over—which made her begin to cry.

Han sighed, and Leia got up with a scowl. "I didn't think we could sit through an entire meal uninterrupted."

She opened the door, and the ornate plasteel plate hummed aside to reveal a hovering messenger droid that bobbed up and down in the corridor, blinking its lights in a swirl.

"Minister Leia Organa Solo, Chief of State Mon Mothma requests your presence immediately in her private quarters for an important consultation. Please follow me."

Back at the table Han rolled his eyes and glowered at no one in particular as Leia was taken from him again. Jaina continued crying, and now Jacen added his own squalls to the racket. Threepio tried to calm the two children down, completely without effect.

Leia looked imploringly at Han, but he gave a short wave of dismissal. "Go on, Mon Mothma needs you."

She bit her lower lip, sensing the bitterness he tried to cover. "I'll cut it short," she said. "I'll be back as soon as I can."

Han nodded and turned to his eating as if he didn't believe her. Leia felt her stomach knot as she hurried after the hovering droid through the arched, well-lit corridors. She felt a simmering annoyance and stubborn resistance build within her, and she walked with purposeful steps.

She agreed to too many things. She bowed her head and trotted anywhere Mon Mothma asked her to go. Well, Leia had her own life, and she had to spend more time with her family. Her career was important too—crucial, in fact—and she vowed to do both. But she had to reestablish some priorities and ground rules.

As she followed the messenger droid into a turbolift that took her to secluded portions of the old Imperial Palace, Leia was actually glad that Mon Mothma had summoned her. She had a few things to say to the Chief of State, and the two of them would have to work out some sort of compromise.

But when the droid transmitted the special unlocking code that caused Mon Mothma's armored door to grind aside, Leia felt a cold fingernail twist in her chest. Mon Mothma's quarters were too dark, lit only by soft greenish glowing lamps designed to be soothing, restful . . . healing. She breathed the sweet tang of odd medicines, and the clinging aftertaste of sickness caught in her throat.

Leia stepped forward into the chambers and saw that they had been filled with bright nova lilies and nebula orchids that showered heady perfumes into the air, masking the unpleasant medicinal smell.

"Mon Mothma?" she said. Her voice sounded small in the enclosed space.

Motion off to her right made her turn her head to see a bullet-headed Too-Onebee medical droid. Mon Mothma looked gaunt and skeletal as she lay on a broad bed surrounded by diagnostic equipment. Another smaller droid monitored the readouts. Everything hung in silence except for the faint hum of machinery.

Leia also saw—feeling foolish for noticing such a small thing—that Mon Mothma kept an array of makeup jars and synthetic skin-coloring agents on her dressing table in a desperate attempt to make herself look presentable in public.

"Ah, Leia," Mon Mothma said. Her voice sounded pathetically weak, a rustle of dry leaves. "Thank you for coming. I can't keep my secret any longer. I must tell you everything."

Leia swallowed. All her indignant arguments evaporated like mist under a red giant sun. She sat down in the small padded chair next to Mon Mothma and listened.

Han had not had time to put the twins to bed before Leia returned. He had felt angry and distracted during the rest of dinner, listless at having her gone again. He had played with the twins, seeking solace in their company.

Threepio was just finishing the kids' evening ripple bath when Leia came quietly through the doors. Han had been sitting in their main living area, looking at the sentimental "Remembrances of Alderaan" framed images he had given her as a gift. Displayed prominently on a small pedestal sat the ridiculous Corellian fast-food mascot statue Leia had bought for him, thinking it a gaudy but important piece of sculpture from Han's homeworld.

When Leia entered, he sat up quickly, brushing his hair with his fingers. But she turned her back to him and worked the door controls, saying nothing. Leia seemed smaller and drawn into herself. She moved with extreme slowness and caution, as if everything might break at any sudden motion.

Han said, "I didn't expect you back until late. Did Mon Mothma let you off the hook?"

When she turned to him, he saw that her eyes shimmered with bright flecks of light from restrained tears. The skin around her eyes looked puffy, and her mouth was drawn.

"What is it?" Han said. "What does Mon Mothma want you to do this time? If it's too much, I'll go tell her off myself. You should—"

"She's *dying*," Leia said.

Han stopped short, feeling his arguments pop like fragile soap bubbles. His mind whirled. Before he could ask again, Leia began to spill her story.

"She has some sort of mysterious wasting disease. The medic droids can't pinpoint it. They've never seen anything like it, and it's pulling her down fast. It's almost as if something is taking her apart genetically from the inside.

"Remember the four days when she supposedly went to a secret conference on Cloud City? She didn't go anywhere. There was no conference. She spent the time in a bacta tank in a last-ditch effort to be healed—but even though the bacta tank completely purged her system, it could do nothing to help. Her body is falling apart. At the rate the disease is taking over, she could be . . . she could be dead in less than a month."

Han swallowed, thinking of the strong woman who had founded the New Republic, led the political side of the Rebel Alliance. "So that's why she's been delegating so many of her responsibilities," Han said. "Why you've had to take over more and more."

"Yes, she's trying to keep up appearances in public—but you should see her, Han! She looks like she can barely stand. She can't keep up the charade much longer."

"So . . ." Han began, not knowing what else to suggest or what he could say. "What does this mean? What do you have to do?"

Leia bit her lip and seemed to dredge up strength inside herself. She came forward and hugged him. He held her close.

"With Mon Mothma weakening," she said, "and Admiral Ackbar in exile, the moderate side of the Council will be gone. I can't let the New Republic turn into an aggressor government. We have already suffered too much. Now is the time for us to strengthen our ties, to make the New Republic firm through political alliances, with planetary systems joining with us—not to go blasting leftover Imperial strongholds in this sector of the galaxy."

"Let me guess who wants to do that," Han said, thinking of a number of the old generals who had reveled in their days of glory during the major battles of the Rebellion.

"I have to bring Ackbar back," she said, looking up to meet Han's eyes. Her face was pale and as beautiful as he had ever seen it. He remembered her staring at him on Cloud City just before Darth Vader had plunged him into the carbon-freeze chamber. Han had spent months locked in a frozen non-existence with only her words "I love you" ringing in his mind.

He tried not to let his disappointment show. "So you're going off to the planet Calamari?"

She nodded, but kept her face pressed against his chest. "I have to, Han. We can't let Ackbar hide at a time like this. He can't keep blaming himself for an accident. He's needed here."

Threepio interrupted them as he walked into the main room. "Oh," he said, startled. "Greetings, Mistress Leia! Welcome home." Runnels of splashed bathwater trickled down his shiny form and dripped onto the soft floor. He held two fluffy white towels draped over his arms. In the back hall two naked children giggled and ran to their bedroom.

"The twins are ready for their evening tale," Threepio said. "Would you like me to select one, sir?"

Han shook his head. "No, they always cry when you choose." He looked at Leia. "Come on, you can listen too. I'll tell them a bedtime story."

With the twins snuggled in their pajamas under warm blankets, Han sat between their small beds. Leia sat in another chair, looking longingly at her children.

"Which story do you want tonight, kids?" Han said. He held a story platform in front of him that would display words and animated pictures.

"I get to pick," Jaina said.

"I want to pick," Jacen said.

"You picked last night, Jaina. It's your brother's turn."

"I want *The Little Lost Bantha Cub*," Jaina said.

"My pick!" Jacen insisted. "*Little Lost Bantha Cub*."

Han smiled. "Big surprise," he muttered. Leia saw that he had already called up the story on the board before the twins made their decision.

He began to read. "After the sandstorm that drove him from home, the little lost bantha cub wandered alone.

"So he walked, and he walked through the desert heat till noon, when he found a Jawa sandcrawler upon a sandy dune.

" 'I am *lost*,' said the bantha cub, 'Please help me find my herd,' but the little Jawas shook their heads and gave their final word."

The twins leaned forward to watch the accompanying images activated by Han's voice and the scrolling words. Though they had heard the story a dozen times already, they still seemed disappointed when the Jawas refused to help.

"So he walked, and he walked till he met a shiny droid. After walking by himself so long, the cub was overjoyed.

" 'I am *lost*,' said the bantha cub, 'Please help me find my herd.' 'I am not programmed to help you,' said the droid, 'Don't be absurd.'

"The droid kept walking straight ahead, not looking left or right; the bantha cub just watched until the droid was out of sight."

Leia listened as the little bantha cub's adventures continued in an encounter with a moisture farmer, and finally a huge krayt dragon. The twins sat wide-eyed with suspense.

" 'I will eat you,' purred the dragon, then he lunged with snapping jaws! So the bantha cub began to run without the slightest pause."

Jacen and Jaina were delighted when the bantha cub finally found a tribe of Sand People, who reunited him with his parents and his herd. Leia shook her head, marveling at the fascination the children showed.

After Han finished telling the story and switched off the platter in his hands, he and Leia each gave the twins a good-night kiss and tucked them in before quietly walking out to the hall.

"I wish you would let me embellish your tale with sound effects," Threepio said, walking beside them. "It would be so much more realistic and enjoyable for the children."

"No," Han said, "you'll give them nightmares."

"Indeed!" Threepio said in a huff, then moved to the kitchen area.

Leia smiled and held Han's arm, hugging him. She kissed him on the cheek. "You're a good daddy, Han."

He blushed, but didn't disagree with her.

14

Small, but infinitely deadly, the
Sun Crusher superweapon entered orbit around the gas
giant of Yavin, flying side by side with the armored New
Republic transport.

Sitting in the streamlined pilot's seat, young Kyp
Durron felt the Sun Crusher's advanced controls respond
to his fingertips. He stared through the segmented
viewport at the eddying orange planet below, a waiting
bottomless pit where the Sun Crusher would be buried
forever.

"Ready to send her down, Kyp?" the voice of Wedge
Antilles crackled across the comm unit. "Straight-line
plunge."

Kyp fingered the controls, feeling a chill of reluctance. The Sun Crusher was such a perfect weapon,
well designed, able to withstand any onslaught. Kyp
felt a strange attachment to the splinter-shaped craft
that had brought him and Han Solo to freedom. But he
also knew that Qwi Xux was right in that the temptation

to use such power would eventually corrupt anyone. Qwi kept the knowledge in her head, vowing to share it with no one. But the functional superweapon itself had to be taken out of everyone's grasp.

He adjusted the sublight course vectors. "I'm setting the nav systems now," he said. "Prepare to dock."

Kyp programmed a set of coordinates that would fire the Sun Crusher's maneuvering jets and send the small ship down in a sharp ellipse to bury it in the turbulent clouds and the high-pressure core below.

"We're ready for transfer," Wedge said.

"Just a minute," Kyp answered. He locked down the controls and caressed the deceptively simple panel one last time. The New Republic scientists and engineers had not been able to understand the machinery inside. They had not known how to deactivate the resonance torpedoes that would spark supernova explosions. Qwi Xux had refused to help them . . . and now the Sun Crusher would be gone forever.

Qwi's birdlike voice interrupted his thoughts over the comm channel. "Make certain all power systems are shut down," she said, "and seal the containment field."

Kyp flicked a row of switches. "Already done." He heard the muffled thump of hull against hull as Wedge brought the armored transport against the Sun Crusher.

"Magnetic fields in place, Kyp," Wedge said. "Open the hatch and come on over."

"Setting the timer," Kyp said. He activated the auto-pilot, dimmed the lights in the cockpit, and clambered toward the small hatch. He opened it and met Wedge's waiting arms as the smiling dark-haired man helped Kyp into the transport.

They sealed the Sun Crusher behind them, then disengaged the docking connection. Wedge moved back to the pilot's seat of the armored transport and flopped into the cockpit chair beside the wispy-looking Qwi Xux.

Qwi sat strapped in with crash restraints. Her pale-blue skin looked splotchy, and she was obviously filled with anxiety. Wedge nudged the attitude-control thrusters and swung the armored transport around so they could watch. The elongated crystal shape of the Sun Crusher increased its distance, drifting closer to the gravitational jaws of Yavin.

Kyp hunkered between Wedge and Qwi, watching through the viewport as the Sun Crusher followed its preprogrammed course. Kyp could see the torus-shaped resonance-field generator at the bottom of the ship's long spike.

The Sun Crusher dwindled to a mere speck that approached the chaotic storms of Yavin. He breathed a sigh of relief to know that this weapon would never be used to destroy any star system.

Qwi sat thin-lipped, silent, intense. Wedge reached over to pat her arm, and she jumped.

Kyp continued to concentrate on the Sun Crusher, watching the speck. He was afraid to look away because he might lose the ship against the titanic field of orange-colored clouds.

He saw the shape plunge into the upper atmosphere, plowing down on its unalterable course toward the planetary core. He imagined the Sun Crusher streaking deeper and deeper into the dense atmosphere. Scorching heat generated by atmospheric friction would throw off ripples and sonic booms as the Sun Crusher went down, down to the gas giant's diamond-thick core.

"Well," Wedge said, sounding cheerful, "we never have to worry about that thing again."

Qwi's elfin face seemed to be a catalog of contradictory expressions. She fluttered the lashes of her indigo eyes.

"It's for the best," Kyp agreed, mumbling his words.

Wedge ignited the thrusters of the armored transport and arced them away from close orbit to the fringes of the system of moons. "Well, Qwi and I are due to go inspect the reparation work on Vortex. Still want to go down to the jungle moon, Kyp?" Wedge said.

Kyp nodded, somewhat uneasy but eager to begin a new phase of his life. "Yes," he answered quietly; then drawing a deep breath, he said, "Yes!" to show his enthusiasm. "Master Skywalker is waiting for me."

Wedge turned back to the craft's controls, arrowing for the tiny emerald circle that was the fourth moon of Yavin. He flashed a grin. "Well then, Kyp, may the Force be with you."

Followed by his group of students, Luke Skywalker emerged from the great Massassi temple to watch the arrival of the transport and their new Jedi student.

Luke had told them all of Kyp's coming. They had responded with measured enthusiasm, glad to have another trainee among their number, yet tempered by the clinging memory of Gantoris's dark and fiery death.

A rectangular ship emblazoned with the scooped blue sign of the New Republic approached through the hazy skies. Its tracking lights flickered on, and broad landing struts extended.

Artoo trundled to the side of the landing grid in front of the Great Temple. Luke approached where the ship was about to set down. Blasts of repulsorlift jets fluttered his hood and ruffled his hair. Luke stared at the ship, blinking grit from his eyes until the transport came to rest.

The boarding ramp extended, and Wedge Antilles stepped out, reaching behind him to help the bluish female scientist descend.

Luke raised his left hand in greeting and turned his attention to the young man emerging from the craft. Kyp Durron was a wiry eighteen-year-old full of energy and eagerness, toughened from years of labor in the spice mines of Kessel.

In the mines Kyp had received a small initiation into the Force through another prisoner there, the fallen Jedi woman Vima-Da-Boda. Kyp had instinctively used those skills to help Han and Chewbacca escape from Kessel and from the Maw Installation. When Luke had tested the young man for Jedi potential, the strength of Kyp's response had thrown Luke backward.

Luke had been waiting for a student like this to come to his academy.

Kyp stepped down the landing platform, averting his eyes at first; but then he paused and looked up to stare into Luke's eyes. Luke saw an intelligence, a quick wit, and a quick temper, survival instincts born from years of struggle—but he also saw unshakable determination. That was the most important factor in a Jedi trainee.

"Welcome, Kyp Durron," Luke said.

"I'm ready, Master Skywalker," Kyp answered. "Teach me the Jedi ways."

15

Staring out the observation window of the orbiting station, Leia thought the Calamarian shipyards looked even more impressive than their reputation had led her to expect.

The starship-construction facilities rode high above the mottled blue planet. Supply platforms sprawled in three dimensions, dotted with winking red, yellow, and green lights that indicated landing pads and docking bays. Small girder impellers pushed huge mounds of plasteel extruded from transorbital rubble shipments from the planet's single moon; the girders would be used in the frameworks of the famous Mon Calamari star cruisers. Crablike constructor pods flitted in and around a tremendous spacedock hangar like tiny insects against the mammoth form of a half-built cruiser.

"Excuse me, Minister Organa Solo?"

Leia turned to see a small Calamarian female wearing pale-blue ambassadorial robes. While the males had bulbous and lumpy heads, the females were more streamlined, with olive-colored mottling over the pale salmon of their hides.

"I am Cilghal." When the Calamarian female raised both of her hands, Leia noticed that the webbing between her spatulate fingers seemed more translucent than Ackbar's.

Leia raised her own hand in acknowledgment. "Thank you for meeting me, Ambassador. I appreciate your help."

Cilghal's mottling darkened in a reaction that Leia recognized as humor or amusement. "You humans have called the Mon Calamari the 'soul of the Rebellion.' After such a compliment, how can we turn down any request for help?"

The ambassador stepped forward to gesture out at the bustling spacedock facility. "I see you have been observing our work on the *Startide*. It will be our first addition to the New Republic fleet in many months. We have been devoting most of our resources to recovering from last year's attack by the Emperor's World Devastators."

Leia nodded, looking again at the splotchy organic shape of the Mon Calamari star cruiser, the New Republic's equivalent of the Imperial Star Destroyer. The ovoid battleship had lumpy protrusions for gun emplacements, field generators, viewports, and staterooms placed at seemingly random intervals. Each star cruiser was unique, modeled after the same basic design, yet altered to meet individual criteria that Leia didn't quite understand.

"All the drive units are installed," Cilghal continued, "and the hull is almost complete. We tested the sublight engines just yesterday, hauling the whole spacedock facility once around the planet. It will take another two months to complete the inner bulkheads, staterooms, and crew quarters."

Leia tore her gaze from the activity and nodded at the ambassador. "As always, I'm astonished at the resourcefulness and dedication of the Calamarians. You have given so much after your enslavement by the Empire, after the attacks you've suffered. I feel reluctant to ask for further help—but I desperately need to speak with Admiral Ackbar."

Cilghal straightened her sky-blue robes. "We have respected Ackbar's request for privacy and his need for contemplation after the tragedy on Vortex, but our people remain proud of him and support him entirely. If you wish to bring further charges against—"

"No, no!" Leia said. "I'm one of his greatest supporters. But circumstances have changed since he exiled himself here." Leia swallowed and decided that she would get further if she trusted Cilghal. "I've come to beg him to return."

Cilghal flushed with an olive tinge. She moved quickly, gliding across the floor of the orbital station. "In that case, a shuttle is ready to take you down."

Leia gripped the widely spaced arms of the passenger seat as Cilghal maneuvered the egg-shaped shuttle through sleeting rain and knotted gray storm clouds. Whitecaps stippled the dull surface of Calamari's deep oceans. Cilghal swung the shuttle lower, seemingly unconcerned with the storm winds. She held her splayed hands over the controls and bent to the viewing panels. The high-resolution viewing instruments had been designed for wide-set Calamarian eyes, and the blunt controls were adapted for the digits of the aquatic people.

Cilghal maneuvered the shuttle like a streamlined fish through water. The vessel curved away from small marshy islands—sparse dots of habitable land where the amphibious Calamarians had first established their civilization. Narrow rivulets of rainwater trickled down the passenger window as Cilghal turned broadside to the wind.

The Calamarian ambassador nudged one of the bulbous control knobs and spoke into an invisible voice pickup. "Foamwander City, this is shuttle SQ/one. Please provide a weather update and an approach vector." Cilghal's voice sounded smooth and soft, as if she hadn't needed to shout in her entire life.

A guttural male voice came over the speaker. "Ambassador Cilghal, we are transmitting your approach vector. We are currently experiencing rising winds that are well within seasonal norms. No difficulties expected, but we are issuing an advisory against topside travel for the afternoon."

"Acknowledged," Cilghal said. "We were planning on making the rest of our journey underwater. Thank you." She signed off, then turned back to Leia. "Don't worry, Minister. I can sense your anxiety, but I assure you, there is nothing to be concerned about."

Leia sat up, trying to quell her nervousness until she put her finger on its cause. "I don't doubt you, Ambassador, it's just that . . . the last time I flew in a storm was on Vortex."

Cilghal nodded somberly. "I understand." Leia sensed Cilghal's sincerity, and the look on her fishlike face was comforting. "We'll be safely landed in a few minutes."

Through the mists and the whipping spray Leia watched them approach a metal island. Lumpy, but smoothed, like an organic coral reef, Foamwander City rose in a hemisphere out of the whitecaps. A forest of reinforced watchtowers and communications antennas rose from the top of the city, but the rest of the drifting metropolis had soft angles and polished outcroppings like a Mon Calamari star cruiser.

The bright lights of thousands of above-surface windows shed jewels of light even through the whipping rain. Below the hemispherical dome Leia knew that the floating cities had underwater towers and descending complexes like the mirror image of a Coruscant skyline. The inverted skyscrapers of dwelling units and water-processing stations beneath the hemisphere made the city look like a mechanical jellyfish.

Starved for raw materials on their marshy islands, the Mon Calamari had not been able to build a civilization until they joined forces with another intelligent species that lived beneath the oceans. The Quarren, a humanoid race with helmet-shaped heads and faces that looked like a fistful of tentacles sprouting beneath close-set eyes, had excavated metallic ores from the ocean crust. Working with the Calamarians, they built dozens of floating cities. Though the Quarren could also breathe air, they chose to remain under the sea while the Calamarians designed starships to explore the bright "islands in space."

Cilghal approached the lumpy hemisphere of Foamwander City, circling to the leeward side, where the bulk of the metropolis protected them from buffeting winds. Whitecaps broke against the dull gray of the city's outer shell, sending arcs of droplets high like a handful of diamonds.

"Open wave doors," Cilghal said into the voice pickup. She aimed the shuttle toward a line of bright lights that guided the ship in. Before Leia could detect the seam, heavy doors split open diagonally like a crooked mouth.

Without slowing, Cilghal shot the vessel into a smooth tunnel, well lit by green illumination strips. Behind them the wave doors closed, sealing the metropolis against the onslaught of the storm.

Leia felt herself swept along as the ambassador moved with a liquid grace, calmly but relentlessly, to the underwater sections of the floating city. Cilghal set a steady, rapid pace that helped Leia hurry but caused no alarm. This was no simple diplomatic mission.

As Leia strode through the curved colorful halls of the upper levels, she was reminded of the corkscrewing chambers inside a gigantic shell. She saw no sharp corners, only rounded edges and smooth, polished decorations made of coral and mother-of-pearl. Even inside the enclosed city, the air had a salty tang, but it was not unpleasant.

"Do you know where Ackbar is?" Leia finally asked.

"Not exactly," the ambassador said. "We allowed him his privacy and did not follow him." Cilghal touched Leia's shoulder with a broad fin-hand. "But do not be concerned. The Calamarians have sources of information that the Empire never suspected. Even during the occupation we were able to keep our collective knowledge intact. We will find Ackbar."

Leia followed Cilghal into a turbolift that plunged down into the deep underwater levels of the floating city. When they emerged, the quality of the corridors had changed. The lighting was dimmer and shimmering, a jewel-blue reflected through faceted glowlamps and thick transparisteel windows that looked out into the ocean depths.

Leia could see divers swimming among the tangle of nets and mooring lines, satellite cages, and small submersible vehicles moving about the inverted towers of the city. The air was thicker and damper. The people in these levels were primarily Quarren, moving about their business, not acknowledging the presence of the visitors.

Though the Quarren and the Calamarians had allied themselves to build this civilization, Leia knew that the two communities did not work together without friction. The Calamarians insisted on their dreams to reach the stars, while the Quarren wished to return to the oceans. Rumors suggested that the Quarren had betrayed their planet to the Empire, but that they had then been treated just as badly under Imperial occupation as the Calamarians.

Cilghal stopped and spoke to a Quarren who stood by a valve-control station. The Quarren looked up at the interruption, flashing dark eyes at Leia, then at Cilghal. The Calamarian ambassador spoke in a high-pitched bubbly language, and the Quarren answered abruptly in kind. He gestured to the left down a steep ramp that corkscrewed to the lower level.

Cilghal nodded her thanks, undisturbed by the Quarren's attitude as she led Leia down the ramp. They emerged into an open equipment bay that had been pressurized to allow easy access to the water.

Five Calamarian males worked on a small submersible hoisted on a tractor beam; they moved together to unload dripping crates from a seatree cargo hold. Quarren, dressed in sleek, flat-black suits that seemed covered with minute scales, dived through access fields into the watery depths. The walls of the equipment bay flickered as traces of dim light wandered up and down the polished surfaces, creating a hypnotic bath of dark green and deep blue.

Cilghal went to a row of small porcelain compartments and opened one. Before she could reach inside, two Quarren workers rushed over, speaking quickly and harshly in their bubbling language. Leia smelled a new, sour scent rising from them.

Cilghal bowed in apology, then moved to a different set of compartments, opening them with more caution. Leia followed, trying to make herself small. She realized she was the only non-native in the entire chamber. The Quarren stared at her, though the Calamarians took no notice.

Cilghal removed a pair of the slithery suits worn by the diving Quarren, handing one to Leia. Leia ran her fingers over the fabric. It seemed alive, clinging and slippery at the same time; the tiny mesh expanded and contracted as if seeking an appropriate shape to best serve the wearer.

Cilghal indicated a narrow closet-sized door. "Our changing compartments are a bit cramped, I'm afraid."

Leia stepped inside, sealing the door behind her as blue-green illumination intensified in the small chamber. She disrobed and slid into the black suit, feeling her skin tingle as the fabric shifted and adjusted, trying to conform. When the crawly sensations stopped, it was the most comfortable garment she had ever worn—warm yet cool, light yet insulating, fuzzy yet slick.

When Leia emerged, Cilghal stood outside the door already wearing her water garment. Without speaking Cilghal fitted a water jetpack over Leia's shoulders, then rigged a crude net for her long hair. Looking at the smooth salmon-and-olive dome of Cilghal's head and the fleshy scalps of the Quarren, Leia said, "I don't suppose you have much need for hair nets around here."

Cilghal made a sound that Leia suspected might be a laugh, and led her over to one of the access fields. Beside a round opening that shimmered with faint static as it held the Calamarian ocean back, Cilghal dipped her broad hands into a bubbling urn. She pulled out a floppy translucent sheet and held it up. Water streamed off its surface, fizzing with tiny bubbles.

"Humans sometimes find this unpleasant," Cilghal said. "I apologize." Without further warning she slapped the gelatinous mass across Leia's mouth and nose. The membrane was cold and wet, clinging to her cheeks, her skin. Leia stiffened in alarm and tried to struggle, but the strange soft gel stuck fast to her face.

"Relax, and you can breathe," Cilghal said. "This symbiote filters oxygen from the sea. It can last for weeks under water."

Starved for air, Leia tried to suck in a deep breath and found that she could indeed inhale clean, ozone-smelling air. Pure oxygen filled her lungs, and as she breathed slowly out, the bubbles percolated back through the symbiote membrane.

Cilghal applied one of the symbiotes to her own angular face and then poked a tiny microphone unit into the soft jelly before adjusting another in her ear hole.

She handed Leia a pair of the small devices. The microphone slid into the gelatinous membrane, but the symbiote held it firmly. When she put the second jack into her ear, Cilghal's voice came through clearly.

"You must take care to articulate your words," Cilghal said, "but this system is quite satisfactory."

Without another word Cilghal took Leia's arm. She could feel the ambassador's grip, every detail of her webbed hands transmitted through the remarkable mesh of the slick suit. Together, they plunged through the containment field and into the deep oceans of Calamari.

As they jetted through the water, Leia felt warm currents on her forehead and around her eyes. The symbiote fed her a steady supply of air, and the fine mesh suit kept her warm and dry and comfortable. Some of her hair broke free of the makeshift netting, and thick strands flipped and flailed around her head as she cruised along.

Behind them, the glittering inverted metropolis of Foamwander City drifted like a huge undersea creature with thousands of tiny figures swimming around it. On the sea floor Leia could see dull orange glows and domed cities, sites of Quarren deep-mining operations in the ocean crust. Above, the light turned milky as it filtered through waves churned by the pelting storm.

Cilghal spoke little, though the radio pickup worked quite well. They left the floating city far behind, and Leia began to feel uneasy at being so far from civilization.

Leia remained close beside Cilghal as their jetpacks bubbled and streamed. Eventually, Cilghal gestured toward a crevasse broken into the ocean crust, surrounded by lumps of coral and waving fronds of red and brown seaweed. "We are going to the Calamarian knowledge bank," Cilghal said through the tiny voice pickup.

They cruised between zigzags of rock overgrown with slow sculptures of coral and hair-fine tendrils of deep plants. The water streamed faster as the rock walls channeled stray currents. Above and around them fleets of bright-colored fish skimmed about, fed upon by larger fish that snapped, swallowed, and returned to feed again.

Leia looked ahead and saw a haphazard bed of shells, polished hulking mollusks a meter across. A faint lustrous glow seemed to come from the shells themselves.

Cilghal unexpectedly switched off her jetpack, and Leia shot past her before managing to stop her own thrusters. Cilghal kicked her broad feet to push herself toward the bottom with long gliding motions.

Leia struggled to keep up as they approached the enormous mollusks. Slowly kicking her feet to maintain her position against the current, Cilghal spread her arms wide as she bent over the largest of the humped shells at the front of the large bed. She hummed, a strange noise that vibrated through the water as much as it moved through the pickup circuit in Leia's ear.

"We have questions," Cilghal said, speaking to the giant shells. "We require access to the knowledge stored here in the great collection of memories. We must know if you have the answers we seek."

The top shell of the largest mollusk groaned open. The crack between its bivalve shells widened until a stream of golden illumination shone out, as if precious sunlight had been captured and held inside the impenetrable shell walls.

Leia couldn't say anything in her astonishment. As the shell cracked open even wider, she saw the soft fleshy mass inside, swirled and curved—not just the meaty lump of a shellfish, but the contours of a brain, an enormous brain that pulsed and shone with yellow light.

A sluggish pulsing sound drummed at Leia's ears through the water, and Cilghal turned to her. "They will answer," she said.

As Leia watched, row upon row of the giant shells opened, shedding rays of warm light into the narrow crevasse and exposing the swirled lumps of other large brains.

"They sit," Cilghal said. "They wait. They listen. They know everything that happens on this planet—and they never forget."

Cilghal began a long, ritualistic communion with the mollusk knowledge bank in a slow hypnotic language. Leia floated in place and watched, mystified and anxious.

Finally Cilghal swam backward, brushing her flipper-hands back and forth as she drifted away. The thick mollusks closed their shells, sealing the golden light away from the shadows of the canyon.

Leia had trouble seeing in the suddenly restored dimness of the depths, but the ambassador's words came crisply through the ear jack. "They have told me where to find him."

Leia could detect no emotion in Cilghal's even voice, but she felt her own thrill of elation.

As they turned to swim upward, Leia stared toward the lip of the crevasse. She froze as she saw a deadly sleek form like an Imperial attack ship above—an enormous living creature with a long bullet-shaped body, spined fins, a mouth filled with fangs. On either side of the mouth streamed whipping tentacles, each tipped with razor-jawed pincers.

Leia began to swim frantically backward. Cilghal grabbed her shoulder and pulled her down. "Krakana," she said.

The monster seemed to notice the bubbles caused by Leia's struggle. A stream of fizz came from the symbiote on Leia's mouth as she panted with terror, but Cilghal held her in a firm grip.

"Will it attack us?" Leia said into the voice pickup.

"If it senses us," Cilghal said. "The krakana will eat anything."

"Then what—" Leia said.

"It won't find us." Cilghal sounded altogether too calm. Fish swam frantically away from the torpedo shape of the predator. Cilghal seemed to be concentrating.

"No, it will get that one," she gestured with one large hand, "the blue-and-yellow-striped kieler. After that it will take that smaller orange one in the middle of the school. By then all the others will have fled, and the krakana will continue on its way. Then we can leave."

"How do you know that?" Leia said, gripping the rough-edged lump of coral on the side of the chasm.

"I know," Cilghal said. "It's a little trick I have."

Leia watched in horrified fascination as the krakana

streaked forward, coming unexpectedly from below as it reached out with its mass of tentacles to grab the blue-and-yellow kieler and rip it to ragged shreds before stuffing its fang-filled mouth.

By the time the monster had grabbed the pale-orange fish, the rest of the school had vanished to hidden corners of the crevasse or fled into the broad expanse of the ocean. The krakana slid away as it cruised the depths, constantly in search of a meal.

Leia stared at Cilghal, amazed at her prescient ability, but the Calamarian ambassador squeezed Leia's upper arm before igniting her water jetpack.

"Now we must go find Ackbar," she said.

16

Leia and Cilghal swam closer to the choppy surface after hours of gliding beneath the waves. Around them leathery seatrees veined with iridescent blue and red swirled in the churning current, stirred by the continuing storm.

The seatree fronds formed a tangled forest around them, filled with thousands of strangely shaped blob-fish, crustaceans, and tentacled things; most were small, but others cast large shadows as they drifted among the fronds, feeding on the air-filled fruit bladders that kept the dense weed afloat.

"When Ackbar was younger, he had a small dwelling here in the wild seatree thickets," Cilghal said. "The fish noticed his return, and though they have short memories, they passed the word from creature to creature until it reached the mollusk knowledge bank."

Leia's arms and legs ached as she continued the long swim, though the wonderful clinging mesh suit seemed to revitalize her muscles. "All I want is to talk to him."

Ahead she saw a spherical dwelling made of plasteel covered with algae and draping weed that had grown up from the spray clinging to its hull. Large valves of water-recirculation equipment, desalination devices, and round viewports dotted the open spaces on the curved walls; a bare deck looked clean and bright, as if recently scrubbed. A white utility submersible, ovoid with a mass of articulated working arms, had been lashed to the side of the deck.

Leia treaded water on the surface in the pelting rain and the whipping wind, still breathing through the symbiote. Cilghal tugged her arm, motioning for her to go down. "The entrance will be below," she said.

They stroked down through the water. Thick seatree trunks anchored the dwelling module in place, rocking it from side to side. Traps and nets dangled beneath the water; some held tiny green fish that could easily swim through the open mesh. From inside, shafts of illumination struck down into the depths like watery spears.

On the bottom of the hull they found an opening like a wide mouth. Cilghal went first through the containment field, and Leia followed, brushing her shoulders against the metal lip. When her head plunged through into the dim interior, she stripped off the symbiote, shook herself, and looked into Ackbar's cluttered home.

He stood up in alarm from a bench made of pitted flowstone, speechless as Cilghal and Leia eased themselves out of the water. Leia dripped for a moment, until the wondrous mesh suit absorbed and dissipated the water in its microthin layers.

Leia sighed with relief to see Ackbar, but she sensed his sudden discomfort at her presence—and something more. All her well-rehearsed speeches drained away like so much seawater splashing to the floor. They stood silently staring at each other for a long moment. Finally Leia recovered enough to speak. "Admiral Ackbar, I'm glad we've found you."

"Leia," Ackbar said. He held his hands in front of him, then withdrew them as if completely at a loss. He turned to Cilghal. "Ambassador, I believe we have met twice before?"

"It was an honor both times, Admiral," Cilghal said.

"Please," he said, "just call me Ackbar. I no longer hold that rank."

His dwelling was like a large, solid bubble with extruded knobs for sitting, pedestals for tables, and cubbyholes for storage. Possessions lay strewn about, though the back of the room was neatly organized, cleaned, polished, as if he had methodically begun repairing and organizing the chaos one square meter at a time.

Ackbar gestured toward the warmly lit galley area where delicious-smelling food bubbled over a heater. "Would you join me? I would not insult a potential Jedi by asking how you found me—but I would like to know what has brought you all the way from Coruscant."

Later they sat finishing bowls of simple but delicious fish stew. Leia chewed on the tender meat, swallowed another mouthful, and licked her lips to taste the burning sweet tingle of Calamarian spices.

She had spent the meal trying to work up her courage, but Ackbar finally addressed the question himself. "Leia, you have not yet said why you are here."

Leia drew a deep breath, then sat up straight. "To speak with you, Admira—ah—Ackbar. And to ask you the same question. Why are *you* here?"

Ackbar seemed to deliberately misunderstand her. "This is my home."

Frustrated, Leia was not ready to give up yet. "I know this is your homeworld, but there are many others who need you. The New Republic—"

Ackbar stood and turned away, gathering the empty stew bowls. "My own people also need me. There has been much destruction. Many deaths . . ." Leia wondered if he referred to the Imperial attacks on Calamari, or his own crash at the Cathedral of Winds.

"Mon Mothma is dying," Leia said abruptly before she could change her mind. Cilghal sat up in the most sudden reaction Leia had yet seen from the calm ambassador.

Ackbar heaved his weary eyes to look at her. He set the stew bowls down. "How can you be certain of this?"

"It's a wasting disease that's tearing her apart," Leia answered. "The medical droids and the experts can't find anything wrong with her. She looks bad. You saw her before you left us. Mon Mothma was covering the worst with extensive makeup to hide how ill she really is.

"We need you back, Admiral." Leia used his rank on purpose. She leaned on Ackbar's small table and stared at him, her dark eyes pleading.

"I'm sorry, Leia," Ackbar said, shaking his head. He indicated the newly refurbished workroom and his equipment. "I have important work to do here. My planet was badly damaged during the Imperial attacks, and there have been many tectonic disturbances. I've taken it upon myself to find out if our planet's crust has become unstable. I need to gather more data. My people could be in danger. No more lives will be lost because of me."

Cilghal turned her head from side to side, watching the debate but saying nothing.

"Admiral, you can't just let the New Republic fall apart because of your guilty conscience," Leia said. "Many lives across the galaxy are at stake."

But Ackbar moved about uneasily, as if trying to shut out Leia's words. "There is so much work to do, I cannot delay another moment. I was just preparing to set some new seismic sensors." He shuffled toward a shelf filled with packaged electronic equipment. "Please, leave me in peace."

Leia stood up quickly. "We'll help you set out your sensors, Admiral."

Ackbar hesitated, as if lonely but afraid to have their company. He turned to meet Leia's eyes, then Cilghal's. "Yes, I would be honored to have your assistance. My submersible can carry the three of us." He blinked his large, sad eyes. "I enjoy your company—even though your requests are most difficult."

Strapped into one of the seats in the cramped utility sub, Leia watched as water sloshed around the upper ports. The sea swallowed the craft, and they descended into the isolated seatree forest until the ocean around them looked like panels of dark-green smoked glass. Leia watched in awe as Ackbar picked a course through thick ropy strands and wide pillars.

Underwater, the seaflowers blossomed in shimmering reds and blues to attract darting creatures that flitted in and out of the fronds. As one of the small fish came too close to a brilliant flower, the petals suddenly contracted like a fist, snatching its prey and swallowing it whole.

"I have only begun deploying my seismic network," Ackbar said, as if to divert the conversation. "I've set up the baseline grid beneath my dwelling, but I need to extend into the seatree forest to get higher-resolution soundings."

Cilghal said, "I am pleased with the important work you are doing for our planet, Admiral." Leia was amused at how the ambassador continued—whether consciously or unconsciously—to use his military title.

"It is necessary to do important things with your life," Ackbar said, then said no more, walling himself off with silence. Behind them, stowed seismic equipment rattled beside the empty nets and sea-harvest baskets.

Leia cleared her throat and spoke, keeping her voice gentle. "Ackbar . . . I understand how you must feel. I was there too, remember?"

"You are kind, Leia. But you do *not* understand how I feel. Were you piloting the B-wing that crashed? Are you responsible for hundreds of deaths?" He shook his head sadly. "Do you hear their voices in your dreams each night, calling out to you?"

Ackbar switched on the sub's depth lights, and a bright cone-shaped beam sliced through the water. The funnel of illumination glanced off colorful fish and strips of seaweed.

Leia spoke more from intuition than from knowledge. "You can't hide on Calamari forever."

Ackbar still would not look at her. "I am not hiding. I have my work. Important work."

They drifted toward the silty ocean bottom near one of the gnarled seatree boles. Rounded hummocks of dark rock thrust out from the milky sand. A coating of algae smoothed every surface, making the sea floor appear soft and soothing. Ackbar hunched forward to stare through the murk, searching for a stable place to implant another seismic sensor.

"Important work, perhaps," Leia said, "but not *your* work. Many Calamarians would gladly help with that research, Admiral. Are you equipped to handle such a task by yourself? Remember that old proverb you used to quote when I complained about all those senseless Council meetings? 'Many eyes see what one alone cannot.' Wouldn't it be best to share your concerns with a team of specialists?"

Cilghal interrupted, leaning forward to indicate some curved half-buried sections of metal, like the ribbed shell of some sort of escape pod. "What's that?"

The edges had corroded, and tracings of algae grew in the protected crevices. "Perhaps a wrecked ship," Ackbar said.

Cilghal nodded. "We fought back when the Imperials tried to enslave us. Many of their ships lie beneath our waters."

Ackbar inserted his hands into the waldo control gloves for the automated metallic claws that extended from the front of the small sub. The sharp jerky motions reminded Leia of the vicious krakana monster near the mollusk knowledge bank.

"If that wreckage has been stable here for years," Ackbar said, "this is a good place to deploy another set of sensors."

Watching the external metal arms, Leia saw Ackbar remove a canister from the external storage bin on the submersible. Ackbar lowered the craft until plumes of pale sand drifted up from the disturbance like a slow-motion Tatooine dust storm. The nimble robotic claws positioned the cylinder upright in the soft silt.

Reversing propellers, Ackbar lifted them away. Craning his neck so he could see better through the front viewport, Ackbar pushed the ACTIVATE button. With a vibrating thump that Leia could feel through the sub's hull, the seismic canister detonated its tiny explosive. A long rod plunged deep into the ocean floor while spraying out a web of secondary detectors symmetrically around the core like a shooting star.

"Now we'll send a test signal," Ackbar said. With a whirr he lifted the sub through the densely tangled seatree forest, moving slowly enough so the fronds could be nudged out of the way, slithering over the rounded hull.

Leia fidgeted, swallowing numerous phrases that sounded flat to her. "Admiral, you know better than anyone on this world how important it is to have the right leadership, to have everyone working toward a common goal. You helped lead a band of Rebels from a hundred different planets, turned them into a united fleet that was able to defeat the Empire, and you guided them as they formed a new government."

Ackbar let the sub drift and turned to meet her gaze. She continued rapidly, hoping to cut off any arguments. "At least come with me to Coruscant and *talk* to Mon Mothma. We've been part of the same team for many years, you and I. You won't stand by and watch the New Republic fall apart."

Ackbar sighed and gripped his controls. Seatree branches flapped against the viewing windows. "It seems you know me better than I had thought. I—"

A pinging alarm beeped from the control panel. Ackbar reacted smoothly and swiftly, slowing the sub. He peered into his widely set stereoscopic sensor displays. "This is interesting," he said.

"What is it?" Leia said.

"Another large metallic mass tangled in the weeds right above us."

"Maybe it's part of that crashed ship," Cilghal said.

"If something fell into the seatree forest, it could have been swallowed up for eternity," Ackbar said. He eased the sub ahead.

As Leia saw the outline of a large multilegged thing wrapped with seatrees and overgrown with algae, she thought it was some kind of alien life-form. Then she recognized the squashed elliptical head, the segmented body core trailing jointed mechanical arms, its nonreflective black surface.

She had seen something like this on the ice planet Hoth, when Han Solo and Chewbacca had stumbled upon the Imperial probe droid. "Admiral—" Leia said.

"I see it. Arakyd Viper Series Probot. The Empire dispatched thousands to all corners of the galaxy to hunt down Rebel bases."

"It must have landed years ago on Calamari," Cilghal said. "The wreckage we found below was its landing pod."

Ackbar nodded. "But when the probe droid tried to rise to the surface, it tangled in the seaweed. It must have shut down." He nudged the sub closer, shining his depth light on the outer surface.

But when the beam struck the probot's rounded head, its entire bank of round eyes blinked to life.

"It's been activated!" Leia said. She could hear the high-pitched vibrating hum of powerful generators as the probe droid began to move again. The head swiveled and directed its own glowing beam at the sub.

Ackbar pushed the propellers into reverse; but before the sub could move away, the probot launched out with its spiderlike claws. Mechanical arms latched on to one of the sub's rounded fins. The head of the probe droid rotated slowly, trying to bring its built-in blaster cannons to bear, but the seatree fronds tangled its joints.

Ackbar threw all the sub's power into pulling away and succeeded only in yanking the probe droid along with him, tearing it free of ancient strands of weed.

Ackbar dug his flippers into the wide gloves that controlled his sub's articulated arms. He brought up two of the segmented mechanical tools, wrestling with the probe droid's gripping black claws.

Through the speakers of the comm unit, a sudden static-filled burst of subspace gibberish blasted out from the probe droid in some kind of powerful coded signal. The long chain of data shouted toward space even as the deadly probot wrestled with Ackbar's sub.

The black droid finally succeeded in rotating its head, bending its laser cannons toward the sub.

Ackbar fired the lateral jets, wrenching them and the probe droid sideways as a volley of vicious laser blasts screamed past them, plowing a tunnel of sudden steam through the water. He tugged at the waldos and brought another of his equipment arms to bear, a small cutting laser.

Its tip heated to incandescent red-white as he slashed through the probe droid's gripping metal claw, severing the plasteel and breaking them free. Ackbar pulled the sub away and brought the cutting laser to bear again just as the probe droid turned to fire a second time.

Leia knew it was hopeless. They couldn't get away, and the cutting laser would do nothing against the far-superior weapons of the probot. And unlike Luke, she had not mastered Jedi skills enough to mount even a feeble defense. But Ackbar, still looking cool and in control, fired two blasts from the cutting laser at the head of the probe droid, attempting to blind its optical sensors. The feeble beams struck—

The probot detonated in an unexpected explosion. Bright concentric waves of light hurled the sub back, tumbling it end over end. They were thrown backward; Leia felt the chair's restraints automatically tighten around her. The shock wave rang against the hull, sending a sound like a gong through the enclosed sub. A fury of bubbles and drifting debris surged around them. Large splintered seatree trunks sank to the ocean bottom.

"The probe self-destructed!" Cilghal said. "But we didn't stand a chance against it."

Leia remembered Han's conjecture on Hoth. "The probe droids have programming to destroy themselves rather than risk letting their data fall into enemy hands."

Ackbar finally managed to stabilize the spinning submersible. Four of the mechanical arms extending from the front of the sub had been snapped off, leaving only frayed edges of broken metal and dead circuitry.

Ackbar blew one of the ballast tanks, and the sub rose toward the surface. Leia noticed three hairline cracks in the transparisteel windowport and realized how close they had come to being crushed by the shock wave.

"But the probot already sent its signal," Cilghal said. "We heard it before the self-destruct."

Leia felt a cold fist of fear close around her stomach, but Ackbar tried to dismiss the peril.

"This probe droid has been here for ten years or more, and that would have been a very old code, almost certainly obsolete," he said. "Even if the Imperials could still understand its message, who would be out there listening?"

17

With her three Imperial Star
Destroyers safely hidden among the ionized islands
of the Cauldron Nebula, Admiral Daala retired to her
private quarters to review tactics.

She sat stiffly in a slick lounge chair, refusing to relax
into the warm contours. Too much comfort made Daala
distinctly uncomfortable.

The holographic image of Grand Moff Tarkin stood
with her in the dim room, unchanged after all these
years. The gaunt, hard man presented his recorded
lectures, his communiqués. Daala had watched them
dozens of times before.

In the privacy of her chambers, she allowed herself to
miss the one person in the Imperial Military Academy
who had seen her talent. Tarkin had raised her rank to
admiral—as far as she knew, the highest rank held by
any female in the Imperial armed forces.

During her years of exile in Maw Installation, Daala
had often replayed Tarkin's messages, but now she

studied them intently. Her eyebrows knitted together, and her bright green eyes narrowed as she concentrated on every word he spoke, searching for some indispensable advice for her private war against the Rebellion.

"Liquidating a dozen small threats is easier than rooting out one well-established center of defiance," his image said, in a speech given on Carida explaining the "Tarkin Doctrine." "Rule through the fear of force rather than through force itself. If we use our strength wisely, we shall intimidate thousands of worlds with the example of a select few."

Daala rewound the holotape to listen to his words again, thinking she had been on the verge of capturing a crucial insight. But the door chime interrupted her. She switched off the holoprojector. "Lights up."

Stocky Commander Kratas stood stiffly at her door, his uniform wrinkle free, his hands clasped behind his back. He was trying to mask a smug grin of satisfaction, but the expression displayed itself in a small facial tick and the slight upturn of his vanishingly thin lips.

"Yes, Commander, what is it?" she said.

"We have intercepted a signal," Kratas said. "It appears to be from an Imperial probe droid transmitting covert data gathered on an important Rebel planet called Calamari, the site of one of their prime starship-building facilities. We can't tell how recent the information is."

Daala raised her eyebrows and let her colorless lips form a smile. With both hands she swept her molten-metal hair behind her shoulders, feeling static electricity crackle through her fingertips, as if generated from the excitement building within her. "Are you certain this transmission is genuine? Where was it directed?"

"It was a broad-spectrum signal, Admiral. My assumption is that these probe droids were deployed in a widely scattered pattern. They would not know the location of any particular Star Destroyer when they transmitted a report."

"Could it be a hoax sent by the Rebels? A trap?"

"I don't believe so. It was heavily encoded. We almost couldn't crack it ourselves until we double-checked against one of the new codes Grand Moff Tarkin delivered on his last visit to Maw Installation."

"Excellent, Commander," she said, brushing her palms down the smooth olive-gray of her uniform slacks. "We've been looking for a new target to strike, and if this is an important starship-construction facility, that sounds like a good candidate. As good as anything, I suppose. I want you and the captains of the other two ships to meet me in the war room. Prepare the Star Destroyers for immediate departure. Recharge all turbolaser batteries. Outfit all TIE fighters.

"This time we will follow Grand Moff Tarkin's strategy to the letter." She punctuated the last phrase with an index finger jabbing the air. "Have everyone review their tapes. I want no mistakes. A flawless attack."

She dimmed the lights as she stepped into the corridor. Her two stormtrooper bodyguards fell into ranks behind her. Their boot heels clicked on the floor in perfect echoing unison.

"We are through practicing," Daala said to Kratas. "After our strike the planet Calamari will be nothing more than a rubble heap."

• • •

Leia piloted Ackbar's open-canopied wavespeeder as they rushed over the oceans of Calamari. The sky was still a congealed soup of dark clouds, but the previous day's storm had run out of energy. The wind remained fresh and cool, tossing droplets of salty spray into their faces—but Leia could not stop smiling with relief just to know that Ackbar had agreed to come to Coruscant with her, if only to speak with Mon Mothma.

She and Cilghal would take him back to Foamwander City, where he could turn over his seismic data to other Calamarian scientists. Sitting in the backseat of the wavespeeder, Ackbar seemed deeply troubled and unsure of himself.

The lumpy hemisphere of the Calamarian city looked like a gunmetal-gray island. Other small seaskimmers drifted in and out, gathering up nets and dashing back to access openings.

Ackbar sat up stiffly. "Listen!"

Over the rushing noise of the wind and waves, Leia heard the sharp tones of an all-hands alarm. She grabbed the comm unit, punching buttons for Foamwander City control. "This is wavespeeder seventeen-oh-one/seven. What is the cause of the alarm?"

Before Leia could receive an answer, a curtain of brilliant light sliced through the clouds, slashing the ocean surface near the floating city. Geysers of suddenly vaporized water plumed into the air with a *whoop*.

"Those are turbolasers!" Leia said.

Ackbar gripped the side of his seat. "We're being fired on from orbit."

"Wave doors are closing," said a maddeningly calm Calamarian voice through the speaker system. "All citizens take shelter immediately. Repeat, wave doors are closing."

Most of the other sea vehicles had disappeared inside the various openings around the hull of Foamwander City. Those who could not make it to the doors abandoned their craft and dived overboard to swim down to submerged entryways.

Many wave doors had already clamped shut like diagonal mouths. Leia aimed for one of the remaining openings and punched the wavespeeder's accelerator. The lurch pressed all three of them back against their padded seats.

Overhead, like a flock of razor-winged carrion birds, came an entire squadron of TIE fighters and TIE bombers. They swooped down in a steep descent with a roaring howl of their Twin Ion Engines.

The TIE bombers released glowing energy packets that exploded in the sea, sending out shock waves and foam and spray. TIE fighters roared over Foamwander City, strafing with their laser cannons. Lances of green light etched smoldering damage into the city shell.

One of the shock waves tossed a wall of water at Leia's wavespeeder. She fought for control but did not slow down, keeping her eyes fixed on the closing wave doors. If they didn't make it through the gap, they would be helpless out on the water, ready targets for the Imperial bombardment.

Ackbar said, "We left a squadron of B-wing fighters to defend the orbiting shipyards. Where are they? I have to learn what's happening up there."

Cilghal maintained a quiet, steady voice. "Perhaps they are otherwise occupied."

"Hang on!" Leia said, and fired emergency thrusters.

The wavespeeder lifted another meter above the surface of the ocean as it flew in a last-ditch effort to get through the closing gap. Leia ducked as the diagonal metal wave doors ground closer and closer. . . .

The bottom layer of plasteel plating scraped off the wavespeeder as Leia struck the sharp edge of the heavy door; then they shot into the protected green-lit tunnel. With the vehicle traveling at such high speed, even that minor impact was enough to send them spinning. Leia wrestled with the controls, trying to slow the vehicle as it caromed off one wall and then the opposite wall, sending out showers of sparks. Finally it ground to a halt. Behind them, with a thunderous echo, the wave doors slammed shut.

Pausing only long enough to confirm that they were all unharmed, Leia picked her way out of the wreckage. Through the thick armor of the floating city she heard the repeated thuds of explosions from TIE bombers and the screams from firing laser cannons.

Ackbar stepped away from the wreckage and turned to Cilghal. "Take me to the control center immediately. I want to be linked with the orbital defense forces." He already looked more alive, more alert. "If I can see what's going on, maybe I can figure out a way to help us all."

"Yes, Admiral," Cilghal said. Leia wondered if she had used his rank intentionally.

Flashing lights and alarm sirens echoed as they hurried through the serpentine corridors. Groups of Quarren rushed past, burbling exclamations through their tentacled faces as they scrambled down access shafts to the underwater levels. Leia had no doubt they were abandoning the city structure, swimming down to where they thought they were safe.

When Cilghal reached a turbolift door, other Calamarians flocked to it, trying to get to the city's protected inner chambers. Cilghal raised her voice, the first time Leia had heard her do so. "Make way for Admiral Ackbar! We must get to Central Command.

"Ackbar," several Calamarians echoed, stepping aside to allow him passage. "Admiral Ackbar!"

Ackbar seemed taller now, without the haunted look he had worn since the crash on Vortex. Leia knew that all Calamarians remembered the nightmare of Imperial attacks—but if anyone could mount a successful defense with what little resources they had, it would be Ackbar.

After the turbolift spilled them out onto the proper level, Ambassador Cilghal led the way. She used her diplomatic access codes to let them into the core of Foamwander City until they finally emerged into the chaotic Central Command.

Seven Calamarian tactical experts sat at command stations, watching the battle overhead. In the center of the room a holographic wireframe diagram of the planet and its moon hovered amid sparkling pinpoints of fighters flying in defensive formation.

Leia stared in awe at the two Imperial Star Destroyers that orbited the planet side by side, firing turbolaser blasts into the oceans. Overhead, TIE squadrons continued to harass Foamwander City. External viewers showed smoldering holes where proton bombs had punctured the city's armored plating. Foamwander's defensive lasers fired upward, burning ship after ship out of the sky—but more attackers kept coming down.

Reeling with shock, the city commander turned from his post and noticed them for the first time. "Admiral Ackbar! Please, sir, help us with our defense. I cede my position."

"Give me a tactical update," Ackbar said, stepping to the holographic projection.

"Cilghal," Leia said, raising her voice over the hubbub, "get me to the comm system. I can use my priority codes to send for New Republic military assistance. On a low frequency the codes can punch through any interference from those Star Destroyers."

"Can their battleships get here in time?" Cilghal asked.

"Depends on how long we can maintain our defenses here," Leia said.

Though Leia could read no specific emotion on Cilghal's face, she sensed some measure of pride. "The Mon Calamari broke the first Imperial occupation using only common tools and scientific implements. This time we have real weapons. We can hold them off as long as necessary." Cilghal motioned to a nearby control panel. "You may use that communication station to send your message."

Leia hurried to the comm station and punched in the override codes to send a tight-beam encoded signal directly to Coruscant. "This is Minister Leia Organa Solo," she said. "The planet Calamari is currently under attack by two Imperial Star Destroyers. We request immediate assistance. Repeat, *immediate* assistance! If you don't get here soon, don't bother to come."

The city commander thrust a webbed hand into the holographic display of the battle. "We positioned the entire squadron of B-wing fighters to defend the shipyards, because we thought that would be the most likely target. But when the Star Destroyers came out of hyperspace, they went into orbit and began an assault on the floating cities. Right now both Star Destroyers are concentrating their firepower on Reef Home City. They've left two squadrons of TIE fighters and TIE bombers to cover Foamwander City. Another three squadrons are currently pummeling Coral Depths."

"Commander," one of the Calamarian tacticians spoke up, touching an implanted microphone at his ear hole. "We've lost all contact with Reef Home. Their last transmissions showed the outer hull breached in at least fifteen separate places, water rushing in. The final image showed a large-scale explosion. Static signature analysis implies that the entire city has been destroyed."

A quiet moan of dismay rippled through Central Command. The city commander said tentatively, "I was about to withdraw defenses from the shipyards to attack the Star Destroyers."

Ackbar looked at the swarms of B-wings still harrying the Imperial fighters. "Good decision, Commander," he said, but stared intently at the map, at the moon, at the two Star Destroyers on the far side of the planet. "Wait a moment," he said. "Something looks very familiar to me."

He paused, nodding slowly as if his great head were too heavy for his shoulders. "Yes, Commander—withdraw the B-wing fighters, all of them. Send them to fight the Star Destroyers. Leave the shipyards entirely undefended."

"Is that wise, Admiral?" Leia asked.

"No," he said, "it is a trap."

On the bridge of the Star Destroyer *Gorgon*, Admiral Daala watched the battle unfold below her, exactly as planned.

In her heart she felt a warm glow of pride for the tactical genius of Grand Moff Tarkin. Beside her ship the *Basilisk* mowed a swath of death across the watery surface. Like a swarm of angry insects, the TIE fighters swept away the pitiful resistance the Calamarians managed to mount.

The Rebel B-wing fighters and some of the midsized capital ships in orbit proved only a minor nuisance. As the *Gorgon* and the *Basilisk* went through their carefully choreographed misleading attack, the Calamarian defense forces had followed along as expected, like marionettes pulled by strings.

She turned to the communications officer at his station. "Contact Captain Brusc on the *Manticore*," she said. "The Calamarian forces have finally left their shipyards undefended. He may begin his attack at once."

Ackbar gestured with his hands and spoke with an undignified rapidity, as if he knew he didn't have much time. "Before I was liberated by the Rebel Alliance, I was Moff Tarkin's indentured assistant. He took great pleasure in telling me exactly how he was going to enslave other worlds. By observing him I learned the fundamentals of space-warfare tactics, including Tarkin's own favorite strategies."

He pointed a flipper-hand into the images of the two Star Destroyers. "Tarkin is dead, but I recognize this trick. I know what the Imperial commander plans to do. Do we have a sensor network on the far side of the moon?"

"No, Admiral," the city commander said. "We had considered it years ago but—"

"I didn't think so," Ackbar said. "So we're blind there, correct?"

"Correct."

"What are you getting at, Admiral?" Leia said.

"There's a third Star Destroyer hiding behind our moon."

When Ackbar said that, half of the chattering voices in the room fell silent. The others turned toward him in amazement. "What proof do you have?"

Leia tried to use her fledgling powers with the Force to sense the hidden enemy ship, but either it was too distant, or she was not skilled enough . . . or it wasn't there.

"The actions of the Imperial commander tell me all I need," Ackbar said. "Their main target is indeed the shipyards. Moments after these two Star Destroyers came out of hyperspace, a third also emerged, concealed in the shadow of our moon. The vanguard attack is designed to lure us away from the shipyards, tricking us into throwing our entire defenses against a feint. When the third Star Destroyer comes in at full sublight speed, the shipyards will be helpless. With one run the third Star Destroyer can obliterate our starship assembly facilities with virtually no losses of its own."

"But, Admiral," the city commander said, "why did you just withdraw all of our forces from the shipyards?"

Ackbar nodded. "Because you are going to give me remote command of *that* ship." He indicated the huge spacedock hangar where the skeletal hull of the new battle cruiser *Startide* hung in orbit.

"But, sir, none of the *Startide*'s weapons are functional."

"But its engines work, if I am not mistaken?"

"Yes," the city commander said, "we tested the sublight engines only last week. The hyperdrive reactor core has been installed, but we have never taken the ship into hyperspace."

"Not necessary," Ackbar said. "Have all the construction engineers been evacuated?"

"Yes, at first sign of the attack."

"Then give me remote operations."

"Admiral—" the city commander said tentatively, then punched in a command-code sequence. "If it were anyone other than you. . ."

Taking control, Ackbar stepped into the field where virtual images were projected with a parallax designed for wide-set telescopic eyes.

The half-constructed ship powered up its engines and locked into drone mode. With an inaudible roar of massive sublight engines the unarmed battleship crawled away from the orbital shipyards, picking up speed as it ascended from the planet's gravity well. The engines were powerful enough to haul along the entire connected framework of the spacedock.

Ackbar didn't mind. The more mass, the better.

Leia bit her lip as the echoes of attack thundered from above, as the external imagers showed the damage to Foamwander's outer shell, as another wave of TIE fighters swooped down to scorch any exposed surface.

Cilghal seemed to have gone into a kind of a trance. Leia wondered if the shock had numbed her. The ambassador stood before the orbital images of swarming fighters, both the B-wing defenders and TIE attackers. She reached out with her fingers, touching seemingly random blips of light.

"This one, now this one . . . now this one," she said. Barely a moment after she touched each one, the screen flared bright, marking the destruction of the indicated ships.

Leia was amazed, unable to believe that Cilghal could pick them so accurately. But with the fledgling abilities Luke had taught her, Leia could feel a tug in the female ambassador, an instinctive working of the Force. She asked, already suspecting the answer, "How are you doing that?"

"Just like with the school of fish," Cilghal said quietly. "It's only a trick—but I wish I could get in contact with our fighters. This one, this one!" With a long finger she traced one of the B-wing fighters that seemed perfectly safe in the midst of its own squadron, but then a damaged TIE fighter out of control spiraled through the group of ships and impacted the doomed B-wing. Cilghal had done the same thing with the school of fish as the krakana monster fed.

The female ambassador looked astonished and stricken. "There's not enough time," she said. "I can't figure it out soon enough."

Despite the fury of the Imperial attack, Leia felt a thread of wonder pass through her. Even without further testing, she knew that Cilghal had the potential to use her powers as a Jedi. Leia would have to send Cilghal to Luke's training center on Yavin 4—if they somehow survived here.

Ackbar felt as if he were part of the massive derelict ship as he controlled it from the core of Foamwander City. He paid no attention to the loud status reports and alarms in Central Command. His entire body was an extension of the *Startide*, and he stared through sensor eyes.

Its engines added velocity to the great hulk. Calamari's moon grew larger as he approached it, then began to streak by close to the airless cratered surface and out of sensor range to the dark side of the moon. Where the third Star Destroyer lay in wait.

Ackbar powered up the *Startide*'s hyperdrive reactors and shut off the automatic coolant systems. Alarms ran through his body as the ship's warning routines screamed at him. But Ackbar increased the power output, trying to hold it in, restraining the seething energy that waited to explode from the great uncompleted battleship.

As he brought the *Startide* around the curve of the moon, Ackbar saw the arrowhead shape of a third Star Destroyer just powering up its weapons batteries. "There it is."

The third Star Destroyer suddenly detected the Mon Calamari battle cruiser and began unleashing a flurry of turbolaser bolts—but Ackbar didn't care.

One of the blasts detonated a joint in the spacedock framework surrounding the *Startide*, and a network of girders dropped into space. Molten droplets flew from the starboard flank where a direct hit vaporized part of the hull.

Ackbar drove on at full speed on his suicide run, heading directly down the Star Destroyer's throat. The Imperial ship continued to fire.

Ackbar released the last safety mechanisms that held the unshielded hyperdrive reactor in check. The super-heated energy furnace would reach its flash point within seconds.

He disconnected himself from the command console and let the laws of physics take their course.

Admiral Daala shouted into the comm system. "Captain Brusc, tell me what's going on!"

The *Manticore* had just begun its triumphant run to destroy the Calamarian shipyards when all havoc broke loose. Alarms interrupted her transmission.

The captain scrambled and shouted orders. "It's another ship, Admiral!" Brusc said, flashing a glance and wanting to bark orders, yet not quite daring to ignore Daala. "It came out of nowhere. They must have known we were here."

"Impossible," Daala said. "They couldn't have known we were there. We left no sensor trace. Ops! Give me the *Manticore*'s tactical sensors."

On the screen Daala saw her third Star Destroy-er and the skeletal Calamarian star cruiser. It looked ridiculously cumbersome, dragged back by heavy construction frameworks—yet it moved inexo-rably. Daala understood the suicide tactic immediate-ly.

"Get out of there!"

The *Manticore* veered to get out of the *Startide*'s path, but the Calamarian cruiser came on too fast. The *Manticore*'s turbolaser batteries did nothing to slow its approach.

Daala held her back rigid, forcing herself not to wince. She gripped the cold rail at her bridge station. Her knuckles whitened. The plasteel floor seemed to drop out from under her. Her dry mouth opened in a wordless shout of No!

The Calamarian battleship struck the underbelly of the *Manticore*. Just before the impact, though, the *Startide* went nova, erupting into blinding waves of energy that tore the *Manticore* apart.

Captain Brusc's transmission cut off abruptly.

Daala turned away, gritting her teeth and refusing to let acid tears of failure well up in her green eyes. She thought of all the weaponry, all the personnel, all the responsibility that had just been destroyed.

She stared into space, blinded by the brilliant double explosion that flowed out behind Calamari's moon, creating an artificial eclipse.

18

Kyp Durron felt exhilarated, yet foolish at the same time. The other Jedi students had stopped their own exercises and dropped back to watch Kyp at work.

Surrounded by the dense foliage of the jungle, with humid air wrapped like sweat around him, Kyp balanced his body. His feet extended straight up into the air, his back rigid; he held himself upright with one hand resting flat on the rough ground. The heel of his palm sank into the soft dirt. Blades of sharp grass stuck between his fingers.

He could balance himself with less difficulty on a more level piece of ground—but that would be too easy. His dark hair hung around his face; droplets of perspiration ran in tiny trickles along his scalp.

With his free hand Kyp supported a moss-covered boulder he had uprooted from the ground. Clumps of dirt pattered to the grass. He held the rock in the air with only a small effort, using the Force to do most of the work.

Artoo-Detoo bleeped in alarm, chittering from high in the branches above. Kyp had levitated him up there as a warm-up exercise, and he would get the little droid down in good time; for now he maintained his concentration.

He blocked out his awareness of the other Jedi trainees. He let his eyes slit halfway closed as he concentrated and raised a fallen, fungus-shrouded tree limb, yanking it from a tangle of blueleaf shrubs and standing it on end beside him.

Kyp blew out a long, slow breath and concentrated on keeping every piece in its place. The rest of the universe focused around him. Highly attuned, he felt a vibration in the Force, a ripple of amazement and pride.

Master Skywalker had come to watch him.

Kyp knew how to feel the Force, how to use it. It came naturally to him. It seemed instinctive, just as navigating the Sun Crusher through the black hole cluster had been. He felt that he had been ready for this all his life, but he could not see it simply because he had never been shown how to use his abilities. But now that Master Skywalker had nudged him, the new skill came flooding into him as if a long-closed valve had been twisted open.

In little more than a week of intensive work, Kyp had surpassed the achievements of the other Jedi students. Kyp shut himself off from socialization among the trainees. He spoke to few of the others, focusing every moment upon honing his Jedi ability, increasing his concentration, developing a rapport with the Force. He hounded Master Skywalker to give him new tasks, to set him greater challenges so he could continue to learn and grow stronger in the Force.

Now, enclosed by the jungle and observed by other trainees, Kyp did not see his exercises as showing off. He didn't care whether Master Skywalker watched him or not. He simply meant to push the boundaries of what he could do. After he completed one set of exercises, he tried another more difficult routine, adding greater challenges. In that way he could continue to improve.

While trapped in the detention levels of the Star Destroyer *Gorgon*, when he had been sentenced to death by Admiral Daala, Kyp had vowed that he would never again allow himself to become so helpless. A Jedi was never helpless, since the Force came from all living things.

Still balancing, dark eyes closed, Kyp felt the other creatures in the jungle, traced their ripples in the great tapestry of the Force. He smelled the plants and flowers and small creatures in the rain forest. He ignored the tiny gnats swarming around his head and body.

He felt the tidal vibrations of the gas giant Yavin and its other moons as he extended his thoughts outward to space. He felt at peace, a part of the cosmos. He pondered what difficulties he could add to his balancing act. But before he could decide, Kyp sensed Artoo-Detoo being lifted from his perch high in the Massassi trees and lowered gently to the ground. The little droid made relieved beeping sounds.

Then Kyp felt the mossy boulder invisibly removed from his hand and set back in its depression. The rotting branch also drifted down, replaced exactly in its former place on the mulch of the jungle floor.

Kyp felt a slash of annoyance at having his exercise forcibly stopped, and he opened his eyes to see Master Skywalker grinning proudly at him.

"Very good, Kyp," Master Skywalker said. "In fact, it's incredible. I'm not sure even Obi-Wan or Yoda would know what to do with you."

Kyp nudged with his levitating skills to flip himself upright so that he landed on his feet. Staring into Master Skywalker's eyes, he felt his heart pounding with exhilaration, filled with far more energy than he knew how to contain.

He spoke breathlessly, blinking as if he had suddenly opened his eyes into the brighter daylight on Yavin 4. "What else can you teach me today, Master?" He felt his skin flush. Droplets of sweat trickled from his dark hair and along his cheeks.

Master Skywalker shook his head. "Nothing more for today, Kyp." The other Jedi candidates stood slumped in exhaustion, resting on broken stumps and overgrown rocks.

Kyp tried not to let his disappointment show. "But there is so much more to learn," he said.

"Yes," Master Skywalker answered with a barely contained smile, "and patience is one of those things to learn. The ability to do a thing is not all there is. You must *know* the thing. You must master every facet of it. You must understand how it fits with everything else you know. You must possess it for it to be truly yours."

Kyp nodded solemnly at the spoken words of wisdom, as Jedi students were expected to do. But he promised himself that he would do everything necessary to make all of these new abilities *his*.

Even in the deepest hours of the night, Kyp did not sleep. He had eaten a bland but filling meal by himself, then retired to his cool quarters to meditate and practice the skills he had already learned.

As he concentrated, with only a small glowlamp in the corner, he sent his mind out to feel between the cracks of all the stone blocks in the Great Temple. He followed the life cycles of the strands of moss. He tracked tiny arachnids skittering through the corridors and vanishing into dark spaces, where his delicate touch could follow them through the blackness into their hidden homes.

Kyp felt as if he had plugged into a network of living things that expanded his mind and made him feel both insignificant and infinite at the same time.

As Kyp thought and dabbled with his fledgling abilities, he felt a great cold *rip* in the Force, like a black gash opening the structure of the universe. He snapped himself back to the present.

Kyp whirled and saw behind him the looming shadow of a tall cloaked figure. Even in the dim room the dark man's silhouette seemed intensely black, a hole that swallowed up all glimmers of light. Kyp said nothing, but as he continued to gaze, he saw the tiny starpoints of distant suns within the outline of his mysterious visitor.

"The Force is strong in you, Kyp Durron," the shadowy figure said.

Kyp looked up, feeling no fear. He had been imprisoned and sentenced to death by the Empire. He had lived in the pitch-dark spice mines of Kessel for over a decade. He had fought against a predatory energy spider. And he had flown through a black-hole cluster. As he looked at the imposing liquid-black outline, though, he felt awe and curiosity.

"Who are you?" Kyp asked.

"I could be your teacher," the dark shape said. "I could show you many things that even your Master Skywalker does not comprehend."

Kyp felt a thrill rush through him. "What things?"

"I could show you techniques that were lost thousands of years ago, secret rites and hidden doorways of power that no weak Jedi Master like Skywalker dares to touch. But *you* are strong, Kyp Durron. Do you dare to learn?"

Kyp felt reckless, but he trusted his instincts. They had served him well in the past. "I'm not afraid to learn," he said, "but you have to tell me your name. I won't learn from a man who is afraid to identify himself."

Kyp felt foolish even as he said it. The shadowy form seemed to ripple as if with silent laughter. His voice boomed out again, full of pride.

"I was the greatest Dark Lord of the Sith. I am Exar Kun."

19

Han Solo dashed into his and Leia's empty sleeping chambers. "Lights!" he shouted so loudly that the voice receptors didn't understand his words. Han forced himself to articulate with brutal clarity through clenched teeth, "Lights," until the illumination came on in the room.

He glanced from side to side, trying to think of everything he would need to bring. After unsealing the coded security chamber atop one of their closets, he snatched a fully charged personal blaster, then grabbed an extra power pack. He pulled out a clean set of clothes, felt a startled pang as he saw Leia's garments hanging untouched in the storage unit.

"Chewie!" he bellowed. "In here."

For some reason the voice-response lights went off again. In disgust he snapped, "Lights on!" for the third time.

See-Threepio strutted into the room with two bawling children in tow. "Sir, must you be so rushed? You're upsetting the children. Will you *please* take a moment to explain what's going on?"

Chewbacca roared from the outer room, and Han could hear him knocking furniture aside as he ran to the bedroom. The Wookiee stood in the doorway, his tan fur ruffled. He opened his wide pink mouth, showing his fangs, and roared again so loudly that it startled the children.

The bedroom lights went off for a second time.

Han saw that Chewbacca carried his deadly bowcaster and a pack of concentrated emergency rations, ready to go. Fumbling in the dimness, Han opened up another small compartment beside the closet and pulled out the trusty automatic medikit he had removed from the *Millennium Falcon.*

"Lights," Threepio said in a calm voice, and the illumination stayed on this time.

"Threepio, where's Lando?" Han said. "Find him for me."

"He's down in the starship bays, sir. He left me a message to tell you that he is not impressed with your standards of maintenance on your former ship."

"Well, he'd better have the *Falcon* running now, that's all I can say," Han said.

Jaina sniffed loudly and between sobs cried out, "Where's Mommy?"

Han stopped as if hit with a stun beam. He knelt, looking into his little girl's face. He brushed aside the tears on her cheeks and placed his hands on her tiny shoulders, giving a squeeze of confidence.

"Daddy's going to rescue her," Han said.

"Rescue her? Oh, dear!" Threepio interrupted. "Why does Mistress Leia need rescuing?" Chewbacca bellowed in answer, but Threepio waved mechanical hands at him. "You're not helping, you know!"

Han turned to the Wookiee. "Not this time, buddy. I need you here to watch over the kids. There's no one else I trust as much." Chewbacca blatted a response, but Han shook his head. "No, I don't have a plan yet. All I know is I need to get to Calamari before the Imperials destroy it. I can't just stay here and let Leia face them alone."

Han stuffed what he needed into a lightweight mesh sack and grabbed the emergency rations from Chewbacca's hairy arms, glancing at the labels to make sure the food was compatible with human digestive systems.

"How long will you be gone, sir?" Threepio asked, trying to stop Jacen from climbing into the open closets.

"As long as it takes to rescue my wife," Han answered.

He sprinted toward the door, taking two steps before he froze. He spun around and returned to his two children. He bent down again and gathered Jacen and Jaina in a big hug. "You two behave for Chewie and Threepio. You have to watch out for each other."

"We *are* good," Jacen answered with a touch of indignation. At that moment the little boy looked heart-wrenchingly like Leia.

"I have recently updated my child-care programming, sir," Threepio said. "We'll have no trouble at all." The golden droid nudged the twins as he tried to usher them back to their own room. "Come, children, I will tell you an entertaining story."

Jacen and Jaina began crying again.

Han took a last longing look at the twins and then ran out of the living quarters, pausing only a moment to straighten the soft chair Chewbacca had knocked over.

The cyberfuse made a popping sound as it clattered on the cockpit floor of the *Millennium Falcon*. Lando Calrissian stared at it in disgust, then turned back to the control panels.

He had finished updating the navicomputer software, but somehow that had caused the cockpit lights to short out. He rummaged around in the small bin of old greasy-smelling replacement fuses and yanked out one that looked appropriate.

The *Falcon* had been cobbled together from so many different parts, he could never keep track of how much spit and monofilament wire kept the ship running. He wondered for the hundredth time why he loved the craft so much.

He popped in the fuse, activated it, and flicked a row of switches that remained glassy dead. "Come *on*," Lando said, smacking the panel hard with the flat of his left palm.

With a humming *whirr* and a blast of cold chemical-smelling air from the recirculating ducts, the controls winked to life. Lando closed his eyes with a sigh. "Good old emergency repair procedure number one," he said.

"Hey, Lando!"

He heard the loud, determined voice from outside in the repair bay. Without looking Lando knew Han Solo had come to shout at him about something.

He felt tired, itchy from sweat and frustrated at how long it was taking to get the *Millennium Falcon* performing up to his exacting standards. He stood up from the open control panels and walked across the short corridor, his boots making impatient clangs on the deck plates. He bent down on the entrance ramp to stick his head out.

"Lando," Han said again, hurrying toward him, his face red with agitation. Sweat clumped his dark hair together, and he marched forward with the unstoppable attitude of an Imperial construction droid.

"Han," Lando said, scowling, "you didn't tell me this junk heap was in such bad shape when we played sabacc."

Han ignored the comment and sprinted up the ramp, carrying a mesh sack of supplies and wearing a blaster at his hip. Lando raised his eyebrows. "Han—"

"Lando, I need the *Falcon*. Now." He pushed past Lando, dropped his sack on the deck plates, and hit the controls for the entrance ramp. Lando had to jump inside as the greased cylinders hauled the slanted metal ramp back into position.

"Han, this is my ship now. You can't just—"

Han went directly to the cockpit and threw himself into the pilot seat. Lando charged up behind Han. "What do you think you're doing?"

Han spun around in the pilot chair and fixed Lando with a stare that skewered him like a pair of stun bolts. "The planet Calamari is being attacked by Admiral Daala at this very moment. Leia's trapped there. Now, are you going to help me go rescue her in the *Falcon*, or do I pick you up by your scruffy neck and throw you off the ship?"

Lando backed off, holding both palms up in a gesture of peace. "Whoa, whoa, Han! Leia's in trouble? Let's go—but I'm flying," he said, motioning for Han to move into the copilot's chair. "It *is* my ship."

Grudgingly, Han unbuckled his restraints and slid over to the right-hand seat normally reserved for Chewbacca. Lando toggled on the comm system. "*Millennium Falcon* requesting clearance for immediate departure."

He raised the modified light freighter off the floor on its repulsorlift jets, hovered, and punched the sublight engines the moment Coruscant Control gave them permission to depart. The *Falcon* shot through the atmosphere and headed out to the stars.

On the planet Vortex, Qwi Xux wandered on the fringes of the reconstruction site of the Cathedral of Winds. Her companion, Wedge Antilles, had joined the other New Republic cleanup crews. The workers wore thick gloves to protect their hands from the razor edges of the crystal shards they hauled to the materials-reprocessing bins, dissolving broken fragments and synthesizing new building material.

Overhead the swirling gray clouds warned of the rapidly approaching storm season. Soon all the winged Vors would take shelter in their low-to-the-ground bunkers and wait out the hurricane-force gales. Already cold gusts hissed across the unbroken plains of pale grasses. Qwi feared that her own ethereal form might take flight, whisked into the air by a sudden powerful gust to join the lacy-winged inhabitants.

The Vors kept away from the New Republic teams, working at the site of the devastated cathedral, reinforcing the foundations and preparing to erect a new network of hollow musical towers. The aliens followed no plan that anyone could see, and had answered only with silence when the engineers asked to study the architectural drawings.

Qwi watched the activity, wishing she could help. The Vors had not demanded aid from the New Republic; in fact, they had barely acknowledged it, simply accepting the new workers and continuing the breakneck pace of their project. The seemingly emotionless Vors had filed no formal protest, made no threats of cutting off relations. It was as if they understood the New Republic bore them no ill will; but as a race they had been stunned and could not return to normal activities until their Cathedral of Winds sang again.

As she walked among the scattered shards of crystal pipes, Qwi found a small, narrow tube, a broken piece of one of the high-pitched windpipes from the tallest pinnacles of the towers. She bent and picked it up with her long fingers, careful to avoid the sharp edges.

The wind gusted around her, rippling the fabric of her tunic, tossing her pearlescent feathery hair around her head. She stared at the tiny flute. Back at Maw Installation, Qwi had often programmed her own computers using musical notes, whistling and humming to set subroutines in motion. She had not played music in a long time. . . .

Over at the materials-reprocessing station, Wedge and two helpers accidentally dropped a large section of crystal pipe, which crashed to the ground. Wedge shouted, and the others jumped out of the way to escape the fragments.

At the construction site the Vors fluttered up in the air in a panic, alarmed by the sound of breaking crystal.

Qwi put the flute to her mouth, taking a tentative breath. The smooth crystal felt cool against her thin blue lips. She blew into the unbroken end and held a finger over one of the holes, letting a test note whistle through the tube. She tried another, and a third, gaining a feel for the songs the crystal flute could sing.

She planted her feet among the crushed glassy fragments on the ground, steadying herself against the blowing wind, and she played. It took her several tries to work the notes into the shapes she wanted, but she closed her large indigo eyes and let the music flow from her.

The Vors flapped through the air, approaching her, circling overhead. Some landed in the whipping lavender grass nearby, turning their angular faces toward her, blinking horny eyelids over pupilless obsidian eyes. They listened.

Qwi thought of the destruction of the Cathedral of Winds, the loss of a great artifact and work of art, the deaths of so many Vors; the music took on a keening tone. In her mind she also saw her own home planet of Omwat, when Moff Tarkin had placed her in an orbital training habitat as a child so she and other talented Omwati children could watch as he destroyed their families' honeycomb settlements if ever the children failed an examination. . . .

Music skirled out of the flute, rising and falling. She heard the flap of Vor wings over the sound of the notes and the wind. Qwi blinked nervously and looked up at her silent audience, but she kept playing.

From his position with the New Republic workers, Wedge came running over to see if she needed help. The other human engineers noticed the attention she had drawn.

As Wedge approached, breathless and wide-eyed, Qwi stopped playing. She took a deep breath and lowered her crystal flute.

Surrounding her, the Vors did not speak. They stared at her, fluttering their wings to keep their balance. Segmented, leathery armor covered their faces, masking any readable expressions. She couldn't think of anything to say.

A large male Vor, obviously a clan leader of some kind, stepped forward and extended his hand to take the flute from her. Still nervous, Qwi placed the delicate instrument in his leathery palm.

With a sudden, violent gesture, the Vor squeezed his hand shut and crushed the flute. The thin crystal sides of the tube shattered. He opened his hand to let the fragments fall to the ground. Thin lines of blood blossomed on his palm.

"No more music," he said. Her entire audience of Vors spread their wings and leaped into the winds, flying back over to the construction site.

The leader kept his gaze on her. "Not until we are finished here," he said, and flew off to join the others.

Stuck in hyperspace, Han Solo could do nothing but wait. He couldn't hurry the passage of time.

He paced around the common area, looking at the battered holographic game board and thinking of when he had first seen Artoo-Detoo playing with Chewbacca. That had been before he had even met Leia, when Luke Skywalker was a wet-behind-the-ears moisture farmer and Obi-Wan Kenobi was just a crazy old man. If he had known how his life would change after that day in the Mos Eisley cantina, Han wondered if he would have taken the risk to pick up two passengers and their droids bound for Alderaan.

But then he would never have met Leia. Never have married her. Never have fathered three children. Never have helped defeat the Empire. Yes, he thought: despite all the turmoil, Han would make the same choices all over again.

And now Leia was in great peril.

Lando came from the cockpit. "She's on autopilot." He looked at the dejected expression on Han's face and shook his head. "Han, why don't you rest? Let's kill some time." Then, as if the idea had just occurred to him, "How about we play a round of . . . sabacc?" Lando raised his eyebrows and flashed one of his famous grins.

Han wondered if his friend was just trying to cheer him up and decided to see how serious Lando really was. "I'm not interested in sabacc right now." He sat down and lowered his voice. "I don't suppose you'd put up my ship as a stake?"

Lando scowled. "It's *my* ship, Han."

Han leaned forward across the holographic chess table. "Not for long, buddy—or are you afraid?"

The *Falcon* shot through hyperspace on autopilot, oblivious to the fact that her ownership was being decided.

Tiny pearls of sweat tickled the back of Han's neck as he stared at his cards. Lando, who prided himself on a perfect bluffing expression, showed concern and uneasiness. For the third time in as many minutes, he wiped a hand across his brow.

The scoring computer held them at ninety-four points each. The time now passed in a flash, and Han found himself so intent on the game that he had not thought about Leia's desperate situation for at least fifteen seconds.

"How do I know you don't have some trick programmed into these cards?" Lando said, staring at the aluminized plates but holding the displays out of Han's line of sight.

"You suggested this game, buddy. These were my old cards, but you degaussed them yourself. They're straight, no tricks." He let a smile creep across his lips. "And this time there's no sudden change of rules during the final scoring round."

Han waited a second longer, then impatiently took the initiative. "I'm keeping three cards," he said, and put two others facedown in the center of the randomizer field. He pressed the scan button to change the value and suit on his cards, then slid them back out of the field to look at what he had drawn.

Lando held out two cards and thought better of it, biting his lower lip, and pulled out a third. Han felt a wave of jubilation. Lando's hand was even worse than his own.

Han's heart pounded. He had a flush of Staves, a low flush with no face cards; but if he could beat Lando, this hand would give him enough points to pass the target score. Lando stared at his own cards, smiling a little bit, but Han thought it was forced.

"Go on," Han said, and slipped his cards one at a time onto the platform.

"Do I get extra points for having a completely random hand?" Lando said, then sighed. He put his elbows on the table and frowned.

Han slapped a hand on his flush. "The *Falcon*'s mine again!"

Lando smirked, as if losing the ship were a mixed blessing. "At least you're getting her back in better condition."

Han clapped his friend on the back and with a light step danced back toward the cockpit. Slowly, with a sigh of satisfaction, he lowered himself back into the pilot's seat.

Now, he thought, if he could just get to Leia in time, this would be a perfect day.

20

Kyp Durron trudged through
the dense rain forest of Yavin 4, trying to find hidden
paths where the jungle would allow him to pass. He
knew exactly where to go. The dark spirit of Exar Kun
had shown him.

With the stirring of the underbrush, reptilian predator
birds burst squawking into flight, disturbed from the
bloody carcass of a kill they had dragged into the
canopy.

Kyp's assigned companion Dorsk 81 stumbled beside
him. The thin, smooth-skinned alien had a much more
difficult time with the steamy air and the steep climbs.

A purple-furred woolamander clambered through the
overhead network of Massassi trees. Dorsk 81 looked up,
startled—but Kyp had sensed the beast minutes before,
feeling its primal panic and indecision build until finally
it had to flee.

Kyp wiped sweat out of his eyes and shook his head,
sending droplets of perspiration flying. He squinted

again and moved forward with greater speed, knowing they had almost reached their destination—though Dorsk 81 had no idea yet.

Insects and small biting creatures buzzed and scuttled around them, but none bothered Kyp. He consciously exuded a shadow of uneasiness around him so that lower creatures had no incentive to come nearer. Exar Kun had taught him that trick too.

Dorsk 81 opened his lipless mouth, panting as he tried to keep up with the vigorous pace. His yellow and olive-green skin was unblemished, his nose flattened and smooth, his ears tucked back against his head as if someone had designed his race in a wind tunnel. The alien looked miserable; his wide-set eyes blinked, and his face gleamed with a sheen of moisture. "I was not bred for this," Dorsk 81 said.

Kyp slowed, but not enough to bring relief to his companion. He softened the tone of his instinctive retort. "You were not bred for anything but bureaucracy and a comfortable life. I don't understand how the planet Khomm could have survived unchanged for a thousand years. Or why your people wanted it to."

Dorsk 81 took no offense and followed Kyp. "Our society and our genetics reached their perfection a millennium ago, or at least that's what we decided at the time. To prevent undesirable changes, we froze our culture at that level. We took our perfect race and cloned them rather than risking genetic anomalies.

"I am the eighty-first clone of Dorsk. Eighty generations before me have been identical, doing the same jobs with the same level of skill, maintaining our level of perfection and not slipping back." Dorsk 81 frowned, and with a burst of surprising energy he pushed around Kyp.

He flung himself into the effort of making a path through the dense brush with all the strength he possessed. "But I was a failure," he said. "I was different."

Kyp gestured to an identical-looking thicket of raven-thorns, spotting the invisible maze of a relatively simple path. "You have the potential to become a Jedi Knight," he said. "How can you consider that a failure?"

Dorsk 81 clawed his way out of the tangle he had become trapped in. Stains from crushed berries and flower petals dotted his uniform. "It is unsettling ... to be different," he said.

Kyp spoke partly to himself and partly to his companion. "Yes, but sometimes it's exhilarating to know you can rise above the others who are trapped down below."

He ducked into the low tunnel of gloomy foliage and dangling mosses. Tiny gnats flew away from his face. The deep shadows suddenly made him think of the black spice mines of Kessel where he had been forced to work as a slave.

"The Empire ruined my life," Kyp said. "My parents were political resisters. They marked the anniversary of the Ghorman Massacre, and they protested the destruction of Alderaan—but by that time the Emperor had lost all patience with political objections.

"Stormtroopers came in the middle of the night, battered their way into our home on the colony of Deyer. They took my parents, stunned them in front of our eyes, leaving them paralyzed and twitching on the floor. My father couldn't even close his eyes. Tears ran down his cheek, but his arms and his legs kept jittering. He couldn't get up. The stormtroopers dragged him and my mother out.

"My brother Zeth was five years older than me. They took him. He was only fourteen, I think. They put stun-cuffs on his hands. They kicked him, pushed him out, and then they stunned me.

"I found out later that they took Zeth to the Imperial Military Academy on Carida. They put my parents and me in the Correctional Facility on Kessel, where we had to work in the spice mines. I spent most of my days in pitch-darkness because any light straying into the mine shafts spoils spice crystals. My parents died there after only a few years.

"I had to take care of myself even when the prisoners overthrew the Correctional Facility and took over. The crime lord there, Moruth Doole, tossed the captured Imperials down into the spice mines. Doole let some of the prisoners out—but not many and not me. Our masters had changed, but we remained slaves."

Dorsk 81 looked at him with his glittering wide-set eyes. "How did you escape?" he said.

"Han Solo rescued me," Kyp answered; warmth filtered into his voice. "We stole a shuttle and fled into the black hole cluster. There we stumbled upon a secret Imperial research installation, and we were captured again—this time by Admiral Daala and her fleet of Star Destroyers. Han got us out of there after Daala had placed a death sentence on me."

Anger curled through him, making his head buzz, making him feel stronger. He tapped into that strength. "You can understand why the Imperials make me so furious," he said. "It seems that every step of my life the Empire has tried to beat me into submission, tried to take away the rights and pleasures that other life-forms enjoy."

"You can't fight the Empire alone," Dorsk 81 said.

Kyp didn't answer for a long moment. "Perhaps not yet," he said.

Before Dorsk 81 could say anything, Kyp parted a dense clump of blueleaf branches. He felt an electric thrill down his spine as the Force told him they had arrived.

"This," Kyp whispered, "this is our destination."

In front of them the jungle gave way to a circular pond that shone like a flat quicksilver mirror, completely free of ripples. In the center of the lake stood a small island dominated by an obsidian split-pyramid of sharp angles showing the distinctive markings of Massassi architecture: another temple, the same one Gantoris and Streen had located weeks before, but Luke Skywalker had not yet explored it. Exar Kun had told Kyp all about it.

Between the bifurcated spire of the tall pyramid stood a colossus, a polished black statue of a dark man, with long hair swept back behind him, the tattoo of a black sun emblazoned on his forehead, and the padded garments of an ancient lord, the Dark Lord of the Sith.

Kyp swallowed hard at seeing the image of Exar Kun.

"Who do you think he was?" Dorsk 81 asked, squinting to stare across the water.

Kyp answered in a quiet, husky voice. "Someone very powerful."

The great orange sphere of Yavin lurked on the horizon with only a fuzzy curve peeping over the tops of the jungle. The system's small sun would also be setting soon. The twin lights in the sky cast intersecting glitter paths across the still lake.

Kyp gestured toward the temple. "We can spend the night there if you'd like," he said.

Dorsk 81 nodded with more eagerness than Kyp had expected. "I would like to sleep inside shelter again," he said, "rather than up in a tree tangled in vines. But how are we going to get out there? How deep is the lake?"

Kyp went to the edge. The water was as transparent as diamond and so deep that it reflected the bottom like a lens, making it impossible to determine how far down the water went. Just below the surface he saw columns of rock rising from the bottom like submerged stepping stones that stopped just barely beneath the water.

Kyp stepped out onto one. The clear water rippled around the bottom of his shoe, but he did not sink in. He took another step to the second stone.

Dorsk 81 stared at him; Kyp knew that he must appear to be walking directly across the surface of the water. "Are you using the Force?" Dorsk 81 said.

Kyp laughed. "No, I'm using stepping stones."

Without hesitation he splashed to the next stone and then the next, eager to reach the temple—a source of new knowledge and secret techniques. On the island he stepped onto mounds of pitted volcanic rock splotched with orange and green lichen that looked like droplets of alien blood. He could already feel the power.

Kyp turned to watch his companion pick his way across the lake. It looked very much as if Dorsk 81 balanced on the fragile membrane of the pool's surface. The illusion was very effective. Around him silence blanketed the island, as if none of the jungle creatures or insects dared to come near the empty temple.

"It's cold here," Dorsk 81 said, shaking water off his feet and looking around. The smooth-skinned alien hunched his head closer to his shoulders.

"You were complaining before about how hot it was," Kyp said. "You should be grateful."

Dorsk 81 clamped his lipless mouth shut and nodded once, but said nothing else.

Kyp walked around, looking at the polished black glass angles of the pyramid, the jutting point at the top. The architecture had been designed as an angular funnel to concentrate the Force, assembled to enhance the powers of Sith rituals.

He stared up at the frozen statue of Exar Kun. The brooding dark lord looked so real to him, so awe inspiring, that Kyp expected the sculpture to bend down and grasp him.

Kyp knew now that the Great Temple was the focal point for the entire Massassi civilization that Exar Kun had built up from primitive decay. The Great Temple had been the headquarters, the prime focus of Kun's battles in the Sith War. But this small, isolated temple had been more of a private retreat, the place where Exar Kun had concentrated on improving his own abilities, strengthening himself.

A cool wind breathed out of the wedge-shaped opening as if the silent temple were some kind of sleeping monster. "Let's go inside," Kyp said.

He ducked his head and took one step into the enfolding darkness. But when he blinked his eyes, the light gradually grew inside the chamber as if lightning bolts trapped within the black slabs of glass continued to send faint sparks visible only from the corner of his eye. When Kyp faced the polished dark walls, he saw nothing in them, only faint etched markings of hieroglyphics in a long-forgotten language. He could not read any of the words.

Deep green tendrils of moss grew like frozen biological flames that worked their way up the polished stones. Against one wall stood a smooth rounded cistern filled with water.

Kyp stepped over to the cistern and dipped his fingers in, surprised and delighted to find the liquid cold and clean. He splashed his sweaty face, and then he drank, savoring the sweetness of the water as it slid down his throat. He sighed.

Dorsk 81 stood just within the opening, looking out at the jungle beyond the lake. The sphere of Yavin had vanished below the treetops, and the sky began to thicken with purple twilight as the distant sun also set. "I'm very sleepy all of a sudden," he said.

Kyp frowned, but thought he knew what was happening. "You've traveled a long way today," he said. "It's cool and dark in here. Why don't you sleep? The floor looks smooth and comfortable. You can curl up against the wall."

As if hypnotized, Dorsk 81 shambled over to a corner and slithered down against the wall until he lay with his back pressed against the obsidian slab. He fell asleep almost before he had settled into place.

"Now you and I can continue in a more appropriate setting." The deep, loud voice echoed like distant thunder inside the chamber.

Kyp turned to see the hooded silhouette of Exar Kun like a black oil stain shimmering in the air. Kyp stood tall, squashing a thrill of terror every time the ancient Lord of the Sith spoke to him.

Kyp indicated Dorsk 81. "Will he wake up? Will he see you?"

Exar Kun raised his shadowy arms. "Not until we have finished," he said.

"All right." Kyp squatted on the cool floor, tucking his robe around him as he found a comfortable position. He knew that his relaxed attitude might appear to be haughtiness or defiance of Exar Kun, but he didn't care.

The ancient Sith Lord began to speak. "Skywalker has taught you everything he knows. He makes excuses, but he can go no further because he has denied himself other options. He cannot grow as a Jedi by blocking out possibilities, by wearing blinders to what can be and what should be."

Exar Kun loomed over Kyp, hovering closer even though he didn't appear to have taken a step. "You have already learned more than Skywalker will ever know, my student."

Kyp felt enthusiasm and pride burn through him, and he tensed his body, wanting to leap to his feet. But he restrained himself.

"Look at what I can show you today," Exar Kun said, gesturing toward the obsidian walls and the incomprehensible hieroglyphs barely visible, black lines against black volcanic glass. But as Kyp looked at them, the words filled with white fire, standing out against the bottomless, opaque background until they burned into his eyes.

And suddenly Kyp could *understand*. The words snapped into focus and filled his mind, an incredible history from four thousand years ago, telling how Exar Kun had begun to learn forbidden teachings, how he had come to the fourth moon of Yavin to find a lost

Sith power object, and how he had enslaved the timid and weak Massassi people, making them build enormous temples for him as focal points for the dark forces he played with.

"The Brotherhood of the Sith could have ruled the galaxy, could have squashed the doddering Republic and turned the other Jedi Knights into mere parlor magicians—but I was betrayed." The shadow of Exar Kun drifted about the floor of the temple, making no sound as he moved. He hovered over the sleeping and helpless form of Dorsk 81.

"When the Jedi combined their might and came here to this moon to fight me, they unleashed such power that I had to drain dry every last one of the Massassi just to trap my spirit within these temples—to survive so that one day I could come back."

Kun's coal-black arms reached down, as if to strangle Dorsk 81. The smooth-skinned clone stirred uneasily in his spellbound sleep, but he made no move to defend himself.

With a thrill of fear and reluctance, Kyp called out, "Exar Kun! *I'm* the one you're trying to teach. Don't waste your time with him."

He was enthralled by the new wonders Kun had shown him, but Kyp was savvy enough to know when he was being manipulated. Exar Kun thought he was playing Kyp like a mesmerized convert. But Kyp was skeptical— Han Solo had taught him that much. He could play his own part, however, to get what he so desperately wanted.

As Exar Kun turned back to face him, leaving Dorsk 81 unharmed, Kyp spread wide his arms in complete acceptance of his new instructor. "Teach me more about the ancient Sith ways."

Kyp swallowed, then made his voice strong, because this was what he really wanted. "Tell me how to use these new powers so I can crush the Empire once and for all."

21

On Coruscant, Chewbacca and Threepio took the twins through the sculpted duracrete columns at the entrance to the Holographic Zoo of Extinct Animals.

At home the pestering children had rapidly worn down even Threepio's patience programming and had driven Chewbacca into a roaring frenzy. Getting Jacen and Jaina outside seemed like a good idea for all concerned. The foursome took transit tubes across the upper skyscrapers in old Imperial City to reach the rooftop levels of the Holographic Zoo.

At the Zoo's gaudy archway Chewbacca let his furry arms dangle behind him; his huge paws engulfed the tiny hands of the children. Chewbacca took two sprawling strides forward, then waited for the twins to catch up before he took two more steps and waited again. Threepio scuttled ahead as if he were in charge. He had just undergone a deep oil bath so that his gold alloy plating gleamed in the artificial lights.

They stepped under the grandiose arches. Threepio went to the cashier kiosk, punching in Han and Leia's credit code. Chewbacca, impatient with Jacen's and Jaina's short legs, scooped up the twins, one in each arm, and strode forward.

They endured a dull preshow in an empty waiting room filled with chairs, cages, and sockets to accommodate the bodies of all alien visitors, until the far doors automatically clicked open. Chewbacca, still carrying the twins, marched down a sloped tunnel to the lower levels. Threepio hurried after, trying to lead the way, but he could not get past the bulky Wookiee.

Arcing, glowing lights shot overhead, inept simulations of stars and comets and planets. As they passed motion sensors, booming godlike voices echoed in stereo from microspeakers in the walls.

"Journey down the corridors of time! Travel the lanes of space! You will experience forgotten wonders from a long time ago and far, far away. You will see extinct creatures lost from our galaxy but recreated here—and now!"

The walls around them darkened. Streaks of light shot out, funneling down in a crude animation of starlines for a fake journey into hyperspace. The floor beneath their feet rumbled and vibrated in the simulation. The children were startled, but Chewbacca groaned at the corniness of it. The illusion ended, and the recorded voice spoke in a conspiratorial whisper. "We have arrived . . . at a universe of possibilities!"

They stood before a choice of several doorways.

"This way children, this way," Threepio said, stepping forward. He had already scanned the data brochures about the exhibits, and after correlating them with the twins' interests, decided exactly which dioramas he would show them first. "Let us go see the mammoth krabbex of Calamari."

As they stepped through the portal, holograms flared, surrounding them with a turbulent oceanscape, a jagged reef thrusting out from white foamy waters. Standing in a swirl of green-and-purple seaweed battered by the rushing waves stood a segmented crustacean, a ten-legged krabbex with dual mandibles in its mouth, twin rows of spines down its back, and eighteen glossy black eyes, four of which were on its front grasping claws. The krabbex reared up and let out a bellow like a wampa ice creature set on fire.

The twins watched as three green-skinned mermen thrashed out of the foaming waves, cocking jagged spears made of pale bone. The mermen hauled themselves onto the reef and attacked.

The spears pierced the exoskeleton of the krabbex, and the monster clipped at them with its pincers. It swung to the left and grabbed one of the mermen, slicing into his smooth green flesh and dragging him out of the water, where his fused finned legs thrashed like the tail of a fish.

"Let's go," Jaina said.

"Next one," Jacen said.

"But, children, I haven't told you the biological background of these creatures yet," Threepio said.

"Go now," Jaina insisted.

They walked right through the surrounding illusion to the far wall, where several more openings presented themselves. Chewbacca urged the children through the left-hand door.

"Oh, not that one, Chewbacca," Threepio said. "I'm not certain—"

But they had already entered the second chamber to be surrounded by the illusion of a desert planet. Waves of invisible heat rippled from a scabbed, dried clay surface. A strange creature scuttled atop a rocky outcropping with a bloodcurdling roar. It had a squarish humanoid head and a massive feline body, huge curved claws, and a segmented tail that thrashed back and forth, capped with a wicked-looking scorpion stinger. As it opened its mouth to bellow again, cracked yellow fangs dripped with venom.

"A manticore?" Threepio said in disbelief. "Well, really! I'm astonished they haven't updated their display yet. That creature was proved to be a jumble of mismatched fossils long ago. Manticores never existed."

Directly behind them in the hologram another manticore echoed the bellowing challenge and climbed over the baked rocks. The twins tugged on Chewbacca's furry arms and headed through the nonexistent creatures toward the next set of openings.

"Let me choose this time, children," Threepio said.

Chewbacca groaned. The twins didn't seem to care.

"Go home," Jacen said.

Jaina nodded in agreement. "I want to go home."

"But, children," Threepio said, "I'm sure you'll enjoy this next one. Let me tell you all about the mournful singing fig trees of Pil Diller. . . . "

After three more dioramas and three more of Threepio's boring lectures, the twins decided that they would much rather play hide-and-seek than continue the tedious expedition through the Holographic Zoo.

While they couldn't communicate telepathically with each other word for word, they did know in a clear but general way what the other was thinking. When Jacen broke away from Chewbacca to run through the glacier eyries of the Snow Falcons, he headed to the left. At the same time, Jaina sprinted in the opposite direction, brushing past a startled Threepio. The twins used their fledgling talent with the Force to guide them into one of the other openings that led to an exit corridor.

Chewbacca bellowed; Threepio called after the children, but Jacen and Jaina met up outside the dioramas, pleased with their escape and giggling. They trotted down the white-tiled corridor as fast as they could go, past icons for refreshments, rest-and-recharge rooms, repair facilities.

At an intersection of corridors, an old maintenance droid worked in an open turbolift. Jacen and Jaina had seen turbolifts before. That was how they got back home once they reached the Imperial Palace.

The maintenance droid was gunmetal-gray with two heads and numerous mechanical arms, each studded with a handful of attachments. The droid's two heads faced each other. One head bore a set of bright optical sensors, while the other face was a blank screen that displayed data, statistics, and official Imperial Building Code specs.

Muttering to itself in binary, the droid searched its back compartment for a particular tool, found it missing from its bin, then puttered down the corridor. It left the turbolift wide open with only a small dangling sign saying Out of Service.

The children ran for the turbolift and ducked inside. They had watched their parents and Threepio use the controls many times.

The panel looked different from the one in the Imperial Palace: much less ornate, discolored with age and rough use, with a wall of buttons marking hundreds of different floors in the kilometer-high metropolis. Since the lower levels of the city had been abandoned and buried long ago, a thick metal plate had been welded onto the bottom half of the panel, sealing off the first 150 floors. But the maintenance droid had removed the barrier plate to check the turbolift circuits.

The children barely knew their numbers, though Threepio had been trying to get them to recognize the primary numerals. The lessons frequently frustrated the protocol droid, but the twins were bright. They had picked up more than Threepio had realized.

The rows of buttons looked like shiny colorful circles to Jacen and Jaina. They stared at them, not knowing which to push, but they did recognize some of the numbers.

Jaina spotted it first. "Number one," she said.

Jacen pushed the button. "Number one," he repeated.

The turbolift door closed, and the floor fell away as the elevator shot downward, humming as it accelerated. Jacen and Jaina looked at each other in momentary terror; then they giggled. The turbolift descent went on and on, until finally the platform came to a stop. The door whisked open.

Jacen and Jaina stood blinking. They stepped out into the shadowy bottom levels of the forbidden metropolitan wilderness. Around them they heard large startled creatures clattering through the fallen debris.

"It's dark," Jacen said.

Behind the twins the turbolift door slid shut as the elevator reset itself and returned to the upper floors, leaving Jacen and Jaina alone.

Chewbacca blasted through the exhibits like a landspeeder out of control. He howled and called out for the two lost children. Threepio scurried behind him, trying to keep up.

"I can't see anything through these holograms," Threepio said. Chewbacca sniffed for the twins. He charged through another opening.

All the shouting and chaos finally brought one of the Bothan zoo attendants. The Bothan fluffed up his white fur and flailed his arms as he tried to get Chewbacca to calm down. "Shhhh! You are disturbing our other patrons. This is a quiet place for enjoyment and education."

Chewbacca roared at him. The Bothan, much smaller, stood on his pointed toes, trying to draw himself up in a laughably ineffective attempt at meeting Chewbacca's eyes. "We never should have let Wookiees into the Holographic Zoo."

Chewbacca grabbed the Bothan by the white chest hairs and hefted him off the ground. He let loose a string of growls, grunts, and howls.

Threepio rushed up to them. "Excuse me, if I might be allowed to translate," the droid said, "my friend Chewbacca and I are currently searching for two small children who appear to be lost. Their names are Jacen and Jaina. They are two-and-a-half years old."

Chewbacca roared again.

"Yes, yes, I was just getting to that. This is really something of an emergency. The children just ran off from us, and any assistance you could offer—"

Chewbacca used both hands to shake the Bothan attendant like a rag doll.

"—would be most appreciated," Threepio finished.

But the Bothan had fainted.

Jacen and Jaina hiked through a forest of fallen girders, orange and yellow toadstools, and lumpy fungus growing in ancient garbage. Unseen feet skittered across fallen beams and webwork structures overhead.

The massive foundations of the buildings looked indestructible, overgrown with thick moss. Things moved in the shadows, but nothing came clear, even as the childrens' eyes adjusted to the shadowy light. Drips of warm, bad-tasting water fell around them in a slow arrhythmic rain.

Jacen looked up, and the enormous buildings seemed to rise forever and ever. He could glimpse only a blurred slice of what might have been the sky.

"I want to go home," Jaina said.

The wreckage of abandoned equipment lay in piles, rusted and corroded. The twins scrambled over crashed vehicles, the hulks of discarded battleships and fighting machines, deep debris left from the previous year's civil warfare.

Jacen and Jaina came upon a half-collapsed wall that had once contained a computer screen. The terminal lay tilted on its side with the screen smashed inward, leaving broken teeth of transparisteel. But the twins recognized it as a data unit similar to the ones inside their own quarters.

Jacen stood in front of the broken panel and put his small hands on his hips, trying to look like his father. He addressed the computer screen—and he knew exactly what to say, after having heard the bedtime story many times before. "We are lost," he said. "Please help us find our home."

He waited and waited but received no response. No lights illuminated the panels. He heard no answer from the torn speaker unit, where glistening black beetles had made a nest.

Jacen sighed. Jaina took his hand, and the two turned around as they heard a slithering sound down the cramped alleyway.

A formless gray-green creature paused behind them, a granite slug with two eyes protruding on gelatinous stalks as if assessing the two children. As it moved, it scoured green sludge off the cracked duracrete alleyway, trailing thick translucent slime.

The granite slug slithered toward them, and the twins backed away. From the bottom of the slug's underbelly, a jagged crack opened up, a quivering lipless mouth that sucked in a long hollow whistle of air.

Jaina stepped up to it. It was her turn this time.

"We are lost," she said. "Please help us find our home."

The granite slug reared until it towered over the little girl. She blinked up at it. Jacen stood by her side.

Then the granite slug seemed to deflate again, hooked its body into a broken passage to the right, and landed on the stones with a wet slapping sound.

A rustle of wind suddenly kicked up, and the granite slug churned down the side alley in alarm. Jacen looked up just in time to see the sharp mantalike wings of a hawk-bat that swooped down from high above, metallic talons outstretched.

The granite slug attempted to burrow into the rusted debris, but the hawk-bat landed on top of the wreckage, ripping and tearing at the fallen hunks of metal with its claws. Its triangular beak bobbed up and down like a piston until it had exposed the granite slug and slashed at the slimy creature. The hawk-bat flapped its broad wings again, heading toward the sky with its squirming, dripping prey.

Jacen and Jaina looked up at the creature, then at each other. The two began trudging through the dark underworld of Coruscant again.

Jaina said, "And he walked, and he walked. . . "

"We must sound the alarm *immediately*, Chewbacca!" Threepio said. But the Wookiee seemed reluctant to admit they had lost the two small children.

They left the unconscious Bothan attendant in one of the holographic dioramas, then made their way to the white-tiled corridor leading to the souvenir shops, refreshment stands, and other parts of the museum. Threepio wondered what the poor Bothan would think when he woke up lying inside the web lair of a cannibal arachnid from Duros.

A maintenance droid finished its turbolift repairs and removed the Out of Service sign. Its two heads began humming a duet to themselves at having completed a satisfying menial task.

Chewbacca pointed to the maintenance droid, but Threepio became indignant. "What could a low-level maintenance droid possibly know about this situation? Those models aren't much smarter than loader vehicles." But a large Wookiee hand dragged him along. "Oh, all right, if you insist."

Chewbacca sprinted ahead and stood in the path of the trundling maintenance droid. Automatic sensors instructed the droid to swerve one way, then the other, but Chewbacca forced it to stop. The maintenance droid emitted a high-pitched whine of confusion.

Threepio came up behind it. "Excuse me," he said, and garbled out a long series of crude binary questions. The maintenance droid answered with a *blat* like a stepped-on steam whistle. Threepio repeated his question, but got the same answer.

"I told you he'd be no use," Threepio said. "Maintenance droids aren't programmed to notice anything. They just do their repairs and wait for new instructions."

Chewbacca moaned, shaking his big hairy head.

Threepio said, "Oh, be quiet, you . . . you big walking carpet—I was *not* talking too much! Besides, *you're* the one who has the life debt to Han Solo."

The maintenance droid continued, oblivious to their bickering. Threepio wished that he could simplify his own programming and be so blissfully ignorant in the ways of the galaxy. He felt his circuits overheating as the full impact of what might happen to him slammed down on his poor head.

"Master Solo will probably remove my legs and make me recompile and alphabetize all the fragmented files in the Imperial Information Center!"

In the dim underworld Jacen pointed to a noisy machine in front of them as the cluttered street widened. "Look," he said. "Droid."

The children ran, waving their hands and hoping to get the droid's attention. But they stopped as the machine continued along a polished path worn through the debris.

The droid was vastly older than the maintenance model up at the turbolift. It had bulkier joints, squarish limbs; large bolts held the pieces together. The antique repair droid was little more than a mobile cart of tools with a torso, arms, and an angled hexagonal head. One of its optical sensors had fallen off. Thick cables ran down its spine and along its neck, corroded and caked with dust and dirt. Moss had begun to grow on its sides. It moved with a stuttering motion as if desperately in need of lubricant.

Along the street a line of corroded poles stood a meter taller than the twins. Atop each pole rested an old glowcrystal, engraved with magnifying facets, but each crystal was a dead translucent gray, shedding no light into the dim streets. Some poles had come loose from their ground-level moorings and tilted sideways.

The repair droid worked its way to the end of the street, stopped at an appropriate position, and ratcheted its torso high on accordion joints so its arms could reach the darkened glowcrystal. The droid removed the burned-out crystal, cradling it carefully in segmented pincers. After placing it in the back of the cart, the repair droid removed another thick glowcrystal from an open bin. Following complex programming, the droid positioned the replacement crystal on top of the pole and activated it.

The new glowcrystal remained as dead and lightless as the first, but the repair droid didn't seem to notice. It moved to the next pole, repeating the process.

Jacen stood in front of the droid, addressing it in his best Daddy voice. "We're lost," he said.

Jaina came up beside him. "Please help us find our home."

The repair droid ratcheted up as if in alarm, then lowered itself down to study the children with its single optical sensor. "Lost?" it said in a clanking voice.

"Home," Jaina insisted.

"Not in my programming," the droid said. "Not my main task." It ratcheted up again and moved to a third malfunctioning glowcrystal pole. "Not in my programming."

Jaina and Jacen began to cry. But upon hearing each other, rather than reinforcing their tears, the twins stopped. "Be brave," Jaina said.

"Brave," Jacen agreed.

The two exhausted twins sat down on a time-smoothed chunk of duracrete in the middle of the open street. They watched the repair droid continue removing dead glowcrystals from poles and replacing them with equally useless lights.

The droid moved all the way to the end of the street, unsuccessful in getting any of the streetlights to work again. Then, picking up speed, it whirred down the worn path it had traveled for a hundred years, back to where it had started.

The droid stopped in front of the first dead glowcrystal pole all over again, ratcheted itself up, and replaced the lightless crystal it had changed only a short while earlier with another one. . . .

22

 Still reeling from the destruc-
tion of the *Manticore*, Admiral Daala slumped against
the bridge rail. She found herself at a loss for words as
the battle on Calamari continued.

"Wipe them out," she said. "Open fire with all
turbolaser batteries from orbit. Target every floating
city." She stared with glassy eyes out the *Gorgon*'s wide
viewport. "Destroy them all."

She couldn't understand what had gone wrong. She
had followed Grand Moff Tarkin's tactics exactly. He
had trained her carefully, giving her all the information she should have needed. But since Daala
had emerged from Maw Installation, she had met
with one disaster after another. The Sun Crusher
fallen into Rebel hands, the *Hydra* destroyed, and
now the *Manticore*. True, she had been successful
in hijacking a small supply vessel, and she had
obliterated an insignificant colony on Dantooine—
but now on her first major attack against a Rebel

world, she had again lost a Star Destroyer through her own overconfidence.

She had failed. Utterly.

Beside the *Gorgon* in a companion flightpath rode the *Basilisk*. Together, they fired volleys of turbolasers into the oceans, incinerating submerged Calamarian structures. In moments they would cross the terminator line between day and night, where they could fire down upon two more of the massive floating cities. They would vaporize the structures, sending all the inhabitants to a watery death.

"Dispatch the last TIE squadron," she said, staring at the fiery battlefield of the ocean world below. "I want to lay this entire planet waste."

"Admiral!" Commander Kratas ran between the sensor and tactical stations and up the two steps to the observation platform. "Rebel battleships have just come out of hyperspace, an entire fleet, more than we can hope to fight."

Daala whirled in disbelief. "They responded to a distress call that quickly?" Then she too saw the glinting figures of large battleships streaking like comets toward them in planetary orbit.

Her breath caught in her throat. The shipyards remained unscathed except for minor sorties. She had not met her primary objective in the attack on Calamari. Still . . . they had destroyed at least one floating city, wrecked another, damaged two more.

"Recall all TIE squadrons," Daala said. "Plot a straight-line vector through hyperspace to the Cauldron Nebula. We'll go back and reassess our tactics, determine our losses." She paused, then raised her voice like a torch of anger. "And we'll prepare our next attack!"

The TIE fighters streamed back into the holds of the Star Destroyers. The Rebel defensive forces swung around in orbit like a pack of carnivores. Daala did not dare risk fighting them, though she wanted nothing more than to rip the throats out of their commanders with her bare hands.

"Ready for hyperspace," she said before the reinforcements could swoop in to attack. Daala watched the starfields elongate into bright white lines that funneled into a vanishing point on the other side of the universe.

Her Star Destroyers entered hyperspace, leaving the New Republic forces hopelessly behind.

Han Solo and Lando Calrissian soared through the skies of Calamari in the *Millennium Falcon,* searching for columns of smoke rising from devastated floating settlements.

They had found Foamwander City, but when they landed on one of the emergency pads, they learned that Admiral Ackbar, Leia, and Ambassador Cilghal had already departed on a rescue mission to the sunken city of Reef Home.

Han, wrapped up in dismay at the devastation caused by Admiral Daala's forces, felt no particular jubilation at being the pilot and owner of the *Falcon.* All exhilaration at winning his ship back had evaporated upon seeing the destruction that had been wreaked on the ocean world.

Lando sat at Chewbacca's station, staring at the navigation charts. "Looks like Reef Home City should be coming up somewhere below. I detect plenty of scattered metallic masses, but nothing that might be a metropolis."

"No, just the remains," Han said in a low voice.

As they skimmed low, he looked out the *Falcon*'s viewports at floating wreckage scattered on the waves. Blackened tracings of blaster scars showed prominently on the fragmented metal. Broken chunks of the floating city, sealed and airtight with flood bulkheads, remained afloat like buoyant coffins; Calamarian and Quarren rescuers swarmed over the self-contained segments, trying to break through to free those inside.

"That used to look like Cloud City," Han said. "Now it looks like leftovers from a garbage masher." He pointed to a smooth chunk of Reef Home's outer shell. "Think we can set down on that section over there?"

Lando gave a nonchalant shrug. "Nobody'd even notice the *Falcon* among all this other junk."

"Hey," Han said.

Lando looked at him. "She's your ship, Han. I just wish I had the *Lady Luck* back."

Han set the *Falcon* down on the rocking plasteel debris, locked down the stabilizers, then broke open the door seals. As he clambered down the exit ramp, he scanned the rescuers to see if he could find Leia. He hadn't held her in his arms in so long.

As usual, when they were forced apart, he thought of all sorts of things he wanted to say to her, the promises and sweet nothings she deserved, though he usually didn't manage to force them through his gruff exterior.

Lando followed him, and they both stared at the wounded who had been dragged onto the floating wreckage of the Calamarian city. Although waves sloshed over the metal edges, for now they had been designated infirmary areas, relatively stable platforms on which the medics could tend the injured.

The smell of blood and salt filled the air, mixed with the chemical stench of laser burns, molten metal quenched in the sea, and smoke from fires that continued to burn.

Tentacle-faced Quarren bobbed up from the waves. Water trickled down their heads as they brought up important components from Reef Home's computer core or personal items rescued from breached living quarters. The Quarren would no doubt claim salvage rights for the entire hulk, and they would sell personal belongings back to the Calamarians.

Han stood with his legs spread wide for greater balance on a drifting fragment. The choppy sea made the platform lurch in slow motion, rocking up and down. He finally noticed a wavespeeder skimming toward the wreckage. Leia piloted it, accompanied by Ackbar and a female Calamarian.

Han waved frantically, and the wavespeeder veered toward him, coming alongside. Leia leaped off the vehicle as Ackbar lashed it to a ragged stump of torn metal. She walked confidently, then ran, keeping her balance as she flung herself into Han's arms. He hugged her against his chest as he kissed her again and again. "I'm so glad you're safe!"

She looked at him. "I know."

"Stop that," Han said. "I'm serious. Daala did this, didn't she?"

"We think so, but we have no proof yet."

He cut her off. "No question in my mind about it. Daala has no political motives—she just wants to destroy things."

The female Calamarian climbed out of the wave-speeder and went to the triage area, glancing at the bleeding Calamarians as far too few medics attempted to tend them. She walked among the injured, making quick pronouncements, as if she could somehow determine their chances for survival.

Two medics worked desperately to resuscitate a Quarren whose arm had been amputated and his chest crushed. She took one glance and said, "He won't survive, and you can do nothing more to make him survive." The two Calamarian healers looked at her and, seeing the absolute conviction on her face, moved to another patient and let the Quarren die.

Like an angel of life and death, she walked among them, staring down, tilting her head and swiveling her round Calamarian eyes from side to side.

Han watched her as she moved. "Who is that?"

"Her name is Cilghal. She's the Calamarian ambassador," Leia said, then lowered her voice. "I think she has Jedi powers. She doesn't know it yet. I'm going to make sure she goes to see Luke." Leia hugged her husband again. "I'm so glad you came."

"I was on my way the moment I heard," Han answered. He cocked an eyebrow as he looked at Lando. "By the way, we played another little game of sabacc en route. This time I won." He offered an arm to his wife. "Would you like a ride home in *my* ship, Leia?"

"The *Falcon*'s yours again?" she said with delight, then slipped her arm through his. Still grinning, she looked at Lando. "Sorry to hear that, Lando."

He shrugged. "It was one way to get him off my back."

Ackbar climbed out of the skimmer and stood on the rocking wreckage. He raised one broad hand to shield his lumpy brow as he looked over the scattered debris of Reef Home City. Han had never been good at telling expressions on the Calamarian admiral's face, but Ackbar seemed devastated.

He went to where Ackbar stood all alone. "Admiral," Han said, "I heard what you did, how you defeated an entire Star Destroyer. Great work."

Leia moved beside him in her white robes. "Admiral, your victory here *must* make up for the simple accident on Vortex. I hope you aren't considering going back into hiding?"

Ackbar shook his massive head. "No, Leia. You've reminded me of one thing with your friendly insistence. I am not the type of person who can hide. I must do what I can, and as much as I can. Hiding is for others. Action is for myself."

Leia placed a hand on the Admiral's thick bicep. "Thank you, Admiral. The New Republic needs you," she said.

But Ackbar shook his head. "No, Leia, I won't be returning to Coruscant. After this attack I can see just how much my own people need me. I must stay here on Calamari to help my people rebuild, to strengthen their civilization, and to tighten their defenses against future Imperial strikes.

"We still have not recovered from the onslaught of the World Devastators, and now a new fleet has laid waste to our floating cities. I can't just leave Calamari now and go back." He turned his circular eyes up into the leaden sky and said, "This planet is my home. These are my people. I must devote my energies to helping them."

Han slipped his arm around Leia's waist and squeezed her. She felt stiff and cold; he knew exactly what she was thinking. "I understand . . . Ackbar," Leia said, finally dropping his military title.

Han could sense her tension, knowing how the loss of Ackbar devastated her. Han gripped her shoulder, feeling iron cords of tension rippling beneath her smooth skin.

With Ackbar's refusal to return to Coruscant, and with Mon Mothma growing weaker day by day, that meant Leia had to face all the problems of the New Republic alone.

23

aylight shone through the rectangular skylights of the Great Temple. Kyp sat on an uncomfortable stone bench in the grand audience chamber, listening to Master Skywalker. He pretended to pay attention, though it became more and more difficult as his opinion of Skywalker's knowledge dwindled.

The other Jedi trainees sat in rapt attention as Master Skywalker placed the small white Holocron on its pedestal. It told yet another story of the ancient Jedi Knights, extolling their heroic adventures, their battles against the dark side—all ultimately ineffectual, because the Emperor and Darth Vader had been stronger than the Jedi Knights, squashing them.

Skywalker refused to learn from that failure. If he meant to bring the new Jedi Knights to greater power, he would have to recognize new abilities, make his Order of Jedi Knights powerful enough to resist a purge like Vader's.

Exar Kun had shown Kyp the ways of the Sith. But Master Skywalker would never adopt those teachings. Kyp wondered why he bothered to keep listening to Skywalker. He seemed so weak, so indecisive.

The other students were a potential wellspring of strength. They had learned how to tap the Force, but they had gone no further than a novice level, mere magicians, playacting in a role that was too big for any of them. They refused to peek behind the doors of greater power; but Kyp was not afraid. *He* could handle the responsibility.

Another holographic gatekeeper of the Holocron appeared and began telling the story of how young Yoda had become a Jedi. Kyp stifled a yawn, unable to understand why they had to keep watching these trivial histories.

He craned his neck to look at the walls of the enormous stone temple. In his mind he tried to imagine the Great Sith War four thousand years ago. He thought of the damp-skinned Massassi race enslaved by Exar Kun, used by him as tools to build the temples that he had reconstructed from even more ancient and forgotten Sith records. Kun had revitalized the dark teachings, granting himself the title of Dark Lord of the Sith, a tradition passed down all the way to Darth Vader, who had been the last Sith Lord.

Exar Kun's temples had been erected across Yavin 4—the last archaeological resting place of the incredibly ancient Sith race—as focal points for his power. Kun had ruled here on the jungle moon, controlling forces that had nearly defeated the Old Republic. But the warlord Jedi Ulic Qel-Droma had betrayed him; and all the united Jedi had swept down in a final battle on Yavin 4, exterminating the Massassi natives, leveling most of the Sith temples, razing most of the rain forest in a holocaust from the skies. But Exar Kun had managed to encyst his spirit here, waiting four thousand years until other Jedi came to awaken him. . . .

Kyp fidgeted and pretended to pay attention. The temple chamber seemed extremely hot. The Holocron droned on and on.

Luke listened with a beatific smile, and the other students continued to observe the images. Kyp gazed at the walls and wondered why he was there.

As half night fell across the jungles of Yavin 4, Luke Skywalker sat back and allowed himself to relax in one of the meeting halls. Smaller than the grand audience chamber, the hall had arched stone ceilings and polished tables, along with serviceable furniture left behind by the Rebel occupation. Bright glowlamps hung in old torch sconces.

Luke felt bone weariness seeping though his body and hunger gnawing in his stomach. For now the students relaxed, recharging their mental energy.

All day long Luke had supervised them through Force exercises, levitation training, visualizing battles and conflicts, sensing other animals and creatures in the forest, learning Jedi history from the Holocron. He was pleased with how well they were doing; though the death of Gantoris still felt like an open wound, he saw that his other students were making great progress. He felt confident in being able to bring back the Jedi Knights.

One of the trainees, Tionne, sat in the corner preparing to play a stringed musical instrument: two hollow resonating boxes separated by a shaft strung with tonal cords.

"This is the ballad of Nomi Sunrider," she said, "one of the historical Jedi Knights." She smiled. Long silvery hair streamed past her shoulders, hanging down to her chest and splitting like a white-capped river down her back. Her eyes were small and close set, glinting with a mother-of-pearl sheen. Her nose was small, her jaw squarish. Luke thought she looked more exotic than beautiful.

Tionne had a great passion for the old Jedi legends and ballads and histories. Even before Luke found her, she had dedicated her life to resurrecting the old stories, digging them out of the archives and popularizing them. Luke had tested Tionne's Jedi talent, and while her potential was perhaps less than the other students', she made up for it with absolute devotion and enthusiasm.

The others found chairs, benches, or just a smooth spot on the floor to hear Tionne sing. She laid the instrument in her lap, and as the trainees listened, she plucked the strings with both hands, setting up an echoing music that fed and subtracted from her lyrics as she sang.

Luke closed his eyes and heard her tale about young Nomi Sunrider, who, after her husband's murder, attended the Jedi training that had been meant for him. Nomi had become a pivotal character in the devastating Sith War that pitted Jedi against Jedi in the ancient days of the Old Republic.

Luke smiled as he heard the music, the resonating notes, Tionne's soft and watery voice as she sang with passion. From the far side of the room, Luke heard a restless stirring and turned to see Kyp Durron, his face stormy with a scowl. The young man sighed, scowled again, and finally stood up, interrupting Tionne's song.

"I wish you wouldn't perpetuate that ridiculous story," Kyp said. "Nomi Sunrider was a victim. She fought in the Sith Wars without ever understanding what the battles were about. She listened blindly to her Jedi Masters, who were afraid because Exar Kun had discovered a way for the Jedi to increase their power."

Tionne set her musical instrument on the flagstones and gripped her knees through the fabric of her robe. Her face looked stricken, her small eyes glinting with confusion. "What are you talking about?" Her voice was thick with discouragement. "I've spent weeks reconstructing that legend. Everyone here knew what I was doing. If you had other information, Kyp, why didn't you share it with me?"

"Where did you learn all this history, Kyp?" Luke said, standing up. He put his hands on his hips, trying to stare Kyp down. The young man had become more and more volatile as he acquired Jedi knowledge. *Calm, you must be calm,* Yoda had said, but Luke didn't know how to make Kyp calm.

Kyp flashed his glance across the trainees, who looked at him in astonishment. "If the Sith War had turned out differently," he said, "perhaps the Jedi Knights would have learned how to *defend* themselves when Darth Vader came hunting, and they wouldn't all have been slaughtered. The Jedi would never have fallen, and we wouldn't be *here,* taught by someone who doesn't know any more than we do."

Luke remained adamant. "Kyp, tell me where you learned all this."

Kyp pushed his lips together and narrowed his eyes. He drew several deep breaths, and Luke could sense the turmoil inside him, as if his mind were working rapidly to come up with an answer. "I can use the Holocron too," he said. "As Master Skywalker keeps telling us, we are all obligated to learn everything we can."

Luke didn't quite believe the young man's words, but before he could ask another question, Artoo trundled in, warbling and chittering in alarm. Luke deciphered some of the electronic language. "No idea who it is?" he said.

Artoo whistled a descending hooting negative.

"We have a visitor," Luke announced. "A ship is landing on the grid right now. Shall we go out to greet the pilot?" He turned to place a firm hand on Kyp's shoulder, but the young man shrugged away. "We'll discuss this later, Kyp."

Relieved to have a distraction that would shatter the tension, Luke led the way. The other Jedi students followed him down the stone steps and through the hangar bay to the cleared landing grid.

A small personal fighter—a Z-95 Headhunter, a sleek metallic cruiser often used by smugglers—circled and eased down into the clearing. The other students stood at the edge of the grid, but Luke came forward.

The cockpit doors swung up like the wings of a great insect and the pilot emerged. Luke saw a sleek silvery suit clinging to the curves of a young woman's body. She stepped down, pulled off an opaque helmet and shook her dark reddish-brown hair. Her angular face had once been pinched with determination, but now seemed softened, her eyes wider, her full lips not entirely unaccustomed to a smile.

"Mara Jade," Luke said.

She tucked the helmet under her left arm, squeezing it against her rib cage. "Hello, Luke." She looked at him with just the hint of a friendly expression, then raised her eyebrows. "Or do I have to call you 'Master Skywalker' now?"

Luke shrugged, holding out his arms to welcome her. "That depends on why you're here."

She left the Headhunter open behind her as she strode across the clearing to take his hand in greeting. Then she swiveled in a military-style maneuver to survey the dozen students that had come to Luke's training center.

"You told me I had the ability to use the Force," she said. "I came here to learn more about it. Jedi powers could help me run the smugglers' guild."

She unzipped a flexible pouch at her side and tugged out a packet of microcompacted folds of cloth, more than Luke could believe would fit inside a tiny package. She shook the brownish folds, unwrapping her garment.

She looked at the identical garments on all of Luke's trainees and then back at him. "See," she said. "I even brought a Jedi robe."

Over a generous meal of spiced runyip stew and bowls of chopped edible greens, Luke watched Mara Jade feed herself as if she were famished. Luke savored every bite, sensing the nutrients and energies as they slowly permeated his body.

"The New Republic is counting on your Jedi Knights, Luke, and things are getting much worse out there," she said.

Luke leaned forward, lacing his fingers together and trying to pick up echoes of her emotions. "What's happening?" he said. "We're starved for news."

"Well," Mara Jade said, still chewing a mouthful of greens. She swallowed and took a drink of cold spring water, frowning at it as if she had expected something else.

"Admiral Daala has continued her depredations. She doesn't seem to be allied with any of the Imperial warlords. From what we can tell, she's just trying to cause a lot of damage to anyone who opposed the Empire—and she *is* causing plenty of damage. You know that she has been hitting supply ships, blowing them out of space? She leveled the new colony on Dantooine."

"Dantooine!" Luke said.

Mara looked at him. "Yes, isn't one of your students from that group of people?"

Luke sat rigid. Some of the trainees gasped in shock. His mind whirled, thinking of all the refugees he had helped relocate to a supposedly safe place from the treacherous world of Eol Sha. But now they had been wiped out.

"Not anymore," he said. "Gantoris died. He was . . . unprepared for the powers he tried to use."

Mara Jade raised her thin eyebrows, waited for him to explain further. When Luke said nothing else, she continued. "The worst part was when Daala struck the planet Calamari. Seems she meant to take out the orbiting shipyards, but Admiral Ackbar recognized her tactics. He blew up one of her three Star Destroyers—but Daala still managed to sink two Calamarian floating cities. Countless thousands died."

Kyp Durron stood up at the far end of the long table. "Daala lost another one of her Star Destroyers?"

Mara Jade looked at him as if noticing the young dark-haired man for the first time. "She still has two Star Destroyers, and no inhibitions. Admiral Daala can still cause incredible destruction, and she has a weapon no one else seems to have: she knows she's got nothing to lose."

"I should have sacrificed myself," Kyp said. "I could have killed her with my bare hands when I was on the *Gorgon*."

He lowered his voice, relating the story Luke already knew. "We stole the Sun Crusher out from under her nose, and we wasted our opportunity. We had a weapon that could have struck a decisive blow against the worlds still loyal to the Empire—but what did we do with it? We threw the Sun Crusher into a gas planet where it won't help us at all."

"Calm," Luke said. He gestured for Kyp to sit back down, but Kyp placed his hands flat on the veined stone table, leaning over to glare at Luke.

"The Imperial threat is not going to go away!" he said. "If we pool our Jedi powers, we can resurrect the Sun Crusher, tear it out from the core of Yavin. We can take it and go hunt the Imperials. What could be a clearer mission for us? Why are we just hiding here on this backwater moon?"

He paused, fuming. When the other students looked at him, Kyp glared back at them. "Are you all stupid?" he shouted. "We don't have the luxury to fine-tune our levitating abilities, or balance rocks, or sense rodents out in the jungle. What good does that do? If we aren't going to use our powers to *help* the New Republic, then why bother?"

Luke looked at Mara Jade, who seemed greatly interested in this discussion. He refocused his attention on Kyp. The young man's meal was practically untouched.

"Because that isn't the Jedi way," Luke said. "You've studied the Code. You know how we must approach a difficult situation. The Jedi do not set out to destroy recklessly."

Kyp turned his back on Luke and stormed toward the door of the dining chamber. At the arched stone entrance to the room, Kyp whirled and said, "If we don't use our power, then we may as well not have it. We're betraying the Force with our cowardice."

He gritted his teeth, and his words came out much more quietly. "I'm not certain what else I can learn here, Master Skywalker." With that, he vanished into the corridor.

Kyp felt his skin tingling with barely contained power, as if his blood had begun to fizz inside of him. He moved down the temple corridors like a projectile, and when he reached the heavy door to his quarters, he used the Force to fling it open and slam it against the far wall with enough strength to flake a long splinter of stone from the blocks.

How could he ever have admired Master Skywalker? What did Han Solo see in him as a friend? The Jedi teacher was blind to reality, ignoring problems, covering his eyes with his Jedi cloak, and refusing to use his own powers for the good of the New Republic! The Empire remained a threat, as Daala's attacks on Calamari and

Dantooine demonstrated—if Skywalker refused to use his powers to wipe out the enemy, then perhaps his convictions were not strong enough.

But Kyp's were.

He could stay at the Jedi academy no longer. He yanked at the collar of his robe to tear it off. From his stash of personal belongings Kyp pulled out a satchel that contained the flowing black cape that Han had given him as a good-bye gift. During his training at the *praxeum,* he had been content to wear the rough old robe Master Skywalker provided. But now he wanted nothing more to do with it.

Exar Kun had shown him how to unleash great powers. Kyp did not trust the Sith Lord, but he could not deny the truth of what the shadow man taught. Kyp could see the power actually working.

For now he had to get away to ponder and sort through the conflicting thoughts in his mind.

He opened up the satchel to look at the black cape. A pair of small, lightning-fast rodents dashed out from their nest in his garment and vanished like hot liquid through a chink in the stone wall.

Alarmed, Kyp lost control of his anger for an instant and let fly a searing blast of power that followed the two rodents down their narrow tunnels and incinerated them as they ran. Blackened bones tumbled forward with the momentum, then slumped to dust in the stone tunnel.

Paying no more heed to the distraction, Kyp pulled out the flowing cape, holding it in front of him. Its embedded reflective threads sparkled as if with hidden power. Kyp wrapped it around himself and gathered a few of his other possessions.

He had to go far away. He had to think. He had to be strong.

Later that evening, when Artoo sounded all the alarms, Luke awoke instantly. He sprinted down the corridors to the outside landing area. Mara Jade ran beside him, already alert, as if she had a good idea of what might be happening.

Luke's eyes adjusted rapidly to the star-strewn sky, which was fuzzy and pale in the south with skyshine from the gas giant Yavin. Mara and Luke stood outside the half-open hangar doors as they watched her Z-95 Headhunter rise from the landing grid with all its running lights darkened.

"He's stealing my ship!" Mara Jade shouted. The Headhunter's sublight engines kicked in, burning white-hot behind the craft as it shot into the sky.

Luke shook his head in disbelief and realized that he had unconsciously extended one hand, beckoning for Kyp Durron to return.

The small ship became a white streak of light that grew smaller and smaller as it reached orbit, then set out among the stars.

Luke felt a devastating emptiness, knowing that he had lost another of his Jedi students forever.

24

E**very flagstone gleamed. Every**
Imperial column had been scrubbed white. Every colorful
banner representing the Empire's most loyal worlds hung
absolutely straight, displayed without a wrinkle. Everything was in order at the main citadel of the Imperial
Military Academy on Carida.

Ambassador Furgan nodded. Just the way he liked
it.

Three hundred crack stormtroopers stood at attention
in the echoing hall, motionless in perfect ranks. Their
white armor glistened like polished bone. They were
identical, intensively trained, precise military machines.
These stormtroopers were the best of the best in the academy. Only the top Imperial recruits even began stormtrooper training, and these three hundred had excelled
in every way.

Ambassador Furgan moved toward the podium to
address them. The smell of oils and waxes on the
synthetic wood seemed potent in the otherwise sterilized

air. Furgan drew himself up, trying to look larger than his stocky stature allowed. The white helmets turned in unison to track him with their black goggles.

"Imperial troops," he said, "you have been chosen to lead the most important mission since the fall of our beloved Emperor. You have endured hardship and passed many tests during your training. I have chosen you as the elite, the best trainees remaining on Carida."

They did not stir, did not congratulate each other. They remained like ranks of statues—which itself attested to the thoroughness of their training.

Since receiving the long-awaited coordinates of the secret planet Anoth, Furgan had plotted this operation with extreme caution. He had studied the personnel data of thousands of his best troops. He had analyzed the records of their training exercises: mock combat in the harsh ice caps of Carida; prolonged sieges out in the baked and waterless deserts; jungle survival tours through dense and uncharted rain forests filled with primitive predators, carnivorous plants, and poisonous insects.

Furgan had culled the names of those stormtroopers who had shown the most stamina, the most initiative, the greatest success, coupled with the strongest willingness to follow every order.

He was proud of his assault force.

"We have obtained secret information regarding the location of a certain baby. A child with enormous potential for using the Force." He paused, expecting to hear them groan, but the stormtroopers made no sound.

"This child is the son of Leia Organa Solo, the New Republic's Minister of State. If we were to apprehend this child, it would deal an enormous psychological blow to the Rebellion—but beyond that, *this boy is the grandson of Darth Vader.*"

There, finally, he thought he heard a rustle of superstitious fear or awe.

"This child could be extremely valuable to the rebirth of the Empire. A child such as this, raised properly and trained properly, could become a worthy successor to the Emperor Palpatine."

Furgan kept talking, faster now as he felt the excitement within him. He was more than just an ambassador; he planned to go along on this assault himself. He would not expose himself to any part of the attack, of course, but he would be there to snatch the young child named Anakin.

"Your unit leaders will provide you with specific assignments. This expedition is currently being provisioned. We have secured transports to take you to the secret location of this world."

Furgan allowed himself a broad grin with his thick purplish lips. "It is also my pleasure to announce that this assault will mark the first combat use of our new Mountain Terrain Armored Transports on which you have been training these past months. That is all. Hail to the Emperor!"

The thunderous response of filtered stormtrooper voices came back at him, rocking the hall. "Hail to the Emperor!"

Furgan slipped behind the hanging purple curtains into a walkway that led down empty glow-lit corridors toward his secure office. Inside his chambers he closed the blast-proof door and sealed it with a cipher lock. He brushed aside models and plans of the deadly new MT-AT attack vehicles. He felt immensely pleased with himself and eager for the assault to start.

Sitting on Carida during the years of turmoil, Furgan had been upset with all the squabbling Imperial commanders since the Emperor's death. Many of the warlords in the Core Systems were extremely powerful, yet they spent their time wrestling for dominance among the remnants of the Imperial fleet rather than fighting against their real enemy, the Rebellion.

Grand Admiral Thrawn had seemed their greatest hope, but he had been defeated; and a year later even the resurrected Emperor had been defeated. The power vacuum of leadership left the Imperial forces with no leadership, no goal, battling only for their own advancement.

Even this surprise new threat by renegade Admiral Daala disturbed Furgan. At least Daala was putting her Star Destroyers to an appropriate use, attacking Rebel worlds and creating as much havoc as possible. But Daala had no overriding plan, no strategy that would bring her ultimate success. She was simply a juggernaut, striking target after target for the satisfaction of causing pain.

Furgan had discovered to his surprise that Daala herself had been trained on Carida. Digging through old records, he had uncovered many disciplinary actions taken against her, reprimands in her file. Even then she had been a maverick, performing admirably but refusing to learn her place, insisting that she deserved promotions instead of others. Furgan had no record of her advancement to admiral, but Moff Tarkin had transferred her to his personal staff after one of his brief inspection tours.

Furgan had no other information about Daala since that time.

It angered him that this admiral continued her attacks on the Rebellion without even attempting to get in touch with Carida. Perhaps Daala considered herself a vigilante, but the Empire needed its soldiers to fight as parts of an immense whole. The Empire did not need vigilantes.

Furgan had tried to contact some of the other battling Imperial commanders to get capital ships for his assault on Anoth. The Emperor and Grand Admiral Thrawn and other depredations had already taken most of the ships available to Carida. On the military training planet, Furgan had access to some of the most sophisticated weaponry and soldiers in the entire galaxy—but because of the perpetual squabbles between the Imperial Army and the spacefaring Imperial Navy, he had no place to go with his troops. This left Furgan in a position of being on the most heavily armed—but useless—planet still loyal to the Empire.

Furgan absently played with one of the articulated models of the MT-AT fighting vehicle. It would be fascinating to see the marvelous new machine in operation. Even with the death of the Emperor, his loyalty to the Empire and the New Order had never been shaken, not even slightly.

Furgan kept doing his best to strike vital blows against the New Republic, one way or another. He was pleased to watch indirect reports that gave him evidence of the inexorable progress of Mon Mothma's "mysterious illness." She would be dead before long.

And as soon as Furgan had the grandson of Darth Vader in his possession, all those still loyal to the Empire would have to listen to him.

25

When Wedge Antilles wasn't looking, Qwi Xux stole a glance at the coordinates displayed on his navigation panel. Sitting in the co-pilot's seat of the disguised personal space yacht, Qwi used her nimble fingers to tap the coordinates into the navicomputer, requesting a full display.

Wedge looked away from the starfield and caught what she was doing. "Hey!" he said, then grinned sheepishly as he lowered his gaze. "This was supposed to be a surprise."

Qwi laughed, a cascade of short musical tones. "I just wanted to know the name of the planet." She frowned as the display came up. "Ithor? Never heard of it."

Wedge chuckled and reached over to squeeze her slender shoulder. She felt the warmth of his touch linger for several moments after he removed his hand. "Qwi, you've never heard of *most* places in the galaxy. You spent your entire life cooped up in Maw Installation."

"Is Ithor a nice place?" she asked.

He sighed. "It's beautiful. A pristine natural world covered with forests and jungles, rivers and waterfalls. We'll be incognito, and you won't have to worry about anybody knowing who you are."

Qwi looked around at the metal-edged control panels of the space yacht, at the synthetic fabric of the seats that felt so smooth and soft. She smelled the recirculated air. Qwi had lived for years inside a completely enclosed environment; she knew nothing about plants and animals and other life-forms. She hoped it would be fascinating.

"Are you sure we'll be safe?" she asked, swallowing hard. Her greatest nightmare was that some Imperial spy might recapture her and haul her back to the black-hole research lab where they would tear the weapons knowledge out of her head, no matter how much she resisted.

"Yes," Wedge said after a long pause. "Ithor is an isolated paradise. It's a world where many young couples"—he paused, then swallowed as if embarrassed by the word he had just spoken—"uh, *tourists* go for vacations. Many people come and go, and the Ithorians welcome everyone.

"The Empire blockaded this world during the Rebellion, causing some damage as a show of force. But after one of the Ithorians gave the Empire access to the agricultural and cloning information they wanted, Ithor was basically left alone."

Wedge looked out at the starfield where the brilliant sun of the Ithorian system gleamed a whitish blue. He increased the thrust from the sublight engines and vectored them toward a bright green planet veined with blue and swathed with white clouds.

"Just pretend we're on vacation," Wedge said. "We'll be tourists, and I'll show you what you've been missing. I can't think of a better place to start."

"I really look forward to it." Qwi smiled warmly at him.

Wedge blushed, then seemed to concentrate furiously on the relatively simple task of entering a low orbit.

Qwi placed her pale-blue fingers against the side viewport as she stared at the lush vistas below. She had never seen such exotic scenery before, so different from the sterile white-walled rooms in Maw Installation.

Below her, between the treetops of a tropical paradise, broad rivers furled with white rapids as the current flowed over broken rocks. The space yacht soared above broad meadows splattered with brilliant colors, blooming flowers in red and yellow, blue and purple. The sheer vibrancy of the growing things dazzled her eyes.

They passed over a chain of oval lakes that glittered and reflected the sunlight, like the string of jewels on the necklace Wedge had given her as a gift a few days earlier. Overhead the sky was a muted lavender.

"Beautiful," she said.

"Told you so," Wedge agreed, giving her a half smile. "You can trust me."

She looked at him, then blinked her indigo eyes. "Yes, Wedge, I trust you."

He cleared his throat and turned away quickly, pointing out the front viewport. "The Ithorians allow no damage to their environment," he said as if reading a data summary. "In fact, they consider it sacrilege even to set foot on the ground of their mother jungle."

"Then how do they live?" Qwi asked.

"Look," Wedge said.

As they soared above the treetops, Qwi made out a strange shape coming over the horizon, rapidly growing larger as they approached. "Is that a city?" she said.

"More than just a city," Wedge said, "an entire enclosed environment. The Ithorians call it the *Tafanda Bay*."

The enormous disk-shaped construction swelled to fill their front viewport, looking larger and larger—and larger, like a fat coin greater in diameter than the entire Maw Installation. Though the city appeared to be made of plasteel, it also seemed at least partially alive.

A chaos of platforms, flight decks, transmission antennas, and roving machinery studded the hull of the Ithorian floating city—but the exposed surfaces were covered with hanging moss; large trees grew out of special pockets on the side walls, rising to the sky and looking thicker and greener than the metallic towers.

On the top flat surface of the disk, greenhouse domes sparkled like a thousand eyes in the sun. Qwi could see through the transparent domes to dense botanical gardens in carefully manicured rows. Small ships flitted like gnats about the landing ports and shipping bays.

Underneath the *Tafanda Bay*, banks of diffused repulsorlift engines kept the entire city hovering over the treetops, casting an elliptical shadow over the leafy surface. The Ithorian city slowly drifted along a wandering course with no destination in particular, without touching the sacred ground.

Wedge keyed in his request for landing coordinates and was answered by an odd echoing voice that Qwi thought sounded like someone speaking through a long empty tube. After a moment the comm system crackled again with the voice—or was it another one?—changing the coordinates.

"Excuse us for the oversight, sir. A special representative will meet you at the landing bay. We hope you enjoy your stay here on our homeworld."

Wedge looked suspiciously at the comm unit. "Why would they be giving us special treatment?" he said to Qwi. "Nobody is supposed to know who we really are."

Qwi looked around, and suddenly the cockpit of the space yacht seemed smaller. "Do you think we're in danger? Should we turn around and find some other place to go?"

Wedge looked as if that was indeed what he wanted to do. "No, it's all right," he said bravely. "I can protect you. Don't worry."

They landed on the pad indicated, and Wedge extended the passenger ramp. He climbed down the gangway first and reached up to take Qwi by the hand, leading her gently down. She could easily have disembarked by herself, but she enjoyed the attention he showered on her.

Surrounding the space yacht were wide-boled gray-barked trees with low branches that spread out to form a long, flat platform. Brilliant white and blue flowers spangled the leaves. Staring around her, Qwi took a deep breath of the moist air. Everything smelled fresh and alive, filled with a symphony of scents that startled her imagination.

"Greetings." Qwi turned to see an exceedingly strange-looking alien hulking toward them, flanked by two ten-year-old human boys. The hunchbacked alien wore a white cape trimmed with braid. Its head looked like a long ladle, as if someone had taken a face made of soft clay and stretched it into an S-curve, looping the front up and yanking out two eye stalks. The mouth was hidden far under the sloping canopy of its head. As Qwi watched, the cumbersome-looking creature took steps forward with a gentle, careful grace.

The two human boys beside the creature wore similar white capes, over bright-green jumpsuits. Pale-haired and blue-eyed, both wore beatific expressions, but neither of them spoke.

Wedge must have seen how startled Qwi was by the alien's appearance. "I guess I should have warned you. The Ithorians are commonly called Hammerheads."

Qwi nodded slowly, thinking about other strange creatures she had seen, from the fish-faced Admiral Ackbar to the tentacle-headed Tol Sivron who had run Maw Installation. Perhaps not all intelligent creatures in the galaxy could be as attractive as some humans . . . such as Wedge.

"Actually," the alien said, stepping closer, "we dislike the name Hammerheads. It seems deprecating to us."

"My apologies, sir," Wedge said, bowing slightly.

"I am Momaw Nadon, and I am honored to be of service to you, Wedge Antilles and Qwi Xux."

Wedge took one step back in panic. "How do you know our names?" he said.

Momaw Nadon made a hollow bubbling sound that came from both sides of his mouth in a stereophonic echo. "Mon Mothma asked me to give you special accommodations."

"Why would Mon Mothma tell you we were coming here?" Wedge said. "We're supposed to be keeping a low profile." As Nadon gave a slight bow, his ladle-shaped head see-sawed up and down. "I have sympathized with the Rebel Alliance since my days of exile on Tatooine, more than a decade ago. My people banished me to the desert planet, where I could tend the sands rather than our beautiful forests. The Empire had demanded certain agricultural information, and I gave it to them to save our forests from being obliterated—but still my people exiled me. I returned here after the Emperor's death, and I have continued to make amends ever since."

Nadon gestured to the two human boys. "Take their luggage. We will show them their staterooms."

The youths moved in unison—without the pell-mell franticness of young boys—entering the space yacht and returning with the slick silvery containers of vacation clothes.

Nadon led them away from the landing bay, ducking his head under the low-hanging branches that surrounded the landing pad. The passage seemed like a living green tunnel.

"I was also in the cantina in Mos Eisley when Luke Skywalker and Obi-Wan Kenobi first met Captain Solo. I did not know my brush with history at that time, but I remember it clearly, though I was preoccupied with . . . other concerns at the time."

"I'm amazed you could recall a meeting like that after so many years," Wedge said.

Nadon indicated a disguised turbolift that opened like a great leafy pod in the wall. They all stepped inside and began to descend deeper within the *Tafanda Bay*.

After a long pause Nadon finally said, "Ithorians have long memories."

He led them through winding corridors, past small domes that contained specimens of plant life from different parts of the planet. Near a delicately spraying fountain, Nadon pointed to two doors across the corridor from each other.

"I have assigned you these staterooms," he said. "Please contact me if you desire other amenities. I am here to serve you." The two mysterious boys deposited the luggage in the corridor and stepped back to stand on either side of Nadon.

Qwi finally said, "You haven't introduced us to the children. Are you their caretaker?"

Nadon made a rumbling bubbly sound in his twin throats. "They are . . . seedlings, grown from the flesh of my enemy. They are also a memory of my days on Tatooine." Nadon hung his ladle-shaped head.

The two boys remained impassive, and Nadon ushered them off. Without a backward glance he left Wedge and Qwi standing outside their staterooms, wondering what he meant.

After nightfall on the upper observation deck of the *Tafanda Bay*, Qwi went with Wedge to watch the moons rise. The lavender skies had turned a deep violet, punctuated by brilliant stars in a wash across the heavens.

A small moon in full phase climbed over the eastern horizon, while the fingernail crescent of a much larger moon hung close to the western sky, following the brilliant colors of sunset over the edge of the world. High up, two other moons showed swollen quarter phases.

Qwi took a deep breath of the humid air, smelling a plethora of spicy perfumes from green plants and night-blooming flowers, like a complex mixture of all the perfumes and all the pleasant cooking herbs she had ever smelled.

The breeze grew paradoxically warmer with nightfall, and she felt her feathery hair drifting about. She straightened it with her slender fingers, knowing that Wedge liked to see her pearly strands glisten in the light. She had changed into a soft wrap swirled with pastel colors that accentuated the ethereal beauty of her wispy body.

The Ithorian eco-city cruised slowly over the treetops. The gentle hum of the *Tafanda Bay*'s banks of repulsorlift engines blended with the simmering night sounds of the jungle below. The breeze rustled leaves in the tall hedges and stands of scale trees around the observation deck.

Other Ithorians arrived, standing in silence or thrumming in their strange stereo language. Wedge and Qwi said nothing to each other.

She stepped closer, brushed against him, then finally let herself snuggle up to his side. Nervously, it seemed, Wedge slipped an arm around her waist and she—Qwi Xux, inventor of the Sun Crusher, co-creator of the Death Star—felt honored to be under the protection of General Wedge Antilles.

She knew that Imperial loyalists would be desperate to regain the secret knowledge locked in her brain. But Qwi realized that here, at least, she felt completely safe.

26

J**acen and Jaina continued their** trek across Coruscant's dank underbelly. They couldn't tell if the dim half light that filtered down from high above signified nighttime or day. The air smelled thick with rotted garbage, dead things, corroded metal, and stagnant water. They walked along the widest streets, dodging rubble, clambering over fallen and ancient wreckage. They had seen nothing familiar for hours, and neither of them knew what to do next.

"I'm hungry," Jaina said.

"Me too," Jacen said.

The deep underground was smothered in a silence overlaid with white noise. Shadowy creatures, startled by the twins, fled into darker hiding spots. Bumping one pile of debris, Jacen and Jaina sparked an avalanche of frightening clatters. The twins ran from the noise, generating further junkfalls that tinkled and clanged from great heights.

"My feet hurt," Jacen said.

"Mine don't," Jaina answered.

Up ahead they finally saw a welcome sign: a cave dwelling made of shored-up wreckage, walls built from piled chunks of duracrete mortared together with a paste of dried algae, mud, and darker substances. Smoky lights burned deep inside the cave, looking enticing in contrast to the forbidding bleakness of the undercity.

Jacen and Jaina moved forward at the same time. "Food?" Jacen asked. His sister nodded.

Outside of the strange slumped cave they saw cables running through lichen-clogged eye bolts mounted at various points. Along the walls and ceilings, metal bands like long fingerbones dangled in a decoration, linked together by sagging segments of chain.

"In here," Jaina said, taking the lead. Dimness folded over them, leading them toward the enticing lights.

Near her head a scratching, scuttling sound came from the shadows. The girl looked to see an elongated spider-roach nearly the size of her head. Bumping against her, Jacen leaned forward to get a better look at the creature. The spider-roach clambered up the lumpy wall and hesitated, turning three glassy amber eyes at them.

Suddenly, with a ratcheting clatter, a fistful of metal flanges from the ceiling swung loose like a prehensile mechanical hand dangling on chains. Dozens of steel fingers slammed against the wall to trap the spider-roach, clamping it into a makeshift metallic cage. The creature thrashed and flailed, clacking its mandibles. Sparks flew as chitinous forelimbs scrabbled against the impenetrable bars.

In panic Jacen and Jaina hurried down the tunnel toward the flickering orange lights. But the twins stopped, simultaneously sensing a thrill of danger.

They looked up just in time to see a much larger cage, all prongs and sharp metal edges, collapse down around them. Mechanical metal claws surrounded them like dozens of fists chained together.

"Trap!" Jaina said.

Shuffling footsteps came toward them—a thud, then a scrape as a large hulking creature emerged from the depths of the lair. The silhouette appeared first, a massive tufted head with enormous arms dragging almost to the ground. One thickly muscled thigh looked the size of a tree trunk, but the other leg was much shorter, twisted and withered.

Jacen and Jaina rattled the sharp metal edges of the cage, but the mechanical claws drew tighter together like scissors. "Help!" Jacen said.

Then their captor came into full view, lit from the side by reflected smoky lights. The creature was covered with a pelt of shaggy hair, showing no distinction between its enormous head and the rest of its torso, as if both pieces had been smashed together into one barrel-shaped mass.

The thing's mouth hung in a long crooked slash, twisted sideways and straightened back only partway. Its left eye was overgrown with a mass of tumors and rotting flesh; the other eye, nearly as large as the twins' fists, shone a sickly yellow, streaked with red lines.

Jacen and Jaina were too afraid to say anything. Their ogrelike captor shambled past, ignoring them for the moment as he rocked back and forth on his stubby withered leg. He picked up the small trap to inspect the frantic spider-roach.

The children could smell the stink from the monster as he next bent toward the bars of their cage, thrusting his giant yellow eye close, but Jacen and Jaina scrambled to the other side of the cage.

The ogre disconnected long chains from the wall, draped them over his shoulder, and dragged the twins' cage clattering down the corridor into his firelit den. The cage rolled and crashed against unseen obstacles, and the twins had to scramble to keep themselves upright.

Inside, gnawed bones from large and small creatures cluttered the monster's lair, some piled in baskets, others cracked and strewn over the broken floor. Smoky red flames came from smoldering pots filled with a rancid-smelling fat.

Chained in a cleared area of the pit sat a tusked ratlike creature covered with bristling fur. Its black rubbery lips stretched back in a perpetual snarl. Gobbets of drool flew from its mouth as it snarled and threw itself to the end of its chain.

A set of broken manacles from a detention area hung on the spike-encrusted walls of the chamber. As the ogre moved about in the brighter light, tatters of an old prison uniform could be seen among his greasy curls of body hair.

The ogre pried open the metal fingers of the small spider-roach trap. He picked up the arachnid with his lumpy bare hands and tossed it to the giant rat-monster. The glossy spider-roach flailed its long legs as it tumbled end over end, and the rat-monster snapped it out of the air. But the bug managed to grab on to the rubbery lips with its sharp legs, and it stung hard.

The rat-creature yelped, gnashing its tusks until it chomped down and split the exoskeleton of the spider-roach with a cracking pop. Then, contented, it slurped the juicy soft meat and licked its black lips.

The rat-creature panted and rolled its wet red eyes at the two children.

Hopeful, the twins peered out from the cage. "We are lost," Jaina said, calling to the ogre from between the bars.

"Please help us find our home," Jacen added.

The ogre fixed its yellow eye on them. A foul wet stench came from his mouth, like slime scraped from the bottoms of a thousand sewers. He spoke in a bubbling voice, slurring the words. "No," the ogre said. "Gonna *eat* you!"

Then he tottered off on his shriveled leg toward a smoldering fireplace. The ogre found a pair of long sharp tongs resting in the hot coals. Holding the implements high, the ogre turned back to the twins.

Jacen and Jaina both looked at the top of their cage. The articulated finger joints were held together by small pins clogged with grease and rust, but smooth enough that the cage could open and close.

The twins each knew which pins the other concentrated on—and used their rudimentary ability with the Force, just as they did when they played tricks on Threepio and played the games that their Uncle Luke showed them.

They popped out the cage pins two at a time in rapid succession. Small pieces of metal flew like tiny projectiles in all directions. Suddenly without support, the long metal fingers fell open to the ground with an incredible clang.

"Run!" Jacen cried. Jaina took his hand and they scrambled toward the tunnel.

The ogre let out a furious roar and stumped after them, but he could not keep up on his uneven legs. Instead he grabbed the thick chain holding the rat-monster to the wall and yanked out the long spike that held its collar together.

Set free, the rat-creature lunged. Turning, it tried to snap its teeth at the ogre—but he used a muscle-swollen arm to bash the rat-thing away from him. He gestured toward the fleeing children.

And they ran, and they ran.

The rat-creature came howling and slavering after them. The twins ran out of the firelit opening and dashed down an alley. Behind them they could hear the steam-engine sounds of the creature as it snorted, following their scent. Its claws clattered on the pavement.

Jaina found a small dark gash in the wall, a hole broken into the layered duracrete. "Here," she said.

Jaina dived into the tiny hole headfirst, and her brother clambered after. Only a second later the rat-creature jammed its tusked snout against the jagged opening, but it could not get its head through the hole.

By that time Jacen and Jaina had scrambled on their hands and knees, burrowing deep into the unexplored darkness.

"Oh, we never should have agreed to baby-sit!" Threepio wailed. "I wonder how often baby-sitters actually lose their children." Chewbacca growled at him.

"Why didn't you listen to me, Chewbacca? Mistress Leia will have all your fur shaved off so she can make a new rug. You will be the first bald Wookiee in history."

Chewbacca bellowed a suggestion as they stormed down the corridors, still searching the Holographic Zoo for Extinct Animals.

"You can go to the control room if you like. I think we should sound the alarm here and now. It is perfectly acceptable to summon help. This is an emergency."

Threepio found the fire alarm and activated it with one golden hand; next, he searched among the holographic exhibits until he also found a security alarm. Without hesitation he pressed the button. "There, that should do it."

Chewbacca growled in Threepio's face with enough force that the droid's audio sensors shut down to reset themselves. Then he manhandled Threepio in his furred Wookiee arms, carrying him bodily down the hall at a fast lope.

"All right, have it your way, then," Threepio said. "We'll go to the control center and shut down all the holograms."

Jacen and Jaina felt the slimy surface of the tunnel as they crawled downward. They had no idea where they were going, but they knew they had to find some other way home.

Jacen reached up, felt no close ceiling, and climbed to his feet. The twins could see nothing in the darkness, only a faint glow ahead. They made their way toward it—cautiously this time, afraid they might find another ogre. Jacen smelled sizzling meat, and he heard guttural words, the first human voices they had heard since deciding to go home without Threepio and Chewbacca.

Jacen started toward the light, but Jaina held on to his arm. "Careful," she said. Jacen nodded and put a finger to his lips as a reminder. They inched forward, hearts hammering. They smelled the delicious scents of cooked food, heard the crackle of fire, the chattering voices.

They reached a corner and peered around it to see a large blasted-out room, a low-level reception area used thousands of years ago. Jacen and Jaina could see a bonfire, tattered figures moving between light and shadow, banks of dimly functioning glowcrystals, and a glimpse of blinking computer equipment. Then suddenly, from all sides, silent hands reached out to grab them.

Firm grips, wiry arms. Five sentries struck at once, snatching Jacen and Jaina and whisking them off their feet before they had a chance to struggle.

The sentries laughed even as the children squealed in terror. A cheer went up from the people around the bonfire as the sentries carried the twins out into the bright light.

Alarms pulsed and whooped in the control center of the Holographic Zoo. Red signals flashed; yellow lights blinked on and off in indecipherable patterns.

Threepio was impressed at the commotion he had managed to cause just by activating a few security systems.

The zoo's control droid sat in the center of an octagonal computer bank. It had a spherical head encircled by optical sensors mounted every thirty-six degrees. From its central station the control droid sprouted eight segmented limbs that scrambled over the panels, pecking at the buttons in a blur of motion like fire-linked blaster cannons.

"Permission denied," the control droid said to them.

Chewbacca roared, but the control droid merely spun its spherical head and ignored the Wookiee's outburst.

"I feel required to warn you," Threepio said to the other droid, "that when Wookiees lose their tempers they are known to rip limbs out of their sockets. I believe Chewbacca here is on the verge of losing his temper."

Chewbacca leaned forward on one of the segmented control panels, gripped it with his hairy paws, and roared again into one set of the multiple eyes.

"Permission still denied," the control droid said.

"But you don't understand!" Threepio insisted. "There are two lost children inside your Holographic Zoo. If you would just shut down the image generators, we could search the habitats and find them."

"Unacceptable," the control droid said. "It would cause too great a disturbance among the other guests."

Threepio indignantly propped his metallic arms on his hips. "But the zoo looked empty when we toured it. How many other patrons are currently using the facility?"

"Irrelevant," the control droid said. "Such an action is strictly forbidden except in conditions of extreme emergency."

Threepio waved his golden hands in the air. "But this *is* an emergency!"

Chewbacca had apparently had enough of formal requests. He bunched his fists together and brought them down on the first control bank, smashing the glossy black coverings and shattering circuit connections.

Sparks flew. The control droid's head spun around like a planet knocked out of its orbit. "Excuse me," the control droid said, "please don't touch the controls,"

Chewbacca went to the second segment of the octagonal board and smashed it as well. The control droid flailed its eight articulated limbs, trying to bypass circuits in the remaining systems.

"I must admit, Chewbacca, that your enthusiasm makes up for any lack of finesse," Threepio said.

In no time the Wookiee had ruined the entire set of panels. Without a single functioning hologram-generating system, the control droid folded all eight of its articulated arms like a dead insect and seemed to sulk.

Chewbacca yanked Threepio's mechanical arm and hauled him back down to the holographic habitats. Now every chamber was empty, white-tiled walls with strategically mounted hologram generators at the vertices of the room. Various guests had dropped garbage in among the illusions, refreshment wrappers, torn scraps of paper, and half-eaten nonorganic treats that had failed to decompose.

"Jacen! Jaina!" Threepio called.

Alarms continued to squawk as Chewbacca and Threepio passed from one habitat to the next. Threepio called up the data brochure inside his computer brain and guided the search, methodically moving from one room to another. Every cell in the deactivated Holographic Zoo looked identical, and they found the children in none of them.

When they finally hurried to the last chamber, hoping against hope that they would discover the twins crouched in the corner and waiting to be rescued, they were suddenly met by the New Republic militia charging toward them in response to all the alarms.

"Halt!" the captain of the guard said.

Threepio instantly counted eighteen humans, all wearing blaster-proof armor. The militia members drew their weapons and leveled them.

In all his adventures Threepio couldn't recall ever having seen so many blaster barrels pointed directly at him.

"Oh, my!" he said.

The feral humans brought Jacen and Jaina before their king. The flickering warmth of the junk-heap bonfire made a pleasant smell. The strips of unrecognizeable meat roasting on long skewers caused both children to lick their lips.

Grimy-faced sentries looked down at the twins and smiled. Their mouths seemed a checkerboard of yellow teeth and black gaps. The king of the underground humans sat on a tall pile of ragged cushions. He laughed. "*These* are the fearsome intruders?"

Jacen and Jaina looked around themselves, gathering details. The refugees in the former reception area had bedrolls, tattered clothing, and stashes of scavenged possessions. Some sat mending rags, others worked on spring-loaded animal traps. Two old men crouched holding small musical instruments cobbled together from old pipes; they blew into the mouthpieces, comparing high whistling notes.

The feral people wore torn and threadbare clothing, some mended, some not, all very old. They had long hair; the men wore bushy beards. Their skin was pale, as if they had not seen sunlight for decades. Some of them might never have seen natural light at all.

The king seemed to have the best materials. He wore shoulder pads and polished white gloves taken from a stormtrooper. His eyebrows were large, his reddish-brown beard wispy. Though his face was the color of raw bread dough, his eyes were bright and alert. His smile also showed gaps from missing teeth, but it contained real humor.

Around and behind the king hung jury-rigged electronic equipment, computer panels, holographic display modules, even one old-model food-processing unit. Ancient generators had been wired into the frayed energy grid of the skyscrapers, skimming power from the main flow through Imperial City. The lost people had obviously been down here a long time.

"Get these children some food," the king yelled, bending down to look at them. "Well, now, my name is Daykim. What're your names?"

"Jaina," Jacen said, indicating his sister.

Jaina pointed to her brother. "Jacen."

A sentry with gray-blond hair tied in a long pony-tail brought a smoking skewer of the roasted meat. He yanked off the red-black pieces of meat with his fingers and dropped them onto a squarish metal platter that had originally been some sort of cover plate. The sentry blew on his fingers, licked the juices, and grinned at the children. He set the platter down in front of them, and the twins sat on the floor, crossing their legs.

"Blow on the meat before you put it in your mouths," the king said. "It's hot."

The twins picked up small morsels, dutifully blowing until the meat was cool enough to chew. King Daykim seemed to delight in just watching them.

"So what were you doing down here all alone? It's dangerous, you know. Would you like to stay here with us?" the king said. "We're all growing old. It's been too long since young people joined us down here."

Jacen and Jaina shook their heads. "We are lost," Jaina said around a mouthful of meat. A thick welling of tears appeared on the edge of her eyelids.

Jacen also started to cry. "Please help us find our home," he said, looking toward the high ceiling. Somewhere up in the distance lay their living quarters.

"Up there?" King Daykim said, comically incredulous. "Why would you want to go back up there? The Emperor lives up there. He's a *bad man*." Daykim shook his head and gestured around him. "We have everything we want here. We have food, we have light, we have . . . our things."

Jacen shook his head at Daykim. "I want to go home."

With a sigh Daykim glanced back at his banks of computer terminals and then flashed them a defeated smile.

"Of course you want to go home. Just finish up your supper. You'll need your strength."

The sergeant of the militia escorted Threepio and Chewbacca back to Han and Leia's quarters in the old Imperial Palace. "Our records indicate that Minister Organa Solo and her husband returned not more than an hour ago," the sergeant said.

Chewbacca moaned dejectedly. Threepio shot a sharp glance at him. "I think *you* should be the one to tell them what happened, Chewbacca. After all, I'm only a droid."

"Rest assured we're doing everything we can," the sergeant said. "We've had our teams combing the Holographic Zoo and the adjoining floors just in case the twins found an emergency staircase. We're checking the logs of the maintenance droid just to be sure that no one used the turbolift that was being serviced." He snapped to attention. "We'll find them, don't you worry."

Threepio used the override code on the doorway to open it. Then he and Chewbacca stepped into the living quarters—to find Han and Leia sitting on the self-conforming chairs, with the twins balanced on their knees.

"Children! Oh, thank goodness, you're home!" Threepio cried. Chewbacca thundered a high-pitched bellow.

Han and Leia both turned to look at them. "Well, there you two are."

Threepio noticed at once that one of the panels from the air-ventilation system had been knocked off, apparently from the inside. A stranger, a large man, dressed in tattered but ornate clothing dashed to shelter behind one of the larger pieces of furniture. He had long reddish-brown hair, a wispy beard, and uncommonly pale skin,

Leia returned her attention to the rag-clad man. "Seriously, Mr. Daykim, I can't tell you how much we appreciate what you've done. I assure you the New Republic will do everything it can to repatriate all your people."

Daykim shook his head. "The Emperor never forgave mistakes, not even accounting mistakes. We saw many of our fellow civil servants either executed or sent off to horrendous penal colonies. As soon as we caught ourselves in a simple but irrevocable filing error, we knew we didn't have long to live—so we grabbed what we could and fled to the underlevels of Imperial City. My people have been living there for years. We're just a bunch of feral bureaucrats who don't know any other life."

"We could find a place for you in the New Republic. We don't punish people for simple mistakes. We could bring you all back," Leia said again. "Look around you, we could give you your own quarters like these. Many of the buildings in the old Imperial City are abandoned."

"We know," Daykim said, "we live there ourselves sometimes. Thank you for your offer." He stood up and cast a suspicious glance toward Threepio and Chewbacca. He patted Jacen and Jaina on the head and flashed his gap-toothed smile. "You're good little children. Your mommy and daddy should be proud of you."

Han cleared his throat and extended his hand in thanks. The tattered man grabbed it and shook vigorously as if pleased to give a firm, businesslike handshake.

"I still don't understand why you want to stay down in those murky lower levels," Han said.

Daykim swung one leg into the ventilation duct and looked around. "It's very simple," he said. "Up here I was just a file clerk—down there I am a *king*!"

With a last smile for all of them, Daykim vanished into the ventilation ducts. They heard him thumping and scrambling as he disappeared down the access tubes.

"Well, everything turned out right after all," Threepio said. "Isn't this wonderful?"

In answer Han and Leia both glared at him.

"We want a story!" the twins said in unison.

27

Kyp Durron brought his stolen
ship into orbit around the small forest moon of Endor,
where the second Death Star had been destroyed.

Ignoring the sensors on board his stolen Z-95 Headhunter, he let his eyes fall closed. He reached out with
his sense ability, seeking across the entire landscape for
shadows or ripples in the Force. He had to find the last
resting place of the only other Dark Lord of the Sith he
knew of.

Darth Vader.

Exar Kun, who had lived long before Vader, was
pleased to know that the Lords of the Sith had continued
for millennia. But Kyp still felt driven to find answers to
the clamoring questions in his mind.

Master Skywalker said that Darth Vader, his own
father, had returned to the light side in the end. From
this Kyp concluded that the powers of the Sith were not
permanently connected with evil. That gave him a thread

of hope. He recognized full well that the dark spirit of Exar Kun had lied to him, or at least misled him. The risk was terrible, but the reward would benefit the entire galaxy.

If he succeeded.

Here on Endor, Kyp felt he could hide from the watchful eyes of Exar Kun. He didn't know how far Kun's power extended, but he didn't think the ancient Sith Lord could leave Yavin 4. Not yet at least.

Kyp instinctively worked the controls of Mara Jade's fighter, bringing the Headhunter lower as he scanned the forests. After the Rebel celebration of their victory over the Emperor, Luke Skywalker had built a pyre for his father near the towering trees, not far from the Ewok villages. He had watched the roaring flames consume the remnants of Darth Vader's mechanical attire.

But perhaps something had survived. . . .

As the Headhunter cruised over the tops of the immense Ewok father trees, Kyp searched with his mind, ironically making use of the exercises Master Skywalker had taught him, how to reach out and touch all life-forms.

He caught the stirrings of the furry Ewoks in their tree cities. He sensed large predators on the prowl: one humanoid behemoth, a giant Gorax, crashed through the trees, black hair swinging from side to side as he searched for Ewok dwellings low enough to grab.

As he flew onward, Kyp's mind ranged far and wide across the Endor wilderness. Then he felt a ripple, an echo of something that definitely did not . . . belong.

Everything else seemed to have its place, but this did not conform. A stain that seemed to absorb all other senses, casting waves of leftover darkness that caused the creatures on Endor to avoid the place instinctively.

Kyp changed course and arrowed to the coordinates, circling once until he found an appropriate clearing. The repulsorlifts whined, and his landing jets kicked up fallen forest debris as he landed the Headhunter in the underbrush.

Afraid and yet eager, Kyp swung out of the cockpit and hopped down, landing with a crunch in the twigs and dead leaves. The breeze died, as if the evening forest were holding its breath around him. Silvery planetshine trickled through the dense leaves, lighting the clearing with a wan, milky glow.

Kyp took four steps and stopped before the scorched site of Vader's funeral pyre.

The ground surrounding the old burned area remained dead and brown. Though the thick forests of Endor were tenacious and fast-growing, no plants dared approach the scar—even after seven years.

The bonfire had been large and hot, incinerating Vader's uniform. Only a few heat-warped bits of body armor had survived, along with tatters of a black cape tangled in broken rocks and time-packed ashes. A twisted lacing of steel reinforcement lay like a torn spiderweb covered.

Kyp swallowed and knelt in the dirt. He reached out tentatively, afraid, until he let his fingertips brush the age-crumbled ashes.

He jerked his hand away, then brought it back. The spot was cold, but the coldness seemed to go away as his hands grew numb.

Kyp used the Force to scatter bits of ash, blowing clear the tiny, buckled residue that had survived the fire, an unrecognizable lump of black plasteel that might have been Vader's helmet. Growing more desperate, Kyp increased his power, scouring away debris and leaving only a sad jumble of wires, melted plasteel, and shreds of tough cloth.

Darth Vader, former Dark Lord of the Sith, had been reduced to only pathetic scraps and nightmarish memories.

Kyp reached out to stroke the remnants. Electric tingles went through his hands. He knew he shouldn't be touching these relics, yet he could not turn away now. Kyp had to find answers to his questions, even if he had to answer them himself.

"Darth Vader, where did you go wrong?" he asked, staring down at the fragments of armor. His voice, unused for more than a day, croaked at him.

Vader had been a monster, with the blood of billions on his hands. According to Exar Kun, Anakin Skywalker had been unprepared for the power he had touched, and it had overwhelmed him.

Kyp recognized that he had begun to walk down a similar path—but he was not so naive. Unlike Anakin Skywalker, he understood the dangers. He could guard himself. He would not be tricked by the temptations and the brutalities that had lured Vader deeper and deeper into the dark side.

Feeling cold and alone in the night, Kyp returned to the ship and took out the long cape Han Solo had given him. He wrapped the fabric around his dark jumpsuit to keep warm, then went back to sit on the barren ground by the ashes of Vader's pyre. The peaceful sounds of the forest gradually returned, chirping and whistling around him like a lullaby.

Kyp was in no hurry. He could wait here on Endor. He needed to make sure he wasn't kidding himself. He was no fool. He knew the dangerous edge he was walking, and it frightened him.

As he sat in peace, running his fingers along the slick, fine fabric of his cloak, Kyp thought of how his friend Han Solo had freed him from the spice mines . . . but even that happy thought twisted around to make him realize just how much of his life the Empire had stolen from him.

Kyp rarely recalled the diamond-edged memories of his youth, when he and his older brother Zeth had lived on the colony world of Deyer. He thought of the raft cities anchored in a complex of terraformed lakes stocked with fish.

Zeth had taken him out many times on a pleasure skimmer to sink crustacean nets or just to swim under the ocher-colored skies. His brother Zeth had long dark hair, eyes narrowed against the brightness of the sun, his body wiry and rippling with lean muscles, his skin tanned from long days spent outside.

The colonists had tried to build a perfect society on Deyer, fully democratic with every person serving a term on the council of raft towns. Unanimously, the representatives on Deyer had voted to condemn the destruction of Alderaan, to request that Emperor Palpatine rescind his New Order. They had worked through the appropriate political channels, naively believing that with their votes they could influence the Emperor's decisions.

Instead Palpatine had crushed the "dissidents" on Deyer, overrunning the entire colony, scattering the people to various penal centers, and taking Zeth away forever. . . .

Kyp found his hands clenched tight, and he thought again of the powers that Exar Kun had shown him, the dark secrets that Master Skywalker refused to consider. He frowned and took a deep breath. The cool night air bit into his lungs, and he let it out slowly.

He vowed not to let Exar Kun twist him into another Vader. Kyp felt confident in his determination, in his own strength of character; he could use the power of the dark side for the benefit of the New Republic.

Master Skywalker was wrong. The New Republic stood on the moral high ground and was justified in using any weapon, any force, to eradicate the last stains of the evil Empire.

Kyp stood up and wrapped the black cape around his chest. He could make amends. He alone could show how well those powers could be used.

Exar Kun was long dead, and Darth Vader lay in ashes on Endor. "Now *I* am the Lord of the Sith," Kyp said. With that admission he felt a cold strength creep up his backbone, as if his spine had turned into a column of ice.

He clambered back aboard his small spacecraft. The determination felt like flames in his feet, making him move, making his heart pound, focusing his resolution into a laser-bright beam.

Now he, and he alone, had the opportunity to solve all of the New Republic's problems—by himself.

28

Reflected glows from the Caul-
dron Nebula made slow dancing patterns on the polished
surface of the *Gorgon*'s war-room table. Admiral Daala
sat alone at the far end, separated from Commander
Kratas, Imperial Army General Odosk, and Captain
Mullinore of the *Basilisk*.

Daala stared at her own drawn and distorted reflection
in the liquid sheen of the table. She kept her emerald
eyes fixedly ahead as she squeezed her fist, feeling the
supple black leather of her gloves. Her head pounded
with a dull ache, like the imagined echoes of screaming
troopers on the exploding *Manticore*. Hot blood roared
through her veins as she thought of how she had also lost
the Star Destroyer *Hydra*. Half of her force obliterated!

What would Tarkin think of her? In her nightmares she pictured his spectre drawing back his open
hand to strike her across the face for her miserable failure. Failure! She had to make up for it.

Commander Kratas drew his bushy eyebrows together in an expression of concern. His Imperial cap rested against his short dark hair. He turned away from Daala's stare, then looked toward the general and the captain of the other Star Destroyer. No one spoke. They waited for Daala, and she tried to summon the courage to speak.

"Gentlemen," she finally said. The words felt like rusty nails catching in her throat; but her voice was strong, startling the three commanders into attention. She eyed each one in turn, then swiveled her chair so she could gaze out at the seething Cauldron gases. A knot of bright blue-giant stars at the heart of the nebula poured out intense energy that illuminated the cloud of gas.

"I have reassessed our mission." Daala swallowed. The words already sounded like defeat to her, but she would not give in to it. "We must somehow differentiate between conflicting priorities. Our original command from Grand Moff Tarkin was to protect the Maw Installation at all costs. That is why we were given four Star Destroyers. Tarkin considered the scientists there a priceless resource for the ultimate victory of the Empire."

She clenched her teeth and hesitated again. Her body betrayed her and started to tremble, but she gripped the edge of the polished table with her glove, gripped it hard until the cramped muscles in her fingers steadied her again.

"But we allowed the Sun Crusher, the most powerful weapon ever designed, to be stolen from our grasp, and we lost one fourth of our fleet in a failed attempt to recapture it. Upon learning of the changed situation with the Rebellion, I decided that it was more important to fight the enemies of the Empire. We left Maw Installation undefended as we harried Rebel worlds. Now, after the disaster at Calamari, I see we have failed in that too."

Commander Kratas rose partway to his feet as if he felt compelled to defend her actions. His skin flushed darker, and Daala noticed a disgraceful hint of stubble on his jaw. If these had been normal disciplinary conditions inside Maw Installation, she would have reprimanded him seriously.

"Admiral," he said, "I agree that we've suffered severe losses, but we have also struck crushing blows against the Rebel traitors. The assault on Dantooine—"

Daala's hand swung up to silence him with the finality of a vibroaxe. Kratas clamped his thin lips shut and slithered back into his chair.

"I am fully aware of the battle statistics, Commander. I see the numbers in my sleep. I have studied the datapads over and over." Her voice rose and became molten with anger. "No matter how much damage we have done to the Rebellion, their losses have been insignificant compared to ours."

Then her voice dropped to such a sudden quiet coldness that she saw General Odosk's watery eyes widen in fear. "And so I intend to use my last resources in one final assault. If successful, it will fulfill both of our missions."

Her gloved fingers worked the controls at the end of the table. From a holoprojector in the center of the black slab rose the computer-generated image she had worked up that afternoon in her private quarters while the image of Grand Moff Tarkin droned on with his prerecorded lectures.

"I mean to stab at the *heart* of the Rebellion," she said. "Coruscant itself."

A high-resolution mapping of the last-known surface topography of the Emperor's planet focused on a world-sized metropolis with frozen polar caps and sparkling chains of city lights on the night side of the planet. She saw spacedocks, curved solar mirrors that warmed the upper and lower latitudes of the planet, communications satellites, large freighters, streams of orbital traffic.

Daala gestured, and two fully rendered images of her Star Destroyers appeared traveling side by side at high speed toward Coruscant.

"I intend to take all ships and all personnel onto the *Gorgon*, leaving only a skeleton crew—of volunteers, of course—on board the *Basilisk*. Our Star Destroyers will come out of hyperspace just beyond the moons of Coruscant. We will drive in at full sublight speed, without hesitation, straight toward our target.

"We will give no warning, and we will fire every turbolaser battery we have, clearing a corridor to head directly for Imperial City. Any ship that stands in our way will become a cloud of ionized metal."

As she spoke, the computer animation demonstrated her tactics. The two Star Destroyers arrowed toward the capital city of the New Republic.

"The Calamarian commander who defeated the *Manticore* gave me an idea with his suicide run, and we shall turn the tables on them." Daala watched the stony face of General Odosk, the appalled look of disbelief on Captain Mullinore, and the stern support of Commander Kratas.

"This will be our deadliest hit-and-run," Daala said. "It will cause enough damage for our names to live forever in the annals of Imperial history. We shall deal a death blow to the Rebel government.

"As we approach in-system, the *Basilisk*'s small volunteer crew will begin a self-destruct countdown. The *Gorgon* will run interference until we reach our target, at which time we will turn aside. At full speed the *Basilisk* will plunge into the atmosphere of Coruscant. It will be unstoppable."

On the simulated image one Star Destroyer split away before touching the skin of air, curving in a tight orbit around Coruscant and then streaking off into space as the first ship plummeted flaming into the atmosphere toward the most heavily populated center on the planet.

"When the *Basilisk* detonates . . ." Daala said. She paused as the planetary image flashed with a brilliant ring of fire that sent ripples igniting through the atmosphere. All the lights on the night side of the planet went dark. Cracks of fire appeared across the land masses.

"The explosion will be sufficient to level the buildings on half a continent. The shock wave traveling through the planetary core could topple cities on the other side of the world. The underground reservoirs will break open. Tidal waves will cause damage along the coasts. For the price of one Star Destroyer, we can lay waste to Coruscant."

Odosk looked grimly admiring at the simulation. "A good plan, Admiral."

"But my ship—" Captain Mullinore said.

"It will be a glorious sacrifice," Commander Kratas said. He steepled his fingers and leaned across the polished table. "I agree."

The simulated death of Coruscant continued, showing spreading fires across the cities, seismic disturbances and destruction that continued long after the *Gorgon* vanished into an incandescent spot of light in hyperspace.

"But what of us?" Kratas said. "What will we d
then?"

Daala folded her arms across her chest. "We wil
accomplish both of our missions, as I said. When th
Basilisk has destroyed Coruscant, the *Gorgon* and all o
our personnel shall return to Maw Installation, where w
will defend it to the death with every resource available
The Rebels know it is there—they will be sure to com
sniffing around."

Daala's need for vengeance forged her heart into
white-hot brand that threatened to burst its way steamin
and pulsing out of her chest. "Grand Moff Tarkin onc
said that setbacks are merely an opportunity for us to d
twice as much damage the second time around."

Captain Mullinore looked even paler than usual; pin
pricks of blood vessels speckled his milky-white skin
His blond hair had been cropped severely close to hi
head, making him seem bald in a certain light.

"Admiral," he said, "let me volunteer to remai
onboard the *Basilisk* for this mission. I will be prou
to captain my ship until the end."

Daala looked at him and tried to determine if h
sought some sort of compassion from her. She decide
he wanted none. "I accept, Captain," she said.

Mullinore sat down and gave a tight nod that jerke
his chin toward his throat.

Daala rose to her feet. The muscles in her thighs an
back felt like tightly bundled wires. Her entire bod
had been a clenched fist since the debacle on Calamari
and she knew the only way to release the crushing ten
sion would be to strike a devastating blow against th
Rebellion.

"Begin the transfer of personnel and equipment," she said. "We must strike Coruscant at once."

Daala glanced once more at the seething nebula that hid her ship, and then she left the war room. She headed to her quarters, where she would review Tarkin's tactical tapes, searching for lost and secret wisdom that would guarantee her victory.

The Calamarian female emerged
from her teardrop-shaped transport pod and swiveled her
head as she took in the thick jungles of Yavin 4, the tall
ancient temples. She waited.

Luke hurried out of the hangar bay and tried to maintain a careful pace across the cleared landing area. Artoo
accompanied him across the packed ground.

He noted that the Calamarian female had a smaller
stature than Admiral Ackbar. She wore yellow-and-
turquoise robes that hung loosely about her frame,
sleeves that flowed like waterfalls. He sensed a sad
determination from her.

The Calamarian female saw Luke and gestured with
a flipper-hand to the unseen pilot of the transport
pod. Behind her the craft rose skyward with a
magnetic hum, leaving her behind. She did not
look up to watch the pod streak back into the
low-lying clouds, but seemed intent on staying right
where she was.

"Master Skywalker," she said with a velvety burr
that put him at ease. "I am Ambassador Cilghal from
Calamari. I have a message for you." She reached into
one of her flowing sleeves and withdrew a gleaming disk
traced with patterns of copper and gold.

"Artoo?" Luke said.

The little droid trundled forward, and Cilghal bent
down to insert the message disk into Artoo's drive. After
a momentary whir Artoo projected a flickering image of
Leia in the air in front of him.

Luke stood back surprised, then looked at Cilghal with
a deeper interest as Leia started speaking.

"Luke, I hope all is well with you. I think I've found
someone for your Jedi training center. Ambassador
Cilghal comes with my highest recommendation. She
has demonstrated to my satisfaction that she has a true
proficiency in using the Force. She seems to have a
knack for healing and for short-range prediction. She was
a great help during the recent battle on Calamari. Please
help her and train her. We need more Jedi Knights."

Her image smiled up at him. "We hope to hear soon
that some of your students are ready to help with our
struggle against the Empire. These are still desperate
times. We can't let our guard slip for a moment."

Her expression softened, and she seemed to look
directly into his eyes. "I miss you. The twins keep
asking when they'll see their Uncle Luke again.
I hope you can visit—or maybe we'll come to
Yavin 4." She straightened, taking a formal tone
again. "I'm sure you'll find Cilghal to be one of
our most promising candidates." She crossed her
arms and smiled as the message flickered and
vanished.

Cilghal stood in silence, waiting for Luke to respond. His mind spun. "Uh, welcome," he finally said.

He had been disturbed since his confrontation with Kyp Durron; Luke did not know where the young man had gone after stealing Mara Jade's ship. The gruesome death of Gantoris, coupled with Kyp's rebellion, had been more than enough to resurrect the old fear in Luke again. His best students were going sour, getting impatient, trying to push the limits of their abilities.

But he had sensed a greater, deeper menace that vibrated within the very stones of the Great Temple itself . . . evil, and well hidden. Working alone, Luke had attempted to find its source, running his fingers along the stone blocks of the walls, trying to tap the cold shadow—but he had found nothing. He had only his suspicions.

How could Kyp have known the details of the Great Sith War? How could Gantoris have learned how to build his own lightsaber? What had Gantoris seen that last terrible night before he was consumed? What dreaded magic had he attempted? Luke was missing an important piece of the puzzle, and until he found it, he could not strike against the threat.

Ambassador Cilghal shifted and looked at him again. "Master Skywalker, you seem preoccupied. Perhaps Leia was wrong in suggesting that I come here to stay?"

Luke looked at her, feeling the weight of responsibility on his shoulders. "No, no," he said, "that's not it. If Leia thinks you have Jedi potential, then I would be honored to teach you here. In fact," he said jokingly, "an even-tempered Calamarian will be a welcome change." He smiled. "Follow me. We'll find quarters for you inside the temple."

• • •

The students at Luke's training center continued their lessons of self-discovery, working eagerly or meditatively, honing their skills.

Newcomer Mara Jade listened intently to Cilghal's firsthand descriptions of the attack on Calamari, pressing the ambassador with detailed questions about the Star Destroyers and the number of TIE squadrons they had carried. Old Streen sat next to Kirana Ti on a rounded bench, listening to silver-haired Tionne practice new ballads. The remaining students sat in other common rooms, or studied in their private chambers, or walked out in the jungles.

Satisfied at their activities, Luke slipped back into the deserted corridors and headed toward his own rooms. Artoo came around the corner and whistled a question at him, but Luke shook his head. "No, Artoo, I don't want to be disturbed for a while."

He stepped inside his stone-walled chamber, the small room where he had stayed as an X-wing pilot in the Alliance. Luke had removed the other bunks, furnished the room to his taste; but the room seemed barren, with only a sleeping pallet and some small Massassi artifacts.

On a ledge of black stone laced with blood-colored impurities sat the translucent cube of the Jedi Holocron.

Luke sealed his door, the first time he had ever locked it since returning to the abandoned temple. He held the Holocron in his palm and activated it, digging deep to seek his information.

"I wish to see Master Vodo-Siosk Baas," he said.

The ghostly image of the nozzle-faced, stunted Jedi Master rose out of the cube, robed and covered with bangles, leaning on a long gnarled stick. "I am the gate-keeper, I am Master Vodo-Siosk Baas," the image said.

Luke squatted in front of the interactive holographic image. "I need information from you, Master Vodo. You were a Jedi during the time of the Great Sith War. You have told us about your student Exar Kun and how he created the Brotherhood of the Sith. You've told us that he fought for dominance over the other Jedi loyal to the Old Republic."

Luke took a deep breath. "I need you to tell me more. How did Exar Kun fall at the end of the war? What happened to him? How did he die—or were you finally able to bring him back to the light side?"

"Exar Kun was my greatest student," Master Vodo said, "yet he was corrupted. He was seduced by the powers available to him through studies of ancient Sith teachings."

Luke nodded gravely. "I am afraid that the same thing might have happened to some of my own students, Master Vodo. Did Exar Kun ever return to the powers of good?"

"That was not to be," the image of Master Vodo said. "Because I was his Master, I alone of the allied Jedi went to confront him, hoping that I could turn him back. I knew it was a foolish mission, but I had no choice. I had to try."

"What happened?" Luke asked.

The image flickered, as if something had sparked inside the Holocron; then Master Vodo reappeared. "Exar Kun destroyed me. He slew his own mas-ter."

Luke was suddenly jarred out of the story, remembering that the gatekeeper images in the Holocron were interactive simulacra with personalities imprinted upon them—not the real spirits of long-dead Jedi Masters.

"Then what happened to Kun at the end of the Sith War?" Luke asked.

"All the Jedi banded together and came to the jungle moon in a united front against the Sith stronghold Exar Kun had built. The allied Jedi combined their power into a massive annihilating strike."

Master Vodo's image flickered again, dissolved into static, then reassembled itself. " . . . which obliterated the surviving Massassi natives and . . . " The image broke up, flickered, re-formed, then broke up again— as if something were jamming it.

"But Exar Kun—what happened to Exar Kun?" Luke demanded. He couldn't understand what was going wrong with the Holocron. He shook the Holocron, tapped it a few times, then set it down on the flat, hard table and stepped back to get a better view of the holographic Jedi Master.

Inside the static-filled cube a dark knot appeared, like a storm gathering within its translucent walls. Master Vodo-Siosk Baas reappeared. "—but Kun was able to—"

Suddenly Master Vodo's image shattered into a thousand glittering fragments of colored light, as if a greater force had torn it apart from within.

The darkness inside the Holocron grew deeper and larger, swelling like a slow-motion explosion. Arcs of red fire struck out in all directions from the black fist. With a high-pitched shrieking noise of discharged energy, the faces of the cube split. The Holocron steamed as it collapsed with a shower of sparks, a stream of black curling smoke, and a stench of melted electronics and organic components.

Luke backed away, raising his hands to shield his eyes from the blaze. For a moment it seemed that a solid black hooded form like a walking silhouette rose up from the Holocron, laughing in a deep subsonic voice. Then it drifted away, dissipating into the stone walls.

Luke felt cold fear grip him. The small white cube of the treasured Holocron lay in a melted lump on the table.

Luke would have to find his own answers—and soon.

30

"Luke, I've had enough of this!"

Luke looked up as Mara Jade emerged from the turbolift in the hangar bay of the Great Temple. She had stayed on the jungle moon a few days, long enough to learn *how* to use her own Jedi skills, but the incident with Kyp Durron and the loss of her personal ship had soured the experience for her.

Luke turned from where he stood next to Artoo-Detoo and two Jedi trainees. Kirana Ti bent over to heft a pack of wilderness supplies as she and Streen prepared for a short sojourn out in the jungles. She wore the reptile-skin garments and ornate lacquered battle helm she had brought from her harsh world of Dathomir.

Streen fidgeted and glanced toward the shaft of sunlight that came in under the half-opened hangar door. He wore the many-pocketed jumpsuit he had kept from his gas-prospecting days on Bespin.

Mara walked briskly toward them, cinching her Jedi robe tighter around her waist. Luke looked at her and thought how different she looked from when he had first met her on the hostile smuggler world of Myrkyr.

Mara stopped in front of him, glanced at the two Jedi trainees waiting to depart on their jungle trek, then ignored them completely. "I can't deny what I've learned here, Luke. But Talon Karrde gave me control of the smugglers' alliance, and I've got too much to do. I can't just meditate all day long." Her narrow chiseled face seemed flushed even in the dim light. "I need to send for another transport to get out of here, since your prize student ran off with my ship."

Luke nodded, partly amused at her predicament but stung by the mention of Kyp Durron's betrayal. "We've got a communications setup in the second-tier war room. You can call Karrde and request a new ship."

Mara snorted. "Karrde only lets me contact him at prearranged intervals. He keeps moving around—says it's because he's afraid someone has a bounty on his head. I suspect he just doesn't want to be bothered. He claims that he's retired from the smuggling life and wants to live as a private citizen."

"You can always contact Coruscant," Luke said in a congenial voice. "I'm sure they'll send a shuttle for you. In fact, we're probably due for another supply run anyway."

Mara pursed her generous lips. "It would be nice to have the New Republic chauffeur *me* around for a change."

Luke searched for any hidden sarcasm in her comment but saw only wry humor instead. He shook his head. "I don't know who you'd get to volunteer for a brutal job like that."

• • •

When Lando came rushing into Han and Leia's quarters without knocking, Han Solo was intent on studying a list of interactive entertainment options for the twins. On the floor Jacen and Jaina played impatiently with shiny self-aware toys that kept trying to run away from the children's grasping hands.

See-Threepio stood nervously next to him. "I am perfectly qualified to make selections, sir. I'm certain I can find something to amuse the twins."

"I don't trust your choices, Threepio," Han said. "Remember how much they enjoyed the Holographic Zoo for Extinct Animals?"

"That was an anomaly, sir," Threepio said.

Lando rushed into the room, looking around. "Han, old buddy! I need a favor—a big favor."

With a sigh Han turned the selection process over to Threepio. "Okay, pick something—but if the kids don't like it, *I'll* let them amuse themselves by running a maintenance check on you."

"I . . . understand completely, sir," Threepio said, and bent to the task.

"What kind of favor?" he asked Lando warily.

Lando flung his cape over his shoulder and rubbed his hands together. "I, uh, need to borrow the *Falcon*—just for a little while."

"What?" Han said.

Lando answered in a rush. "Mara Jade is stuck on Yavin 4, and she needs a lift. I want to be the gallant gentleman who rescues her. Let me take the *Falcon*. Please?"

Han shook his head. "My ship isn't going anywhere without me. Besides, if you're trying to impress Mara Jade, taking a ship like the *Falcon* isn't the way to do it."

"Come on, Han," Lando said. "I took you to rescue Leia when Calamari was under attack. You owe me one."

Han sighed. "I suppose I could use an excuse to go see Luke and Kyp at the Jedi academy." He turned and smirked at Threepio. "Besides, this time at least *Leia's* here to watch out for the children."

When the *Millennium Falcon* landed in front of the great Massassi temple, Han emerged to see Luke sprinting toward him wearing an expression of boyish delight. Han grinned and stepped down the entry ramp, his boots clomping on the metal plates. Luke came forward to hug him in an enthusiastic embrace that was distinctly undignified for a Jedi Master.

Han said, "Enjoying your little vacation away from the thick of galactic politics, Luke?"

Luke's expression became troubled. "I wouldn't exactly say that."

Lando Calrissian emerged from the *Falcon* after taking an extra few moments to groom his hair, straighten his clothes, and make certain his appearance was as dashing as he could make it. Han had rolled his eyes, convinced that suave gentility was no way to win the affections of Mara Jade.

Though her scalding anger seemed to have cooled somewhat, Mara still showed a rough-edged hardness that made Han wonder why Lando would get so excited about the woman who had once called herself "The Emperor's Hand." With a flash of insight Han realized that Leia herself had come across as a mixture of fiery temper and icy coolness when he had first met her—and look at how that had turned out!

Mara Jade's slender figure emerged from the half-open hangar doors at the base of the blocky stone ziggurat. She carried a satchel slung over her shoulder.

Lando hurried down the ramp and cursorily clapped Luke on the back. "How you doing, Luke?" He practically tripped over himself as he trotted across the landing pad to meet Mara. "We hear you need a lift," he said, offering to take her satchel. "What happened to your own ship?"

"Don't ask," she said, then smiled wryly at him before handing over her heavy bag. "So you finally found something you're qualified to do, Calrissian. Baggage handler."

He carried her satchel over his shoulder and gestured to the *Falcon*. "Right this way to the VIP shuttle, madam."

Han stepped back from Luke and looked around at the steaming jungles and the vine-covered Great Temple. "So, where's Kyp?" he asked.

Luke looked down at his feet, and then, as if gathering courage through some kind of Jedi exercise, he looked up to meet Han's gaze. "I've got bad news for you. Kyp . . . disagreed with me about how fast he should learn dangerous new skills and how best to develop his ability with the Force."

"What do you mean?" Han asked. He grabbed one of the piston supports of the entry ramp to keep himself upright. "Was he hurt? Why didn't you call me?"

Luke shook his head. "I don't know what happened to him. He's been practicing certain techniques that I fear may lead him to the dark side. I'm very concerned, Han. He's the most powerful of all the students I've had here. He stole Mara Jade's ship and left Yavin 4. I have no idea where he is now or what he's doing."

Han forced his mouth into a thin line, but Luke continued. "Kyp has a great deal of power, and a great deal of anger and ambition—but little understanding or patience. That's a dangerous combination."

Han felt helpless. He barely noticed as Lando escorted Mara Jade up the ramp into the *Falcon*. "I don't know what to do, Luke," Han said.

Luke nodded grimly. "Neither do I."

The *Millennium Falcon* cruised through hyperspace with a vibrating hum of hyperdrive engines. Lando tried to keep his voice down as he leaned close to Han in the cockpit.

"Just let me tinker with the food-processing units, Han. Please? I've memorized some programming from the finest Cloud City casinos, and I can generate recipes that would make Mara Jade float with pleasure."

"No." Han scanned the chronometer that counted down how much time remained on the journey back to Coruscant. "I like the food processors the way they are."

Exasperated, Lando slumped into the copilot's chair and sighed. "They're all programmed for greasy, heavy Corellian recipes. Someone like Mara needs exotic food, special preparation. Not nerf sausage and dumplings with soggy charbote roots."

"Lando, that's the food I was brought up on—and on *my* ship, I want the food-prep units to make dishes that *I* like. I already wasted the whole journey to Yavin helping you scrub the living compartments in the back, polishing the holochess table, and perfuming the whole ship with disinfectant."

"Han," Lando said, "the ship was filthy, and it stank."

"Well, I *liked* it that way," Han insisted. "It was my dirt, and my stink, on my ship."

"Only because you got lucky in sabacc." Lando stood up, straightened his cape, and smoothed his purplish jumpsuit. "I let you win. You could never do it again."

Han and Lando glared at each other across the hastily cleared game board. Lando kept flicking glances toward Mara Jade as he randomized the rectangles of Han's old sabacc deck.

Mara had ignored Lando for most of the journey to Coruscant. She had rebuffed his attempts to prepare dinner, find musical selections for her, and engage her in conversation. Now as she watched them playing cards to settle a dispute over the ownership of the *Falcon*, she scowled as if they were no more than two little boys scuffling in a child's amusement pen.

Lando took the pack of glittering metallic cards so that the crystalline faces showed and held them toward Mara. "My lady, would you care to cut the cards?"

"No," she said, "I would not."

"I'm getting tired of this, Lando," Han said. "First I won the *Falcon* from you in a sabacc game on Bespin, then you won her back from me in the diplomatic lounge on Coruscant, and I won her back from you en route to Calamari. Enough is enough. This is our *last* hand."

"Fine with me, old buddy," Lando said, and started dealing the cards.

"No rematches," Han said.

"No rematches," Lando agreed.

"Whoever wins this time keeps the *Falcon* from now on."

"You got it," Lando said. "The *Millennium Falcon* belongs to the winner to do with as he pleases. No more borrowing, no more arguing."

Han nodded. "Loser gets a lifetime of Coruscant public transport." He picked up his cards. "Shut up and play."

Han tossed down the cards that had betrayed him and stood up to hide the devastating sense of loss coursing through him. He felt as if his heart had been crumpled like a piece of discarded paper and then stuffed back into his chest. "Go ahead and gloat, Lando."

Cool-faced, Mara Jade had watched the entire game with less indifference than she pretended to show. Now she scowled as if she expected Lando to stand up and cheer in triumph. Han anticipated the same reaction.

Halfway to his feet, Lando stopped and calmed himself, straightening in a dignified fashion. "That's it," he said in a slow, rich voice. "End of game. We'll never play for the *Falcon* again."

"Yeah," Han said in a barely audible voice, "that's what we agreed."

"And the *Falcon* is mine, to do with as I please," Lando said.

"Go ahead and gloat," Han said, again, using sarcasm to mask his own despair. He kicked himself for being lured into another stupid game. He had been an idiot, with nothing to gain, and now he had lost everything. "I should have known better than to play with you."

"Just like vornskyrs hissing at each other in a territorial dispute," Mara said, shaking her head. Her exotic spice-colored hair hung to one side. She did nothing to make herself look attractive, yet somehow it worked to her advantage.

Lando glanced at Mara, then turned partly aside as if ignoring her. With a grand flourish he spread his hands wide and gestured to Han.

"But since you're my friend, Han Solo, and since I know that the *Falcon* means even more to you than she does to me"—Lando paused for effect and stole another glance at Mara Jade before continuing—"I choose to *give* the *Millennium Falcon* back to you. A gift from me to you. A testimony to our years of friendship, and all that we've been through together."

Han collapsed back into his chair, feeling his knees turn weak and watery. His throat shriveled, and he opened and closed his mouth several times, completely at a loss for what to say.

"I'm going to the food-prep units," Lando said gallantly. "*If* Han will let me adjust the programming, I'll see if I can prepare the finest repast your units can manufacture, and we'll all have a nice meal together."

Han felt too stunned to argue, and Lando didn't wait for an answer. He cast a second look back at Mara Jade as he went toward the galley.

Still in shock, Han saw her raise her eyebrows and look after him with a surprised and mystified smile, as if completely reassessing her opinion of Lando Calrissian—which, Han concluded, must have been Lando's plan all along.

31

The Hammerhead Momaw Nadon arranged for Wedge Antilles and Qwi Xux to go sight-seeing across the pristine Ithorian landscape in an open-air skimmer. On the transit landing platform, the dazzling morning sky was a pale whitish purple with high wisps of cloud that masked several dim moons still riding the sky.

Qwi strapped herself into the plush vegetable-fiber seat and looked into the sunshine. "Why didn't you want Momaw Nadon to guide us?" she asked, studying the topographic information and the scenic highlights Nadon had suggested. "He seems very proud of his world."

Wedge concentrated on the control panel, though the vehicle looked rather simple to operate. "Well, because he's very busy, and because . . ." His voice trailed off, and he looked up at her with a faint smile. "I kind of wanted to be alone with you."

Qwi felt a giddy elation rising within her. "Yes, I think that would be nicer."

Wedge lifted their skimmer off the pad, and the
soared away from the great disk of the Ithorian eco-ci
and across the treetops. The *Tafanda Bay* had drifte
many kilometers during the course of the night, an
Wedge had to recalibrate the skimmer's coordinate
Daylight warmed their faces as the wind breathed co
drafts against their skin.

They headed for a low ridge where the dark-gree
jungles fell away into a paler forest. "What are yo
taking me to see?" Qwi asked.

Wedge leaned forward, staring at the horizon. "
large grove of bafforr trees that was half-destroyed b
the Imperials during their siege many years ago."

"Is there something special about those trees?" Qw
asked.

"The Ithorians worship them," he said. "They're sem
intelligent, like a hive mind. The greater the forest grow
the more intelligent the trees become."

As they skimmed closer, Qwi could see that a
aquamarine crystalline forest glowed faintly in th
sunlight, covering part of the hillside. Wedge le
the skimmer hover as they bent over the sides 1
gaze down at the glassy trunks, at the smooth y
sharp webs of bafforr branches. Scattered around th
perimeter, large, dark cylinders had toppled to th
ground and broken like tubes of burned transpariste
It reminded her of the debris scattered around th
site of the smashed Cathedral of Winds on Vorte
Tiny saplings like inverted icicles protruded from th
rocky earth.

"The forest seems to be growing back," Wedge sai
The thin saplings glowed a whiter blue than the rest
the forest.

"I see people down there!" Qwi said, pointing off to the
[si]de. The smooth grayish forms of four Ithorians dashed
[fo]r the cover of the thick undergrowth on the side of the
[ri]dge. "I thought they weren't supposed to set foot in the
[ju]ngle."

Wedge stared down at them, baffled. He raised the
[sk]immer higher, but the four renegade Ithorians had
[al]ready vanished into the tree cover. His brow furrowed
[as] if searching for an answer. He drew in a quick
[br]eath.

"I seem to remember something about the Mother
[Ju]ngle summoning certain Ithorians. It's a rare calling
[th]at no one can explain. They leave everything behind
[an]d live in the wilderness, forbidden to return to their
[ec]o-cities. In a way, they become fugitives. Since the
[It]horians consider it such sacrilege to touch the forest,
[th]e calling must be pretty strong."

Qwi looked down at the burned glasslike trunks of
[th]e bafforr trees destroyed by Imperial turbolaser fire.
["I]'m glad to know they're tending the forest, though."
[Sh]e wondered how much of the bafforr forest's collective
[in]telligence had returned. "Let's go somewhere else,
[W]edge, so they can get back to their work."

Wedge took Qwi to a high plateau studded with
[fl]at gray and tan rocks, covered with vermilion scrub
[br]ush and black vines. A confluence of three rivers
[ca]me together in a great sinkhole on the edge of
[th]e towering cliff, pouring into a spectacular triple
[w]aterfall that plunged into the plateau's deep pit.
[A]t the bottom of the plateau, water spilled out
[of] a thousand broken caves, flowing into a turgid,

foamy marsh filled with swaying reeds and leaping fish.

Wedge circled the open-air skimmer above the enormous sinkhole on the plateau, and Qwi gaped at the fabulous waterfall. Curtains of spray rose from thundering echoes of plunging water. Rainbows sparkled against the lavender sky.

Qwi turned her head this way and that, trying to look at everything at once. Wedge grinned like a daredevil and took them over the center of the three waterfalls, hovering and then lowering them down the core of the sinkhole.

Qwi laughed as the thick, cold mist blanketed them, drenching their clothes. Wedge dropped the skimmer to where all three rivers crashed against the rocks with a sound like exploding planets. Green batlike creatures flitted through the spray, catching insects and tiny fish that tumbled over the falls.

"This is fantastic," Qwi shouted.

"It gets better," Wedge said, "if Momaw Nadon gave us good information."

He steered the skimmer toward a cluster of slick black outcroppings that jutted from the side of the pit. The overhang sheltered them from most of the cold spray and cyclonic winds swirling in the rock-walled chimney. The booming echo of water became a constant background.

Wedge brought the skimmer in among the rocks to a sheltered place where shafts of sunlight pierced the rising swirls of spray. "Nadon said we could land here."

He reached into a compartment under the seat, pulled out two translucent waterproof capes, and removed two packages of self-heating meals Nadon had also provided. Wedge helped Qwi fasten one of the waterproof garments over her narrow shoulders, then fastened his own. He picked up their lunches and indicated the smooth rocks under the overhang.

"Let's have a picnic," he said.

At the end of an exhausting day Qwi stood outside her vine-covered stateroom door on the *Tafanda Bay*. Wedge looked into her indigo eyes and shuffled his feet.

"Thank you," Qwi said. "This has been the most wonderful day of my life."

Wedge opened his mouth and closed it three times, as if searching for something to say. Finally he bent forward, touched her silky mother-of-pearl hair, then kissed her. He let his warm lips linger on hers for a long moment. She pushed closer to him and felt delight surge through her.

"And now you've given me one more interesting thing," she said in her quiet musical voice.

Blushing, Wedge backed away from her and said, "Uh, I'll see you in the morning." He turned and practically fled back to his own stateroom.

With a wistful smile Qwi watched his door close. She opened her stateroom and slipped inside, feeling as if she had repulsorlifts in her feet. She leaned against the door as it closed and shut her eyes as the gentle illumination in her room slowly brightened. She heaved a contented sigh.

And opened her eyes to see a dark man rising from his crouch in the shadowy corners of the room.

The looming silhouette approached her, and she froze in terror at the sight of the swirling black cape that flowed around his body.

Darth Vader!

She tried to shout for help, but her voice locked in her throat as if an invisible hand had stilled her vocal cords. She whirled for the door and hung in midstride, yanked back by unseen spiderwebs.

The dark man was closer now, gliding toward her. What did he want? She couldn't scream. She heard his hollow breathing echo like the snarl of a beast.

A hand reached out for her, and Qwi couldn't move, couldn't duck away as the fingers wrapped around the top of her head. She felt him pressing there. The other hand, cold and supple, grasped her face. She blinked her wide eyes and looked up to see the face of Kyp Durron, eyes blazing, his expression soulless.

He spoke in a freezing voice. "I have found you, Dr. Xux. You hold too much dangerous knowledge," he said. "I must make certain no one can ever again create the weapons you've been responsible for. There must be no more Death Stars. No more Sun Crushers."

His fingers clamped down harder on her forehead, on her face. Her skull seemed ready to shatter. Waves of pain plunged through her brain like the claws of a nightmare monster. She felt the sharp points of metal talons scraping through her mind, digging, prying up and ripping out memories and scientific knowledge she had accumulated over the course of many years.

Qwi finally managed a scream, but it was a weak, watery cry that faded as she fell down a long, dark tunnel into forgetfulness. She slumped against the vine-covered wall of her quarters.

As her sight turned dim in front of her, the last thing she saw was the black-shrouded form of her attacker.

as he opened her stateroom door and stalked out into the night.

Next morning Wedge whistled to himself as he dressed, smiling into a reflection plate as he straightened his dark hair. He ordered an exotic breakfast for two. Qwi was an early riser, especially now that she was excited about the sight-seeing they would do on Ithor. Momaw Nadon had promised them the open-air skimmer for another day.

He sauntered across the corridor, signaled at her stateroom door, and waited. No answer.

He signaled again and again until, alarmed, he tried to open the door. Finding the entrance to Qwi's room unlocked, he was even more alarmed. Had someone come to assassinate her in the night? Did the Imperials know her location, after all? He pushed the door open and rushed inside. Darkness and shadows filled her quarters.

"Lights!" he yelled. Sudden illumination bathed the room in pale peach-colored light.

He heard Qwi before he saw her. She sat crouched in a corner, sobbing. She clutched her pearlescent hair with both hands, squeezing her temples as if trying to hold thoughts inside that kept slipping through her fingers.

"Qwi!" he shouted, and ran to her. Bending down, he took her wrist and gently forced her to turn her head. He stared into her wide, blank eyes. "What happened?"

She didn't appear to recognize him, and Wedge's stomach sank with horror. Qwi looked confused and devastated. She frowned as if searching her memory. She shook her head slowly, then closed her big eyes, squeezing them tight as she fought with her own thoughts. Tears ran down her cheeks, oozing in small drops, then larger splashes as she bit her lip in furious concentration. She blinked up at him again, finally finding the name that had eluded her.

"Widj? *Wedge?*" she said at last. "Is your name Wedge?"

He nodded numbly, and with another great weeping cry she threw herself into his arms. He held her, feeling her body tremble with sobs. "What happened?" he repeated. "Qwi, tell me!"

"I don't know." She shook her head, and featherlike hair flowed in a slow wave from one shoulder to the other. "I barely know *you*. I can't remember. My mind feels so empty . . . filled with blank spots."

Wedge held her tight as she said, "I've lost everything. Most of my memory, my life—is gone."

32

Kyp Durron returned to the fourth moon of Yavin in the heartbeat stillness of the jungle night. Filled with a power he had decided to use to its fullest, he felt ready to explode in an exhilarating outpouring of the Force—but he could not let such childish demonstrations seduce him. He had a mission to accomplish, one that would affect the future of the entire galaxy.

Without running lights or landing beacon, he brought the Z-95 Headhunter he had taken from Mara Jade to a gentle rest on the slightly overgrown landing pad in front of the Great Temple. Kyp had no interest in reacquainting himself with the other weak Jedi trainees or even with the misguided and cowardly Master Skywalker. He simply needed access to the ancient Massassi temples Exar Kun had designed as focal points for concentrating the power of the Sith.

Above him the night sky was lush with stars, and the stirrings of the surrounding jungle wove a tapestry of hushed sounds. But the insects made their music more quietly, and few large animals crashed through the underbrush. The entire rain forest seemed stunned by Kyp's return.

Kyp tossed the oddly glittering black cape over his shoulders. Time to be about his business.

Leaving the Headhunter fighter behind him, he approached the monolithic ziggurat of the Great Temple. Rust-colored vermiform vines writhed out of his way, avoiding Kyp's footsteps, as if his entire body exuded a deadly heat.

Chisel-cut stone steps ran up the side of the pyramid. He set one foot in front of the other, climbing slowly, listening to the soft echoes of his breathing. Anticipation built within him.

In his mind Kyp heard cheering ghosts, saw visions like a videoloop from four thousand years ago when Exar Kun had found the last resting place of the ancient Sith. Kun had rediscovered their teachings. He had built great temples, establishing the Brotherhood of the Sith among disillusioned Jedi Knights. Here on Yavin 4, Kun had used the Massassi people as expendable resources, power conduits to redefine the chaos and corruption of the Old Republic. He had challenged the foolish Jedi who followed their incompetent leaders without thinking simply because they had sworn to do so. . . .

Now Kyp would finish the battle, though the enemy was no longer the incompetent, decaying Republic, but the fraudulent New Order and the repressive Empire that had taken the Old Republic's place. While Master Skywalker limited the training of his new Jedi Knights, Kyp Durron had learned more. Much more.

He reached the second tier of the ziggurat and paused to look down at the insectile shape of his Z-95 fighter resting in the center of the landing grid. No one had yet stirred from inside the temple.

A pastel glow crept into the sky at the horizon as the rapid rotation of the jungle moon brought planetrise closer. Kyp continued to climb the long series of steps, staring toward the apex of the Great Temple.

Kyp had already struck his first blow by erasing dangerous knowledge from the Imperial scientist, Qwi Xux. Only Qwi had known how to build another Sun Crusher—but Kyp, using his bare hands and his newfound power, had torn that knowledge from her brain and scattered it into nothingness. No one could ever find it again.

Next, he would apply a poetic justice that delighted his sensibility, that made him thrill with revenge for all that the Empire had done against him and his family and his colony world. Kyp would resurrect the Sun Crusher itself and use it to obliterate the remains of the Empire. He would be accountable to no one but himself. He trusted no one else to make the hard decisions.

Kyp reached the summit of the Great Temple just as the huge orange ball of Yavin heaved itself over the horizon. Misty and pale, the gas giant swirled with tremendous storm systems large enough to swallow smaller worlds.

The temple's diamond-shaped flagstones covered the small observation platform above the grand audience chamber. Vines and stunted Massassi trees poked up from the corners of the old stones.

Kyp looked skyward. The small plants and animals filling the jungles of Yavin 4 were insignificant to him.

They mattered nothing in the grand scheme of what he was about to undertake. The importance of his vision far exceeded the petty needs of any single planet.

As the sphere of Yavin rose into the sky, Kyp lifted his arms, and the slick black fabric of his cape fell behind him. His hands were slender and small, the hands of a young man. But inside, power sizzled through his bones.

"Exar Kun, help me," Kyp said, closing his eyes.

He reached out with his mind, following the paths of the Force that led to every object in the universe, drawing power from the cosmic focal point of the Massassi temple. He searched, sending his thoughts like a probe deep into the storm systems of the gas giant.

Behind him Kyp felt the black-ice power of Exar Kun arise, tapping into him and reinforcing his abilities. His own feeble exploratory touch suddenly plunged forward like a blaster bolt. Kyp felt larger, a part of the jungle moon, then a part of the entire planetary system, until he burrowed into the heart of the gas giant itself.

Pale orange clouds whipped past him. He sensed pressure increasing as he plummeted down, down to the incredibly dense layers near the core. He sought the tiny speck of machinery, a small, indestructible ship that had been cast away.

When he reached the bottommost levels of the atmosphere, Kyp finally found the Sun Crusher. It stood out like a beacon, a bull's-eye in the funneling field lines of the Force.

Size matters not, Master Skywalker had repeated. Kyp engulfed the Sun Crusher with his mind, surrounding it, touching it with his limitless, invisible hands. He thought about heaving it back up, dragging the Sun

Crusher out of the depths of Yavin. But he discarded that thought.

Instead, with the assistance of Exar Kun, he used his innate skill to power up the controls again, to move control levers, push buttons to alter the course stored in the Sun Crusher's memory, bringing it out of its entombment.

Kyp continued to watch the weapon's progress, focusing on the sphere of the enormous planet as it crested the misty treetops. The Sun Crusher appeared as a silvery dot, seeming no larger than an atom as it emerged from the highest cloud layers and streaked across space toward the emerald-green moon where Kyp waited.

He stared upward and waited, opening his arms to receive the indestructible weapon.

The Sun Crusher approached like a long, sharp horn of crystalline alloy, cruising upright on its long axis. The toroidal resonance-torpedo launcher hung at the bottom of the long hook. It looked beautiful.

The Sun Crusher descended through the jungle moon's atmosphere, straight down—like a spike to impale the great Temple. Kyp controlled it, slowed its descent, until the superweapon hovered to a stop, suspended in front of him.

As the sky brightened with planetrise, the alloy hull of the Sun Crusher seemed as pristine as a firefacet gem, scoured of all oxidation and debris by the intense temperatures and pressures at the core of Yavin. The Sun Crusher looked clean, and deadly, and ready for him.

"Thank you, Exar Kun," Kyp whispered.

•   •   •

Luke Skywalker awoke from another series of night mares. He sat bolt upright on his pallet, instantly aware He had felt a great disturbance in the Force. Something was not right.

He got up, moving cautiously as he sent out his thoughts to check on his students: Kirana Ti, Dorsk 81, the new Calamarian arrival Cilghal, Streen, Tionne Kam Solusar, and all the others. Nothing seemed amiss They slept soundly—almost too soundly, as if a net of sleep had been cast over them.

When he reached out farther, he was stunned to feel a cold, black whirlpool of twisted Force around the peak of the temple. It stunned him.

Luke sprinted to the door of his chambers, hesitated then stepped back to retrieve his lightsaber. He marched down the corridors, smoothing his fear as he rode the turbolift to the upper levels of the ancient pyramid.

Calm, Yoda had said, *you must remain calm.*

But the sight that greeted him under the dawn sky nearly overwhelmed Luke.

The Sun Crusher hung suspended over the temple still steaming in the morning air, resurrected from its tomb at the core of the gas giant. Kyp Durron spun around to stare at Luke, his black cape swirling with the rapid motion.

Stunned, Luke reeled backward. "How dare you bring that weapon back!" he said. "It goes against all the Jedi knowledge I have taught you."

Kyp laughed at him. "You haven't taught me very much, Master Skywalker. I've learned a great deal beyond your feeble teachings. You pretend to h a great instructor, but you're afraid to learn for yourself."

He looked back at the Sun Crusher. "I will do what must be done to eradicate the Empire. While I make the galaxy safe for everyone, you can stay here and practice your simple Jedi tricks. But they are no more than children's games."

"Kyp," Luke said, keeping his voice even and taking a step toward him, "you've been lured by the dark side, but you must return. You were deceived and misled. Come back before its grip becomes too strong." He swallowed. "I went over to the dark side once, and I came back. It *can* be done if you're strong enough and brave enough. Are you?"

Kyp laughed in disbelief. "Skywalker, it's embarrassing for me to listen to you talk. You are afraid to risk anything yourself, yet you want to call yourself a Jedi Master. It doesn't work that way. You've stunted the training of your other Jedi candidates because of your own narrow-mindedness. Perhaps I should just defeat you here and now, and then *I* can take over their training."

With trembling hands and a deep-seated dread in his heart, Luke reached to his side and wrapped his hand around the slick handle of his lightsaber. He pulled it free, igniting it with the familiar *snap-hiss*. The brilliant green blade extended, humming and ready for battle.

A Jedi could not attack an unarmed opponent, could not resort to violence before all other avenues had been exhausted—but Luke knew the deadly potential of his most talented student. If Kyp had fallen to the dark side, he could become another Darth Vader. Perhaps even worse. . . .

"Don't make me do this," Luke said, raising his lightsaber, but unsure what to do. He couldn't just cut down his student, who stood unarmed at the top of the temple. But if he didn't . . .

"We have to send the Sun Crusher back," Luke said. "At one time you yourself insisted that it should never be used."

"I spoke out of ignorance," Kyp said, "just as you do."

"Don't make me fight you," Luke said in a low voice.

Kyp made a dismissive gesture with one hand, and a sudden wave of dark ripples splashed across the air like the shock front from a concussion grenade.

Luke stumbled backward. The lightsaber turned cold in his hand. Frost crystals grew in feathery patterns around the handle. At the core of the brilliant green blade a shadow appeared, a black disease rotting away the purity of the beam. The humming blade sputtered sounding like a sickly cough. The black taint rapidly grew stronger, swallowing up the green beam.

With a fizzle of sparks Luke's lightsaber died.

Trying to control his growing fear, Luke felt a sudden brush of cold behind him. He turned to see a black hooded *silhouette*—the image that had impersonated Anakin Skywalker in Luke's nightmare . . . the dark man who had lured Gantoris into a devastating loss of control.

Kyp's voice came as if from a great distance. "At last, Master Skywalker, you can meet my mentor—Exar Kun."

Luke dropped his useless lightsaber and crouched. His every muscle suddenly coiled and tensed. He rallied

all the powers of the Force around him, seeking any
defensive tactic.

With the Sun Crusher looming behind him, Kyp
stretched out both hands and blasted Luke with lightning
bolts like black cracks in the Force. Dark tendrils rose
up from gaps in the temple flagstones, fanged, illusory
vipers that struck at him from all sides.

Luke cried out and tried to strike back, but the shadow
of Exar Kun joined the attack, adding more deadly force.
The ancient Dark Lord of the Sith lashed out with waves
of blackness, driving long icicles of frozen poison into
Luke's body.

He thrashed, but felt helpless. To lose control to anger
and desperation would be as great a failure as if he did
nothing at all. Luke called upon the powers that Yoda
and Obi-Wan had taught him—but everything he did,
every skillful technique, failed utterly.

Against the full might of Kyp Durron and the forbidden weapons of the long-dead spirit of Exar Kun, even a
Jedi Master such as Luke Skywalker could not prevail.

The black serpentlike tentacles of evil force struck at
him again and again, filling his body with a pain like lava
coursing through his veins. As he screamed, his voice
was swallowed by a hurricane from the dark side.

Luke cried out one last time and crumpled backward
to the blessedly cool flagstones of the Great Massassi
Temple, as everything turned a smothering, final black
around him. . . .

33

Near the center of the Caul-
dron Nebula, the two surviving Star Destroyers hung
poised and ready to launch their attack on Coruscant.

Admiral Daala stood tall on her bridge platform, filled
with an electrifying new self-confidence and determination. She had not slept in the past day.

Her officers sat at their stations, keyed up and anxious. A double complement of stormtroopers marched
up and down the *Gorgon*'s halls, fully armed and battle
ready. They had had a decade of drills, and now they
would use their training to strike the greatest blow they
could imagine for their cause.

"Commander Kratas, report," Daala said.

Kratas snapped to attention, barking out his report.
"All equipment and weaponry have been transferred
from the *Basilisk* to the *Gorgon*. Only a skeleton
crew of volunteers—all stormtroopers—remains on the
Basilisk. Captain Mullinore reports he is ready for his
final mission."

Daala turned to the lieutenant at the comm station. "Patch me through to Captain Mullinore."

The image of the *Basilisk*'s captain appeared in front of her. The hologram wavered, but the man himself seemed completely rigid and in control, looking stoic as he met Admiral Daala's emerald eyes. "Yes, Admiral," he said.

"Captain, is your ship ready?" She paused, clasping her hands behind her back. "Are *you* ready?"

"Yes, Admiral. We have reconfigured all weapons systems to increase power to our shields. The stormtrooper crew has rigged the self-destruct mechanism into our primary hyperdrive reactors." He paused as if gathering courage, but his close-cropped blond hair showed not a glimmer of sweat. "The *Basilisk* is ready whenever you give the word, Admiral."

"Thank you, Captain. History will remember your sacrifice—I swear it."

She turned to the rest of her crew and switched on the intraship comm system. Her clipped voice rang throughout the *Gorgon*. "All hands, battle stations! Prepare to begin our run. We will destroy Coruscant and strike a death blow to the heart of the Rebellion."

Kyp Durron piloted the Sun Crusher to the core of the Cauldron Nebula, where Exar Kun had told him Admiral Daala's fleet lay in wait.

The controls of the Sun Crusher felt cool and familiar as he sat forward in the hard, uncomfortable pilot seat, looking through the segmented viewpanels. He had helped fly the superweapon during the escape from Maw Installation with Han Solo.

During that battle they had taken out one of Daala's Star Destroyers. Now he would use the Sun Crusher to obliterate the rest of her fleet.

Igniting an entire nebula seemed like an excessive blow to squash an Imperial insect, but Kyp appreciated the irony of destroying them with their own weapons. And it would signal to the rest of the fragmented Empire what was about to befall them as Kyp continued his purge.

The Sun Crusher's sensor panels became useless in the ionized discharge from the knot of blue-giant stars that illuminated the Cauldron Nebula. The front viewscreens dimmed to filter out the blazing light.

Kyp stretched out with the Force, dropping his inhibitions and letting the power burst from him like compressed gas. After the effort of yanking the Sun Crusher from the core of Yavin, finding a few Star Destroyers seemed a simple exercise.

After only a moment he sensed the arrowhead-shaped silhouettes of two Imperial battleships.

He piloted the Sun Crusher toward the bloated supergiants at the heart of the nebula. The titanic blue stars were huge, and young, and ripe for destruction. On a cosmic timescale they would burn hot, but briefly, ending their lives in supernova explosions that would send shock waves through an entire region of the galaxy.

With the Sun Crusher, though, Kyp could ignite the supernovas *now*, rather than in a hundred thousand years.

He stared across the soothing rainbow sea of gas and thought of the splashed-color sunsets on his colony world of Deyer, the placid terraformed lakes around the peaceful raft towns where he and his brother Zeth had played. But the Empire had broken into Kyp's home and taken him and his family away—without warning.

Years ago the Death Star had approached the quiet and pristine planet of Alderaan and had blown it to pieces with its planet-destroying superlaser—without warning.

Admiral Daala had captured Kyp and Han and Chewbacca after they had passed through the black-hole maze; but because Kyp had possessed no "worthwhile" information for her, she had sentenced him to death.

Daala deserved no warning. None at all.

Kyp increased the radiation shields on the Sun Crusher and approached the mammoth blue-giant stars, seething in their ocean of star material. He powered up the targeting display in front of him.

A recessed section of the control panel slid aside. A screen popped up, displaying a diagram of closely orbiting spheres. Seven enormous stars crowded in the middle of the nebula, circling in complex orbits as they stole gas from each other. Their intense radiation shone through the scattered hydrogen, oxygen, and neon clouds.

Kyp's face was a grim mask as he flicked a row of red activator switches. He knew exactly how the Sun Crusher worked; he had stolen those memories from Qwi Xux.

Warning beacons flashed across the command-system panels, and Kyp confirmed his intentions to the onboard computer. The torus-shaped generator at the long end of the Sun Crusher powered up, crackling with blue plasma.

Kyp remembered the New Republic engineers attempting to determine how the superweapon worked, how they had panicked at the sight of a simple message cylinder. The resonance torpedoes that triggered stellar explosions were dense packets of energy, programmed and modulated to make the core of a star unstable. The torpedoes could initiate a collapse and rebound of the outer layers of star material, unleashing a tremendously violent explosion that would rip a star apart.

Kyp targeted the cluster of blue-giant stars. He did not hesitate. He knew in his heart what he had to do.

He pushed the activation buttons. The Sun Crusher shuddered as the superweapon launched seven high-power resonance torpedoes.

Against the muted swirls of the Cauldron Nebula, he saw sizzling ovoid shapes of electric green, white, and yellow fire. The energy torpedoes streaked out, plunging into the boiling surfaces of the giant stars.

Kyp dimmed the segmented viewport and fixed his gaze on the blue giants. The cluster would explode simultaneously, and the shock waves would ignite vast oceans of nebular material in a galactic wildfire. It would be a perfectly clear signal to the remnants of the Empire.

But it would take hours for the torpedoes to tunnel to the stellar cores and set up the chain reaction. The wave of destruction would boil up from the depths of the stars until a flash of incredible force spewed brilliant light, high-energy radiation, and star matter into the Cauldron. The entire sector would become an inferno.

Kyp felt a cold fist clench inside his stomach. He could not turn back now. Once launched, the resonance torpedoes were irrevocable. These seven stars were doomed to explode in a few hours.

He pulled away at a leisurely pace, killing time. The Sun Crusher was so small that few sensor systems could detect it, especially within the electromagnetic chaos of the Cauldron Nebula. The weapon was designed to flit into a system, drop its torpedo into a star, and vanish without a battle, without loss of ordnance or personnel. A simple first—and final—strike.

Admiral Daala would never detect his presence.

Kyp's gaze wandered back to the chronometer, impatient to watch Daala's ships being wiped out in the murderous waves ripping through the nebula. He had the most powerful weapon ever invented, and he had the powers of the Sith that Exar Kun had shown him.

Where others had failed against the Empire, Kyp Durron would succeed. Completely.

As he drifted away from the blue-giant cluster, he noted that only about an hour remained before the massive explosions would begin. The waiting seemed to go on forever. He sent out his thoughts again, wishing he could taunt Daala.

Then, unexpectedly, her Star Destroyers began to move. The *Basilisk* and the *Gorgon* powered up their sublight engines and started a slow drift, aligning themselves to a hyperspace path, as if they were ready to launch another attack.

Kyp felt a flame of anger sear through him. "No—she can't leave now!"

He could not go back and stop the explosion of the core stars. Daala *had* to stay where she would be trapped!

Kyp slapped at the Sun Crusher's weapon-control systems, powering up the defensive laser cannons mounted at sharp angles on the weapon. Then he shot forward at full thrust.

When he and Han had first escaped from the Maw cluster, Daala had thrown all of her fighters at him in a desperate attempt to recapture the Sun Crusher.

Kyp figured it would take little more than a few potshots to give her the incentive to stay around.

Admiral Daala raised her right hand, looking at the navigator. "Prepare to engage hyperdrive," she said.

"Admiral!" the lieutenant at the sensor station cried. "I've detected an intruder!"

A tiny ship streaked across the bow of the *Gorgon*, blasting at them with puny laser strikes.

"What?" Daala said, turning. "Viewscreen," she called, "Enhance."

A shimmering image of Captain Mullinore from the *Basilisk* appeared at the comm station beside her. "Admiral, we have just detected the Sun Crusher," he said. "Shall we engage?"

"The Sun Crusher!" Daala took a second to accept the information. She could not answer before the small ship flitted in front of the *Gorgon*'s bridge tower again, blasting at the turbolaser batteries. She instantly recognized the thorn-shaped ship, the tiny superweapon bristling with defensive laser turrets. But the Sun Crusher's lasers had too little power to cause damage to a Star Destroyer.

"Launch two TIE squadrons," Daala said, feeling a new excitement. "I want the Sun Crusher recaptured. This changes everything in our strategy against the New Republic."

The stormtroopers, already keyed up from a day's worth of red-alert status, swarmed across the decks. Moments later the bottom bay of the *Gorgon* opened and spewed out a hundred plane-winged TIE fighters soaring through the curling gas of the nebula.

Daala watched the small battle unfold. The Sun Crusher had been designed to be extremely swift and maneuverable. With its indestructible quantum armor, the superweapon seemed to laugh at the attack she sent against it. It was only a matter of time, though.

"But why does he attack us at all?" Daala said, tapping black-gloved fingers on the bridge railing. "Something's wrong here. He provoked us, but he has no way of causing us damage. Why did he call attention to himself," she mused, "and how did he find us here?"

Commander Kratas answered her, though she had been muttering to herself. "I can't speculate on that, Admiral."

"Bring the Star Destroyers about," she said. "Lock a tractor beam on the Sun Crusher next time it passes."

"The Sun Crusher's pilot is maneuvering at speeds much too high for us to be certain of a firm lock," Kratas said.

Daala glared at him. "Does that mean you're unable to try?"

"No, Admiral." Kratas turned and clapped his hands, directing the tactical officers on the bridge. "You heard the Admiral! Set to it immediately."

"Admiral, the Sun Crusher is signaling us," the comm officer said. "Voice-only transmission."

Daala whirled. "Put the pilot on."

With a crackle the thin voice of a mere boy echoed through the *Gorgon's* command center. "Admiral Daala, I'm Kyp Durron—remember me? I hope so. You put me under a death sentence. That made quite an impression on me. I hope it made some sort of impression on you."

Daala recalled the wiry, dark-haired youth who had been taken prisoner along with the Rebels who had blundered into the Maw Installation. She motioned for the comm officer to open a channel.

"Kyp Durron, if you surrender immediately and deliver the Sun Crusher intact, we will take you to the planet of your choice. You can be free. Don't be foolish."

"Not a chance, Admiral." Kyp laughed at her. "I'm thumbing my nose at your supposed Imperial superiority. I'll take my chances." He cut off the transmission and streaked by again, firing darts of laser energy that bounced harmlessly off the shielded hull of the Star Destroyer.

"Tractor-beam lock—" the tactical officer said, " . . . lost it."

"Admiral!" the sensor chief broke in, his voice filled with urgency. "I'm picking up unusual readings from the star cluster. The blue giants are fluctuating, all seven of them, I've never seen anything like—"

Daala froze. Her mouth dropped open in horror as she suddenly realized the terrible plan this . . . this *boy* had put into effect against her fleet.

"Full about!" she shouted. "One hundred eighty degrees, maximum speed. Get out of the nebula, now!"

"But, Admiral—?" Commander Kratas said.

"He's used the Sun Crusher!" she screamed. "The stars are going to explode! He's just trying to stall us here so we'll be trapped."

Kratas scrambled to the navigation station himself. The *Gorgon* lurched as the sublight engines kicked in, spinning the enormous Star Destroyer about.

"We no longer have our navicomputer lock on Coruscant," the navigation officer said. "When we turned to strike at the Sun Crusher, we lost our alignment."

"Get us out of here now," Daala said. "Any vector! Inform the *Basilisk*."

The sublight engines powered up, blasting as they lumbered away from the center of the nebula, picking up speed. The hyperdrive engines were primed, gathering power. The Star Destroyers began to move away—

Then all the stars exploded.

Kyp Durron watched the Star Destroyers wheel about and flee like wounded banthas.

"You can't get away fast enough." He smiled. "Not fast enough."

The *Gorgon* and the *Basilisk* began to heave themselves through the nebula at top speed, abandoning scores of TIE fighters. The small Imperial fighters veered off in a panic when their mother ships suddenly turned to run.

Kyp ignored the rest of the TIE fighters and punched his engines to twice the Sun Crusher's maximum-rated capacity, shooting straight up and out the plane of the nebular cloud.

When the cluster of blue giants detonated, concentric shock waves of blinding light and searing radiation blasted outward like a cosmic hurricane.

The *Gorgon* had managed to pull two ship lengths ahead of the *Basilisk*.

Hauling on the controls, Kyp continued the Sun Crusher's race upward, confident that the quantum armor would protect him from the worst. The incredible surge of energy from the supernovas darkened his viewports to near opacity.

Curtains of fire overtook the *Basilisk,* washing over the Star Destroyer and igniting it like another tiny nova erupting in the nebula, as the firestorm front swept on.

The viewscreen blackened, but where the *Gorgon* had been Kyp saw another flash—and then the firestorm obliterated all detail.

After his screens opaqued completely, Kyp used the onboard navicomputer to set a new course. This was just the beginning.

Leaving the galactic inferno behind him, and awed by the power of the Sun Crusher, Kyp moved off to seek out those remaining worlds that still swore allegiance to the Empire.

Now, without doubt, he had all the power he needed.

34

With the morning coolness of Yavin 4, Ambassador Cilghal rose in her austere quarters and basked in the shadowy dampness of the stone temple.

She had been at the Jedi *praxeum* for only a few days, but already she felt as if the whole universe had opened for her. Master Skywalker's exercises in attuning her mind to the Force had shown her how to turn her gaze in a new direction, to see things in full view that she had previously only glimpsed out of the corners of her eyes. He had given her a nudge down a long, smooth slope of discovery; the more she learned, the easier it was to learn more.

She splashed tepid water across her face, moistening her rubbery skin, scrubbing the delicate tendrils that hung beneath her slit of a mouth. Though the air of the jungle moon was thick with humidity, she still felt more comfortable when she could keep her exposed skin moist.

Cilghal left her quarters and moved to join the dozen other Jedi candidates in the dining hall, where each would consume a small breakfast of fruits or meats compatible with his or her biochemistry.

Dorsk 81 sat at a table contemplating colored rectangles of processed nutrients. Because he had lived for so long on a self-contained, environmentally controlled world, the cloned Jedi trainee could not digest foods that had not been heavily processed.

The gaunt, hardened Jedi Kam Solusar attempted to talk to wild-haired Streen, who kept flicking his gaze from side to side as if distracted.

The rest of the Jedi trainees sat by themselves or in small groups, talking uneasily. Cilghal did not see Master Skywalker among them. He was usually the first to enter the dining hall, waiting for his students to join him. The other Jedi trainees seemed disconcerted by the change of routine.

Cilghal worked the food-processing unit to prepare a breakfast of diced smoked fish and a pungent-tasting grain mash she enjoyed. Finally she asked the students in general, "Where is Master Skywalker?"

The trainees looked at each other as if they had been wanting to ask the same question.

Streen stood up and looked around in alarm. "It's too quiet," he said. "Too quiet. I wanted it quiet, but this is too much. I can't hear Master Skywalker. I could always sense voices in my head. I *hear* all of yours. It's too quiet." He sat down again as if embarrassed. "Too quiet."

Tionne rushed into the dining hall, clutching her twin boxed musical instrument. Her silvery hair streamed behind her in a wild mass, and her pearly eyes were wide and panic-stricken. "Come quickly! I've found Master Skywalker."

Without question, without confusion, all the Jedi trainees rose in a coordinated, flowing movement. They moved together and sprinted after Tionne as she ran down the winding moss-grown halls. Cilghal attempted to keep up with the more athletic members, such as Kirana Ti and Tionne.

They ran through the echoing grand audience chamber where vines covered the walls and the long polished seats stood empty in shafts of sunlight.

"This way," Tionne said. "I don't know what's happened to him."

They reached a back staircase of worn stone steps that led to the observation platform at the top of the ziggurat.

Cilghal drew up short as she noticed the robed figure sprawled on the flagstones under the sky. His hands were thrown back as if to defend against something.

"Master Skywalker!" she called. The other trainees rushed forward. Cilghal pushed through the gathered students and knelt beside the fallen man.

Luke's face seemed curdled in an outcry of pain or fear. His eyes were squeezed shut, his lips were curled back in a grimace.

On the stone floor beside him lay his lightsaber, as if it had proved useless against whatever enemy he had fought.

Cilghal propped Luke's head up, touching his pale-brown hair. Rivulets of cold sweat glistened on his face, but she felt no warmth on his skin. She probed, using her newfound abilities in the Force, desperately searching.

"What happened to him?" Dorsk 81 said in great alarm.

"Is he alive?" Streen asked. "I can't hear him."

Cilghal probed with her sensing abilities and shook her orange and muddy-green head. "He's breathing. I can sense very little heartbeat, just the faintest pulse. But I can't find *him* inside. When I touch him with the Force, all I find is a great empty spot. . . . "

She turned to look at the others with her sad round Calamarian eyes. "It's as if he has left us."

"What can we do?" Kirana Ti asked.

Cilghal cradled Luke's motionless head in her lap and blinked her huge Calamarian eyes, unable to speak for a long moment.

"We are all alone now," she finally said.

About the Author

'or the past ten years KEVIN J. ANDERSON has worked
s a technical editor and writer at the large govern-
nent weapons research lab, Lawrence Livermore Nation-
l Laboratory . . . which he insists has nothing to do with
he large Imperial weapons research lab, Maw Installa-
ion, in JEDI SEARCH. He is also the author of 18 sci-
nce fiction or fantasy books, including three co-written
vith Doug Beason for Bantam—LIFELINE, THE TRINITY
PARADOX, and ASSEMBLERS OF INFINITY. His works have
ppeared on numerous Best of the Year lists, as well
s preliminary or final ballots for the Nebula and Bram
toker Awards. In addition to the three novels in the
Jedi Academy" trilogy, he is also at work on various
ther STAR WARS projects, including THE ILLUSTRATED
TAR WARS UNIVERSE, an art book featuring many new
aintings by artist Ralph McQuarrie showing daily life
n the planets in the STAR WARS universe. He is
lso editing three anthologies of short stories, the first
f which—TALES FROM THE MOS EISLEY CANTINA—
ells the stories of all the bizarre characters from the
amous STAR WARS Cantina scene.

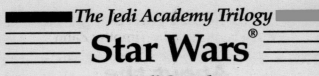

The Jedi Academy Trilogy

Star Wars®

Jedi Search
by Kevin J. Anderson

As the war between the Republic and the remnants of
Empire continues, two children—Jedi twins—will come
their powers in a universe on the brink of vast changes
challenges. In this time of turmoil and discovery, an extra
dinary new *Star Wars* saga begins....

While Luke Skywalker takes the first step towards set
up an academy to train a new order of Jedi Knights, I
Solo and Chewbacca are taken prisoner on the pla
Kessel. But when Han and Chewie escape, their fli
leads to a secret Imperial research laboratory—and fr
one danger to a far greater one....Luke picks up their
only to come face-to-face with a weapon so awesome, it
wipe out an entire solar system. It is a death ship called
Sun Crusher, invented by a reclusive genius and piloted
none other than Han himself....

STAR WARS®
A three book cycle by Timothy Zahn

Heir to the Empire (29612-4 * $5.99/$6.99 Canada)

e years after the events of *Return of the Jedi* Leia Organa and
n Solo have shouldered the burdens of creating the new
public. Luke Skywalker is the first in a hoped-for new line
Jedi Knights. But many light years away, the last of the
peror's warlords has taken command of the remains of the
perial fleet to launch a campaign to destroy the Republic.

Dark Force Rising (56071-9 * $5.99/$6.99 Canada)

ssention and personal ambition threaten to tear the Repub-
apart. As the pregnant Princess Leia risks her life to ally a
ud, lethal alien race with the Republic, Han and Lando
e against time to find proof of treason inside the Republic
uncil. But most dangerous of all is a new Dark Jedi,
isumed by bitterness...and throughly insane.

The Last Command (56492-7 * $5.99/$6.99 Canada)

ile Han and Chewbacca struggle to form an uneasy
ance of smugglers for a last-ditch attack against the Em-
e, Leia fights to keep the Alliance together and prepares for
birth of her twins. But the odds are against them: Admiral
rawn's resources are huge, and only a small force led by
ke to infiltrate Thrawn's power base has any hope of
ppling the last remnants of the Empire or of challenging
aoth, the Dark Jedi.

The adventure is only beginning!

STAR WARS®

THE TRUCE AT BAKURA

by Kathy Tyers

In the wake of the death of Emperor Palpatine and th
destruction of the second Death Star, the Alliance ha
begun to heal its wounds. But no sooner has the flee
regrouped than a new threat looms over the galaxy.

From a far-flung Imperial world called Bakura comes
desperate plea for help. It is the first planet to encoun
ter the cold-blooded Ssi-ruuk, reptilian invaders who
once allied with the dead Emperor, are infiltrating
Imperial space with only one goal: total domination
With the Imperial fleet scattered, Princess Leia sees th
plea for help as an opportunity to achieve a diplomat
victory for the Alliance. But it assumes even greater
importance when a vision of Obi-Wan Kenobi appear
to Luke Skywalker with the message that he *must* go
Bakura—or risk losing everything the Rebels have
fought so hard to achieve.